The BORN QUEEN

By Greg Keyes

The Chosen of the Changeling
THE WATERBORN
THE BLACKGOD

The Age of Unreason
NEWTON'S CANNON
A CALCULUS OF ANGELS
EMPIRE OF UNREASON
THE SHADOWS OF GOD

The Psi Corps Trilogy
BABYLON 5: DARK GENESIS
BABYLON 5: DEADLY RELATIONS
BABYLON 5: FINAL RECKONING

Star Wars®: The New Jedi Order
EDGE OF VICTORY I: CONQUEST
EDGE OF VICTORY II: REBIRTH
THE FINAL PROPHECY

The Kingdoms of Thorn and Bone
THE BRIAR KING
THE CHARNEL PRINCE
THE BLOOD KNIGHT
THE BORN QUEEN

Books published by The Random House Publishing Group
are available at quantity discounts on bulk purchases for
premium, educational, fund-raising, and special sales use.
For details, please call 1-800-733-3000.

The BORN
QUEEN

BOOK FOUR OF THE KINGDOMS OF
THORN AND BONE

GREG KEYES

DEL
REY

BALLANTINE BOOKS • NEW YORK

2009 Del Rey Books Mass Market Edition

Copyright © 2008 by J. Gregory Keyes

All rights reserved.

Published in the United States by Del Rey Books, an imprint of The Random House Publishing Group, a division of Random House, Inc., New York.

DEL REY is a registered trademark and the Del Rey colophon is a trademark of Random House, Inc.

Originally published in hardcover in the United States by Del Rey Books, an imprint of The Random House Publishing Group, a division of Random House, Inc., in 2008.

ISBN 978-0-345-44073-0

Map illustration by Kirk Caldwell

Printed in the United States of America

www.delreybooks.com

OPM   9   8   7   6   5   4   3   2   1

For Nell,
again

PROLOGUE

✛

FOUR BRIEF TALES

HARRIOT

A SHRIEK OF PAIN lifted into the pearl-colored sky and hung on the wind above Tarnshead like a seabird. Roger Harriot didn't turn; he'd heard plenty of screams this morning and would hear quite a few more before the day was done. Instead he focused his regard on the landscape, of which the west tower of Fiderech castle afforded an expansive view. The head itself was off to the west, presently on his left hand. Stacks of white stone jutted up through emerald grass, standing high enough to obscure the sea beyond, although as they slouched north toward town, the gray-green waves became visible. Along that slope, wind-gnarled trees reached their branches all in the same direction, as if to snatch some unseen prize from the air. From those twisty boughs hung strange fruit. He wondered if he would have been able to tell what they were if he did not already know.

Probably.

"Not everyone has the stomach for torture," a voice informed him. He recognized it as belonging to Sacritor Praecum, whose attish this was.

"I find it dreary," Roger replied, letting his gaze drift across the village with its neat little houses, gardens, and ropewalk. Ships' masts swayed gently behind the roofs.

"Dreary?"

"And tedious, and unproductive," he added. "I doubt very much it accomplishes anything."

"Many have confessed and turned back to the true path," Praecum objected.

"I'm more than familiar with torture," Roger told him. "Under the iron, men will confess to things they have not done." He turned a wan smile toward the sacritor. "Indeed, I've found that the sins admitted by the victim are usually first in the guilty hearts of their interrogators."

"Now, see here—" the sacritor began, but Roger waved him off.

"I'm not accusing you of anything," he said. "It's a general observation."

"I can't believe a knight of the Church could have such views. You seem almost to question the resacaratum itself."

"Not at all," Roger replied. "The cancer of heresy infects every city, town, village, and household. Evil walks abroad in daylight and does not bother to wear a disguise. No, this world must be made pure again, as it was in the days of the Sacaratum."

"Then—"

"My comment was about torture. It doesn't work. The confessions it yields are untrustworthy, and the epiphanies it inspires are insincere."

"Then how would you have us proceed?"

Roger pointed toward the headland. "Most of those you question will end there, swinging by their necks."

"The unrepentant, yes."

"Best skip straight to the hanging. The 'repentant' are liars, and those innocents we execute will be rewarded by the saints in the cities of the dead."

He could feel the sacritor stiffen. "Have you come to replace me? Are the patiri not pleased with our work?"

"No," Roger said. "My opinions are my own and not popular. The patiri—like you—enjoy torture, and it will continue. My task here is of another nature."

He turned his gaze to the southeast, where a light saffron road vanished into forested hills.

"Out of curiosity," Roger asked, "how many have you hung?"

"Thirty-one," Praecum replied. "And besides these behind us, twenty-six more await proving. And there will be more, I think."

"So many heretics from such a small village."

"The countryside is worse. Nearly every farm-and-woodwife practices shinecraft of some sort. Under your method, I should kill everyone in the attish."

"Once an arm has gangrene," Roger said, "you cannot cure it in spots. It must be cut off."

He turned to regard the whimpering man behind him. Roger first had seen him as a strong, stocky fellow with ruddy windburned cheeks and challenging blue eyes. Now he was something of a sack, and his gaze pleaded only for that dark boat ride at the border of the world. He was tied to a wooden pillar set in a socket in the stone of the tower, his arms chained above him. Six other pillars held as many more prisoners, stripped and waiting their turn in the spring breeze.

"Why do you do your work up here rather than in the dungeons?" Roger wondered.

The sacritor straightened a little and firmed his chin. "Because I believe there *is* a point to this. In the dungeons they contemplate their sins and yearn for sunlight until they wonder if they really remember what it looked like. Then I bring them here, where they can see the beauty of the world: the sea, the sun, the grass—"

"And the fate that awaits them," Harriot said, glancing at the gallow trees.

"That, too," Praecum admitted. "I want them to learn to love the saints again, to return to them in their hearts."

"You filthy whoreson," the man on the pillar sobbed. "You vicious little sceat. What you did to my poor little Maola . . ." He shuddered off into sobs.

"Your wife was a shinecrafter," Praecum said.

"She was never," the man croaked. "She was never."

"She admitted to tying Hynthia knots for sailors," he shot back.

"Saint Hynthia," the victim sighed. His energy seemed to be ebbing as quickly as he had found it.

"There is no Saint Hynthia," the sacritor said.

Roger tried to bite back a laugh, then thought better of it and let it go.

The sacritor nodded in satisfaction. "You see?" he said. "This is Roger Harriot, knight of the Church, an educated man."

"Indeed," Roger said, his mind changed again by the sacritor's smugness. "I'm educated enough to—on occasion—consult the *Tafles Nomens,* one of the three books available in every attish."

"The Tafles Nomens?"

"The largest volume in your library. The one on the lectern in the corner with the thick coat of dust on it."

"I fail to see—"

"Hynthia is one of the forty-eight aspects of Saint Sefrus," Roger said. "An obscure one, I'll grant you. But I seem to recall that one ties knots to her."

Praecum opened his mouth in protest, closed it, then opened it again.

"Saint Sefrus is male," he finally said.

Roger wagged a finger at him. "You're guessing that, based on the Vitellian ending. You've no idea who Saint Sefrus was, do you?"

"I . . . there are a lot of saints."

"Yes. Thousands. Which is why I should wonder that you didn't bother to check the book to see if Hynthia was a saint before you started accusing her followers as shinecrafters."

"She gave sailors knots and told them to untie them if they needed wind," Praecum said desperately. "That reeks of shinecraft."

Roger cleared his throat. "And Ghial," he quoted, "the Queen, said to Saint Merinero, 'Take you this linen strand and bind a knot in the name of Sephrus, and when you are becalmed, release the wind by untying it.'"

He smiled. "That's from the Sacred Annals of Saint Merinero. Was he a heretic?"

The sacritor pursed his lips and fidgeted. "I read the Life of Merinero," he said. "I don't remember that."

"The Life of Merinero is a paragraph in the *Sahtii Bivii*," Roger said. "The *Anal* is a book of seven hundred pages."

"Well, then I can hardly be expected—"

"Tell me. I've noticed you've a chapel for Mannad, Lir, and Netuno. How many sailors make their offerings there before going out to sea?"

"Few to none," Praecum exploded. "They prefer their sea witches. For twenty years they've spurned—" He broke off, his face red, his eyes bugging halfway from their sockets.

"Truth?" Roger asked mildly.

"I have done what I thought best. What the saints wished of me."

"So you have," Roger replied. "And that clearly is neither here nor there as concerns the truth."

"Then you have come to, to . . ." His eyes were watery, and he was trembling.

Roger rolled his eyes. "I don't care about you, or this poor bastard's wife, or whether every person you've hanged was innocent. The fact that you're an ignorant butcher *is* the reason I'm here, but not for any of the reasons you fear."

"Then why, for pity's sake?"

"Wait, and I promise you will see."

A bell later, his promise was kept.

They came from the south, as Harriot reckoned. There were around half a hundred of them, most in the dark orange tabards of the Royal Light Horse, riding boldly out of the forest and up to the gates of the castle. As they drew nearer, he saw that ten of them wore the full lord's plate of knights. There was a single unarmored fellow appareled in the Vitellian manner, complete with broad-brimmed hat. Next to him was the most singular of the riders, a slight figure in a breastplate, with short red hair. At first he thought the person a page or squire, but then, to his delight, he realized who it actually was.

I was right, he thought, trying not to feel smug.

"It appears Queen Anne herself has come to pay you a visit," he told the sacritor.

"Heresy," the sacritor muttered. "There is no Queen Anne."

"The Comven crowned her," Harriot pointed out.

"The Church does not recognize her authority," Praecum countered.

"I'll enjoy hearing you tell her that," Harriot replied. "You and your fifteen men."

"Up there," a clear feminine voice shouted. "Is one of you the sacritor of this attish?"

"I am," Praecum replied.

From his vantage, Harriot couldn't make out much about her features, but even so he felt a wintry chill, and her eyes seemed somehow dark.

"M—Majesty," the sacritor said. "If you wait but a moment, I can offer you the humble hospitality of my poor attish."

"No," the woman replied. "Wait where you are. Send someone down to show us the way up."

Praecum nodded nervously at one of his men, then began rubbing his hands nervously.

"That was a quick change of mind," Harriot observed.

"As you said, we're outnumbered."

"Not if the saints are on our side," Harriot replied.

"Do you mock me?"

"Not at all."

The sacritor shook his head. "What can she want here?"

"You haven't heard about Plinse, Nurthwys, and Saeham?"

"Towns in Newland. What about them?"

"You've really no better ear for news than that?"

"I have been quite occupied here, sir."

"So it appears."

"What do you mean?"

Harriot heard clattering on the stairs.

"I think you'll find out in a moment," he remarked. "Here they come."

Harriot had never met Anne Dare, but he knew quite a bit about her. She was seventeen, the youngest daughter of the late William II. Reports by Praefec Hespero and others described her as selfish and willful, intelligent but uninterested in using her intelligence, least of all for politics, for which she had no inclination whatsoever. She had vanished from sight around a year earlier, only to turn up at the Coven Saint Dare, where she was being trained in the arts of the Dark Lady.

Now it seemed she took a great deal of interest in politics. Perhaps it was the slaughter of her sisters and father that had spurred it, or the numerous attempts on her own life. Perhaps it was something the sisters of Saint Cer had done to her.

Whatever the case, this was not the girl he had read about.

He hadn't expected freckles, although he knew she was fair-skinned and red-haired, and those things usually went together. Her nose was large and arched enough that if it were a bit bigger, one might call it a beak, but somehow it fit pleasantly below her sea-green eyes, and though she wasn't classically beautiful like her mother, there was an appeal about her.

She focused her gaze on Praecum. She didn't say anything, but the young man at her side placed his hand on the hilt of his rapier.

"Her Majesty, Anne I of Crotheny," he said.

Praecum hesitated, then went down on his knee, followed by his men. Harriot followed suit.

"Rise," Anne said. Her gaze wandered over the tortured souls on the rooftop.

"Release these people," she said. "See that they are treated for their sufferings."

Several of her men broke away from her group and began to do that.

"Majesty—"

"Sacritor," Anne said. "These people are my subjects. Mine. My subjects are not detained, tortured, or murdered without my consent. I do not remember you asking my consent."

"Majesty, my instructions come from z'Irbina and the Fratrex Prismo, as you must know."

"Z'Irbina is in Vitellio," she replied. "This is Hornladh, in the Empire of Crotheny, and I am its empress."

"Surely, Majesty, the holy Church is above temporal rulers."

"Not in Crotheny," she said. "Not according to my father, not according to me."

The sacritor lowered his head. "I am a servant of the Church, Majesty."

"That's immaterial to me. You are accused of torture, murder, and treason. We will try you tomorrow."

"As you tried the sacritors of Plinse, Nurthwys, and Saeham?"

Her gaze switched to him, and he felt another, deeper chill. There was still something of a girl in there, but there was something else, too, something very dangerous.

"Who are you?" she demanded.

"Sir Roger Harriot," he replied. "Knight of the Church, in service to His Grace Supernnirus Abullo."

"I see. Sent by z'Irbina to aid in this butchery?"

"No, Majesty," he replied. "That's not my business here."

"What is your business, then?"

"I and forty-nine other knights of the Church were called to aid His Majesty Robert in keeping the peace."

"Yes," Anne said. "I remember now. We were wondering what happened to you."

"We got word that things had changed in Eslen."

"And so they did," Anne replied. "The usurper is fled, and I have taken the throne my father meant me to have." She smiled thinly. "Did you think you would be unwelcome?"

"That occurred to my liege," Harriot admitted.

"Have your companions returned to z'Irbina, then?"

"No, Majesty. We have been waiting."

"For what?"

"For you."

Her eyebrows lifted, but she didn't say anything.

"You're an unusual queen," Harriot went on. "You personally led the invasion of Eslen castle. Since taking the crown, you have managed a number of these visits to interfere with the resacaratum. We thought that given your pattern, our friend Praecum here would eventually prove irresistible."

"Well, you were right about that," Anne said. "So this was all a trap, then."

"Yes, Majesty. And now you are surrounded. I urge you to surrender to my custody, and I promise you will not be harmed."

"Not until I've been convicted of shinecraft, you mean?"

"That I cannot speak to."

Praecum had regained a little color. "You were serious, Sir Harriot! The saints are with us. Forty-nine knights—"

"Each with a guard of ten, all mounted," Harriot finished.

"That makes . . ." Praecum's lips moved silently. "Five hundred."

"Yes," Harriot replied.

Anne smiled. "How convenient that I brought two thousand, then."

Harriot felt his heart all but stop in his chest.

"Majesty?"

"This was indeed a trap, Sir Harriot," she said. Something tightened around her eyes, and then she reached forward so that the heel of her hand came against his forehead.

He felt the bones in his skin go suddenly heavy and febrile. He fell to his knees, but she did not release the contact. His skin everywhere stung, his lungs seemed full of flies. And in his head . . .

He saw St. Abulo's host in their camp, waiting for the morning, some sleeping, some on watch. He seemed to be one of the watchmen, suddenly crushed by this same black torpor, and he watched, uncaring, as nimble shadows slipped into the camp, slitting the throats of the sleeping and waking alike. Some woke and managed to fight, but it wasn't long before all five hundred were dead. The eyes he watched through dimmed, and he felt himself dragged along as if by a swift river, and screamed . . .

He came back to the sunlight gasping, watching the distant corpses swinging from their branches. His breeches were wet.

He looked up at the queen, and her smile broadened into a terrible thing.

"Now about your surrender," she said.

Harriot summoned a dogged reserve of will. "Do you understand what you've done?" He gasped. "The full wrath of the Church will fall on you now. There will be holy war."

"Let z'Irbina come," she replied. "I have seen enough of their work. Let them come and receive the justice they deserve."

Harriot steadied his breath and felt his fever fade. "That's bold talk," he said. "How is the Hansan fleet?"

"Encamped along our coast, as you must know," Anne replied.

"And you truly believe you can fight Hansa and the holy Church?"

Her gaze intensified, and he flinched. It took all he had in him not to cower.

"What do you think?" she asked softly.

I think you are mad, he silently opined, but he could not say it.

She nodded, as if she had heard him, anyway. "I've a mind to let you return to z'Irbina," she said. "So you can tell them what was done and said here. And let me add this: From this moment, all servants of the Church in z'Irbina shall either renounce their allegiance to that corrupt institution or leave our borders within the nineday. Beyond that time, any churchman, regardless of rank, will be arrested, imprisoned, and tried for treason against the empire. Is this clear enough for you to repeat, Sir Roger?"

"Very clear, Majesty," he husked.

"Very well. Go. As you've pointed out, I've other things to attend to now."

They let him keep his horse and arms. He went to the camp and found the bodies where they had fallen, most still in their blankets. The field was thick with ravens, and the clouds threatened rain.

Roger sat there for a few moments as the earth seemed to tilt. He didn't know if Anne really understood what would happen now; even he couldn't imagine the full scope of the slaughter that was now inevitable. The five hundred who had died here weren't even a start.

HESPERO

His footsteps rang on the red marble, drifted up into the great dark hollow of the Caillo Vaillaimo, and came back to him like whispers from death.

I am come, they seemed to say.

Death walked with him, but fear came creeping behind.

Be still, he told himself. *Be still. You are Marché Hespero, praifec of Crotheny. You are the son of Ispure of the Curnaxii. You are worthy.*

"The holiest of holies," the man a step behind him and to his left breathed.

Hespero glanced at him and saw that his gaze was wandering around the arching buttresses, the thousands of niches with their gilded saints.

"That?" Hespero waved at the architecture. "Are you talking about the building, Brother Helm?"

"The Caillo Vaillaimo," Helm replied. "Our most perfect temple."

Hespero felt his brow pinch in a frown. He heard Sir Eldon, on his right, sigh, but the other six men in his entourage remained silent.

"You've learned nothing," he told Helm.

"Your grace?" the brother asked, his voice sounding chastised but puzzled.

"Hush now. Be silent as we approach his eminence."

"Yes, your grace."

Hespero waved him off. Brother Helm's mistake was a common one. The building had been built to impress, and it did, but in the end the structure was only a symbol. The real holy of holies was underneath the red marble and ancient foundations. He could feel it as he never had before with each touch of his foot against the stone: aching, awful power that made his bones feel burnt and his flesh rotten. His mouth tasted of soot and decay.

But Helm couldn't feel that, could he? Death wasn't with Helm.

On down the sacristy hall they went, but before they reached the grand nave, their guide led them to a side passage and up a staircase into the prayer halls with their writing lecterns and smell of lead, then around a corner, past the lesser scriftorium. He realized with a chill that they were making their way to the private suites of the Fratrex Prismo, but not by the most direct route.

"There's no one here," Brother Helm whispered. He had noticed it, too. "The corridors are all empty."

"Quite," Sir Eldon agreed.

Their escort didn't glance back, but he surely had heard. Not that it mattered.

He'd been in this part of the Caillo only once, very long ago, when Niro Pihatur had been the Fratrex Prismo.

He thought he knew where they were going.

They came into a lozenge-shaped room, ostensibly a chapel to Lady Lasa; her winged and wreathed statue stood at the far end, smiling a knowing smile. At the moment, however, the place was filled not with worshippers but with Mamres monks. They were armed, and not with ceremonial weapons. At their head stood a figure in dark indigo robes and a black three-cornered hat that somewhat resembled a crown.

"Brother Mylton," Hespero said, favoring the man with a short bow.

"I am a tribiceros now," the cleric corrected.

"Yes, I see the hat," Hespero said. "But you are still a brother, like all of us."

Mylton smiled indulgently. His bulging eyes and narrow face had always made Hespero think of some sort of rodent. The hat didn't really change the impression.

"You will submit to blindfolding, all of you," Mylton said.

"Of course," Hespero replied.

As the monks knotted darkness to his face, Hespero felt the floor beneath him thin even further, and his body shivered as if aching to tear itself into pieces.

Someone took him firmly by the arm.

"Step down," a voice he did not know whispered.

He did, once, twice, thrice. In the end, he counted eighty-four steps, just as he had the last time. Then there was turning this way and that in air that tasted stale, until at last they stopped and the blindfolds were removed.

Perhaps they don't plan to kill us, a small part of Hespero thought as his eyes adjusted to his new surroundings. *Why bother keeping the way secret if we're never coming out?*

But another part of him knew that was stupid. It was ritual. Any intelligent, attentive person—and certainly any initiate of Decmanus, for instance—would be able to find his way back here, blindfolded or not. Only initiates and sacrifices made this journey to the place beneath, to the real Caillo Vaillaimo.

He began picking out details in the guttering light of the torches that plenished two score wall sockets. The chamber was carved into the living stone the temple was built upon, its natural sandy hue made orange by the firelight. Rows of semicircular benches climbed before him, but all were empty save for three seats raised up at the back and the throne behind them. Two of the three were occupied by the other two tribiceri, and as Hespero watched, Mylton completed their number.

The Fratrex Prismo sat the throne, of course.

"Where are we?" Brother Helm asked.

"The Obfuscate Senaz of the Hierovasi," Hespero replied.

The Fratrex Prismo suddenly raised his voice:

Commenumus
Pispis post oraumus
Ehtrad ezois verus Taces est.

"Izic deivumus," the others chorused, and Hespero realized with faint surprise that he had responded along with everyone else.

Well, he had been in the Church a long while. Much of what he did was reflex.

Niro Fabulo had been in the clergy longer than Hespero. The Fratrex Prismo was almost eighty. The hair streaming from beneath the black-and-gold crown was white, and his eyes, once blue, had been bleached to tinted ice. He had an arched Vitellian nose and a persistent tick in his sagging left cheek.

"Well," Fabulo said, almost sighing. "You surprise me, Hespero."

"How so, your grace?"

"You've delivered yourself here after all of your crimes. I thought I would have to have you brought in by the ear."

"You don't know me very well, then," Hespero said.

"Don't be impertinent," Fabulo snapped. He leaned back in his chair. "I'll never know what Niro Lucio saw in you, I really won't. I know you took your vows together, but that was more than thirty years ago."

"I don't understand what you're implying," Hespero said.

"When you left the college, you went off to some tiny attish in the Bairghs and distinguished yourself in no way whatever. But Lucio stayed here and rose in rank. When he was lustrated as praifec, he called for you. He swayed the senaz to make you amplulo of Crotheny and later praifec."

"I'm flattered you know so much about me."

"What I know does not flatter you," he snapped. "And yet I knew Lucio. He was loyal, above all loyal to the Church. He was not one who usually counted friendship toward a qualification. I wonder if something more than friendship did not prompt your rise in position."

"Does my record since that time suggest I was unqualified?"

Niro Fabulo shook his head. "No, indeed. You have been exemplary in every way, or at least that is what the record reflects. Until the last year or so, that is, and there things go very wrong. Shall I catalogue your major failures?"

"If it pleases you, your grace."

"It does not, but I shall do so." He leaned forward.

"You failed to stop William from naming his daughters as heirs. You promised to manage that mistake, yet again you failed. Not only is one of the daughters still alive, she now sits the throne. Now, that in itself is enough failure for a lifetime, Hespero. You failed to quicken the faneways of the shrouded lords in the King's Forest. And despite all of this"— he mopped his brow with his sleeve—"despite all of this, my predecessor, your dear friend Lucio, entrusted you with the arrow of Aitas in order to slay the Briar King. This also you failed to do, and now the arrow is lost to us."

Hespero started to retort to that last accusation, but thought better of it. What was the point? It was mostly true, especially as concerned Anne. He could only blame himself for choosing such unstable allies in the matter. The faneways were of little consequence, really, and Lucio had known that.

But Lucio was dead, most probably at the hand of the man now accusing him. Niro Fabulo didn't begin to understand Hespero's real failure.

"Finally," the *prismo* concluded, "you took cowardly flight from your post in Eslen."

"Did I?"

"Yes."

"Interesting. In what month do your reports have that happening?"

"Just after Yule."

"That was when King Robert was on the throne and months before Anne raised her army. What do you imagine I was fleeing?"

"You left no explanation of your whereabouts," Fabulo said. "What are we to assume?"

"Does it matter?" Hespero asked, his voice sounding eerily calm and uncustomarily blunt in his own ears. "You've murdered Lucio, and now you're purging his friends. I'm one of them. Why all this talk?"

"Lucio was a fool," Fabulo said. "Lucio never really understood the prophecies or what must be done now. He was too much of the past. But I think you and he were up to something. And I rather want to know what that was."

"A failure like me? What could I be up to?" Hespero asked.

"That's what we're going to find out," Fabulo said.

Hespero felt his throat go dry, and for an instant the words stuck in his throat, coming out as a sort of gasp.

"What?" the *prismo* demanded.

Hespero took a deep breath and raised his head.

"You *are* going to find out," he repeated, clearly this time. "But not the way you'd like."

Hespero saw Fabulo's brow descend and his mouth open to speak.

I am Hespero, he thought. He clenched his teeth, then relaxed and let the incantation come.

"Shadowed saints who walk all ways, know all fanes. Be with me."

He let the cold waters beneath the world rush in through his feet, and they went numb, followed quickly by his legs, crotch, and belly. He felt his heart stop, and he knew he did not have long. Then the numbness reached his head, and the voices around him dropped away. He could still see, but the figures before him appeared tiny, the torches like little brass jewels. He felt hollowed and stretched by the power of the fane beneath him.

What was he doing? Who was he? Faces were fading in his mind. He glanced at the man beside him and could not remember his name. The place itself no longer seemed familiar.

Now he felt a current tug; the tide had come into him, and now it was going out. When it went, it would take him with it.

Unless . . .

There was an "unless," but he couldn't remember what it was. But he did see something across the unfamiliar space, something his eye told him was the shape of a man but was also something else. It was a river, a stream, a swift bright current. It was beautiful, and he reached for it like a man dying of thirst.

Everything else was paling. The spring was too far away, and the pull inside him was so *strong*. He realized he had stopped breathing, and suddenly he no longer cared. He could rest, forget, sleep.

No. I am still Marché Hespero. Son of . . .

He couldn't recall. With an inchoate cry, he flung himself at the effulgent waters, and something in him reached farther than his paralyzed body, and he felt the stream that wasn't a stream with fingers that weren't fingers, and he drew it into him as if drinking. The separation of his soul and corpse eased, and he drank deeper, opening himself completely as everything faded into black.

Impossible, someone seemed to say.

Hespero felt his grin, a grim crescent slicing through two worlds.

Impossible. You have not walked the faneway. Only I . . .

"You're right," Hespero said. "But I am attuned to it."

Not as I am.

Hespero suddenly felt the chill replaced by fever, and his body stiffened, then began to dissolve.

"No," he gritted.

Yes. You surprised me . . .

"Yes," Hespero gasped.

But I am the more powerful here.

Hespero clenched his fists, but the strain tore his fingers loose from his hands. An instant later his shoulders sagged, and both arms dropped off.

No.

His spine wobbled and then began to crumble, and his torso almost gently collapsed as his knees dissolved. His body broke apart, the black current towing the pieces away.

Shivering with fear, Hespero renewed his grasp on the brightness even as he began to stretch thinner and thinner, becoming a stream himself.

"Here," a voice suddenly said. He couldn't see anything, but he suddenly felt something shivery and hot.

"I remember," he murmured. "I remember this."

"Then hurry. You will soon forget."

The voice was right, for even as Hespero struck with the thing, he was no longer sure what he was doing, or why, or—

Something like a scream, and then, and then . . .

Revelation.

Images came first, fractured and whole. Scents, textures, pain and pleasure, the stuff of matter, the stuff of life but peeled off of life, adrift.

But no longer adrift. In him, now.

The first came from Fabulo: fear and exhilaration. Yes, it had been murder, Lucio's death, subtle poison, but then, it was all too fast, a life falling backward, flashes jumping out. The electric tingle of the faneway of Saint Diuvo, the stroke of a woman's fingers, running through a field of tall wheat, the tap of his head on the cold marble of a chapel in z'Espino, shivering, hot, confused in chaffing blankets, the softness of linen, wonder, a face that was the universe, the sweet scent of mother's milk, pain, light . . .

And then, for a long while, Hespero could not think at all as the well of knowledge opened, filled him, and—just as he thought he could endure no more—closed.

Something spasmed, and he felt his fingernails biting into his palms, a painful vise on each arm, and in his chest a terrible shuddering.

My heart, he thought. *My heart.*

It shuddered again, and his chest felt crushed.

Then a thump, pause, thump-thump, pause, thump.

And the agony eased to hurt, then relief. Gasping, he opened his eyes.

"You did it," Sir Eldon said. The knight was holding him up by his left arm. Brother Helm had the right.

He fought his gaze up the tiers of benches. Niro Fabulo slumped in his chair, eyes wide, skin already turning blue.

Mylton was just turning from the dead *prismo,* his jaw dropping.

"How?" he asked.

"The saints rejected him," Hespero wheezed. "They chose me."

"But you haven't walked the faneway," Mylton objected. "How could you use the holy source?"

"The saints make their will known through me directly," Hespero asserted.

"That's impossible."

"It is a fact," Hespero managed. "You all saw. You must have felt."

"Yes," another of the tribiceri—L'Ossel—said. "Don't you see? Don't you remember? It's true. The prophecy says, 'and he will draw the power of Saint Diuvo, although he has not walked in his steps.'"

A general murmur went up from what had been a stunned silence.

"He is the real Fratrex Prismo," L'Ossel went on. "He is the one meant to lead us in the final days."

Hespero rallied what little remained of his strength and shook himself free of the supporting hands.

"I will not brook doubt," he said. "Time is short, and too much has to be done. If anyone else would challenge me, let it be now."

He lifted his chin. Against all odds, he had survived both the fane and Fabulo. He had nothing left now. If even the weakest of them challenged him, it was all over.

But instead, they all went to their knees.

And a few days later, he was titled Fratrex Prismo Niro Marco.

It had a nice ring to it.

DARIGE

Stephen snapped awake, his heart thundering in his chest.

"What?" he gasped.

But no one answered. Something had awakened him— something loud, or bright, or painful—except that he couldn't quite remember whether it had been a sound, a light, or a feeling. Had it been in the waking world or across the night divide? His scalp and palms tingled, and he felt like an insect mired in molasses.

Then the wind came in the open window, cool and clean, and the liminal moment faded.

He pressed the page of the book he'd been studying, realizing that he'd literally fallen asleep with his nose in it, and, as the waking terror faded, felt like chuckling at himself. What would Zemlé say?

She would make some joke about him being obsessed, but she understood. He tucked a ribbon to mark his place in the tome, then regarded the sheet of lead next to it with its faded engravings. It was the epistle, the letter that had led him to this place. Although he had translated the cipher it was written in long before, he felt something basic was escaping him, hidden in the text, some clue to the secret for which he was searching.

He rose and went to the east window and then paused. Hadn't he left it shuttered?

A glance around the room revealed no intruder or any place that might conceal one. It was an open, airy space, carved of living stone but with enormous windows for each direction of the wind, hung with framed crystal thicker than the length of his thumb. Closed, they were translucent, suffusing the chamber with ample pleasant light during the day, but open, they offered a rare view. So far as he could tell, this was the highest room in the vast complex of caves and tunnels that riddled Witchhorn Mountain, hollowed out from a spindly upthrust on the east side of the peak the Aitivar—the inhabitants of the place—called the Khelan, or "spit." He didn't know what they called this upper room, but he'd named it the aerie. Sunrises were splendid from there, pulling above the jagged peaks of the Bairghs, and he fancied on a clear day he could see almost to the Midenlands south and as far east as the inlet of Dephis, because at times he thought he saw the liquid shimmer of a great water, although that could well be a trick of the light.

He shrugged. He must have left it unlatched, and the wind had blown it open.

It was dusk now, and the Witchhorn cast its long shadow out toward the blue haze of the horizon. North and south of the mountain's umbra, the pikes and ridges burned orange, and a few stars were furtively appearing in the deep of the sky.

He savored a long, happy breath and put his palms on the marble sill, leaning forward a bit.

It was as if he had placed his hands on a hot stove, and he yelped from the pain and surprise. He stumbled back, staring at his hands in shock.

In a few heartbeats he began to calm down. The stone hadn't been hot enough to burn his skin from such a brief contact; it had been mostly the surprise. He ventured back and touched the sill again. It was still very warm.

He felt the near wall, but it was as cool as the evening air.

He glanced around uneasily. What was going on? Had he unwittingly triggered some ancient Sefry shinecraft? Were volcanic vapors rising through the mountain? Curious, he continued along the wall toward the next window, then the next. There wasn't anything unusual there, but when he came to the stone stair that descended farther into the mountain, he found the banister unusually warm, too.

He went back to the eastern window, knelt, and touched the floor. There it was, a warm spot. And a little more than a kingsyard farther there was another—a trail of them, leading to the steps . . .

His scalp was tingling now.

What had come through here? What had walked past him as he slept?

Now he wished he hadn't wanted to be alone and had allowed some of the Aitivar to accompany him.

Whatever it was, it had ignored him when he was at his most vulnerable. Surely it wouldn't hurt him now.

He strained his saint-blessed senses. He didn't hear anything, but there was a faint scent a little like burning pine, but with a musky, animal component, too.

He looked back out the window, examining the drop that stayed sheer for two hundred kingsyards. Whatever had come, it must have flown.

He glanced back at the stair, and then he remembered. Zemlé was down there where whatever it was had gone. Maybe it had left him alone because he was asleep, but if she was awake . . .

He suddenly heard dogs barking—Zemlé's hounds—and everything went pale.

He wasn't a fighter by nature, but he wished he had thought to carry a weapon: a knife, at the very least.

Swearing that from now on he would do so, he grabbed his lantern and started down the stairs.

The dogs suddenly stopped barking.

The aerie wasn't the only chamber in the Khelan. The whole thing was rather like a small castle or mansion or, perhaps more aptly, a wizard's tower. Fifty-seven steps brought him to the next chamber, which he and Zemlé had dubbed the Warlock's Bedroom. It was carved in a high vault, and although there were no windows as such, numerous long shafts brought light in from different directions, depending on the time of day, offering not only illumination but also a rough sort of clock.

The scent was stronger on the stairway, cloying in his nostrils, and when he burst into the chamber, he had the start of a good panic. Zemlé's three great beasts were at the far end of the room, facing the hall where the stair continued down. They weren't making a sound, but the hair on their necks was up.

"Zemlé!"

He could see her on the bed, one bare leg thrown out from beneath the quilt. She wasn't moving, and she didn't respond to his shout. He raced to her side.

"Zemlé," he repeated, shaking her.

Her lids fluttered open. "Stephen?" Then her brows dropped. "Stephen, what's wrong?"

Gasping for breath, he sat on the bed.

Zemlé sat up, reaching for his arm. "What?"

"Nothing, I—I think something came through here. I was afraid it might have hurt you. Didn't you hear the dogs?"

"They started up," she murmured, rubbing her eyes. "They do that. This place spooks them." Then her vision seemed to clear. "Some*thing*?"

"I've no idea. I fell asleep, upstairs—"

"Nose in your book."

He stopped. "You came up?"

"I guessed. If you'd gone to sleep on purpose, I rather think you would have come down here with me." She shrugged. "Or do I flatter myself?"

"Ah, no, you don't."

"But go on."

"The, umm, the window ledge was hot."

She arched an eyebrow. "Hot?"

"I mean *really* hot. Burning, almost. And the banister of the stairs and the floor, in places, as if something really blistering walked through."

"Like what?"

"I've no idea. But what with all of the greffyns and utins and waurms and generally ancient nasties I've seen lately, it might be anything. A salamandra, maybe."

She stroked his arm. "Well, it didn't hurt you and it didn't hurt me, did it? Or even the dogs. So maybe it's a friendly burning-invisible thing."

"Maybe. Or maybe friendly like Fend."

"Fend hasn't made the slightest false move," she pointed out.

"He tried to kill me."

"I mean since he became the Blood Knight and swore himself to your service."

"Well, right, but . . . he *will,* mark my words. Anyway, it's been less than a month. He's up to something."

She shrugged. "Do you want to keep trailing this beastie of yours? I can get dressed."

He blinked, suddenly understanding that in sitting up she hadn't brought the covers with her and was quite nude.

"That's something I'd hate to ask," he murmured.

"And generally untypical of men," she replied.

"Still . . ."

"Just wait." She swung her slim legs off the bed and stepped onto the floor, crossing a few paces to a dressing gown that lay rumpled there. As she slid it over her head and her white body vanished into it, he felt a strong stirring. Why should it be more erotic for her to dress than the opposite? But there it was, a fact.

He shook that off. She pulled on her buskins, and together they set off in search of the apparition, the dogs padding silently behind. Stephen wondered if she even believed him or if she was just being as deferential to him as the Aitivar and Fend appeared to be. He hoped not; he had been attracted by her strong and independent spirit, not her pliancy. In fact, she had been very much in control of the relationship in the beginning. Now, it sometimes almost felt that he was. It was as worrying as any other unfamiliar thing, especially considering the reverence with which the Aitivar seemed to treat him.

"Seemed," because they had brought him here by force, and he hadn't forgotten that.

But there hadn't been anything like that since. His word was law, and so far as he could tell, no part of the mountain was off limits.

Except the parts he couldn't find.

"What's wrong?"

It was disconcerting how well Zemlé could read his mood.

"Watch your step," he muttered, "not me."

"Come on. You're distracted."

"I'm just wondering again why the Aitivar don't know where the Alq is," Stephen said. "It's supposed to be the heart, the treasury of this place, and no one can point me toward it despite the fact that that's what I came here to find."

"Well, treasuries are usually hidden or well guarded or both," she pointed out. "And the Aitivar were latecomers here, too."

"I know," he said.

They'd reached the next landing and a series of galleries that might have once been ballrooms or banquet halls, so grand were they.

He listened, but his once supernatural hearing had been damaged by an explosion a few months before. He could still hear better than the average mortal, though, and now he didn't notice anything out of place. Feeling about, he couldn't detect any warm spots, either.

"Well, it could have gone ten ways from here," he said. "Maybe I should just alert the guard."

"That's what they're for," Zemlé said.

He nodded. "I'll find them; they're just another flight down. Maybe they even saw it. You go on back up."

She smiled. "Fine. I've a mind to undress again. Will you be joining me?"

Stephen hesitated.

She rolled her eyes. "We'll find the Alq, Stephen. As you said, it's been less than a month. You spent all last night reading. Spend another night so, and I'll begin to doubt my charms."

"It's just—it's urgent. The Revesturi expect I can find the knowledge here to keep the world from ending. That's a bit of a responsibility. And now this . . . intruder."

She smiled and partly opened her dressing gown.

"Life is short," she said. "You'll find it. It's your destiny. So come to bed."

Stephen felt his face burning.

"I'll be right up," he said.

LEOFF

Leovigild Ackenzal eased back onto a cushion of warm clover and closed his eyes against the sun. He drew a deep breath of bloom-sweet air and let the solar heat press gently on him. His thoughts began to lose their sense as the dreams hiding in the green began to tiptoe into his head.

A thaurnharp began sounding a delicate melody that blended with the birdsong and bee buzzes of the afternoon.

"What tune is that?" a familiar voice softly asked, startling him.

"She's improvising," he murmured.

"It sounds a little sad."

"Yes," he agreed. "Everything she plays these days is sad."

Warm, supple fingers wrapped around his own stiff and ruined digits. He opened his eyes and turned his head so that he could see Areana's red-gold hair and dark-jeweled orbits.

"I didn't hear you come up," he told her.

"Bare feet don't make much sound on clover, do they?"

"Especially feet as dainty as yours," he replied.

"Oh, hush. You don't have to win me anymore."

"On the contrary," he said. "I'd like to win you again every day."

"Well, that's nice," she said. "Good husband talk. We'll see if you feel that way in ten years as opposed to ten days."

"It's my fondest wish to find out. And again in twenty, thirty—"

She cupped her hand over his mouth. "Hush, I said."

She looked around the glade. "I'm going to start calling this your solar. You always want to be in the sunlight these days."

Don't you? he wanted to ask. She had spent months in the dungeons, just as he had. And just as he had, she had heard—

No. He didn't want to remember.

"I'm sorry," she said. "I didn't mean to remind you. I just—I wonder what you will do when winter comes."

He shrugged. "It's not here yet, and I can't stop it coming. We'll see."

She smiled, but he felt it turn in him.

"Maybe I can write a bright music."

"I'm sorry," she said. "I've ruined your nap."

You have, he thought, his bitterness growing. *And why carp about winter?*

"Still," she went on, her tone changing, "all you do is nap, it seems."

He sat up, feeling his breath begin to fire. "How do you—"

And then a bee stung him. The pain was very simple, very direct, and he found himself on his feet howling, swatting at the air, which was alive with the swarming insects.

He understood now. The pain of the sting had wakened his sense.

"Mery," he shouted, striding toward the girl where she sat with her little thaurnharp.

"Mery, quit that."

But she kept playing until Leoff reached down and stopped her hands. They felt cold.

"Mery, it's hurting us."

She didn't look up at first but continued to study the keyboard.

"It doesn't hurt me," she said.

"I know," he said softly.

She looked up then, and his chest tightened.

Mery was a slight girl; she looked younger than her eight winters. From a distance she might be five or six.

But she wasn't at a distance now. Her eyes had been azure when they had met. They were still blue, but they seemed filmed over somehow, sometimes vacant, sometimes sharp with subtle pain a child her age should not know. Up close, Mery might be a hundred.

"I'm sorry," she said.

"What were you trying to do there?"

She shrugged. "I don't know."

He knelt and stroked her hair.

"Robert won't find us again."

"He took it with him," Mery said, her voice just audible. "He tricked you into writing it, and he took it with him."

"It's all right," Leoff said.

"It's not," Mery replied. "It's not. When he plays it, I can hear it."

The hairs went up on Leoff's neck. "What?"

"He doesn't play it well," she whispered. "But now he has someone else to do it. I can hear it."

Leoff glanced over at Areana. She hadn't said anything, but tears were running quietly down her face.

"I thought you would fix it," Mery said. "Now I see you can't."

"Mery . . ."

"It's okay," she said. "I understand."

She lifted the thaurnharp off her lap, took it by its carry strap, and stood up.

"I'll play someplace else," she said.

"Mery, please don't go," Areana said.

But the girl already was trudging off.

Leoff watched her leave and sighed. "She expects me to do something," he said.

"She expects too much," she said.

He shook his head. "We were there, but she *played* it. I used her—"

"To save our lives," his wife gently reminded him.

"I'm not sure I saved hers," he said. "I thought she would get better, but she's slipping away, Rey. It's worse every day."

She nodded. "Yah."

"I should go after her."

"She wants to be alone right now," Areana said. "I think you'd better let her. She was a solitary sort of person even before."

"Yes."

"Stay here. Rest. I need to go to the market to gather a few things for dinner. I'll see if I can find something Mery might like. A ribbon or some *drop.*"

Ribbons and candy won't help, he thought, but he smiled and gave her a kiss.

"I *am* a lucky man," he managed.

"We all are lucky," Areana said. "Even Mery. We have each other."

"I'm not certain about that," Leoff said.

Areana frowned. "What can you mean?"

"I had a letter yesterday from Lord Edwin Graham. Mery's mother was his sister."

"They mean to take her away? But the duke put her in our charge."

"I'm not sure what he wants," Leoff replied. "He's sending his wife here to tell us. She'll arrive on Thonsdagh."

Lady Teris Graham was tall, taller than Leoff. She had unsettling sea-green eyes and a face spotted by rusty freckles, which made her dark, nearly black hair somehow surprising. Her face was strong-boned and long like her body, and she had come in a dark green and black traveling gown that looked expensive. She had two servants and two bodyguards with her, which also spoke of money. She was younger than he had expected. Areana had seated her in their small parlor, which up until then they really hadn't used for anything. Then she went for tea while the lady sized up Leoff.

"You're the man that wrote that sinfonia?" she said at last. "The one that started the riot in Glastir?"

"Yes," Leoff confirmed. "I'm afraid so."

"And the other thing, the play that the *people* liked so well?" The way she said "people" made it clear that it wasn't a term that included everyone—not, for instance, herself.

"Yes, lady."

"Yes," she repeated drily.

Areana arrived with the tea, and they sat sipping it in uncomfortable silence for a few moments.

"How well did you know my sister-in-law?" Lady Graham asked abruptly.

Leoff practically could feel Areana stiffen and a warmth flush his face.

To his surprise, the lady laughed. "Oh, dear," she said. "Yes, Ambria was a generous soul in some ways."

Leoff nodded, not knowing what to say, his mind suddenly filled with the sensations of that night, the warmth of Ambria's skin . . .

And, a few days later, her pitiful murdered gaze.

"Not to the point," Lady Graham said, shrugging. "The thing now is what's to be done with Mery."

"I think she should stay with us," Leoff said.

"Personally, I'm inclined to agree with you," the lady said. "I've no use for another brat underfoot. It's bad enough taking her brother in, but we'll soon have him married off. Still, she is William's bastard, and she is family, so my husband has other thoughts on the matter."

"She's safe here," Areana said. "And she's still heir."

"And you will be her parents?"

"Yes," Leoff said.

"In fact, perhaps. But technically, hasn't Duke Artwair made her his ward?"

"That's true," Leoff said.

"One would imagine Artwair would have reason for doing that. And for giving you this lovely house on the grounds of his even more lovely estate."

"My husband and the duke are friends," Areana said. "The house was a wedding gift."

"I'm sure it was," Lady Graham sighed. "But he's also keeping her close." She looked up sharply. "What's wrong with the girl, by the by? I've heard some very strange stories. Something about a music that kills?"

Leoff pursed his lips. The story had gotten around, somehow, but he didn't know if he should confirm it.

"They say that Prince Robert forced you to write a melody that slays anyone who hears it, and that Mery played it and did not die," she amplified.

When he didn't react to that, she sighed and signaled for her maidservant, who produced a folded paper sealed with wax.

He took the proffered document and found Artwair's seal on it. He broke it and read the contents.

Dear Friend, feel free to relate any and all particulars concerning Mery to Lady Teris Graham. She deserves to know the facts of the matter, and I trust her to be discreet.

—A.

Leoff looked up, feeling abashed. "Sorry, lady," he said.

"Your discretion does you credit. But do go on."

"It's as you said, except that Robert did not commission the piece. He wanted—or claimed to want—another singspell, one that would counteract my earlier work and make him popular with the people again. I think he always knew I would try to kill him."

"Ah. He tricked you into writing it. But it didn't kill him because he's already dead."

"Something like that. But it slew everyone else in the room."

"Except you and your bride here—and Mery."

"The music advances," Leoff said. "It's not a single sound but a progression that leads toward death. The last chord kills, but only if the entire piece is heard. I taught Mery and Areana a counterchord to hum to dilute the effect. We almost died, anyway. And Mery—she was playing the hammarharp, so she got the worst of it."

"Yes, I suppose she did." Lady Graham leaned back and had another sip of tea. "What do you suppose Robert will do with the music?"

"Something very bad," Leoff said.

"I'm trying to imagine. A band of pipers marching across the battlefield? A choir of trumpets, and everyone on the defending wall dropping dead?"

"It's not impossible," Leoff replied, feeling sick. "Hard to coordinate, but someone skilled enough in arranging and composing could do it."

"Someone like yourself?"

"Yes."

"Maybe that's why you're here, so well protected. Maybe Artwair has commissioned you to write the piece again."

"I won't. He knows that. He knows I would die first."

"But Mery might remember it?"

"No."

"She is a prodigy."

"No," he repeated, almost shouting.

"Not even to save Crotheny?"

"You stay away from her," he snapped.

Lady Graham nodded and drank a bit more tea. "What about your counterchord? Could you compose a music to neutralize whatever Robert may be up to? If he is up to anything other than his own amusement?"

"I don't know," he said.

"Have you tried?"

I don't want to be tricked again. He wanted to shout. *I don't want to be used again.*

"You let something terrible into the world, Leovigild Ackenzal. You're responsible for that."

"Who are you?" Areana asked suddenly. "You didn't come here to talk about the custody of Mery."

The lady smiled. "I admit to practicing a bit of deception," she replied. "But I've come here to tell you certain things and to perhaps give you a bit of a slap in the face."

"Who are you?" Areana repeated, looking askance at the lady's armed guard.

"Hush, child, so I can tell your husband something important."

"Don't speak to her like that," Leoff said.

The lady set her cup down. "Don't you wonder why, since the days of the Black Jester, no one has ever discovered what you discovered?"

"Robert placed certain books at my disposal."

"Yes, my point. There are books! They describe armies being slain by choirs of eunuchs and water organs. They explain how the modes function. These books are well known to scholars. Do you think in all of this time no one else with the talent to do so has attempted what you did?"

"I hadn't thought about it," Leoff admitted.

"It didn't happen because it wasn't possible," Graham, or whoever she was, said. "The music you created can only exist when the law of death is broken, as it was during the reign of the Black Jester. As it is now."

"The law of death?"

"The thing that separates life from death, that makes them different states."

"Robert!" Leoff exploded.

"Robert wasn't the first, but before him the law was only compromised. His return from death was the breaking point, and once broken, the law is more easily violated again and again, until the boundary between quick and dead is entirely gone. And when that happens—well, that's the end of us all. Imagine the law as like a dike, holding back deadly waters. When it's first compromised, there's just a small leak. Left alone, the hole gets wider no matter what. But when vandals start poking at it with shovels, it widens very quickly, and eventually the whole thing collapses."

"Why would anyone do that?"

"Well, you might put a small hole in a dike to run a water mill, yes? And you turn a profit and need a bigger mill, a larger stream of water? There is great power in violating the law of death. Robert can be stabbed in the heart and keep walking. You can write a sinfonia that murders, and that's only the start. As the law grows weaker, those who break it grow stronger. This is especially true now, as other powers of destruction are waxing."

"Why are you telling me this?"

"Your music made the hole, so to speak, considerably wider."

"But what can I do? How was the law of death mended before?"

She smiled. "I've no idea. But consider the possibility that if the right song can weaken the law—"

"Then another might strengthen it," Areana finished.

The lady stood. "Precisely."

"Wait," Leoff said. "That's not nearly enough. Why should I even believe any of this?"

"Because you do."

"No. I've been duped before. I'm not off on another fool's errand that might make everything worse."

"If that's true, there is no hope," the lady replied. "In any event, I've said what I came to say."

"Wait a moment."

"No, I shan't. Good luck to you."

And despite his further protests, she left, mounted her carriage, and was gone, leaving Leoff and Areana staring after her.

"Artwair knew she was coming," Areana said. "Perhaps he can shed some light on this."

Leoff nodded and absently realized he still had the duke's letter in his hand. He held it up, and blinked.

What had earlier appeared to be Artwair's seal was only an unmarked dab of wax.

PART I
✥
THE UNHEALED

The land bristles shadow and shrugs off the sun
Frail voices sing beneath the wind
It all ends soon
In health, courage comes easily
Death is still a dream
But I watch now
I see the true heroes
Stagger up on shaking limbs
And face what must be faced
Unhealed
—ANONYMOUS VIRGENYAN POET

Iery cledief derny
Faiver mereu-mem.
Even a broken sword has an edge.
—LIERISH PROVERB

CHAPTER ONE

✣

THE QUEEN
OF DEMONS

ANNE SIGHED with pleasure as ghosts brushed her bare flesh. She kept her eyes closed as they murmured softly about her, savoring their faintly chilly caresses. She inhaled the ripe perfumes of decay and for the first time in a very long time felt a deep contentment.

Anne, one of the phantoms simpered. *Anne, there is no time.*

A bit irritated, she opened her eyes to see three women standing before her.

No, she realized. They weren't standing at all. Feeling a weird tingle that she knew ought to be more, she turned her gaze around her to see what else there was.

She was *elsewhere,* of course, couched on deep, spongy moss grown on a hammock in a blackwater fen that went beyond sight in every direction. The branches of the trees above her were tatted together like the finest Safnian lace, allowing only the wispiest of diffuse light through to glisten on the dew-jeweled webs of spiders larger than her hand.

The women swayed faintly, the boughs above them creaking a bit from their weight.

One wore a black gown and a black mask, and her locks were flowing silver. The next wore forest green and a golden mask, and her red braids swayed almost to her feet. The third wore a mask of bone and a dress the color of dried blood. Her hair was brown.

Their undisguised lips and flesh were bluish-black above

the coils of rope that had cinched about their necks and wrung out their lives.

The Faiths, those obtuse creatures, were dead. Should she be sad? Part of her thought so.

Anne.

She started. Was one of them still alive? But then she felt the ghosts again, tickling against her. Now she knew who the ghosts were.

Should she be frightened? Part of her thought so.

"You're dead," she observed.

"Yes," the faint voice replied. "We fought to linger here, but too much of us is gone. We had something to tell you."

"Something useful? That would be the first time."

"Pity us, Anne. We did what we could. Find our sister."

"That's right, there are four of you," Anne remembered. Was she asleep? She seemed to be having trouble recalling things.

"Yes, four. Find—ah, no. He's coming. Anne—"

But then a cold wind started in the depths of the quag, and the canopy was alive with strange dark birds, and Anne was suddenly alone with the corpses.

But only for a moment. Then she felt *him,* as she had another time when in this place. All of her blood seemed to gather on one side of her body, and all of the branches of the forest yearned toward his invisible presence.

"Well, there you are, little queen," the voice said. "It's been too long."

"Stay back," she said. "You remember last time."

"Last time, I was weaker and you had help," the voice replied. "This is not last time."

"What do you want?"

"Your company, sweet queen. Your hand in marriage."

"Who are you?"

"Your king."

"I have no king," Anne bristled. "I am queen, regent in my own right."

"Look deeper in your heart," the voice purred.

"Who are you?"

"You want my name? What do names matter when one is as we are?"

"There is no 'we,' " Anne protested. But her belly tingled, as it had when Roderick had kissed her there.

The presence moved closer, and though she could not see him, she felt as if the shadow wore a wicked smile.

"Why did you kill the Faiths?"

A deep chuckle rustled through the branches, and the water stirred into circles all about.

Then a ruddy light fell on the broken surface of the fen, and Anne felt heat behind her. With a shriek, she turned to confront him.

But it was no male thing that stood behind her; there was no mistaking that. The body that shone like a white flame was willowy but certainly female, dressed only in locks that billowed and curled like strands of liquid, living fire. Her face was so terrible in its beauty that Anne felt as if icicles had been driven through her eyes and deep into her brain. She screamed so loudly, she felt her throat was tearing.

"Hush," the woman said, and Anne felt her larynx instantly close. Then the horrible gaze went through and beyond her.

"Leave," she commanded.

"You only delay the inevitable," the male voice muttered.

"Leave," the woman repeated.

Anne felt the weight of him lessen.

"I didn't kill your friends," he said, and was gone.

Anne felt the woman's gaze on her but could not look up.

"Who are you?" she whispered.

"The Kept gave you my true name," the woman replied. "He gave you some of my old epithets—Queen of Demons, and so on."

"Yes. But I don't . . ." She trailed off in confusion.

"You wonder rather *what* I am. What I want. Why I've helped you."

"I guess so," Anne said weakly, feeling suddenly presumptuous.

"Am I demon or saint?" the woman sighed, so close that Anne could feel her breath.

"Yes," Anne barely managed.

"If there were a difference, perhaps I could tell you," she replied.

"And the man . . ."

"He's quite right, you know," the woman went on. "He didn't kill the Faiths. I did. For you."

"What do you mean?"

"You led me to them. You rejected them, withdrew your protection, and I ended their existence. All but the one, and I shall find her."

"But why?"

"You don't need them," she said. "You never did. They were poor councillors. And now you have me."

"I don't want you," Anne protested.

"Then say my name. Tell me to leave."

Anne swallowed.

"You won't," the woman said. "You need my help. You need all the help you can get, because *he* will come for you and will either make you his or destroy you. Which means you must destroy him. And that you cannot currently do. Your friends will fall first, then you."

"And if I believe you, how can I stop that?"

"Strengthen yourself every way you can. Let me teach you the ways of your power. When he comes, you will be ready, if you trust me."

"Trust you," Anne murmured, finally lifting her gaze to the woman's face.

This time it wasn't so terrifying. There was something in the set of the woman's eyes that seemed truthful.

"Give me a reason to trust you," Anne said.

A smile slit the woman's face. "You have another enemy, one you haven't noticed yet, one that even I have difficulty seeing, for he—or perhaps she—sits deep in the shadows of the Reiksbaurg Palace. Like you, he is able to look across leagues and through time. Haven't you wondered why you manage to surprise the forces of the Church but Hansa is always one step ahead of you?"

"Yes," Anne replied. "I assumed spies and traitors were involved. How can you be certain it's shinecraft?"

"Because there is a place I can never see, and that is the sign of a Hellrune," the woman replied.

"A Hellrune?"

"A Hellrune sees through the eyes of the dead, who do not know past from present. Because the law of death has been broken, that is an even more powerful gift than it once was. But you get your visions directly through the sedos power. You can be stronger: See the consequences of his visions and act against them. In time, you will even be able to command the dead to give him false visions. But before you achieve that mastery, he can do much harm. If you act as I say, you may stop him sooner."

"How is that?"

"Send an embassy to Hansa, to the court of Marcomir. Send your mother, Neil MeqVren, Alis Berrye—"

"I'll do no such thing," Anne snapped. "I just got my mother back; I won't send her into danger."

"Do you think she isn't in danger in Eslen? Try to dream about that. I promise you that you will not like what visions come."

A sick dismay was starting to grip Anne, but she tried to stay strong. "You're less use than the Faiths," she said.

"No, I'm not. Your mother is going to ask to go, anyway; she thinks there is a chance for peace. You'll know by that that I'm telling you something useful. But further, I'll tell you this: If you send your mother, the knight, and the assassin to Kaithbaurg, I foresee an excellent chance for them to end the threat of the Hellrune and thus weaken Hansa. If you do not send them, I see you weeping over your mother's body in Eslen-of-the-Dead."

"An 'excellent chance'? Why can't you see whether they kill him or not?"

"Two reasons. The first is that since you haven't decided

to send them, the future is cloudy. But the deeper reason is that as I told you, I am not able to see the Hellrune. But I know the opportunity can arise. Try seeing it yourself."

"I can't direct my visions," Anne said. "They just come."

"You can direct them," the woman insisted. "Remember how once you had to be summoned *here*? Now you come and go as you please. It's the same. Everything you need is *here,* especially now that the Faiths aren't mucking around."

"Where is *here*?" Anne asked. "I've never understood that."

"Why, inside the sedos," she replied. "This is where the world is moved from, where the power flows from. It is given form only by those who live here. It is your kingdom now, and you can shape it as you want. Hansa, the future, the past—all are here. Grasp the reins of power. You need not take my word for anything I've just said. Discover it for yourself."

And like a fire blown out by a wind, she flickered and was gone.

Anne stood there for a moment, looking at the dead faces of the Faiths.

Was it possible? Could she really free herself from the whims of the forces around her? Could she actually steer them herself, be free of doubt, finally chart her own destiny without the meddling of untrustworthy wights?

"Why didn't you tell me any of this?" she asked the Faiths. But their whispering was over.

"Well," she murmured. "Let's see if she's telling the truth."

And she saw, and woke with tears streaming on her face, and knew some things had to be done.

She rose to do them.

CHAPTER TWO

AN EMBASSY

WHEN NEIL MEQVREN saw the dragon banner of Hansa, his heart sped and his hand shivered for killing. Pain stitched up his side, and he couldn't keep back a gasp.

"Easy, Sir Neil," Muriele Dare said.

He tried to smile at her. In the sunlight a bit of her age was showing: wrinkles at the corners of her eyes and on the line of the chin, a few strands of silver in her black hair. Yet he had never seen her look more beautiful than now, in an emerald Safnite riding habit and embroidered black buskins. A simple rose gold circlet settled over her brow told her rank.

"Sir Neil?" she repeated.

"Majesty," he replied.

"We aren't here to fight, so stray your hand away from that sword." Her brow creased. "Perhaps you shouldn't be here at all."

"I'm hale, Majesty."

"No, you aren't," she retorted. "Your wounds are still fresh."

"He's a MeqVren," Sir Fail de Liery said. "Like his father and his before. Men stubborn as an iron prow."

"I know I can't fight," Neil said. "I know I'll split open at the seams. But I still have eyes. I might see a knife in time."

"And *then* split open your seams," Fail grunted.

Neil shrugged, and even that hurt.

"You're not here to step between me and a knife, Sir Neil," Muriele said.

Then why am I here? he wondered silently. But he felt the

tightness in his arms and legs and knew. Like the leics who had tended him, the queen mother believed he might never be able to wield a blade again. She was trying, as it were, to teach him another trade. So now, while the kingdom girded for war, Neil found himself gazing on the faces of the enemy, trying to count them.

He estimated a full Hanzish wairdu, about a hundred men, on the field between them and the white walls of Copenwis, but that would be only a fraction of their army. Copenwis was occupied, and though he could not see them, Neil knew that a sizable portion of the Hansan fleet was anchored in the harbor and along the shore of the great port. Six thousand, perhaps. Ten? Twenty? There was no way to know from here.

In his own party there were twenty, not twenty thousand. To be sure, they had nearly two thousand men behind them, but they were more than a league behind. The queen had not wanted to tempt the Hansans into battle. Not yet, anyway.

So the northerners glared at their flag of parley, and they waited. Neil heard them muttering in their windy tongue and remembered dark nights in his childhood, creeping up on Hanzish positions, hearing the same hushed language.

"Copenwis has fine walls," Sir Fail observed.

Neil nodded and glanced at his old patron. Not long ago, he'd still had a trace of black in his hair, but now it was less gray than white. He wore it long, in the fashion of the isles, bound back with a simple leather thong. His cheek was pitted from the shatters of a spear shaft, and one of his brows lifted oddly from the time a Weihand sword had all but flensed that part of his forehead from his skull. Neil had first seen him with that purple, loose flap of skin and his eye swollen shut. He'd been six and had thought he was seeing Neuden Lem Eryeint, the battle saint, come as flesh on earth. And in the years since, serving him, in his heart of hearts he still thought of Fail that way: immortal, greater than other men.

But Fail looked old now. He seemed to have shrunk a bit. It unsettled Neil.

"It does," he agreed, tracing his gaze along the stout bastions of white stone.

"I lived there for a time," Alis Berrye said.

"Did you?" Muriele asked.

"When I was eight. I stayed here with an uncle for a few months. I remember a pretty park in the midst of the city, with a fountain and the statue of Saint Nethune."

Neil studied Alis from the corner of his eye. Her tone was light, but a little pucker between her eyes made him guess the young woman was trying to remember more: how the streets were laid out, where the gates were, anything that might help her protect and defend Muriele. For despite her youth, charm, and beauty, if the petite brunette was anything like her predecessor, she was dangerous, and the more knowledge she had, the more dangerous she could be.

Neil wasn't sure he trusted her. Her past did not speak well of her.

He suddenly found Alis staring straight into his eyes and felt a flush on his face.

I caught you, she mouthed, then smiled cheerfully.

"Stout walls, anyway," he said, sheepishly returning her smile.

"This poor city has changed hands so often, I wonder why they bother with walls," Muriele remarked. She stood a bit in her stirrups. "Ah," she said. "Here we are."

Neil saw him, coming through the Hanzish ranks, a large man mounted on a charger in gleaming barding enameled black and sanguine. He wore a breastplate made in the same colors displaying an eagle stooping. It looked more ceremonial than useful. A cloak of white bearskin hung on his shoulders, and his oiled sealskin boots gleamed.

Neil knew him. He'd first seen that pink, corpulent face at his own introduction to the court of Eslen. It was the Archgreft Valamhar of Aradal, once ambassador to the court of Crotheny.

"Saint Rooster's balls," Fail muttered under his breath.

"Hush," Muriele hissed, then raised her voice.

"Archgreft."

The Hanzish lord nodded and dismounted, aided by four of the eight young men in his livery who had come with him to the field. Then he took a knee.

"Majesty," he said. "I must say, I am glad the Ansus have kept you well. I worried and prayed for you during your captivity."

"I'm sorry you were troubled," Muriele told him. "I do so dislike being the cause of disturbance."

Aradal smiled uncertainly. "Well, I am all better now," he replied.

"Yes. And rather camped in one of our cities," she said, nodding at Copenwis.

"Oh, yes, that," Aradal said. "I'm thinking that is what you've come to discuss."

"You are as brilliant as ever, my lord," she replied.

"Well, it must be the company I keep," he said.

"Perhaps," Muriele replied. "In any event, yes, I've been empowered by Empress Anne to take the terms of your withdrawal from our northern port."

"Well, Majesty, that's a bit sticky," Aradal said. "You see, we had the king's permission to take Copenwis under our protection."

"By king you mean my brother-in-law Robert?" Muriele asked. "Robert was a usurper, never a lawful sovereign, so that's easily cleared up. His word never came from the crown, and so you've no right or reason to be here."

Aradal scratched his ear. "It's rather more complicated than that, don't you think?"

The queen drew back a bit. "I don't see how. Take your fleet and your men and go home, Aradal."

"Well, they aren't my men or my fleet, are they, Majesty? They belong to His Majesty Marcomir III, and he recognizes Robert as king and emperor of Crotheny."

"If you've given shelter to that hell-hearted bastard—" Fail began, but Muriele silenced him with a frown before turning back to the archgreft.

"If Robert has taken refuge with your liege, that is another matter," she said, her voice sounding a bit strained.

"But for now, I think bringing our countries back from the brink of war should do."

Aradal lowered his voice. "Majesty, you assume that war is to be prevented. I rather think it will happen."

"Marcomir's avarice has been known for a long time," Muriele said, "but—"

Aradal shook his head. "No, there is more to it than that, Majesty. Your daughter has murdered churchmen, Muriele. William defied the Church, but Anne has denied and *attacked* it. Our people are devout, and the signs are all around us. There are those who say that it is not enough to conquer Crotheny; they say it must be cleansed." His voice lowered further. "Majesty, I have tried to tell you before, I am friendly to you. Take your daughter and those you care for and go to Virgenya or someplace even farther. I . . ." He broke off. "I have said too much."

"You will do nothing?"

"I *can* do nothing."

Muriele shrugged. "Very well. Then I must speak with Marcomir."

Aradal's brows raised. "Lady . . ."

"By the most ancient law of nations, by the covenant the free peoples created when the Skasloi were destroyed, you *must* provide me safe passage to the court of your king, and you must conduct me safely out of it. Even the Church itself cannot subvert that most basic law."

Aradal's cheek twitched.

"Can you do that? Can you uphold the ancient covenant?"

"I can give you my word," he finally said. "But my word does not travel very far from me these days."

The queen's eyes widened. "You cannot be implying that Marcomir would kill me or take me prisoner."

"I am saying, lady, that the world has gone mad, and I can promise nothing. My liege is a man of law, I assure you, and I would stake my life that he would not treat you ill."

"But?"

"But I can promise nothing."

Muriele took a deep breath and let it out. Then she

straightened and spoke in her most courtly tones. "Will you arrange for my party to travel to the court under flag of truce so that I can press the case for peace before His Majesty? Will you do that, Archgreft?"

Aradal tried to meet her gaze and failed, but then something strengthened in him, and he lifted his head. "I will," he replied.

"I will return in the morning with my chosen companions," she said.

"No more than fifteen," he said.

"That will be sufficient," Muriele assured him.

On another day the Maog Voast plain might have seemed pretty, Neil reflected. Four months had passed since his wounding in the battle for the waerd. It was the fifteenth of Ponthmen, and summer was just coming into its own. The fields were glorious with the white spires of lady's traces, yellow oxeyes, purple thrift, and a rainbow's hoard of flowers he didn't recognize. They mingled their sweet scents with that of wild rosemary, bee fennel, and something that reminded him of apple, although there were no trees in sight on the flat landscape. Still, the riding of a league was a long time for Neil to have the army of Hansa at his back, and he glanced behind often despite the lack of cover for an ambush. But that lack of cover went two ways, and Neil felt rather as a mouse might, wondering if a hawk was about to come out of the sun.

Muriele noticed.

"I don't think they'll attack us, Sir Neil," she said.

"No," Fail snapped. "Why should they when you'll deliver yourself to them tomorrow?"

"The old law—"

"Even Aradal won't vouch for its keeping," the duke pointed out.

"Niece, you've just escaped one prison. Why must you hurry back into another? They'll hold you hostage to better bargain with Anne. Lady Berrye, reason with her."

Alis shrugged. "I serve at the pleasure of Queen Muriele," she said. "I find her reasonable enough."

"And don't forget, we have hostages of our own," Muriele added.

"Schalksweih?" Fail muttered. "How could I forget? It was I took him captive and his ship a prize. But against you . . ."

"He's a favorite of Marcomir's," she said. "They have sued for his release."

Fail looked heavenward, shaking his head.

"Why are you really doing this, dove?"

"What else should I do? Knit stockings while my daughter rides into battle? Arrange flowers as army after army arrays against us?"

"Why not, Majesty?" Neil interjected.

"Excuse me, Sir Neil?"

"Why not?" he repeated. "The fleet of Hansa is inside our borders, and their land army is on the march. What can you say that will deter them? Sir Fail is right: You've suffered enough, milady."

"How much I've suffered is not at issue," Muriele countered. "And although I'm not flattered by your opinion of my political abilities, I see a chance to stop this war, and I will take it. I've discussed this with Anne. She will not yield one grain of our dirt if I am taken hostage."

"She fought like a demon to retrieve you from Robert," Fail pointed out.

"Things have changed," Muriele said.

Anne has changed, Neil reflected. Muriele was probably right in that: The empress would not be intimidated even by threats to her own mother.

He wondered where she was now: on the throne or off killing churchmen. The latter had become almost a sport to her.

"Well," Fail said. "I'll go."

"One of our best sea commanders? It's out of the question. You're needed here, guarding our waves. Anyway, the strain of keeping your sword sheathed would split the vein on your forehead. You're not much of a diplomat, Uncle."

"And you are?"

She shrugged. "I've seen it done, and I have the station for it, even though I am a woman." She paused. "Anne *wants* me to go, Uncle. One of her visions. She says there's a chance."

"Visions," he snorted.

"She knew you were coming with the fleet," Neil said. "She knew when. It's why we knew we had to take down Thornrath so quickly."

"Aye," Fail muttered, chewing his lip. "Maybe her visions are true. But your own daughter, sending you to the viper's den—it's hard to fathom."

"Majesty," Neil said. "I know I'm not much use—"

"Oh, you're going," Muriele said. "Why do you think you're here? If it were my decision, you would still be abed."

Neil frowned. "You mean to say the empress wants me to go to Hansa?"

"She was quite adamant about it."

"I see."

Muriele shifted in her saddle.

"Do you feel slighted, not being in her guard?" she asked.

That took him by surprise. "Milady?"

"Are you disappointed at being returned to my service?" she amplified.

He shook his head. "Majesty, I always considered myself in your service. When I was guarding Anne, I was following your orders. I am your man and do not hope to be anyone else's."

He didn't add that he found Anne more than a little uncanny, and although he knew firsthand that some in the Church had turned to darkness, he was happy not to be directly involved in Anne's vendetta against z'Irbina.

Muriele took in his speech without a hint of changed expression, then nodded slightly.

"Very well. Once we return to camp, pick the men who

will accompany us. In the morning we'll begin our journey
to Hansa."

Neil nodded and began thinking about who to take along.
More than ever, he felt like prey beneath a hunter sky.

CHAPTER THREE

THE END
OF A REST

ASPAR WHITE tried to match his breath to the faint breeze
through the forest fringe, to be as still as a stump as the
monster approached. It was just a shape at the moment,
about twice the size of a horse and slouching through the
narrow white boles of the aspens. But he smelled autumn
leaves although it was high summer, and when its eyes glittered like blue lightning through the branches, he felt the
poison in its blood.

It wasn't a surprise. The world was made of monsters
now, and he had fought plenty. Sceat, he'd met their mother.

A few jays were shrieking at the thing, but most of the
other bird sounds were gone, because most birds weren't as
blind, stupid, brave as jays.

Maybe it'll just go by, he thought. *Maybe it'll just pass
on by.*

He was already tired; that was the damned thing. His leg
ached, and his lungs hurt. His muscles were all soft, and his
vision kept going blurry.

Half a bell he'd been out there, at the most, working himself no harder than a baby taking pap. Just looking across
the meadow.

Pass, he thought. *I don't care what you are or where
you're going. Just pass.*

But it didn't, of course. Instead, he heard it pause and snuffle and then saw the actinic flash of its eyes. It stepped from the trees and into the field, moving toward Aspar as he waited in the cover of the trees on his side.

"Hello, *luvileh*," he muttered, quickly thrusting four more arrows into the soft earth before him. No point imitating a stump anymore.

It was something new, not a monster he had seen before. From a distance, the thing resembled a bull crossed with a hedgehog. Bony spines bristled from it everywhere, and it was massively front-heavy, with colossal bunches of muscle above forelegs easily twice as long as the hind legs. Its head was blocky, with a single horn spearing forward so that it looked almost like an anvil. The eyes were set deep in bony plate.

He had no idea what to call it. Besides the eyes, he didn't see anything that might be soft.

It bellowed, and he noticed sharp teeth. Were all sedhmhari carnivores? He hadn't met one that wasn't.

"You make pretty babies, Sarnwood witch," he grunted.

And here it came.

His first shot skittered off the armored skull, as did the second. The third lodged in the eye socket—or he thought it did, but after a heartbeat it fell out, and the eye was still there.

It was *fast* and even bigger than he'd thought. It bellowed again, a sound so loud that it hurt his ears. He had time for one more arrow but knew even as he released it that it was going wide of the eye. The monster bounded even faster, hit the ground, and crouched for the final leap, its forelimbs lifted up almost like a man's, reaching for him . . .

Then the ground collapsed beneath it, and this time it shrieked in surprise and anger as it fell hard onto the sharpened stakes four kingsyards below. A catch snapped above Aspar, releasing a sharpened beam that had been suspended above the pit. He couldn't see it hit but heard a fleshy thud.

Aspar let out a long breath, but an instant later a massive paw—a thick-fingered hand, really—clawed up over the edge of the hole. Aspar scooted back against a tree and used his bow to lever himself up.

The other hand came up, followed by the head. He saw even more of a family resemblance to the utin he once had fought, but if it could speak, it didn't. It strained, blood blowing from its nostrils, and began to crawl from the pit.

"Leshya!" Aspar snapped.

"Here," he heard her say. He felt the wind as another massive log came swinging down, this one aimed to skim along just above the trap. It hit the beast in the horn, crushing it back into its skull, and it vanished into the hole again.

Aspar turned at Leshya's soft approach. Her violet eyes peered at him from beneath her broad-brimmed hat.

"You're all right?" she lilted.

"No worse than I was this morning," he replied. "Aside from the indignity of being bait."

She shrugged. "Should have thought of that before you went and got your leg broken."

She walked over to the pit, and Aspar limped after her to see.

It didn't know it was dead yet. Its flanks were still heaving, and the hind legs twitching. But the head was cracked like an egg, and Aspar didn't imagine it would breathe much longer.

"What in Grim's name do we call that?" he grunted.

"I remember stories about something like this," she said. "I think it was called a *mhertyesvher*."

"That the Skaslos name for it?"

"I couldn't pronounce the Skaslos name for it," she replied.

"Notwithstandin' that you are one," he said.

"I was born in this shape, with this tongue," she said. "I've never heard the language of the Skasloi. I've told you that."

"Yah," Aspar assented. "You've told me." He looked back at the dying beast and rubbed the stubble on his chin. "Well," he mused, "I think it's a manticore."

"As good a name as any," she said. "Now, why don't we go rest."

"I'm not tired," Aspar lied.

"Well, there's no reason to stay here. It'll be days before the poison clears out, even if it rains."

"Yah," Aspar agreed.

"Come on, then."

He slung the bow on his back and looked around for his crutch, only to find Leshya holding it out for him. He took it silently, and they began walking back through the trees. It got harder when the slope turned upward, and they followed a little switchback trail up an ever-steepening way. At last it opened onto a rocky ridge that gave a good view of the scatters of forest and meadow below. A deep ravine fell from the other side of the crest, and across that, white-capped mountains rose against the turquoise sky. The western horizon was also bounded in peaks. With their back to the chasm and a view for leagues in every other direction, it was here they usually spotted the monsters when they came; that was why Leshya had picked the spot to build the shelter. It had started as a lean-to made of branches, but now it was a comfortable little four-post house with birch-bark roof.

Aspar didn't remember the building of it; he'd been deep in the land of Black Mary, in and out of a fever that jumbled three months into a haze of images and pain. When it was finally gone, it left him so weak that even without a broken leg he couldn't have walked. Leshya had tended him, built traps, fought the monsters that appeared more and more frequently.

The climb left him winded, and he sat on a log, looking out over the valley below.

"It's time to go," he said.

"You aren't ready to travel," Leshya said, poking the banking of the morning's fire, looking for embers.

"I'm ready," he said.

"I don't think so."

"You came after me with your stitching still wet," Aspar said. "I'm in better shape than that."

"You're wheezing from a little walk," the Sefry pointed out. "That ever been the case before?"

"I've never been flat on my back for four months," Aspar replied, "but I can't spare any more time."

She smiled, slightly. "Are you that much in love with her?"

"None of your business," he said.

"Us leaving now could get us both killed. Makes it my business."

"I want to find Winna and Ehawk, yes. But there's more to it. I have duties."

"To whom? To that girl-queen Anne? You've no idea whether she's alive or not. Or who sits the throne of Crotheny. Aspar, the Briar King is dead. There's nothing left to check the sedhmhari. There are more of them every day."

"Yah. And sitting here killing them one at a time won't help."

"What do you think will?"

"I don't know. I've thought I might go back to where he was sleeping, find something."

"In the Mountains of the Hare? That's twenty leagues from here as the eagle goes, and we aren't eagles." Her eyes slitted. "Do you have some reason to think you should go there?"

"No."

"No?" She sighed. "I know you, Aspar White. You just want to die fighting for the King's Forest. This one here isn't good enough."

"It's not—" He stopped. *Not mine,* he finished silently, imagining the great ironoaks of his youth rotting into putrid jelly, the bright streams clogged with death, the ferny glens choked in black thorn. Did he really want to see that?

"You came to find me," he said, "all those months ago. You talked about having a duty other Sefry have abandoned. What is it?"

She had found some coals and was coaxing them to life and adding tinder from a pile near the pit, stirring up the scent of hickory and juniper. "I don't know," she said. "I don't know if I can tell you that."

"I already know what you and your kind really are. After that, what secret is worth keeping?"

"I told you, I'm not sure. I'm trying to maun it out."

"Well, fine; find me when you do. I'm going now."

"You don't even know where we are," Leshya said.

"Well, I reckon if I head south, I'll eventually come across someplace I know," he replied.

"We're lucky I remembered this place," she said. "Otherwise they would have caught us long ago."

"Who? Fend?"

"And his people."

"Your people."

She acknowledged that with a bow of her head.

"Well, I'm sure they've stopped looking by now," he replied.

"I doubt that," she said. "You were with the Briar King when he died. He might have told you something."

"What do you mean? So far as I know, he can't speak."

"That doesn't mean he didn't tell you something."

Aspar remembered the shocking rush of visions he'd had as the Briar King died.

"Yah," he said. "But if he told me anything, I don't know what it was."

"Yet."

"Sceat," he muttered.

"Aspar, you could be the most important man in the world right now. You might be the only one who can stop what's happening—save the King's Forest, if that's the only thing that means anything to you."

"Is that why we're still here? You're hopin' I'll have some sainty vision?"

"I can't think of any other hope to cling to. It's why I've kept you safe."

He looked at her. "That you have," he said. "And I'm grateful. But there's no need for you to take my part anymore. I'm strong enough now."

"You aren't, and you know it."

"I won't get stronger sittin' about here," he said. "And

you know that. Now, if you think I'm so important, I reckon
you can come with me. But I *am* going."

She had a fire now. "Rabbit for supper," she said.

"Leshya."

She sighed. "Another four days," she said.

"Why?"

"You'll be four days stronger, and the moon will be dark.
We'll need that, I think."

Aspar nodded and looked back to the east. He pointed at
a nearly invisible talus slope that vanished behind a ridge.

"Is that the pass we came in through?" he asked.

She nodded.

"I reckoned."

"The only way in or out unless you're a bird or wild-
buck."

He nodded, then squinted. "We might not get that four
days," he said.

"Ilshvic," Leshya snarled. He didn't know what she'd
said but could make a pretty good guess.

A line of mounted figures was coming through the pass,
a lot of them.

CHAPTER FOUR

✦

PROPOSITION AND
DISPOSITION

THE BROADSWORD cutting toward Cazio was moving
almost too fast to see, and he suddenly understood the nasty
grin on the monk's face. Cazio reacted from years of training, jabbing his lighter but longer weapon out in a stop-
thrust that should have pierced the man's sword wrist. It
didn't, though, because—impossibly—the monk checked

his swing. He stepped back and regarded Cazio for a moment, just out of measure.

"Interesting," he said. "I've never met a swordsman like you. Are you from Safnia?"

"They have butchers in Safnia," Cazio panted, trying to both watch the man and check his peripheral vision. Sounds of battle were everywhere. "But the only swordsmen in the world come from Vitellio."

"I see." The fellow grinned again. "Vitellio. Home of the father Church."

The man had gray eyes, darkish skin, and an accent Cazio couldn't place.

"Tell me," the man went on. "Why do you follow this heretic queen, you a man from the very birthplace of our faith?"

"I like the color of her hair," Cazio replied, "and the sort of people she associates with."

"When I move next," the man warned, "you won't have time to see the cut that kills you. Lay down your arms and you will be well treated."

"I'm already well treated," Cazio replied.

"You know what I mean."

Cazio sighed and relaxed his guard.

"See there," the man said. "I knew you looked sensible."

Cazio nodded and lunged, throwing his front foot forward and pushing with the back.

The monk blurred toward him, and as Cazio let his lunge collapse into a forward duck, he felt hair shaved from the top of his head. The monk ran onto his rapier so hard that the hilt slammed into his solar plexus and the grip was wrenched from Cazio's hand. The monk fell, hit, rolled, and sprawled, eyes glazing and blood pumping.

"As long as I can draw you into attacking when and where I want," Cazio informed him, "I don't need to be able to see you."

The monk jerked his head in affirmation. Cazio could see that his spine was broken.

"Come get your sword," the monk suggested.

"No, I'll wait a moment," he replied.

"You don't have a moment," the man pointed out.

Cazio followed his gaze and saw that he didn't. Two of the man's brethren were rushing toward him.

Grimly, he started toward the fallen broadsword, only a yard away.

Then he felt something like a thousand spiders racing across his skin. His windpipe closed, and his heart shuddered, stopped, and started again, faster than before. He gasped and fell to one knee but fought back up.

But there was no need. His attackers were sprawled motionless on the ground, their corpses twisted unnaturally.

He turned and found Anne two kingsyards behind him. Her eyes were green ice, looking somewhere he couldn't see. Her body was taut beneath her black and ocher riding habit, like the string of a lute tightened almost to breaking.

She shifted her gaze to him, and his heart suddenly went strange again.

Then her face softened and she smiled, and he swallowed as the pain in his chest eased. He started to say something, but he saw she wasn't looking at him anymore but instead studying the grounds of the monastery.

"That's it, then," she said softly. "That's all of them."

"That's what we thought before," Cazio said, lifting himself to his feet. "Before these fellows came up from behind."

"True," Anne murmured. "I miss things still. They just arrived, I think—from the forest."

"And there could be more. Anne, you ought to get inside. Your Sefry can sweep the woods around."

She shot him a smile that he suddenly suspected was condescending. But then, she had just killed two men without touching them, and it wasn't the first time.

"You can still bleed," he pointed out. "An arrow can still kill you. I can't quite catch an arrow."

"True," Anne said. "Secure me. I am at your disposal."

The monastery Saint Eng stood on a small hill surrounded by wheat fields and pasture, save for one dark finger of forest that prodded up to it from the south. The clock tower of the town of Pale could be seen in the west, near the line of the same forest. It wasn't a big place, just a few outbuildings and barns scattered around a squat, squarish structure with a single rather inelegant tower rising from the southeast corner.

Before they had taken ten steps, five of Anne's cowled Sefry guard were with them, led by their amber-eyed captain, Cauth Versial.

"Majesty," Cauth said, taking a knee. "Apologies. They drew us away from you."

"It's nothing," Anne said. "You see my Cazio was able to handle it."

My Cazio? Why had she phrased it like that?

"Nevertheless," the Sefry said, "I shouldn't have left you with only one guard. But the inside of the monastery is secure now."

"Good," Anne replied. "We'll go there, then. And I think I'd like to dine."

"It's nearly that hour," the Sefry said. "I'll have something fetched."

By the next bell Cazio was sitting with Anne in a small room on the west side of the building. St. Abulo was driving the sun down the Hesper sky, but he still had a few bells to go this long summer day.

"I'll miss this," Anne sighed, gazing out the window and sipping her wine.

"Miss what?"

"These outings."

"Outings? You mean our fights with the Church?"

"Yes," she replied. "Just sitting on the throne is dull, and the details of war—well, the generals don't really need me to work those out. This feels *real* to me, Cazio. I can see the faces of those we rescue."

Cazio sniffed his wine, then raised it up.

"Az da Vereo," he toasted.

"Yes," Anne agreed. "To the real."

They drank.

"This is Vitellian," he murmured. "From the Tero Vaillamo region if I'm not very wrong."

Anne tilted her head. "Why does it matter? Wine is wine, isn't it?"

For a moment Cazio had no idea what to say. He'd known Anne for almost a year and been almost constantly at her side during that time. He'd formed a pretty good opinion of her and had certainly never suspected she was capable of what could even charitably only be called a moronic statement.

"I, ah, you're kidding with me," he finally managed.

"Well, there's red and white, I suppose," she went on. "But really, beyond that I've never been able to tell the difference."

Cazio blinked, then held up his cup. "You can't tell the difference between this and the frog blood we drank at that inn on the way here? You really can't?"

She shrugged and took a large swallow, then looked thoughtful.

"No," she said. "I like this, but I liked the 'frog blood,' too."

"It must be like being blind or deaf," Cazio said. "I . . . it's really absurd."

She pointed the index finger of the hand holding the glass at him. "That's just the sort of comment *some* queens might have your head struck off for," she said.

"Yes, well, I'd rather have it struck off if I couldn't discern *Dacrumi da Pachio* from Piss-of-the-Cat."

"But you *can*," Anne said, "or say you can, so best start walking backward now."

"My apologies," Cazio said. "It's just that this wine—" He tasted it again and dropped his eyelids. "Close your eyes," he said, "and taste it again."

He heard Anne sigh.

"It's five, maybe six years ago," he began. "The hills in the Tero Vaillamo are purple with the blooms of wild oregano and lavender; the juniper trees are swaying in a slight breeze. It's hot, and it hasn't rained in a month. The vines

are heavy with little purple grapes so ripe that some have already begun to ferment. The *familia* is picking them, old
men, young men, girls and boys, handling each grape like a
little jewel, fruit from the same stock their grandparents and
great-grandparents picked two hundred years ago and more.
They put the grapes in a big vat, and as the afternoon cools,
they feast on roast pork, they open last year's wine, and
there's music while they smash the grapes with apple-wood
pestles. They ferment it carefully, the way they've done it
for centuries. They take their time, and the method never
leaves the family. They let it ripen in a cellar, not too cool,
not too hot. Perfect." He took another sip. "Taste. The
oregano, the lavender, the juniper. The smoke is their cooking fire, where they roasted the boar for the vatting feast.
The art, the care . . ."

He suddenly felt breath on his lips.

"Hush," Anne said as she kissed him.

She smelled like the wine and apricot and fresh green apple. Her tongue searched against his, and his whole body
flashed hot. He fumbled his wine down and stood, reaching
for her head, cupping behind her ears, and drawing her up
against him. She laughed and pressed close.

Cazio took a breath—and lifted his head.

"Wait," he said. "What—*what*?"

"I had to shut you up," she said, reaching back up with
her mouth. "You would have gone on like that all night.
Come on; you know you wanted this."

He released her and stepped back a little. "Well, yes," he
said. "But you weren't interested, and then Austra . . ." He
floundered off.

"So all of those things you said in Vitellio, when we met,
and on the road home were nothing, just lies?"

"No," he said. "No, but it was before I knew who you were
and before—"

"Austra," Anne finished, crossing her arms. "Before you
and Austra." She frowned. "You're no good for her."

"No good for her but fine for you?"

"I'm different," Anne said. "Austra—you could hurt Austra."

"But not you?"

"Once, maybe. Not now."

"Well, I've no intention of hurting Austra," Cazio said.

"No. Otherwise you might do something like, oh, kiss her best friend."

"You kissed *me*!"

"That's how *you* tell it," Anne replied.

"Now, wait," he began, suddenly feeling that everything was out of control.

Anne suddenly laughed and picked her wine back up. "Hush, drink," she said. "Your virtue is safe. I just wanted to know."

"What?"

"If you really love Austra. If you're really faithful to her. If you can be trusted."

"Oh," he said, his head whirling. "Then this was all for her?"

"Well, it certainly wasn't for you," Anne said. "Now *ta-cheta,* and drink your wine, and don't try to explain it to me anymore."

Cazio did as he was told, desperately trying to sort out what had just happened. He'd felt more competent on his brother's boat, and he not only knew nothing about the sea but never felt adequate around his brother. He tried to sneak a glance at Anne, to see what the expression on her face was, but was a little afraid to.

When he'd first met Anne, she'd been in love with a man named Roderick, or thought she was, the way girls often did with their first paramours. Still, Cazio had always felt he had a chance. Anne had never given him much hope, though, and when he'd discovered she was in line to be queen of one of the most powerful nations in the world, he'd given up the matter for lost. Besides, his feelings for Austra had been strengthening that whole time, and he was happy with her, missed her even now.

So why did he want to grab Anne and return her kiss? Why did he find it so hard to picture Austra at the moment?

A light rap at the door caught his attention. He glanced up and saw that it was one of Anne's Sefry pages.

"Majesty," he said. "Duke Artwair of Haundwarpen begs a word."

"Yes, of course; send him in."

A moment later the duke appeared, an imposing man with steel-gray eyes and close-cropped hair. One of his hands was made of wood.

"Majesty," he said, bowing.

"Cousin, it's good to see you. To what do I owe the pleasure?"

He smiled uncomfortably. "I was riding in the area."

"That's an odd coincidence. This place is rather out of the way."

"Indeed. I was riding in the area because reports were that you were here."

"I see. You've come to collect me. Is that it?"

"You are the empress," Artwair said, "I cannot 'collect' you. But you are needed in Eslen. Your people need you on your throne."

"My people have seemed rather pleased to see me freeing their towns from torture and oppression."

"Yes, I agree. Your . . . adventures . . . have made you very popular. But now some begin to wonder if you are neglecting the larger issue of the war that seems sure to come."

"I've you to general my army."

"And you've an army to do the sort of thing you've been risking your life at these last few months. And this place— why did you come here? A monastery in the country, not so far from the Hansan border. Have you any idea how exposed you are here?"

Anne nodded. "I won't be here long. And this is the last."

"The last what?"

"The last of my 'little adventures,' as I was just telling Cazio. When I'm done here, I'll return to Eslen, I promise."

"Well, you've reduced the place," Artwair pointed out. "What more did you have in mind?"

"Don't you know where we are?" Anne asked. "The saint this faneway is dedicated to?"

The duke's eyes widened. "You wouldn't—"

"Why wouldn't I?"

"B-because that is the business of the Church," Artwair sputtered.

"A Church I have stripped of authority in my kingdom," she pointed out.

"Of temporal authority, yes," Artwair said. "But this is different. Here you are definitely stepping into the realm of the sacred."

Anne shrugged. "So be it. The Church abused the boundaries first, not me."

"I don't understand," Cazio said.

Anne turned to him. "This monastery is committed to Saint Mamres, the bloody saint of war," she said. "His faneway is here. As we control it now, the Church will be making no new warrior-monks. And indeed, perhaps I will make a few of my own."

Artwair's face was still red, but the expression on it was turning thoughtful.

"It's an interesting idea," he said, "but a dangerous one. Forget the ire of the Church—"

"Done," Anne pronounced.

"Well. Forget it, then. But you aren't the first worldly ruler to try this, you know. Twenty years ago, Marhgreft Walis bribed the monks to let his bodyguard walk this faneway."

"And?"

"There were ten of them. Seven died walking it. Another went mad immediately."

"And the other two?"

"Were very good bodyguards. But the sacrifice—"

"Even bribed, I expect, the monks were loath to give up the power they guarded," Anne said. "I imagine they neglected to mention some sacaum or such that needed doing.

We have a few of them to question on the matter, so we won't be missing any information."

"I'm just urging caution, Majesty."

"I know. But the enemy has Mamres monks and knights that cannot die and other monsters in number. I feel we need some of the same benefits."

"Nor do I dispute it. Just be cautious."

"I shall. And then I shall return to Eslen, I promise you, Cousin."

Artwair left, and Cazio stayed close on his heels, looking more than a little relieved to be leaving her presence. She poured herself more wine, took a swallow, and went to the window.

"What have I done?" she whispered to the faintly visible evening star. She closed her eyes, but lightning seemed to flash there and made her mind busy. Her body was humming head to toe with desire.

She and Austra had been best friends for all of her life. She loved her like a sister and in a moment had betrayed her.

She wasn't entirely stupid. She'd known her feelings for Cazio had been changing these last few months. Despite her first impressions of him, he'd proved more reliable and noble than any knight she had ever known with the possible exception of Neil MeqVren. He was also handsome, amusing, and intelligent.

And Austra's now. She'd tried to keep that firmly in her mind. But Austra should have known better, shouldn't she? Austra knew what Anne felt before she did. Austra, her best friend, had snapped up the swordsman before Anne could sort out her own feelings.

"What sort of friend is that?" she wondered aloud.

She knew that she probably wasn't being completely fair, but who was there to hear her?

Austra had no place in a fighting force and had proved that by getting injured on their first ride against the gallows of Brithwater. Nothing serious, but she'd sent her back to

Eslen. These last few weeks, without her maid around, she'd felt that something was happening between her and the swordsman, something inevitable.

And when he'd kissed her back, she'd been really happy, like a girl again, ready to forget her duties, the coming war, the strange things happening in her mind and body as she gained more and more command of the powers Saint Cer had given her.

But no, he'd been surprised, and he'd remembered Austra *very* quickly, and so she had been wrong about their growing closer.

How foolish that must seem to him, and how intolerable to seem foolish.

And how tiring, how very tiring, to be still a virgin. Maybe she should have someone she didn't give a fig about fix that for her and then have him exiled or beheaded or something so that she could see what the fuss was about. Austra knew well enough, didn't she? Because of Cazio.

She shook that away. With all that was going on in her kingdom—in the world—didn't she have better things to worry about? If Eslen fell, if the dark forces gathering against her triumphed, it wouldn't matter who Cazio had or hadn't loved.

"Majesty?" a soft voice whispered. She turned to find Cauth regarding her.

"Yes?"

"We've found the map of the faneway."

"Excellent," she replied. "We should begin immediately. Have you picked your men?"

"I—Majesty, I thought you knew."

"Knew what?"

"Sefry cannot walk faneways. Our constitutions forbid it."

"What does that mean?"

"No Sefry has ever survived the attempt," he replied.

"Really? Not just this faneway but any?"

"That's correct, Majesty."

"Wonderful," she said sarcastically. "Send for the Craftsmen, then."

"Very well. Is there anything else?"

Anne turned and rested her head against the windowsill.

"I'm changing, Sir Cauth," she said. "Why is that?"

"I haven't known you long," he said, "but I expect being queen changes you."

"No. That's not what I mean. How much did Mother Uun tell you?"

"Not everything, but enough. You mean your blessing."

"Is it a blessing?" she asked. "I'm stronger, yes. I can do things. But I'm changing. I think things I never thought before, feel things I've never felt . . ."

"You are touched by great powers," he said. "That's only natural."

Anne shivered. "Some of my visions are terrible."

"I'm sorry for your pain," he said. He sounded sincere.

She shrugged.

"It's lonely," he ventured. "No one understands you."

"That's true," she murmured, taking a sideways glance at the Sefry.

She had first seen Cauth when he and his troops had saved her from her uncle Robert's men and, much to her surprise, he had pledged his life and loyalty to her. The Sefry had enabled her to win back her throne. She owed Cauth and his men a great deal.

But the Sefry were so strange, and despite their help and constant presence, she hadn't really gotten to know any of them.

Nor had any of them spoken to her as Cauth was speaking now. It was a surprise but also something of a relief. The Sefry always had walked in that borderland between the mundane and the very strange. The unnatural was natural to them.

"People fear to speak to me," she said. "Some are calling me the witch-queen. Did you know that?"

"Yes," he said. "But your friends—"

"My friends," she repeated. "Austra has always been my friend. But even she . . ." She shied away from the subject. Who had really betrayed whom?

"We are less now."

"What of Casnar de Pachiomadio?"

"Cazio?" She shrugged. "He doesn't understand, either."

"But he might."

"What do you mean?"

"If he was touched by great powers, as you are. Then perhaps—and forgive my impertinence—then he might truly be worthy of you."

She felt her face go hot. "That *is* impertinence."

"I beg your forgiveness, then."

"And it is dangerous, I'm told."

"Not for a true swordsman," Cauth replied.

"You know this?"

Cauth bowed. "I've spoken when I should have kept silent," he said. "Please understand; it was only my concern for you speaking."

"I forgive it," she said. "When we are alone, you may speak your mind. I need that, I think, to stay honest myself." She tilted her head. "Sir Cauth, why do you serve me?"

He hesitated. "Because you are our only hope," he replied.

"You believe that?"

"Yes."

"I wish you did not. I wish no one did."

He smiled thinly. "That's why you are worthy."

And then he went. She returned to the window to think.

Cazio as a knight of Mamres, at her side. *Her* knight, not one on loan from her mother. Cauth was right: She needed someone more than merely mortal, someone else touched by the saints.

A knight of the dark moon for the Born Queen, a woman's voice whispered. Anne didn't bother turning. She knew she would find no one there.

CHAPTER FIVE

TESTAMENT

STEPHEN HAD SPENT months expecting Fend to kill him. Now that the moment had arrived, he felt that he had no right to be surprised, but there he was, watching in frozen shock as the kneeling Sefry's blade came free of its ancient sheath. Stephen tried to back away, but of course he was sitting down in a chair carved of granite. He wondered if the guards behind him were rushing toward the assassin or if they were part of the plot. He wondered if Fend would kill Zemlé, too, and hoped not.

The weapon darted toward him—and stopped. Stephen realized that it was the hilt end and that the one-eyed Sefry was holding the blade in his black-gloved hand.

The shock passed through him, pulling rage in its wake.

"What?" he heard himself snap. "What the *sceat*—" He cut himself off. "Sceat" was not a word he used. In the dialect he had grown up speaking, it wasn't even a word. No, he'd gotten that from Aspar White, and his Oostish brogue.

He swallowed, feeling the anger already replaced by relief.

"What is this, Fend?" he asked, more controlled.

Fend's eye glittered. "I understand we aren't the best of friends," he began.

Stephen coughed a mirthless laugh. "No, we're not," he affirmed.

"But you are Kauron's heir, and I am the Blood Knight. It is my duty to serve you. But since your distrust for me stops you doing what you must, I see I will serve you best by letting another bear this sword and wear my armor."

"You're the Blood Knight because you drank the blood of the waurm," Stephen said, "not because of those arms. And the waurm is dead."

"The waurm's blood is still quick in mine," Fend said. "So drive this sword into my heart, collect my blood, and feed it to a champion you like."

Stephen stared at the hilt of the weapon and, almost without thinking, took hold of it. He felt dizzy and odd and thought he smelled something sharp and dusty.

Killing Fend seemed like a good idea. The man was a murderer many times over. He nearly had killed Aspar, had treated Winna with great cruelty, and had had a hand in the slaughter of two young princesses.

Oddly, Stephen found himself reviewing those facts without much passion. The best reason to kill Fend was that he, Stephen, could rest easier at night. He shrugged and started to thrust.

What am I doing? he suddenly wondered, and stopped.

"Pathikh?" Fend gasped.

Stephen felt a little smile play on his lips. He'd frightened Fend. *He* had frightened *Fend.* He dropped the tip of the weapon.

"I don't believe you," Stephen said.

"What do you mean?"

"I don't believe you're willing to sacrifice your life for a higher purpose. I think you expect to get something out of this or, rather, *more* out of it, since the waurm's blood has already made you something more than you were. No, Fend, you have a goal, and it isn't to die."

"I've offered you my life," Fend said.

"What happens when I stab the Blood Knight? I don't know. I've seen a man that no blade can kill."

"I'm not like that."

Stephen lifted his hands. "You know I don't trust you. You just said so. Do you imagine this charade has changed that?"

Fend's eyebrows rose.

"What?"

The Sefry grinned a little. "This isn't the Stephen Darige I met at Cal Azroth," he said. "You're getting some steel."

Stephen started to retort, but Fend's words struck home. He wasn't afraid of the man anymore. He hadn't actually been afraid even when he had thought Fend was about to kill him.

"This is about the faneway, then," Stephen said.

"Exactly, pathikh."

"I've walked one faneway and been nearly killed by another," Stephen said. "I'm reluctant to travel this one until I know more about it." But even as he said it, he suddenly felt like the old, timid Stephen again.

"What do you need to know?" Fend challenged. "You are Kauron's heir. The power of this mountain is yours. It is well past time for you to take it."

"I haven't found the Alq yet," Stephen temporized. "I've found some interesting texts in the old section."

"Pathikh," Fend replied. "The Alq will show itself to you after you've walked the faneway and not before. Didn't you know that?"

Stephen stared at the Sefry while he tried to absorb that.

"Why hasn't anyone mentioned this?" he asked, glancing back at Adhrekh, his valet.

The other Sefry looked surprised, too. "We thought you knew that, pathikh," he replied. "You're Kauron's heir."

Stephen closed his eyes. "I've been looking for the Alq for three months."

"That wasn't clear to us," Fend replied.

"What do you think I've spent all of my time doing?" Stephen asked.

"Reading books," Fend said. "Reading books when you're right here in the mountain."

"It's a big mountain . . ." Stephen started, then waved it away. "From now on, don't take for granted that I know anything, please."

"Then you'll walk the faneway?"

Stephen sighed. "Fine," he said. "Have someone show me the route."

Fend blinked. His mouth opened, and his eyes darted past Stephen to Adhrekh.

"What?" Stephen asked.

"Pathikh," the Aitivar said, "we don't *know* where the faneway is. Only Kauron's heir knows that."

Stephen turned and stared at the man for a moment and saw he was serious. He looked back at Fend, and then the absurdity was suddenly too much to contain, and he started to laugh. Fend and Adhrekh didn't seem to think it was funny, which made the whole thing even funnier, and soon he had tears in his eyes and the back of his head had begun to ache.

"Well," he said when he could finally speak again, "there we go. Quite a situation. So my answer to you, Fend, is that I will walk the faneway when I find it. Do you have any further dismissive comments regarding the need to do research in the library?"

Fend glowered for a moment, then shook his head.

"No, pathikh."

"Wonderful. Now leave me, please, unless you've got another bit of absolutely crucial information you've failed to mention to me."

"Nothing I can think of," Fend replied. He knelt, stood, saluted, and returned his weapon to its sheath. Then he held up a finger. "Except this. I've word of where Praefec Hespero is hiding," he said. "I'd like to personally take charge of his capture."

"Favor for an old friend?"

Fend stiffened. "Hespero was never my friend. Only a necessary ally for a time."

"Find him, then," Stephen said. "Bring him here."

He watched the Sefry leave. Was he really going after Hespero?

It didn't matter. Fend was leaving, and that was good.

He retired to the library, where he felt safest. His guard of four followed quietly behind him.

They made him almost as nervous as Fend did. Sefry were nothing new to Stephen. When he was growing up in Virgenya, they had been a fact of life.

But at a distance. The Sefry of his experience traveled in caravans. They danced, sang, told fortunes. They sold things from far away and counterfeit relics. He'd rarely seen one with a sword.

They did not come calling, they did not go to school, they did not pray in chapels or visit fanes. They moved in the world of men and women, but rarely did they socialize with them. Of all the former slaves of the Skasloi, they were the most apart.

The Aitivar did not sing or dance, so far as he knew, but they could fight like monsters. Twelve of them had routed three times their number in the battle below the mountain. They were decidedly unlike any of their race he had ever known, but then, he never had really known a Sefry, had he? Aspar had. He'd been raised by one, and he held that they were all liars, absolutely not to be trusted. Fend certainly bore out that assertion. But the Aitivar—he still didn't know what motivated them. They claimed to have been waiting for him, Kauron's heir, but they were a bit gray as to why.

He noticed they were still bunched around him.

"I'm going to do a bit of research," Stephen said. "I don't need you right at my elbow."

"You heard him," Adhrekh said. "Take posts."

Stephen turned to the vast collection of scrifti. A better collection he had never seen, not in any monastery or scriftorium. At this point, he had only the faintest idea of what was here or how it was organized. He'd found a very interesting section in an early form of Vadhiian he had never encountered before, and there were at least fifty scrifti in the section. Most seemed to be accounting records of some sort, and as much as he wanted to translate them, it seemed more pressing to divine the secrets of the mountain.

Still, daunting as the scriftorium was, the instincts and intuition of his training and saint-given gifts seemed to lead him roughly toward what he wanted. When he thought of a subject, there seemed a certain obvious logic that took him to it, although he found he couldn't explain to Zemlé the workings of that logic.

And now, considering the mysteries of the Sefry, he found himself standing before a wall of scrifti, some bound, some rolled and sealed in bone tubes, some of the oldest placed flat in cedar boxes.

Sefry Charms and Fancies. Alis Harriot and the False Knight. Secrets of the Halafolk. The Secret Commonwealth . . .

He scanned along, looking for a history, but most of the books continued in the same vein until he came across a plain black volume with no title. He felt something like the sort of shock one often got on cold winter days when walking on a rug and touching something metal. Curious, he drew it forth.

The cover was only that, a brittle leather case enclosing a lacquered wooden box. The top lifted off easily, revealing sheets of lead tissue. He suddenly knew he had something very old. Excited, he peered more closely.

No one had ever heard the Sefry language; under the Skasloi, they seem to have abandoned their ancient tongue or tongues and adopted cants based on the Mannish languages around them. But Stephen had a sudden hope that that was what he might be holding, for the faint script impressed into the metal was not one he had ever seen before. It was flowing and beautiful but utterly unknown.

Or so he thought until he noticed the first line, and there something looked familiar. He had seen this script before, in simpler form, not flowing together but in distinct characters carved in stone.

Virgenyan tombstones, the oldest.

He blinked as the first line suddenly jumped out at him: "My Journal and Testament. Virgenya Dare."

He choked back a gasp. This was the book he'd been sent here to recover. It was the reason he'd been trying to find the Alq, the hidden heart of the mountain, because he'd assumed that was where such a treasure would be.

Maybe it wasn't the real thing. Surely there had been many fakes.

Hands trembling, he took the box to one of the stone tables, lit a lamp, and found some vellum and a pen and ink to take notes. Once that was all assembled, he gingerly lifted the first sheet and held it to the light. The impression was faded, the script very difficult to make out, and the Virgenyan incredibly archaic. Without his saint-touched sense, he might not have been able to read it.

MY JOURNAL AND TESTAMENT. VIRGENYA DARE.

MY FATHER HAS TAUGHT ME TO WRITE, BUT IT IS DIFFI-
CULT TO FIND SOMETHING TO WRITE ON OR THE CHANCE
TO DO IT. I WILL NOT WASTE WORDS. MY FATHER HAS
DIED OF GALL ROT IN THE FESTER. HERE IS HIS ONLY
MONUMENT, AND I GIVE IT WITH THE YEAR AS HE RECK-
ONED IT.

ANANIAS DARE
HUSBAND AND FATHER.
B. 1560 D. 1599

I HAVE FOUND MORE LEAD TISSUE.
FATHER SAID I SHOULD WRITE, BUT I'M NOT SURE WHAT
TO WRITE.
I AM VIRGENYA DARE, AND I AM A SLAVE. I WOULD NOT
EVEN KNOW THAT WORD IF MY FATHER HAD NOT TAUGHT
IT TO ME. HE SAID NO ONE USES IT BECAUSE HERE, THERE
IS NO OTHER CONDITION TO COMPARE OURS TO. THERE
ARE THE MASTERS, AND THERE IS US, AND THERE ISN'T
ANYTHING ELSE. BUT FATHER SAID THAT WHERE WE
COME FROM, SOME PEOPLE WERE SLAVES AND SOME WERE
NOT. I THOUGHT AT FIRST HE MEANT THAT IN THE OTHER
WORLD SOME MEN WERE ALSO MASTERS, BUT THAT ISN'T
WHAT HE MEANT, ALTHOUGH HE SAID THAT WAS TRUE
ALSO.

I HAVE LIVED WITH THE MASTER SINCE I WAS FIVE. I DO WHAT PLEASES HIM, AND IF I DO NOT, I AM HURT, AND THAT SOMETIMES PLEASES HIM, TOO. HE CALLS ME EXHREY (I INVENT A SPELLING HERE), WHICH MEANS "DAUGHTER." THE MASTERS DO NOT HAVE CHILDREN OF THEIR OWN, BUT MY MASTER HAS HAD MANY MANNISH CHILDREN, ALTHOUGH ONLY ONE AT A TIME. I HAVE FOUND THE BONES OF MANY OF THEM.

I SLEEP ON A STONE IN HIS CHAMBER. SOMETIMES HE FORGETS TO FEED ME FOR A FEW DAYS. WHEN HE WILL BE GONE FOR A LONG TIME, HE LEAVES THE DOOR OPEN SO THE OTHER HOUSE STAFF CAN TAKE CARE OF ME. IT WAS TIMES LIKE THAT I USED TO SEE MY FATHER, FOR THEY WOULD SMUGGLE HIM TO THE OUTER COURTS. I HAVE TEACHERS, ALSO, WHO SCHOOL ME IN THE ANTICS THAT PLEASE THE MASTER. IN THE WAYS OF THE SKASLOI CHILDREN WHO ARE NO MORE. SOMETIMES I AM LEARNT OTHER THINGS.

That brought Stephen to the end of the first sheet. He lifted it and went to the next and saw that it was different. The hand was the same, but the characters weren't all Virgenyan and neither was the language.

"Like the epistle," he murmured. "A cipher."

He lifted his pen to begin the work of translating it and realized with a start that his hand had been in motion while he'd been reading. He looked to see what he had written, and when he did, crawlers went up his neck. It was in Vahiian, and the hand was an oddly angular scrawl not at all his own:

SOMETHING TERRIBLE IS IN THE MOUNTAIN. IT DOES NOT MEAN YOU WELL.

TELL NO ONE YOU'VE FOUND THE BOOK.

CHAPTER SIX

✦

A MESSAGE
FROM MOTHER

ASPAR DROPPED belly-down when he saw the greffyn. That put it out of sight, but he still could feel the burn of its yellow eyes through the trees. He glanced up at Leshya in the branches above him. She touched her eye with two fingers, then shook her head no. It hadn't seen him.

Gradually he raised his head until he was peering down the streambed.

He counted forty-three riders. Three of them were Sefry, the rest human. But that didn't end the count of the procession. He'd spied at least three greffyns: horse-size beasts with beaked heads and catlike bodies, if one discounted the scales and coarse hair that covered them. Four vaguely manlike utins loped alongside the horses, mostly on all fours, occasionally raising their spidery limbs to grasp and swing from low branches. A manticore like the one he and Leshya had killed that morning finished up the unlikely company.

Grim, Aspar wondered, *is all of that really for me?*

He all but held his breath until they had passed. Then he and Leshya compared their count.

"I think there may be one more greffyn or something about that size and shape," she said. "Following a few dozen kingsyards behind and deeper in the woods. Other than that, that's about the size of it."

"I wonder what they left up in the pass."

She thought about that for a moment. "The lead riders. Did you get a good look at them?"

"They were Sefry. Your lot?"

"Yes. Aitivar. But the three leading, those were all three *Vaix*."

"Vaix?"

"Aitivar warriors."

"Only three?"

She shook her head. "You don't understand. The Mannish are probably fighting men. But there are only twelve Vaix at any given time. They aren't ordinary warriors. They're fast, strong, very skilled, very hard to kill."

"Like that Hansan knight?"

"Hard to kill, not impossible. But they have feyswords and other arms inherited from the old times." Her mouth quirked. "My point is, Fend has a quarter of his warriors out looking for you. You should be flattered."

"Not flattered enough. He's not with them." He frowned. "How do you know Fend is their master?"

"Because I believe he drank the blood of the waurm you killed. I think he's the Blood Knight, which means the Aitivar have won."

"I'm not following you."

"Well, this isn't the time to talk about it," she said.

"No, that would've been sometime in the last four months."

"I told you—"

"Yah. When there's a chance, you're telling me. But sceat, yah, now we've got to get out of here. So, back to the question: How many do you think they have in the pass?"

"Too many," she said. "But I can't think of another way to leave."

"I can," Aspar said.

She lifted an eyebrow.

Aspar grabbed at a scraggly yellow pine as the rotten shale under his foot shifted and then snapped. He watched it turn in the air, the flat fragments almost seeming to glide on their long way down.

He felt the pine start to pull up from the roots and, with a grunt, pushed with the foot that still had purchase—and fell forward.

His target was a sapling growing up from the narrow edge below. He caught it, but it bent like a green bow, and he lost his grip and went back out into the air, turning, flailing for any purchase at all. Everything seemed to be out of reach.

Then something caught him. At first he had the impression of a giant spiderweb because it sagged as his weight went into it. He lay there for a moment, blinking, feeling the air all around him. The almost vertical slope stretched twenty kingsyards above, shattered stone and crevices filled with soil supporting a tenacious forest. Higher, the sky was simple and blue.

About four kingsyards up, Leshya's face peeked down from where she was braced in the roots of a hemlock.

"That was interesting," she said. "How I wonder what you will do next."

A quick survey showed Aspar that he'd fallen into a sort of hammock of wild grapevines. Just below, the stubborn forest gave way to a gray stone cliff. If the vines failed to support him, there was nothing between him and the jumble of fallen rock a hundred yards below. He couldn't even see the river at the bottom of the gorge, so there wasn't much hope of hitting that.

He looked back in the direction from which he'd fallen. He and Leshya had been working their way down a groove worn by water running off the plateau. Not quite as perpendicular as the rest of the precipice, it was cluttered with enough debris to offer purchase, or at least so it had seemed from above. It was starting to look more dubious now as the water track steepened. The gray stone was harder, it seemed, than the shale above.

"What can you see from there?" Leshya asked.

"The channel hits the gray rock and gets steeper," he said.

"Steeper?" she said dubiously. "Or impossible?"

"Steeper. Work your way to the deepest cut and there should be handholds. Below that, there's a talus slope, like I reckoned."

"How far below that?"

"I maun thirty kingsyards."

"Oh, is that all? Thirty kingsyards of wedging our fingers and boot tips in cracks?"

"If you've got a better idea . . ."

"I do. Let's go back up and fight them all."

Aspar grabbed the thickest vine and carefully pulled himself to a sitting position. The natural net creaked and sagged, and leaves and chunks of rotting wood fell silently past him. Then he started working his way toward the rock face, cursing Grim in advance should a vine come unanchored and send him to the bonehouse.

He reached the wall and managed to scrabble sideways to the ledge, where he spent a few moments appreciating having something solid between him and the earth's beckoning.

He turned at a slight noise and found Leshya on the shelf just above him.

"How's the leg?" she asked.

Aspar realized he was wheezing as if he had just run for half a day. His heart felt weak, and his arms already were trembling from fatigue.

"It's fine," he said.

"Here," Leshya said, holding out her hand.

She helped him up, and together they sat, regarding the descent still before them.

"At least we don't have to go *up* it," Leshya said.

"Sceat," Aspar replied, wiping the sweat from his brow.

It had looked somehow better from the other angle. Now he could see the river.

"You might make it to the talus slope," she said. "But the river . . ."

"Yah," Aspar snarled.

The river had dug itself down another hundred kingsyards. Although he couldn't see the canyon wall on his side, the other side looked as smooth as a fawn's coat.

"We need rope," he said, "and lots of it." He glanced back at the vines.

"No," Leshya said.

He didn't answer, because she was right. Instead he scrutinized the gorge, hoping to find something he had missed.

"Come on," Leshya said. "Let's make it to the slope. At least there we'll be able to camp. Maybe we'll see a way to the river, maybe we won't. But if they don't think to look down here, we could survive for a while."

"Yah," Aspar said. "You said this was a stupid idea."

"It was the only idea, Aspar. And here we are."

"From here I might be able to get back up. Certain you could."

"Nothing up there we want," the Sefry replied. "Are you ready?"

"Yah."

They started from the ledge at middagh, and it was almost vespers when Aspar finally half fell onto the jumble of soil and rocks, his muscles twitching and his breath like lungfuls of sand. He lay looking up from the deep shadow of the gorge at the black bats fluttering against a river of red sky, listening to the rising chorus of the frogs and the ghostly churring of nightjars. For a moment, it almost felt normal, as if he could rest.

It sounded right. It looked right. But he could smell the disease all around him. It was all poisoned, all dying.

The King's Forest probably was already dead without the Briar King to protect it.

He should have understood earlier. He should have been helping the horned one all along. Now it was too late, and every breath he drew felt like wasted time.

But there had to be something he could do, something he could kill, that would set things right.

And there was Winna, yah?

He pushed himself up and began to limp his way down to the next broad ledge at the bottom of the slope, where he could see Leshya already searching for a protected campsite.

In the fading light, from the corner of his eye, he saw something else. It was coming down the way they had, but quickly, like a four-legged spider.

"Sceat," he breathed, and drew his dirk, because he'd bundled his bow and arrows and dropped them down before the most arduous part of the climb. They were still ten yards down the slope.

He relaxed his grip and shoulders, waiting.

The utin changed course suddenly, leaping from the rock face into the tops of some small poplars, bending them in a nightmare imitation of Aspar's earlier stunt. As the trees snapped back up, he saw it land effortlessly on the slope downgrade of him.

He let his breath out. It hadn't seen him.

But his hackles went back up when he saw that its next leap was going to take it right to Leshya.

"Leshya!" he howled, coming out of his crouch and starting to run downhill. He saw her look up as the beast sprang forward. Then his leg jerked in a violent cramp and his knee went down, sending him into a tumble. Cursing, he tried to find his feet again, but the world stirred all about him, and he reckoned that at least he was going in the right direction.

He shocked against a half-rotted tree trunk and, wheezing, came dizzily to his feet, hoping he hadn't broken anything new. He heard Leshya screaming something, and when he managed to focus on her, he saw her below him, backed against a tree, grimly stringing her bow. He didn't see the utin until he followed the Sefry's desperate gaze.

The tree-corpse that had stopped him was part of a jumble clogging a water cut in the slope. He was on top of a natural dam.

The utin was two kingsyards below him. Something seemed odd about the way it was moving.

Aspar got his footing and leaped.

It was really more of a fall.

The utin was on all fours, and Aspar landed squarely on its back. It was very fast, twisting even as the holter locked his left arm around its neck and wrapped his legs around the hard barrel of its torso. He plunged his dirk at the thing's neck, but the weapon turned. That didn't stop him; he kept stabbing away. He saw something bright standing in the utin's chest, something familiar that he couldn't place at the moment. He also noticed that the monster was missing a hind foot. Then the night was rushing around him at great speed. He leaned back to avoid the creature's armored head slamming into his face and felt his weapon drive into something. The ear hole, maybe. The beast gave a satisfying shriek, and they were suddenly in the air.

Then they hit the ground hard, but Aspar had already blown out the breath in his lungs. He tightened his grip and kept thrusting.

Then they were falling again for what seemed like a long time, until the utin caught something, arresting their descent so hard that Aspar actually did loosen his grip around its windpipe. He expected to be flung off, but suddenly they were plummeting again. He managed to throw both arms around its neck.

It fetched against something else, howled, and fell again, twisting in the holter's grip like some giant snake. Aspar's arms were numb now, and he lost his clench again. This time he didn't find it before something astonishingly cold hit him hard.

"Holter."

Aspar opened his eyes, but there wasn't much to see. He hadn't lost his senses in the fall, but it had been hard keeping hold of them since. He'd been lucky in hitting the river where it was deep and relatively slow. From the rushing he heard up- and downstream, that easily could have not been the case.

Once he had dragged himself out, his abused body had finally given out. The warm air soon had taken the water's chill, and the forest had worked to soothe him to sleep. He'd fought it but had drifted into and out of dream, and he wasn't sure where he was when the voice spoke.

"Holter," it croaked again.

He sat up. He'd heard an utin speak before, and this was just what it sounded like. But he couldn't tell how far away it was. It could be one kingsyard or ten. Either way it was too close.

"Mother sends regards, Mannish."

Aspar kept quiet. He'd lost the dirk and was unarmed. However badly the utin was hurt, if it could move at all, he doubted very much he could fight it with his bare hands. His best chance was to stay still and hope it was bleeding to death. Failing that, morning might give him a better chance.

He heard something sliding through the undergrowth and wondered if the monster could see in the dark. He hoped not, but that seemed like a thing monsters ought to be able to do.

"Mother," the voice sighed again.

Something tickled the back of Aspar's neck, something with a lot of legs. He stayed frozen as it explored around his ear, across his lips, and finally down his chin and across his jerkin.

It was quiet save for the gentle *shush* of the river, and after a time the sky above began to gray. Aspar turned his head slowly, trying to piece together his surroundings as the light came up. He made out the river first and then the reeds he'd crawled through into the shelter of the trees. The cliff across the water came into focus, and the boles nearest him emerged from darkness.

Something big fell behind him, brushing limbs and breaking sticks. He whipped his head around and saw something bright, glittering.

It was the thing in the utin's chest. The creature itself lay collapsed only a kingsyard away. It had been right above him.

The thing in its chest, he saw now, was a knife, and he suddenly remembered, months before, a battle in an oak grove in Dunmrogh where a knight had wielded a sword that shone like this, a sword that could cut through almost anything.

The utin wasn't moving. Carefully, Aspar leaned forward, soundlessly shifting his weight until his fingers touched the hilt. He felt an odd, tingling warmth, then took hold of it and pulled it out.

Blood spurted in a stream. The utin's eyes snapped open, and it gave a horrible gurgling scream, starting toward Aspar but stopping when it saw the weapon.

"Unholy thing," it said.

"You're one to talk."

It started an odd gulp and hiss that might have been a laugh.

"Your mother," Aspar said. "The Sarnwood witch. Did she send you?"

"No, no. Mother not sending us, eh?"

"But you work for Fend?"

"The Blood Knight calls us. We come."

"Why?"

"How we are," the utin said. "How we are, it's all."

"But what does he want?"

The utin had shoved its fist into the knife hole. It wasn't helping much.

"Not the same as Mother, I think," it said. "Not at end of things. But doesn't matter. Today he wanting you. Today, you." It looked up suddenly and released a deafening, ululating shriek. Howling himself, Aspar drove forward, slicing through the exposed throat so deeply that the head flopped backward like the hood of a cloak. Blood jetted from the stump of its neck, pulsed another few times, and stopped.

Aspar tried to still his own panting and reckon whether he'd been wounded by the thing. He didn't want to take his eyes off it, so he was watching when its mouth started moving again.

"Holter."

Aspar flinched and raised the knife back up. The voice was the same, but the timbre of it was somehow different.

"Another of my children dead by you."

"Sarnwood witch," he breathed.

"Each one is part of me," she said.

He remembered her forest, how he'd felt her in every

limb and leaf, how she'd laid her invisible weight on him so that he couldn't move.

"He tried to kill me," he pointed out.

"More coming," she said. *"They may kill you. But if they don't, you have a promise to keep."*

Aspar felt an even deeper chill settle in. Months earlier, to save the lives of his friends, he had made a bargain.

"I won't ask for the life of anyone you love. I won't ask you to spare one of my children."

"That's what we agreed," Aspar said. "I remember."

She'll ask for my life, he suddenly thought. But no, it wasn't going to be that simple.

"Here is your geos," she said. *"The next human being you meet, you'll take under your protection. And you will take that person to the valley where you found the Briar King sleeping."*

"Why?"

"That's not in the bargain, holter. I honored my part; now it's time for you to honor yours."

He sighed, trying to think what the witch could mean. Leshya was right; he'd been thinking about going back there anyway. But what could the Sarnwood witch be up to?

But he'd given his word, and she *had* kept hers.

"Yah," he said. "I'll do it."

"Yes, you will," she replied. The utin seemed to sag further, and a long soft exhalation escaped its lips. *"If you live . . ."*

Already Aspar could hear something else coming through the trees. He pushed himself up, every part of him shaking, and held the knife before him.

CHAPTER SEVEN

✛

THE TOWN BETWEEN

HIS BLOOD soaks this ground. But his soul is with the Draugs.

Muriele stared at the sungilt waves and wondered what to feel. William had been a good man, a fair king. As husband he hadn't been mean or abusive, but he often hadn't much been there, either. Maintaining several mistresses tended to be draining. Against the grain she had loved him, and she mourned for him. She could remember the scent on his clothes even now.

Alis took her hand. It felt good, the young, honest warmth of it. She looked at the girl, a pretty brown-haired creature of twenty.

"Robert came one night," Muriele said. "When I was alone. When he thought you dead. He was drunk and even more cruel than usual, and he told me how William died."

"He might have lied," Alis said.

"He might have," Muriele agreed. "But the details make me think he was telling the truth." She took a step so that they stood at the edge of the cliff. She looked at the waves breaking far below.

"It was an ambush, and William had fallen wounded from his horse. Robert dragged him here and meant to gloat and kick him over the edge. But William managed to enrage him with taunts, tricked him into stooping down, and then Wil struck him in the heart with his *echein doif*. That was how Robert learned he could not die." She squeezed her friend's hand. "Why would Robert tell a lie so unflattering to himself?"

"Robert does not like himself very well," Alis said. Her voice sounded odd, and when Muriele looked up, she saw tears in the younger woman's eyes.

"You loved my poor husband," she said.

"I don't know," Alis admitted. "But I miss him."

"Well, at least he has Gramme to keep him company," Muriele said, feeling suddenly mordant.

"Muriele . . ."

"Hush. It's past. To tell the truth, if I could have him back, I wouldn't mind if you were his mistress. At least not so much as I did before."

"I hope your next husband feels the same," Alis said lightly.

Muriele gave her a hug, then turned back to the sea.

"Good-bye, William," she called.

Together they walked back to where the others waited.

Neil watched the two women stride toward the party, remembering his own recent ghosts: Fastia, Muriele's eldest daughter, who had died in his arms; Erren, the coven-trained assassin who had protected the queen when he first had met her. He had loved the first and respected the second, and both had been lost to the hands of fate the same day King William was slain.

Erren and Muriele had been together so long when he met them that they had seemed sisters to Neil. Alis was something different. She had been one of William's mistresses, for one thing. And now, suddenly, she was Muriele's maid, bodyguard, best friend. Aside from Muriele, he was the only one in the party who knew the girl claimed coven training. But what coven? Who was her mestra? She wouldn't say.

"Thank you, Aradal, for that detour," Muriele said to the archgreft.

"It hardly took us out of our way," the Hansan replied. He gestured north and east. "The old Nean Road is just over that hill, and that will bring us to the Vitellian Way in a few bells."

"Thank you just the same."

"William was a good man," Aradal said. "An opponent, usually, but I liked him. I am sorry for his loss, Muriele."

She smiled a thin smile Neil had come to understand was her alternative to screaming.

"Thank you," she said. "And now, by all means, let us go. I would not have us miss the feast you describe that awaits us at the inn at Bitaenstath."

"I would not have you miss your first taste of Hansan hospitality," the duke replied.

Muriele's smile tightened, and this time she did not reply.

And so they went on, the road taking them through fields of spelt and wheat that rose high enough to hide an army of murderers. Neil saw a malend high on a hill, its four great sails turning rather quickly in the breeze from the sea. It was the first he had seen since leaving Newland, where they were used to keep water out of the poelen. But what was this one doing? Why was it here?

As promised, within a few bells they met the Vitellian Way, the longest road in the world. It had been built by the Hegemony a thousand years before, and it stretched more than a hundred leagues from z'Irbina in Vitellio to Kaith-baurg in the north.

Neil had traveled the southern portion of the road and had found it well kept, stoutly embanked, and wide enough for two carriages to pass.

Here it was hardly more than a pair of deep wain ruts. The old Vitellian bed of the road seemed barely there.

The women stayed in saddle for a bell or so and then re-tired to the carriage that the Hansans had brought along with their twenty horses.

Why only twenty?

He became aware of another rider at his flank.

"Sir Neil," the young man said. "I don't know if you re-member me."

"I know the name of every man in this party, Sir Edhmon,"

Neil assured him. "When I saw that you had joined the Craftsmen, I picked you for this duty."

"But you hardly know me, Sir Neil."

"You fought on my left flank at the battle of the waerd," Neil replied. "I do not need long walks in the gardens with you to know what I need to know."

The young man blushed. "It was my first battle," he said. "You inspired me to something I never dreamed myself capable of."

"Whatever you are, it was in you before you met me," Neil replied.

"I don't know about that," Edhmon said, shaking his head.

"Well," Neil said, searching for a reply.

They rode on in silence.

They reached the looming fortress of Northwatch while the sun was settling into a bed of high western clouds. The sky was still blue, but the slanting light was copper and brass, and the white walls of the castle, the verdance of the fields, and the still-blue sky made such a pretty picture that war seemed very far away.

And yet Northwatch, despite its sunset patina, had been built for nothing but war. Its walls were thick and from the top it would appear as a six-pointed star, so that the outside of each section of wall was defensible from the inside of another. It was a new design, and Neil reckoned the ramparts were no more than ten years old.

The keep was a different story. Its weathered and vine-etched stone formed four walls with a squat tower at each corner. Clearly a fancy new fortification had been thrown up around a very old castle.

Six riders met them, four of them in lord's plate. As they approached, they doffed their helmets, and the oldest-looking one let his horse step forward.

The carriage door swung open, and Muriele stepped out. The riders dismounted and knelt.

"It's good to see you, Marhgreft Geoffrysen," Muriele said. "Please rise; let me embrace you."

The marhgreft looked to be sixty-five at least. His iron-gray hair was cropped to his skull, and his eyes were that blue that always startled.

"Highness," he said, rising. Muriele crossed to him and gave him a perfunctory embrace. Then the marhgreft bowed again, this time to Aradal, with a good deal less enthusiasm.

"My lord," Aradal acknowledged.

"I rather expected to see you riding in from the other direction," Geoffrysen said.

"Well, if one comes, one must go back," Aradal replied.

"Not necessarily," Geoffrysen said with a wicked little smile.

"But today," Aradal replied, wagging a finger.

"Today," the marhgreft agreed. "And I'd be pleased if you would take the hospitality of my house."

"We've accommodations arranged in town," Muriele told him. "But your offer is more than kind."

Geoffrysen looked surprised. "In town? Not in Suthschild?"

"It will be too dark before we reach Suthschild and past the dinner hour," Aradal said. "No, we shall be at the Wexrohzen."

"On the Hansan side."

"I suppose it is. But can you think of a better accommodation?"

"Mine," the marhgreft said stubbornly.

"I am in good hands, Marhgreft," Muriele assured the old man. "Aradal is my escort to Kaithbaurg. I leave these matters to him."

"Better leave the watching of piglets to a wolf," Geoffrysen blurted. "Stay here, Majesty, and tomorrow let me escort you safely home."

Neil tensed and with a sidewise glance caught Sir Edhmon's eye.

"Marhgreft," Muriele said softly, "that is uncalled for. For one thing, I am not a piglet."

"Majesty, they have gathered troops at Suthschild. They are marching even now in the north."

"That will be enough, my lord," Muriele said. "I hope to enjoy your hospitality on my return."

Geoffrysen was red in the face. He swallowed hard, then nodded. "As you say, Highness."

"It is," Muriele gently agreed.

Neil could almost hear muscles relaxing. He nodded a salute at the marhgreft as they rode past.

After a moment's thought, Neil rode up alongside Aradal.

"Sir Neil," Aradal acknowledged.

"My lord. May I have a word with you?"

"Of course."

"What did the marhgreft mean by 'the Hansan side'?"

"Ah. Never been to Bitaenstath before?"

"No, my lord."

"Well, there it is."

They had been riding over an old earthwork, probably the remains of an earlier castle, but now Neil could see houses and shops. Most of them hugged the road closely, but some sprawled out from it. Beyond, perhaps a third of a league distant, he saw the towers of another castle.

"That's Suthschild, our counterpart to Northwatch," he said. "The border of our countries is out there. I think long ago there were two towns, one near each fortress, but over the years they've grown together. After all, a miller doesn't care which side buys his flour, nor a whore whose soldiers she's servicing."

"But what happens during war?"

"It hasn't come up in a hundred years," Aradal pointed out. "But castles always have villages, and villages are always at risk when war comes." He nodded. "This is Southmarket. When the marhgreft needs beer or broadcloth, it's here he'll likely get it. But if he throws a feast, he'll want mead or svartbier, and to get that he'll send to Northmarket."

"There are no border guards?"

"Do you see a border?"

Neil didn't. There was no wall, no standing stones, no pickets to mark where Crotheny became Hansa.

Most of Southmarket seemed to be shutting down for the evening, except for the inns and bierrohsen, from which issued cheerful singing and the savory scents of roasting beef. Some of the patrons had taken their cups into the street and stood in little circles, talking and laughing. Many looked like farmers, still in their sweat-soaked shirts. Others were cleaner and more neatly dressed and seemed likely to be tradesmen. The few women he saw appeared to be working, not drinking.

As they moved toward the center of town, the look of the people appeared richer. The taverns had tables and chairs outside and lanterns to keep the night away. The houses and shops were grander, too, some with glass windows. The road went from dirt to gravel to paved, and not much later they found themselves in a largish village square, which at one end had an imposing, high-timbered hall with great doors swung open and dance music playing within.

"Just in time," Aradal said, pointing up.

Neil looked and saw the first stars appearing in the rose sky.

"That's our destination?"

"The Wexrohzen. I promise you, you'll find no better bread, butter, pork, or ale in the world than right there." He slapped his rotund belly. "And I've looked."

"Not even in Kaithbaurg?"

"Fancier. Not better. Too many dumplings."

"This hardly seems the place for the queen," Neil said, lowering his voice. "Too busy, too crowded."

"William stayed several times," Aradal said. "Muriele was with him at least once, and I don't think she complained."

Neil felt a hand settle on his shoulder.

"It's perfectly fine," Muriele told him.

"Majesty . . ."

"As I told Geoffrysen, we're in the archgreft's care now."

"Yes, Majesty."

And so they entered the Wexrohzen, and the music dropped away as every head in the hall turned toward them.

Aradal raised his voice. "Welcome, all, Her Majesty Queen Muriele."

To Neil's surprise, a great shout went up, and flagons were raised as the crowd answered with a welcome.

Aradal patted his shoulder and leaned close to his ear. "They don't, after all, know who will win the war," he said.

"I suppose they don't," Neil replied, but he already was frowning as some commotion seemed to be moving toward them, and space suddenly was cleared on the dance floor.

And in that space stepped a man with close-cropped red hair and a sharp beard. He wore a sable tunic displaying a lion, three roses, a sword and helm.

The hairs on Neil's neck pricked up, because he knew the man.

The fellow lifted his chin and addressed Muriele.

"Your Majesty, I am Sir Alareik Wishilm af Gothfera, and your knight and I have unfinished business."

CHAPTER EIGHT

THE NATURE OF
A SWORDSMAN

ANNE FOUND Cazio in the hen yard of the monastery, thrusting and stamping on the packed, swept earth. The chickens at the edge of the yard clucked protests but kept a respectable distance.

He hadn't noticed her yet, and Anne waited a moment, watching his graceful movements. If she hadn't seen him kill so many people with those deft, clever movements of his feet, she might think he was practicing some sort of dance.

She remembered the first time she had seen that dance, when two armed and armored knights had attacked her. Against such machines of war, Cazio had stood little chance, yet he'd put himself between her and them, anyway, and since then he'd never stopped.

But it hadn't just been her, had it? Austra had been there, too.

The color of the sunlight seemed to change, becoming less like gold and more like brass.

He is Austra's love, but he is my man, she thought.

"Cazio," she said.

He stopped in midaction, turned, and saluted her with his sword.

"Majesty," he said.

For a moment she felt breathless and silly. Her attempt to seduce him flashed vividly in her mind's eye.

She cleared her throat. "I'm told it requires three days to walk the faneway of Mamres, and as you know, I am pressed to return to Eslen."

He nodded, an odd look on his face, but didn't answer. She felt a flash of pique. Surely he understood what she was getting at. Did she have to make everything clear?

Apparently.

"You need to start walking the faneway today," she said. "Within the hour."

Cazio sheathed his sword.

"I don't want to," he said. "I'm sorry."

But he didn't sound apologetic.

"What do you mean?" she asked.

"You said I could walk it if I wished," he replied. "I don't wish."

Now she thought she understood his tone. "You're angry?"

He paused, then stared her in the eye. "I'm offended," he replied. "When has my sword failed you? When have I not defeated your enemies with my own strength and skill?"

"You would have failed yesterday if I hadn't helped you."

You will fail when he *comes. You will die; I have seen you dead.* But she couldn't say that.

He flushed brightly. "Maybe so," he admitted. Then: "Probably. But I am a dessrator, Majesty. I am not a killer or a mere swordsman but an artist. Would you give a singer a different voice? A painter a different pair of eyes?"

"If they could make better work, yes."

"But it wouldn't be theirs, would it?"

"Cazio, with the skills you already have and the blessing of Saint Mamres, you could be invincible."

"I have beaten such invincible men. Their physical abilities made them foolish."

"But you are not so foolish."

"I think if I had that power I might become so."

"Cazio . . ."

"Majesty, whatever gifts this faneway can give me, I do not want and I do not need."

"But I want them, Cazio. I want them for you. I'm sorry if I've offended your pride. You are certainly the greatest swordsman I have ever known. I only want you to be the best swordsman you can be. How else can you guard me against the things that are to come? How else can you survive them?"

"The way I always have. With my blade and my wits."

"That is no longer good enough," she said softly.

"If you wish another bodyguard—"

Something had been welling up in her throughout the whole conversation, something hard in her belly and throat. She felt deeply shaken by something, frustrated by Cazio's inability to *listen*. Now she suddenly convulsed and felt tears on her face.

"Cazio," she managed. "Do not be so selfish. I need you. I need you with the blessing of Mamres. Would it be so bad to be lustrated by a saint? How is that wrong?"

He stepped toward her. "Don't cry," he said.

"I'm angry," she snapped. "Sometimes I cry when I'm angry. Do not mistake these tears. I'm offering you something, something—you aren't afraid, are you?"

"Afraid?"

"Of the faneway. Afraid you might die?"

One of his eyebrows lifted. "You're calling me a coward?"

"Ten of my Craftsmen are walking it as we speak. Three of them are already dead."

"That's terrible."

"They just weren't worthy, Cazio. You are. By the saints, if anyone was ever worthy of the blessing of Mamres, it is you."

"Who has died, Majesty?"

"I told you. Some of my Craftsmen."

"Which ones? What were their names?"

It hit her like a punch in the gut, pushing the anger out of her. Her knees went weak, and she felt as if there were no longer anything in her at all. She put her hand against the wall, but it would not support her, and the next thing she knew, she was on the ground.

What was happening to her?

But then Cazio had her cradled in his arms. He smelled both clean and sweaty, which seemed odd.

"I'm sorry," he said.

"No," she managed. "I should know, shouldn't I? I should know who died. I don't understand what's wrong with me, Cazio."

"There's a lot going on," Cazio said. "A lot to worry about."

"I feel—I'm sorry I asked you to walk the faneway, Cazio. I'm sorry. I couldn't bear to lose you."

"I want you to understand—" he began.

Something suddenly tumbled into place, and Anne nearly gasped with understanding.

"No, hush," she said, knowing what she needed to do. "We won't talk of this again." She tapped his shoulder. "You can put me down now," she said. "I'm fine. Pack your things. We'll leave for Eslen by noon. Time for me to really act like a queen."

Cazio cast a look back over his shoulder at the monastery. Besides the Craftsmen still walking the fanes, they had left it invested with nearly two hundred men. The Church was sure to attempt to take it back.

He glanced at Anne. Her face was composed and freshly powdered. He had no idea what she was thinking.

He wasn't sure what *he* was thinking. First the sudden kiss, then her request that he make himself unnatural.

It had been very simple once. He had pledged to keep two girls alive, and with the help of his mentor, z'Acatto, he had managed to do it. But since Anne had come back into her kingdom, surrounding herself with knights, lords, and Sefry, he had been less sure of his footing. He had found his place in continuing to be her bodyguard, and he thought he had done tolerably well at it.

But she didn't seem to think so. He had shocked her into withdrawing her request, but she had made it and could not take it back.

He glanced back again. Should he?

But the mere thought sickened him.

They traveled all day, following the banks of the Warlock River, stopping for the night at Tor Aver, a small castle just beyond the edge of the forest. They had stayed there a few nights before when preparing the assault on the monastery, and the knight who had charge of it, Sir Robert Taverner, had a feast prepared for them by the time they arrived. It wasn't bad, but one of the discoveries Cazio had made in his travels was that good cooks were vanishingly scarce in this part of the world. The meat was heavy, greasy, more often boiled than roasted, and rarely provided with a proper sauce. The bread was grainy and dull, fruit nonexistent, cheese depressingly similar from place to place and meal to meal. The fare was better and more varied at court, of course, but then, he had spent hardly any time at court.

The wine was often undrinkably sweet, especially the white, and so far he hadn't found much to like about beer or mead, which tasted to him like rotted bread and bear piss, respectively. Not that he had tasted bear piss, but now he didn't have to.

Sir Robert's meal did not set itself above the standard, but Cazio managed to fill himself without any unpleasant incidents. He didn't feel much like talking, so he watched Anne, trying to gauge her mood. He had known her for more than a year and in many trying circumstances, but he had never known her to be so suddenly changeable as in these last few days.

But she seemed at ease, chatting with Sir Robert and the guests he had invited. The anger and remorse of the morning seemed forgotten.

And so, feeling heavy with the sweet wine, he excused himself to the chamber provided for him and lay there, wishing he were drunk on a better vintage, wishing for other things.

He was nearly asleep when the door cracked open. Blinking, he saw Anne's face in the candlelight, and with a guilty start he realized that one of his wishes had come true. He opened his mouth to attempt another denial, but the words glued themselves there.

"Cazio?"

"Majesty."

"Just Anne, for the moment," she said.

"Ah," he managed. "Anne." How was it he once had felt comfortable saying her name?

"Don't worry," she said, "I haven't come to test your virtue again. May I enter?"

"Of course."

He was still in his clothes, but he somehow felt he ought to cover himself.

She stepped in, shuffled her feet another half step, and stopped.

"I was wrong to ask you to walk the faneway, Cazio. I want you to know I understand. There are so many people around me I don't really know, much less trust. But I trust you. Today you've only proved that I can trust you to protect me, even against myself."

"I'm glad you understand."

She nodded, and something odd worked behind her eyes. She cleared her throat softly. "So," she said. "I need you to go to Dunmrogh."

Cazio blinked, wondering what he had missed. His king's tongue was still not so good.

"Dunmrogh."

"Yes. I want you to take a garrison there to guard the fane. I want you to command it."

"I don't understand," Cazio said. "I'm not a commander. I'm a swordsman, that's all."

"You're a swordsman I trust," she said.

"To guard *you*," he said.

"I have my Sefry," she said. "And the Craftsmen."

"Mamres knights."

"Two or three of them might make one of you," she said. "But I shall have to make do."

"This doesn't make sense to me," he said. Was she trying to shame him into walking the faneway?

"It's only for a while," Anne said. "I know you'll miss Austra, but I'll send her to be with you. I know you want to guard me. But I'm asking you, as my friend, to do this."

Cazio struggled for something to say. His chest was tight. This felt like an attack from nowhere, one he had no parry and riposte for.

"Won't you reconsider?"

"Cazio," she said softly, "you aren't one of my subjects. Everything you've ever done for me, you did because you wanted to. I'm not ordering you to do this, just asking." She sighed and closed her eyes. "I had a vision. I need you there."

Her eyes remained shut for a long moment, and he examined her face, thinking how familiar it had become and how strange that was. How had he come to this place? Shouldn't he be back in Vitellio, sunning himself in some piato, seducing girls and starting duels? Guarding her was one thing, but this war—was it really his? Did he care about it if Anne and Austra were removed from the equation?

He didn't know.

But he nodded when she opened her eyes. "Very well," he sighed. "I shall do as you ask."

Even as he said it, he felt something turn in him and knew that he had never agreed to anything in his life that felt more wrong.

CHAPTER NINE

ZEMLÉ'S TALE

STEPHEN WOKE paralyzed, a shriek of terror fused in his throat. Invisible things crawled in the darkness, and just at the corner of his vision a hard red light sparked. He couldn't look at it because he knew that whatever it was was so terrible that his heart would stop from the sheer horror of it.

He felt tears start in his eyes as he tried again to scream but could not.

Then, abruptly, the light vanished, and his whole body seized. He flailed his arms at the dark things, and finally the shriek tore from his throat.

Something grappled at his arms, and he sobbed another low howl, striking frantically at his attacker.

"Stephen! Stephen!"

At first he couldn't identify the voice, but he was suddenly free of groping fingers.

"Why?" he heard himself shout.

"Stephen, it's a Black Mary. Do you understand? It's me, Zemlé. It's me."

"Zemlé?"

"It's me, meldhe," she said more softly, using her lover's name for him. "It's only me. You were thrashing in your sleep."

"Where are we?"

"In our bed," she said. "Wait, let me kindle the lamp."

A moment later, features appeared and the darkness backed into the distance.

But it wasn't Zemlé's face.

* * *

When he woke again, every lamp and candle in the room was glowing. Zemlé sat across the bed from him, looking concerned.

"What?" he murmured.

"Well, at least you didn't scream at me this time," she said.

"It wasn't you," he tried to explain.

"Black Mary follow you back, then?"

Stephen nodded without understanding. Zemlé offered him a cup of something that smelled minty.

"Saint Weylan's root and siftras," she explained. "That will chase off the Mary."

He nodded and took a sip. "There's something wrong with me," he murmured.

"Everyone has bad dreams."

He shook his head. "Do you remember what I saw in the scriftorium in Demsted? The face in the flame?"

She nodded reluctantly.

"And the thing that passed through our room a few months ago?"

Her brow crinkled. "Meldhe, that might have been a dream, too," she said softly.

"I wrote something in someone else's hand," he said, knowing it sounded quite mad. "It was a warning against that thing, I think, against something evil come into the mountain."

"Who do you think was warning you?"

"Kauron," he said. "I think he's helped me before, on the way here. Maybe before that. And these Black Marys—I've had those before, too.

"I know," she said. "More and more often. Almost every night now. But not usually so violent."

He nodded and took another sip of the tea, then noticed something.

"What happened to the side of your face?" he asked.

She turned away, but it was too late to hide the red mark that by the morning would be starting to purple.

"I did that?" he asked.

"You did not mean to."

"That's no excuse!" he cried. "Saints, Zemlé, I've hurt you."

"You were in a terror. You didn't know me."

"That's . . . " He reached forward. "I'm so sorry," he said.

He was afraid she would flinch, but she let him touch her face.

"I know," she said. "Believe me, if I thought you did it on purpose, you would know it." She touched his arm lightly as she said it. "Now, tell me more. About today."

"I found the journal."

"The journal. Virgenya Dare's journal?" Her voice pitched up.

"Yes."

"Where?"

"In the shelves, like any other book. I thought it would be hidden away in a secret compartment, but I just happened upon it."

"That was lucky."

He shook his head. "I don't think it was luck. I think I was led to it. I started reading it, and when I stopped, I found that I had been writing."

"And that was a warning about something come into the mountain."

"Yes. And not to tell anyone about finding the journal."

"Which you just did," she pointed out.

"Well, yes. But if I can't trust you . . ."

The remainder of the thought cloyed before it reached his tongue.

"What?" she asked softly. "Do you think you've made a mistake?"

He stared at her for a moment, then stood and paced across the room, hands folded behind his back.

Maybe he had.

"Stephen. Talk to me."

He turned. "When we first met, you told me you had attended a coven. A coven not sanctioned by the Church."

"And you didn't believe me."

"I believe you now. Tell me about it."

Her face went blank. "This whole time you've never asked me about that. Why now?"

"Why now? A very good question. You talked me into coming here. No woman has ever shown all that much interest in me, but you were kissing me the first night we met. That doesn't make any sense, does it?"

"Stop it, Stephen," she cautioned. "Don't walk that trail. Think. Why are you suddenly so angry with me?"

"I'm not angry," he said. "But it wouldn't be the first time you kissed a man to—"

"Stop it right there," she said. "You don't want to say that."

You slept with Hespero, his mind urged him to continue, but part of him knew she was right, and so he stopped.

"Sorry," he said.

She nodded. "You're not entirely wrong," she said. "I wanted to win your trust. But I kissed you because I wished to. Maybe no one was ever attracted to you before, but more likely you were too inexperienced to see it. I am bolder than most women, Stephen. I don't wait for the things I want."

He sat on a stool and passed his palm across his eyes.

"I know," he said. "I know. I told you there's something wrong with me." He looked straight at her then and saw a tear on her cheek.

"Look," he sighed. "When you met me, you had an interest in all of this. You may have liked me, but you still had an agenda. And you weren't working alone. Zemlé, I need to know who you work for. If the coven isn't the place to start . . ."

"It is," she said. "It's the place to start."

"Well, then please start."

She wiped the tear away and pulled the covers about her like a cloak.

"It was the Coven Saint Dare," she said.

"As in Virgenya Dare."

"Yes."

"Go on."

"You know that Virgenya Dare unlocked the secret of the sedos power and used it to defeat the Skasloi. You know that she ruled the first Kingdom of Man and that one day she walked away from it and never came back."

"Everyone knows that story."

"It's easiest to start there, Stephen, because here is where the story my coven tells is different from the one your Church does. According to canon, Virgenya left the throne to her husband, and it was he who founded the Church and became the first Fratrex Prismo, Niro Promom."

"You dispute that?"

"My order does, yes. According to our teachings, Saint Dare had a council of four women and two men known as the *vhatii.* She left them in charge when she vanished. For half a century, the majority of highest officials of the Church were women."

"The Revesturi told me a similar tale," Stephen said. "Except they mention only one woman ruling, like a fratrex."

"That's true. When the *vhatii* finally understood that Saint Dare would never return, they elected a *mater prisma,* because Virgenya taught that a woman must rule the church."

"Why a woman?"

Zemlé frowned. "I don't know. The sisters believed that women rule with more mercy, but I can't recall any text that says that. Doesn't the journal say?"

"I haven't gotten that far. She's still a girl, a Skasloi slave."

"How can you resist skipping to the end?"

"It's in cipher, and the cipher changes as I go along. Besides, I don't want to miss anything."

"Well, read faster."

"I will. Go on with what you were saying."

"The arrangement didn't sit well with some of the men, but the older generation respected Virgenya's wishes. But eventually a *mater prisma* was elected who was really little more than the mistress of a powerful sacritor named Irjomen. She died soon after—murdered, probably—and he assumed the title of Fratrex Prismo. The *vhatii* objected, and war followed, but Irjomen had been planning his rebellion for some time. The loyal were slain, the male *vhatii* joined the fratrex, and the women fled into exile. Women were eliminated from all positions of power, and the covens where they once had been trained became their only homes in the Church. Certain covens remained true and were destroyed or went into hiding. Mine was one such coven."

"And your mission is to bring women back to power in the Church?"

"No. The church is hopelessly corrupt. Our mission was to watch the heirs of Virgenya Dare until the arrival of the next Born Queen, the woman who will re-create the Church, remake the world, and set all right."

"Anne Dare?"

"So my coven believes. When the sedos throne emerges, she must take its power and rule."

"But what has that to do with me?"

"You're supposed to find the throne," she replied. "Her throne. And keep *him* from claiming it."

"Him? Who would that be? The Blood Knight? The Demon Lord you mentioned when we first met?"

"The Vhelny is your great enemy, Stephen. He wants to destroy the world, all of it and everyone in it. But there is another foe, a man who would claim the sedos throne for himself."

"Hespero."

"That's what I think," she replied.

"Well, Fend says he's found Hespero and is off after him. If that's true, we won't have to worry about him much longer. But if he's lying, if he's gone to join forces with him . . ."

"If he was going to do that, why wouldn't he have done it months ago instead of battling him?"

"Maybe they needed me to find the journal. Maybe the battle was a ruse to make me feel safe and in charge. Maybe Fend is stark raving mad. That wouldn't surprise me in the least."

"Or maybe, as some of the legends say, the Blood Knight is your servant and ally," she said.

He nodded. "That's his claim."

"The thing in the mountain—suppose that's the Vhelny? What if it's here, watching, waiting?"

She paled. "I hadn't considered it. I've thought of all of this as prophecy for so long, as an ancient and distant thing. In my mind's eye, the Vhelny would come like a dragon, all flame and shadow, not sneak about like a thief. But no tale or legend describes him." She rubbed her forehead. "Saints, it's likely, isn't it?"

"Yes," he said, reaching for his clothes.

"Where are you going?"

"To read more of the journal. Virgenya Dare found this place. She walked the faneway I'm supposed to walk. Let's see what she has to say about it."

SLAVES HAVE SECRETS, AND THIS IS ONE OF THEM, THIS CIPHER. WILL AND I INVENTED IT TO WRITE EACH OTHER. WILL'S MASTER MAKES LEAD TISSUE, AND SO HE FINDS IT IN PLENTY.

WILL'S MASTER BROUGHT HIM HERE WHEN I WAS TWELVE, BY MY FATHER'S RECKONING. THEY PUT US IN A ROOM TO-GETHER, AND WE KNEW WHAT WE WERE SUPPOSED TO DO. THE MASTERS WERE WATCHING, BUT THEY COULDN'T HEAR WHEN WILL WHISPERED AND TOLD ME IT WOULD BE OKAY. HE WHISPERED A LOT ABOUT HOW OUR FATHERS KNEW EACH OTHER, ABOUT WHERE HE LIVED. IT HELPED ME FORGET WHAT WAS GOING ON AND HOW SCARED I WAS. AFTER THAT I WASN'T SCARED. I LOOKED FORWARD TO OUR WHISPERED CONVERSATIONS. IT WAS LIKE MY BODY WASN'T THERE AT ALL. WILL STARTED TEACHING ME THE SECRET LANGUAGE THE SLAVES IN HIS FORTRESS HAVE, AND I MADE UP THESE LETTERS FOR IT. WE PASS EACH OTHER NOTES WHEN WE MEET. I'LL SEE HIM AGAIN NEXT WHEN THE MOON IS FULL.

I DIDN'T BLEED THIS MONTH, AND WILL DIDN'T COME. THE MASTER SAYS I WILL HAVE A YOUNGLING. THE HOUSE SLAVES TELL ME THAT A LOT OF WOMEN DIE WHEN THEY DO THAT. I DON'T WANT TO DIE, BUT I AM OFTEN

SICK. MY FATHER SAID WE ESCAPE THE MASTER WHEN WE DIE. I WONDER IF THAT IS TRUE.

I HAVE SEEN WILL AGAIN. THEY RACED HIM, WITH FIFTY OTHERS. THEY DROVE THEM WITH CHARIOTS, AND IF ANY FELL, THEY CUT THEM TO PIECES. WILL RAN HARD; THEY DIDN'T CATCH HIM. MY MASTER KEPT ME CHAINED AT THE FRONT OF HIS FLYING BARGE, SO I WOULD HAVE TO WATCH HIM, BUT I DIDN'T WANT TO LOOK AWAY. TWO DAYS THEY RAN, WITHOUT SLEEPING OR EATING. BY THE END OF THE SECOND DAY, ONLY THREE WERE LEFT, AND ONE OF THEM WAS WILL. I WAS SO PROUD OF HIM. I WAS PROUD TO HAVE HIS DAUGHTER IN MY BELLY.

SIX MOONS HAVE WAXED AND WANED. MY BELLY IS LARGE, AND THE MASTER HAS TAKEN ME TO THE MOUNTAIN FORTRESS FOR THE REST OF MY PREGNANCY. IT IS A HABIT FROM THE OLD DAYS, WHEN MASTERS COULD HAVE CHILDREN. I HAD NOT SEEN MOUNTAINS BEFORE, AND I LOVE THEM. THEY MAKE ME THINK STRANGE, LOVELY THOUGHTS. AND THERE IS SOMETHING IN THE FORTRESS, OR DEEP BELOW IT, SOMETHING THAT MAKES MY BELLY TINGLE AND SOMETIMES SETS MY TEETH ON EDGE.

I HAD A DREAM LAST NIGHT. I DREAMED I WAS A MOUNTAIN, AND MY FEET PULLED LOOSE OF THE EARTH, AND I WALKED, CRUSHING EVERYTHING BENEATH ME. I CRUSHED THE MASTER. WHEN I WOKE, I WAS FRIGHTENED HE WOULD FIND OUT AND PUNISH ME, BUT HE DIDN'T. I ALWAYS THOUGHT HE COULD SEE MY DREAMS. HE HAS TOLD ME WHAT I DREAMED BEFORE. BUT THIS DREAM WAS DIFFERENT. I THINK SOMEHOW THE MOUNTAINS HAVE TAUGHT ME HOW TO DREAM IN SECRET. THAT WOULD BE NICE.

IT HURT, JUST AS THEY SAID IT WOULD. IT HURT SO MUCH, I ALREADY CAN'T IMAGINE THE PAIN. AND THERE WAS BLOOD, A LOT OF IT. EVERYTHING WENT DARK, AND

I THOUGHT I HAD DIED AND WAS IN A STRANGE
PLACE. THERE WERE TWO RIVERS THERE, A BRIGHT
BLUE-GREEN STREAM AND A BLACK ONE. I STOOD WITH
A FOOT IN EACH, AND I WAS TALL, LIKE A MOUNTAIN. I
WAS TERRIBLE.

THEN I WOKE, AND THERE WAS MY DAUGHTER, AND I FI-
NALLY UNDERSTOOD WHAT MY FATHER MEANT BY THE
WORD "LOVE."

I WON'T WRITE WHAT THEY DID. I WILL NOT. IT IS DONE.
But I'm going to kill them. I'm going to kill all of them.

Stephen gasped and pulled his fingers away as the lead
scrift was suddenly too hot to touch. The purest hatred he
had ever felt scalded through him, so uncontainable in its
fury that he found himself shrieking. And as that awful rage
trembled through him, he turned and caught a motion from
the verge of his eye. He spun to find a boiling, kinetic darkness like black oil poured in water and almost a shape. Then
his gaze rejected it and turned his head away, and when he
was able to look again, it was gone.

The anger burned away as quickly as it had come, replaced
by shivering fear. He sat, quaking, for long moments, his
brain refusing to tell him what to do. Where was the thing?
Was it still here, perhaps a fingers-breadth from him, hiding
in the air itself, waiting to strike?

You don't have to be afraid, a voice whispered. *You never
have to be afraid again.*

"Shut up," Stephen muttered, rubbing his shaking hands
together.

It took a long time for him to manage to stand, and when
he did, his body felt light enough to blow away on the wind.

He flipped through the journal until he found what he was
looking for.

A little later he heard a slight scuffing and saw that Zemlé
was watching him from the stairwell.

"What's wrong?" she asked.

He closed his eyes. "Enough," he said. "Enough."

"What?"

"Call Adhrekh. I'll start walking the faneway. Tonight."

CHAPTER TEN

THREE THRONES

ASPAR SHIFTED his grip on the knife a bit and licked his dry lips. He'd heard—or thought he'd heard—something coming through the dense bottomland forest, but now all he could make out was the rushing of the stream and the scraping of branches in low wind.

But then, behind him, he caught the faintest hiss of fabric on wood and whipped around to face whatever it was.

He found himself staring down an arrow shaft at Leshya's violet eyes.

"Sceat," he muttered, sagging against the rough, twisty bark of a willow.

"I took the longer way down," she explained.

"Yah."

She glanced at the corpse of the utin. "You're still alive," she said.

"Yah."

"I've lived a long time, Aspar White, and been almost everywhere. But you, my friend, are unique." She shook her head. "Any open wounds need stopping? Broken bones?"

"I don't think so."

"I noticed a rock shelter not far from here. Let's go there and take a look."

He nodded wearily.

* * *

He winced as her fingers prodded the tissue of his leg, but actually it almost felt good, like sore muscles after a hard hike.

"Well, you didn't break it again," she said.

"Well, Grim must love me, then," he said.

"If he loves anyone, I'd say so," she replied. "Now let's have your shirt off."

He didn't feel like he was capable of doing much more than raising his arms, but she shucked it off with a few sharp tugs. He felt a jagged pain in his side.

"Need a bath," she said.

"Sefry bathe too much," he replied. "Unhealthy habit."

"But we smell good," she said.

In fact, she smelled of sweat and leather, and it did smell good.

"Ah, there's a home for gangrene," she said.

Aspar looked down and saw a ragged but not particularly deep cut on his ribs. Blood had glued his jerkin to the wound, which was what he'd felt when she had dishabilled him.

He took deep breaths and tried to stay relaxed as she cleaned out the gash with water and then pressed some sort of unguent from her haversack into the cut.

"You saved my life," she said, her voice sounding oddly soft.

"Yah. You've saved mine a time or two."

"You're important, Aspar. You're worth saving."

Without thinking, he caught her hand. "You're worth saving, too," he said.

Her startled gaze met his and settled there, and he felt a sort of jolt, and in an instant he was gazing into the deepest forest in the world, more impossible to enter than the Sarnwood, even less possible to leave. He felt beaten, and happy to be beaten, happy to finally go home.

He saw the path in for perhaps ten heartbeats, and then the trees closed ranks. She pulled her hand away, and he knew that if she had just squeezed his fingers, he would have acted foolishly.

Sceat, he thought. At a time like this he was thinking about women? Two of them? Was he seventeen?

"I don't think we have all that long," Aspar said. "The utin said Fend sent him. If Fend is leading that motley up above—"

"He is the Blood Knight, then."

"Yah, whatever the sceat that means."

"I'll tell you, I promise. But right now we need to go. And quietly."

"Soon," he said.

"Soon."

The valley narrowed to the point where they were always on a slope. Aspar's leg ached even with the new crutch Leshya had cut him, and as the way turned more and more downhill, his knees began to hurt as well.

In the back of his mind he'd always reckoned that after a while he'd be back to his old self, but now he was starting to wonder. He was past forty winters, and at his age, when things broke, they didn't necessarily get fixed.

They came at last to steep, shallow shoals with nothing but cliffs on either side.

"We'll be getting wet," Leshya said.

They went down basically sitting, letting their boots find the rocks. The mountain water already had winter in it, and before they were a third of the way down, Aspar's extremities were numb. Halfway, his boot slipped and the current got control of him, sweeping him down until he lodged hard against a log.

The sky was wider there. Two white-tailed eagles turned high above. Treetops peered down at him from the gorge's rim.

It's still alive here, he thought. *Despite the monsters. Why should I go back to the King's Forest, where everything is dead? Why not stay here, fight, die, sink into the earth?*

It was only when something struck him across the face that he realized there was water in his mouth and lungs. His body understood then, and he started hacking it up in long, painful coughs.

"Get up," Leshya said. "You're not done, Aspar White."

They made it the rest of the way down, and he took a few minutes to finish clearing his lungs.

"Sceat," he managed weakly.

"You've got to help me more than this, Aspar," Leshya said. "You've got to try harder."

"Sceat on you," he muttered, and for a moment he wanted to kill her just for seeing him like this. It was the most humiliating thing he could imagine.

Up until now, at least. Now he could envision more worlds waiting for him as the years crept by. Why, there was Winna, still young enough to bear children, rolling him over to change the linens under him, the ones he'd just soiled . . .

He pushed himself up with the crutch, then threw it away.

"Let's go," he said.

The valley broadened out into a gentle, ferny glen where the warmth of the sun took the chill from his bones. Dragon-flies whirred over the water and its sedge of horsetails. Snakes and turtles lazily quit their perches as the two travelers neared them. The cliffs became slopes, and trees walked down them; soon they were able to move out of the marsh and travel on drier ground.

He also began seeing more signs of man. Some of the forest bore old farming terraces, and they passed several hunting shelters. The rinn was joined by several others, and some had the scent of manure in them.

He felt the geos of the Sarnwood in his belly, cold, waiting. Who would it be?

All the while, the terrain turned them south.

It was getting dark when they heard dogs and smelled smoke. Soon they saw, on a rise some distance from the stream, a fenced yard and a large cabin built of split cypress.

To Aspar's relief, Leshya gestured away from that and upslope, where in time the trees thinned into pasture. The stars began to appear, although the sun was barely gone behind the mountain they just had come down from. Aspar found himself looking back often, and once something caught his eye. He thought at first that it was a bat, but then he kenned he'd misunderstood the distance; if it was a bat, it was a very big one.

He suddenly felt like a hare on a broad plain.

"Ah," Leshya said. He found her staring at the thing as it vanished into shadow.

"Any ideas what that might be?"

"No. But I reckon we'd better sleep in tonight."

"Go back down to the cabin?"

"No. This is winter pasture. There ought to be something up here."

She was proved right before the darkness was total; they found a small sod house in good repair. It was even sparely furnished with firewood, a cooking pot, a cask of somewhat weevily oats, and a little dried meat. Cobwebs testified that all of it was from the last season.

They didn't build a fire, and so the oats stayed where they were, but the dried meat proved hard to resist, thievery though it was.

"Blood Knight," Aspar said as he lay back on a straw mat and pulled the ragged bits of a blanket over his legs.

"Right," she said.

He couldn't see her at all in the darkness. "And you can throw in as a bargain where you got this witchy knife."

"That's easier," she said. "I found it on a dead man back at the mountain. One of Hespero's men."

"Where are they getting those things?"

"Old places," she said. "There were once quite a lot of them."

"When your folk ruled the world."

"When we were being beaten by yours," she replied. "The fey weapons were forged by humans. Virgenya Dare found the knowledge of their making. The Skasloi wouldn't use such weapons."

"Why?"

"Because they draw on the sedos power. The Skasloi wouldn't have anything to do with that."

"Why?"

She sighed. "You know we don't really write things down, we Sefry. But we live a long time. Seventy generations have come and gone for your kind since you won your freedom. But my mother was born four hundred years ago, and her mother was born six hundred before that. Three more generations back—"

"You were Skasloi. Yah."

"So our memories are better. But there's still a lot we don't know. Things our ancestors intentionally didn't pass on and others they may have lied about. So understand that everything I'm about to tell you might not be true."

"I grew up with Sefry, remember? I know a thing or two about their lies."

She shrugged. "We couldn't have survived all of these centuries without a talent for dissembling. If we had been found out—if the Mannish races ever knew what we really were—we would have been slaughtered."

"Yah," Aspar said drily. "I reckon."

"Anyway, what I was getting to. My ancestors did use the sedos power once. But they discovered that using it isn't without cost. Each time it's drawn on, it leaves a poison behind it. The pollution builds up over time like dead fish in a stream, and things begin to die. Almost everything died once, before my ancestors understood the consequences of the sedos power and forswore its use."

"But the Skasloi were supposed to be demons, with lots of strange shinecrafting."

"The Skasloi had magicks, yes. They found another source of power, one without the same ill effects as the sedos. But by that time the world was a wasteland. They discovered a way beyond the lands of fate to another place, an otherwhere, and they brought plants to make the world green again. They brought animals, too, and in time they brought your people."

"To use as slaves."

"Pets at first.. Curiosities. But eventually slaves, yes."

"Until the pets found the sedos power."

"Exactly."

A thought struck him. "So the monsters, the black thorns, the things destroying the world—that's from using the sedos power?"

"Yes. You told me about the boar you saw in the Sarnwood, how it gave birth to a greffyn. The sedhmhari are born from natural things poisoned by sedos power. Some say they are shadows of the elder beasts that walked the world before the great dying, the ancient life trying to push through the new, but tainted by the venom of the sedos."

He remembered the Sarnwood again, the strange plants that grew in its heart. "The Sarnwood witch," he murmured.

"We don't know what she is, but she is very, very old. Older maybe than my race."

"She's from the old forest. The one your people destroyed. The one my forest replaced."

"Maybe," she said cautiously. "As I said, we don't know much about her."

"What does she want?"

"We don't know."

Aspar nodded, but he had an idea he already knew. If *he* was the witch of the Sarnwood, he knew what he would want.

"What's all this got to do with Fend?"

"That's another legend, a prophecy, really. There are seasons larger than the ones you know, seasons that last hundreds and thousands of years. The powers—we call them thrones—of the world wax and wane with those seasons. When Virgenya Dare found the sedos power, it was strong. But over time it weakened, and the other thrones waxed, bringing on the Warlock Wars and all sorts of havoc. But now the sedoi swell very powerful, more powerful than ever. They say that whoever controls the sedos throne at its peak will be able to subjugate the other thrones forever and end the long, slow change of seasons."

"And these other powers—these thrones—what are they?"

"There are only three. The sedos we've been talking about. The second is the power your folk call shinecraft and witchcraft, and it comes from the abyss beneath the world. It makes unlikely things likely and the certain impossible. It can bring a rain of fire from heaven or stop water freezing even though it is bitter cold. It brings things together that belong apart and pushes things apart that belong together. That was the throne the Skasloi mastered, and after them the warlocks. We called that throne the Xhes throne."

"And the third power?"

"That's the one you've felt in your bones every day of your life, Aspar White. Generation and decay. Death and birth. The energy that makes life into dirt and dirt into life. We called that throne the Vhen throne."

"The Briar King's throne."

"Not anymore," she said softly.

"Because Fend killed him. Why did he do that?"

"According to the elders, the master of the Xhes throne is a creature we know as the Vhelny, a demon. The Blood Knight is said to be his servant. He is the foe of the masters of the other thrones."

"So now that he's slain the Briar King, he'll go after the sedos throne. Who is the master of that?"

"No one. The Church has used the sedos power, but the throne hasn't been occupied since the time of Virgenya Dare. But it will be soon. That's what all of this is about."

"The Briar King was fighting the sedos power."

"Of course. It was destroying his forest."

"But the Xhes throne wasn't, yah? So it seems like he and this Vhelny should be allies against the sedos throne when it rises. Why kill the Briar King now?"

"Because the Vhelny wants all the thrones, of course."

"Ah," Aspar murmured, rubbing his forehead. He wished he could see Leshya's face, but he knew he still wouldn't be able to tell if she was having him on.

"You don't know how much of this is pure sceat?" he finally said.

"Not really," she said. "You asked, and I told you what I know. I've never lied to you, have I?"

"Knowing all this and not mentioning it earlier is very much like a lie, I maun," he replied.

"To have told you earlier, I would have had to tell you what the Sefry really are. After that, you wouldn't have listened to anything I said. But after Fend let the secret slip, and after all the time we've been together . . ."

"You reckoned I'd be more gullible."

"I didn't ask you to believe it," she snapped.

"Yah," he muttered, waving at the darkness. "So Fend's after me because he works for the Vhelny thing and he's afraid the Briar King might have told me something or other."

"Either that or Fend's just using his power to indulge a personal vendetta. You did take one of his eyes."

"Not a lot of love between us," Aspar admitted. "Not much at all."

"Any other questions?" Leshya asked, her voice sounding stiff.

"Yah," he said. "Just what are you hoping the Briar King passed on to me?"

She nodded and was still for a long moment. "We made the Briar King," she finally said.

"What?"

"The Skasloi. The Xhes and sedos thrones existed before any history I know. We may have created them, or some elder race, but we believe they were created."

"I thought the saints created the sedoi."

"Not the saints as your people worship them. We simply don't know. But the Vhen—the essence of life and death— that was in everything, and it had no throne, no being that controlled it. After we brought the world back from the brink of death, the Skasloi decided that the Vhen needed its own guardian, its own focus. So they created the Briar King—or, more specifically, they created the Vhenkherdh, the heart of life, and from that he was born."

"And you hope he told me where that place is?"

"Did he?"

"No."

But suddenly he *did* know.

She saw it on his face. "You've been there. That's why you want to go back. Not to just die there."

"It's only a feeling," he said.

"Of course. I've been stupid. He wouldn't have put a map in your hand."

"But he's dead. What can we do now?"

"Without his protection, everything will die. But if he is reborn, we might have a chance."

"You think that's possible?"

"I don't know. But it's something, isn't it?"

"Then why haven't you been in more of a hurry to leave?"

"Because I think you're the key to whatever must happen, and I didn't want you to die before you knew where to go or die on the journey from starting too early."

"Well," he said. "Well. I need to chew on all of this for a while."

"Fine. Shall I take first watch?"

"I'll take it."

She didn't say anything else, but he heard the rustle of her situating herself. He suddenly felt heavy and stupid. He listened to her breathing.

"Thanks," he said. "I don't always mean to be like I am. I just—I like things simple."

"I know," she replied.

He went outside. The stars were out, but the moon was no more than a faint glow in the west. He studied the sky, watching for something dark moving against the constellations, straining his ears for any distant warning.

The Aitivar had been mounted. If they stayed that way, they would have to go back up and out of the pass and wind their way here. That could put them far behind, but if he really had seen some sort of flying beast . . .

But he didn't see or hear anything, so he let his thoughts wander ahead. Tomorrow they ought to be out of the hills and into the river plain of the White Warlock. If they were where he thought they were, another day or two would get them to Haemeth, where he'd left Winna and Ehawk.

But if he was dragging a war band of monsters after him, was that really what he wanted to do?

What *did* he want to do?

That hardly mattered, did it? Because he would have to do what the Sarnwood witch had geosed him to do.

He hadn't told Leshya about that, had he? Why?

He didn't have the answers, and if the stars and the wind did, they weren't telling. And so his watch passed, and then he slept.

The next morning he and Leshya marched across the Fells, hugging the thin tree lines that followed streams for cover, keeping their thoughts to themselves. But at midday they were working their way down the last line of leans, and he caught a glimpse of the Warlock in the distance before they slipped beneath the comforting branches of a small wood. There wasn't much old growth. Wood was cut here, and often. Mannish trails were everywhere. Still, it kept them out from under the sky, at least for a little while.

But after about a bell, things went quiet—all the birds, even the jays—and a shadow passed. Aspar looked up and caught a glimpse of something big.

"Sceat," he said.

They crouched beneath huckleberry bushes and waited for it to return, but instead, after a moment, Aspar heard a shriek. Without a thought, he suddenly found himself running and wondering why.

"Aspar!" Leshya snapped, but he ignored her.

He bounded down a series of old terraces and broke into a clearing, and there was the thing, gleaming black and green, its wings folding down as its claws came to earth. But in that terrible moment, that was not what held his attention. It was Winna, coming shakily to her feet next to a fallen horse, her eyes wide, a knife in her outstretched hand.

She was in profile, and so he could see the round bulge of her belly.

CHAPTER ELEVEN

A CHALLENGE

THE HANSAN KNIGHT stepped nearer, and Neil tried to keep his hand off Battlehound's hilt. A hush settled over the room, more profound by far than the earlier pause in the revelry that had greeted his lady.

"Sir Alareik," Neil acknowledged. "We've met before, it's true. I can't recall any unfinished business between us."

"Don't you? The Moonfish Inn at the docks in Eslen?"

"I remember," Neil said. "I was Sir Fail's squire, and he sent me to ask you to dine with us. You refused."

"You insulted me. Since you were a squire, honor forbade me taking the field against you. That is no longer the case."

It didn't stop you sending three of your squires to ambush me in the stables, Neil remembered, but he didn't think it best to bring that up.

In fact, before he could reply at all, Aradal broke in.

"Sir Alareik, this man is a member of an embassy and therefore a guest of our king. You will treat him with all the respect that comes with that position. Whatever grievance you have with him can be settled later."

"I'll not attack him out of hand," the Wishilm knight replied. "But there's nothing in the old code that says he can't agree to meet me with honor. There's no law in the world that forces a man to hide behind skirts and pretty words rather than step out and take arms like a knight. Well, maybe in Crotheny that's how they do things, but I'd rather think that even there knights are knights."

A general mutter went up at that, and a few shouts of agreement. Neil sighed.

"Sir Neil," Muriele whispered in Lierish.

"It's too late," he replied in the same tongue. "I can't refuse this."

"You certainly can," she said. "Your injuries—"

"Don't matter, Majesty. Don't you see? It's not the insult to me that's the problem; it's the insult to you and to Crotheny. If we're weak here, we'll be weak before Marcomir. There's no helping it."

"Nonsense. We just show we won't be distracted from our purpose. You're not that wise in politics yet, Sir Neil."

"Maybe not, but I know men of war, Majesty. I know knights, and I know Hansans."

"What's your mother say there, sir knight?" Sir Alareik shouted to general laughter.

Muriele lifted a glare at the man. "You've no manners, sir," she replied. "You're no better than a beast. You've interrupted a perfectly fine evening in the most boorish manner possible."

"I've approached your knight in an honorable way, Your Majesty," he replied. "Which is more than I can say about how he dealt with my poor squires, whom he set upon from hiding. What sort of satisfaction can I have if I can't fight him?"

To Neil, Muriele seemed to pause for an instant.

"Oh, you can fight him," she replied. "I was only pleading with him to spare your life when the moment comes."

The Wishilm knight's brow arched in surprise, and then he smiled. But Neil saw something in the man's eyes. It looked like worry.

He thought I would refuse, Neil realized. *He doesn't want to fight me.*

"Shall we wait for the sun?" Neil asked. "Or would you rather have it now?"

"The morning is fine," Alareik replied. "On the green. Mounted or not?"

"Your choice," Neil replied. "I don't care."

Alareik stood there for a moment.

"Was there something else?" Muriele asked.

"No, Majesty," the Wishilm knight replied. He bowed awkwardly and vanished into the crowd. The music struck up again, and the rest of the evening was all beer, food, and song.

Neil lifted himself from bed after the midnight bell tolled. He put on his gambeson, took up Battlehound, and made his way back down to the great hall and through its doors to the dark street. He took the sword and made a few passes, trying not to wince at how weak the arm felt. An arrow had struck him from above, piercing bone and muscle, and even after the head finally had been withdrawn, fever had nested there for more than a nineday.

Experimentally, he shifted to a left-favoring hold, but that was worse, because the muscles in his upper arm seized into a ball of pain. He'd taken a spear there, and the blade had cut one of the tendons that attached muscle to bone. Apparently those didn't grow back.

He saw something move from the corner of his eye and found a silhouette watching him. Not surprisingly, the shadow had a familiar hulking shape.

"Good evening, Everwulf af Gastenmarka," Neil said. "Come to do your master's dirty work again?"

He couldn't see the face, but the head moved from side to side.

"I'm much ashamed of that," the man growled. "You taught me a proper lesson that night. You could have killed me, but you didn't."

"You were never in danger of that," Neil said.

"Ney, nor was I ever in danger of beating you," the fellow said, "not even with my friends to help me."

"I was lucky."

"Oh, no. I was there. And who hasn't heard of the battle on Thornrath? You butchered our men there, and one of them was Slautwulf Thvairheison. You've made a large reputation in a small time."

"It's the past, Everwulf. No need for you to worry over it."

"Oh, but there is. My lord sent us after you, do you understand? To punish you and affront Sir Fail de Liery. And when you beat us, two of us quit him and went in search of more honorable masters. That's the humiliation that stings him now, that forces this fight, even with you injured."

"What makes him think I'm injured?"

"The battle for the waerd is famous, Sir Neil. And the tale says that you were bleeding from six wounds and lay three months abed. That's not long enough, Sir Neil. You can't be fully mended."

"It is if I didn't really bleed from six wounds," he replied.

"His squires watched you approach. Do you really think he would fight you if he didn't think you were infirm?"

"I think he thought I would back down, and now he isn't sure I'm injured at all."

"Yah. I'm sure you're right there. He's trembling. But he's challenged you in public. He'll fight you."

"There's no talking him out of it?"

"No."

"Well, I'll fight him, then."

Everwulf's voice dropped a bit lower. "Rumor is your legs are good, that your worst injuries were to shoulder and arm. If that were me, I would choose to fight on foot. Quick feet can make up for a slow arm, and I know you have quick feet."

"Thank you," Neil said.

"May the Ansus favor you," Everwulf replied, taking a step back. He paused, then turned and walked quickly off.

"Well, that was interesting," another voice murmured from the darkness, this one feminine. Heat flashed through Neil's veins, and he lifted his blade before recognizing the voice.

"Lady Berrye," he acknowledged.

"You might as well call me Alis," she replied softly.

"You were here for all of that?" he asked.

"Yes."

"Shouldn't you be guarding the queen?"

"I am," she replied.

"By watching after me?"

"I never thought she ought to be on this fool's errand in the first place," Berrye said, "and I think it was a mistake to bring you. The embassy is hardly under way, and already you've endangered it just by being who you are. Every knight between here and Kaithbaurg is going to want to fight you."

"I know," Neil replied.

"Well, then put a stop to it now. Admit your injuries and withdraw."

For a moment Neil honestly thought she was joking, but then her tone registered.

"That's impossible," he said. "That's what Sir Alareik wants."

"Yes. It's what I want, too."

"Is this the queen's word?"

"No. She bleeds the same hot island blood you do, and you convinced her. I think she really believes you will win."

"And you don't?"

"You can barely move your sword arm. Even a little exertion leaves you gasping."

"Well, then I'll lose," Neil said. "That's still better than not fighting."

"You're her champion. If you fight and fall, it weakens her. If you refuse to fight, it shows she's really determined to carry out this embassy, to avoid distraction, that she has *you* under control."

"If she orders me to withdraw, I will."

"She won't."

"She won't because you're wrong," Neil replied. "Anything I do other than fight and win will weaken her. So I'll fight and I'll win."

"That's pure genius," Berrye said, her voice larded with sarcasm.

He didn't see much point in replying, and after a moment she sighed.

"Very well. This fellow you just spoke to—was he really trying to help you? If you chose to fight on foot, won't that just let Wishilm know about the trouble with your arms?"

"Probably. But I don't think Everwulf came to trick me."

"Why, then?"

"To make his peace with me and tell me good-bye."

"You can still stop this," Alis murmured.

Muriele nodded absently. The sun was breaking through the mist, crowning the poplars and firs at the edge of the green, which lay on the eastern outskirts of town. It wasn't, of course, very green but rather an expanse of muddy ground churned up by horses and wagons, soldiers practicing, and children playing games. There were bits of grass here and there, but on balance Muriele thought it probably ought to be called a "brown."

There was no seating as such, although a chair had been provided for her. Everyone else—and it really did look as if it might be everyone in town—was standing or squatting around the perimeter, waiting expectantly. The Wishilm knight was already on the field, his suit of lord's plate beginning to pick up the gleam of the rising sun. Neil hadn't appeared yet.

"He'll be killed," Alis pursued.

"He's a knight," she replied.

"A badly injured knight. A knight the leics said should never fight again. A knight you brought along to ease into less martial professions."

"He will be of no use to me if I allow Hansa to brand him a coward," Muriele said.

"I cannot believe you are so cold," Alis said.

Muriele felt a flare of anger but let it flicker down.

"I love that boy," she said after a moment. "He has more heart and soul than any man I have ever known, and I owe him more than I can possibly say. But he is from Skern, Alis. I could make him turn from this, but it would wither him. It would destroy him. For a man like him, death is better."

"So you send him to his death?"

Muriele forced a little laugh. "You did not see him at Cal Azroth," she said.

The crowd suddenly erupted in cheers and heckling that were nearly matched, and Muriele wondered if Neil's hounds were from the south part of town and his ravens from the north. But nothing about Bitaenstath seemed so neatly divided.

Neil wore armor easily as bright as Sir Alareik's. It should have been: It never had been worn before. His last harness had had to be cut from him after the battle of the waerd. The new armor was very plain, made in the style of the islands, without ornamentation, formed for battle and not for court.

He was mounted as Wishilm was, but something about the way he sat seemed strange.

Alis caught it first. "He's got it in his left," she said.

That was it. Neil had his lance couched under his left arm. His shield rested heavily on his right.

"That doesn't make sense," she said. "That puts point against point. His shield is useless; it's on the wrong side of the horse."

"The same is true for Wishilm," Alis pointed out.

"What is this?" Sir Alareik muttered as they raised visors. "You've got your spear in the wrong hand."

"It's the hand I want it in," Neil shot back.

"It isn't done."

"You challenged me, and yet I let you choose the place and the weapons. Now you're going to begrudge how I choose to wield my spear?"

"This is some trick. It won't work."

Neil shook his head. "It's not a trick," he said. "My right arm is hurt. I think you know that. I can't hold a lance in it, and in fact I don't think I would be able to hold a shield up to take a blow."

Alareik's puzzlement was plain. "Do you wish to withdraw?" he asked.

"Withdraw? No, Sir Alareik. I'm going to kill you. This isn't a formal list; I'll stay to your left, where your shield won't be of any use to you. If you try to bring it around, you'll hit your horse in the head, won't you? So we'll come together point to point, and I'll drive my spear through one of your eyes, and that will be that."

"I'll do the same."

Neil smiled thinly. He leaned forward, keeping his gaze fixed on the man's smoke-blue eyes.

"I don't care," he whispered.

Then he turned his horse and rode for his end of the list. He reached it, turned, and waited.

He patted his horse's neck. "I don't care," he confided to his mount.

The horn blew, and he gave Ohfahs the heel. His left arm was starting to hurt. If he lifted or extended it, he knew it would cramp, but it worked just fine for couching a lance. As the stallion gathered speed, he let his shield fall away, concentrating only on putting the point where he wanted it.

PART II

MANIFESTATIONS
OF SEVERAL SORTS

He found her there beneath the cliff
In the shallows of the sea
Her body like a white, white swan
All still and cold was she

He kissed her on her pale wet lips
And combed her bonny hair
He cut twelve golden strands of it
And strung his harp with care

The harp it sang of murder
The harp it sang of blood
It rang across the lands of fate
To the darkling western wood
—FROM "THOS TOE SOSTEREN," A FOLKSONG
OF NEWLAND, TRANSLATED INTO KING'S TONGUE
BY STEPHEN DARIGE

A butterfly, as it turns out, is only a thing for making
more worms.
—FROM THE AMVIONNOM OF PRESSON MANTEO

CHAPTER ONE

EMPRESS OF
THE RED HALL

ANNE STOOD on the bow of the royal ferry and stared up at the walls and towers of Eslen, wondering at how alien they seemed. She had lived all but one of her seventeen winters on that hill, within that fortress. The island's forests and greens had been her playground. Shouldn't she feel like she was coming home?

But she didn't. Not in the least.

When they reached the slip and the boat was secure, her horse, Faster, was brought around. She mounted it for the procession through the city but paused at the great Fastness gate, frowning at the massive stone of its construction.

"Majesty?" Cauth asked. "Is something the matter?"

Her pulse was thumping strangely in her neck, and she couldn't seem to draw a deep breath.

"Wait," she said. "Just wait a moment."

She turned and looked back the way they had come, across the slow flood of the Dew River and the green fields of Newland beyond, to the malends on the distant dike turning against the blue sky. She knew that all she wanted to do was cross that water again and ride, keep riding until she was so far away that no one had ever heard of Eslen or Crotheny or Anne Dare.

Instead she turned, set her shoulders, and rode through the portal.

Crowds had collected along the Rixplaf Way, and each square was full of merriment, as if it were a holiday. They chanted her name and threw flowers before her horse, and she tried to seem pleased and smile for them, when it was the best she could do not to bolt faster through the throngs at a dead run.

When she had returned from exile the previous spring, almost no one had recognized who she was. At the time she had been surprised and a little chagrined that so few people knew what their princess looked like. Now that anonymity was another precious thing forever lost to her.

By the time they reached the castle itself, Anne wanted nothing more than to hide in her rooms for a time, but she knew there wouldn't be any peace there; that was where Austra would be, and she didn't quite feel like facing her oldest friend. Better to confront her counselors and find out just what was being blamed on her absence this day.

"I'll give an audience in the Hall of Doves," she told Cauth. "I'd like to see Duke Fail de Liery, Duke Artwair, John Waite, Lord Bishop, and Marhgreft Sighbrand. Have them there in half a bell, would you?"

"It's done, Majesty," the Sefry replied.

John Waite, of course, was already waiting in the Hall of Doves when Anne arrived there. Plump, balding, pleasant of expression, John had been her father's valet. He'd been imprisoned and apparently forgotten by Robert, which was a better fate than most of the late king's staff had received.

"Majesty," he said, bowing as she entered the room.

"Hello, John," she replied.

"I understand you wanted to speak with me, Majesty."

She nodded. "Yes, John. I was going to wait until everyone was here, but we may have something of a delay while they're all found." She took a seat in what once had been her father's armchair, a straight-backed affair with arms carved to resemble feathered pinions. Made of white ash, it fit well in the white marble and abundant light of the Hall of Doves.

"My father trusted you more than anyone, John, and I know the two of you were close."

"That's very kind of you to say, Your Majesty. I miss your father a great deal."

"I do, too," she said. "I wish he were in this chair right now, not me. But it is me, as that's how it is."

"It's what your father wanted."

Anne almost laughed. "I'm sure he imagined Fastia here, not me. No one imagined it would be me here, I'm sure. Was I horrible to you, John?"

He smiled indulgently. "Just a bit of a prankster," he said. "But I always knew you had a good heart."

"I was horrible," Anne contradicted. "And I may be horrible yet; I'm still learning. But I hope you will consider being gardoald and keybearer of the house Dare."

The old man's eyes widened. "Majesty—I—I haven't the blood for that position."

"You will when I create you lord," she replied.

John reddened. "Your Highness, I've no idea what to say."

"Say yes. You won't thrust a knife in my back, John. I need men like that."

He bowed deeply. "I would be most honored," he replied.

"Good. We'll discuss particulars later, but the first thing I'd like you to do is see to finding me some ladies-in-waiting and a female head of staff. Someone absolutely trustworthy, you understand? Someone whom I don't have to worry about and who will not bother me much."

John bowed again, but when he straightened, he had a puzzled expression. "Your young maid, Austra. I should consider her for head of staff."

"No, I have other plans for her."

His eyebrows shot up in surprise, but he nodded. "As you wish."

"Thank you, John. Please arrange for some wine to be brought and then rejoin me here. As my gardoald, these discussions will concern you."

"Yes, Majesty."

She heard footsteps approaching and looked up in time to see Artwair come in.

"Well, Cousin," she said. "Here I am, just as you wished."

"I am pleased," he said. "We need our empress here, Anne."

"I'm here," she replied. "When the others arrive, we'll discuss those matters you deem most urgent."

"Who else is coming?"

"John will be back. I'm making him gardoald."

"That's not a bad choice," Artwair said. "You'll have to title him."

"I know. Can you think of a good one?"

Artwair frowned. "Haul Atref, I should think. One of Robert's puppets slaughtered the former Lord Haul and all his kin. The castle is garrisoned but masterless."

"Then I shall create him Lord Haul," Anne said.

"Well, here's my grandniece, back from her adventures," a low-timbred voice said.

"Grannuncle Fail," Anne said, allowing him to gather her in a hug. "I trust all went well at Copenwis."

"As well as it could. I still don't like it, but I imagine they're in Hansa by now."

"Mother will be fine," Anne said. She heard more foot-steps and saw that the others had arrived.

"My lords," she said. "Let's begin, shall we? Tell me what I need to know. Duke of Haundwarpen, you first."

Artwair drew himself up and clasped his wooden hand with his living one. "Hansa continues to occupy Copen-wis, and they are massing ships there and in Saltmark. My guess is that they will disembark ground forces for a march on Eslen and send their navy against Liery. There are also reports of an army gathering at Schildu, on the Dew River. Their intention there is probably to cut off our river trade, then use the river to move down into New-land."

"A familiar strategy," Anne said. "That's like what we did."

"Precisely, Majesty."

"Do they have the men to come at us from all of these directions and deal with the Lierish fleet as well?"

Sir Fail cleared his throat. "If I may?"

"Spell on," she said.

"They haven't the ships to take Liery, not alone. But there is rumor that a fleet is assembling at z'Espino. Moreover, it is nearly certain that Rakh Fadh is allied with Hansa, although there's no way of knowing how many ships they have or will send."

"What about our allies? Or do we have any?"

"Riders tell us that an embassy from Virgenya will arrive soon, probably sometime tomorrow."

"An embassy? I'm their empress. I don't want an embassy; I want the ships and troops we asked for three months ago."

"You may take that up with the Virgenyans," Artwair said. "Of all of the parts of the empire, they are the most independent, and they like to make a show of it."

"There will be a show," Anne muttered more or less under her breath. Then she turned to the other two men.

"Lord Bishop, Marhgreft Sighbrand, I trust you are well."

"Very well, Your Highness," Bishop replied.

"Lord Bishop, we made you master of the treasury, did we not?"

"You did, Majesty."

"What is the state of it?"

Lord Bishop's lips tightened. "Robert did a bit of looting before he fled the city, it seems."

"Can we pay and supply our troops?"

"For the time being. But if we have another levy—even a modest one—it will make our belts very tight."

"Even with the confiscated Church properties?"

"Even with that, yes," he replied.

"I see. Well, we need to find some more silver, don't we?"

"Yes, Majesty."

She turned to Sighbrand. "Marhgreft?"

"Majesty."

"The duke tells us that troops are gathering at Schildu. That is very near your greffy of Dhaerath, isn't it?"

"It is. Very near."

"I called you here to ask you to be my prime minister. I've been advised you would make a good one."

Sighbrand's lips twitched. "I'm honored, Majesty."

"Yet I wonder if your heart would really be in the job when your lands are in danger, so I will give you a choice instead. You may serve here as my adviser and defender of the keep, or you can take command of the armies of the east and defend us from there."

The old warrior's eyes brightened a bit. "I am a man more suited to action, Your Majesty, than arranging court appearances and the like."

"So I thought. Very well. You will answer to Artwair, who is supreme general of my forces, and you will answer to me. Beyond that, you have leave to organize the armies of the east as you see fit to guard our borders. I will have your title and powers drafted before this afternoon."

"Thank you, Majesty. I will not fail you."

"I don't expect you to," she replied. "I don't expect any of you to." She settled her hands on the tops of her thighs.

"Now," she said. "All of you. Can this war be stopped?"

"You did appoint an embassy," Artwair pointed out.

"Yes, based on the recommendation of the Comven and on an idea of my own. But you are not the Comven; you are men I respect. I'm not a general. I don't know much about war. So tell me what to think."

"There will be war," Artwair said. "They have come too far to turn back, and Marcomir is old. He has the backing of the Church. This is his chance, and he knows it."

"The rest of you agree?"

The others nodded their heads yes.

"Very well, then. It seems foolish to give them any more time to make things as they want them. We will take the war to them, gentlemen. Where shall we begin?"

Artwair frowned. "You mean now? But Your Majesty—"

"I won't wait until we're completely hemmed in," Anne said. "You say there are ships at Copenwis? Copenwis is our city, our port. Let those ships become ours or burn."

"Now, that's her de Liery blood talking," Duke Fail said. "I've been saying that for months."

"I'm settled on it," Anne said. "Make preparations. I would like to march within the nineday."

"Surely you aren't planning to go," Artwair said. "You promised you were done with adventures."

"This isn't an adventure. This is the war you've been asking me to fight. And Copenwis isn't so very far from Eslen. I can return at will."

Artwair looked unconvinced.

"You need me, Duke. I promise you. You need my gifts."

He bowed stiffly. "As you say, Majesty."

She rose. "Tomorrow, gentlemen."

Then she did go back to her rooms.

Just as she expected, Austra was there to fling herself into her arms and kiss her cheeks.

Austra was a year younger than Anne, a pretty young woman with hair the color of sun on grain. She had forgotten how good, how natural it felt to be with her; she felt her intentions falter a bit.

"It's been so strange here without you," Austra said. "In our old rooms, all alone."

"How is your leg?"

"Mended, almost. And things went well at the monastery?"

"Well enough," Anne replied.

"And is everyone, ah, well?"

"Cazio is fine," Anne replied. "You'll see him soon, although not as soon as you wish, I'm sure."

"What do you mean?"

"He didn't come back with me. I sent him to Dunmrogh."

Austra's face seemed to sag. "What?" she said faintly. "Dunmrogh?"

"I still don't fully trust the heirs to that place. They might yet give the Church the dark fane there, and I can't risk that. I need someone I can rely upon watching the place."

"But he's your bodyguard."

"I have other bodyguards now, Austra. And you cannot tell me you wouldn't be happier with Cazio safer."

"Happier, yes, but in Dunmrogh? For how long?"

"He doesn't know it yet, but I'm giving him Dunmrogh. I'm making him greft there and sending him the men he might need to hold that title should what remains of Roderick's family object."

"He won't be back, then?"

Anne took Austra's hand. "Don't worry," she said. "You're going there, too. You have my blessing to marry if you wish."

"What?" Austra's eyes were like plates, and her throat was working oddly.

"You once told me that although I felt we were like sisters, we never would be, not really, because you're a servant and I'm—well, now I'm queen, aren't I? And if something were to happen to me, what would become of you? As a girl I always assumed you would be fine, but I know better than that now. Well, under the law, there's no way for me to give a woman a title. But I can give Cazio one, and he can make you an honest woman, and your children will be nobles of Crotheny."

"But that means you're sending me away. I won't be your maid anymore."

"That's true," Anne said.

"I don't want that," Austra said. "I mean, it would be wonderful to marry and be a greffess and that sort of thing, but you can't send me away!"

"You'll thank me one day," Anne said.

"Give Cazio a castle in Newland or make him ward of some part of the city. Then we can all stay together!"

"Now you're wanting the dress and the cloth it was made from," Anne said. "No. You will go to Dunmrogh. I've said it."

Austra's eyes were full of tears. "What have I done? Why would you do this? Anne, we've always been together."

"As children. We aren't children anymore. Austra, this is for the best. You'll see. Be ready to leave by tomorrow."

She left Austra crying, went into her chamber, and shut the door.

* * *

The next morning she took her breakfast in the solar, accompanied by her new ladies-in-waiting. She'd put Austra on the road that morning, with Sir Walis of Pale and fifty men-at-arms. She hadn't gone down to see her off, fearing her resolve would weaken, and she reckoned they were a league away by now.

She noticed that all the girls were looking at her and none were eating.

"Ah," she said. She picked up a piece of bread and spread some butter and marmalade on it. "There. The queen is eating."

Lize de Neivless, one of the few Anne knew by name, giggled. A Lierish girl of fifteen, she had dark, curly hair and a stubby little nose.

"Thank you, Majesty. I was so hungry."

"In future," Anne said, "don't wait for me to start. I won't have you beheaded, I promise. Not for that, at least."

That drew a few more giggles.

Lize tucked into the rolls and cheese, and so did the others.

"Your Majesty," began a slender young woman with wheat-colored hair and oddly dark eyes, "I wonder if you could tell us about Vitellio. Was it wonderful and strange? Are all the men as handsome as Sir Cazio?"

"Well, not all of them," Anne said. "Miss . . . ?"

"Cotsmur, Majesty. Audry Cotsmur."

"Well, Miss Cotsmur, there is no lack of comely fellows there. As to the rest, yes, I suppose I thought it was strange and exotic at first."

"And is it true you worked as a scrub maid?" another asked.

"Hush, Agnes," Lize hissed, clapping her hand over the mouth of a girl who looked about thirteen. "That's not to be brought up; you know that." She looked at Anne. "I'm *so* sorry, Majesty. Miss Ellis often talks without thinking."

"Miss de Neivless, it's no matter," Anne said. "Miss Ellis

is quite right. When I was hiding in z'Espino, I did scrub pots and pans and floors. I did what needed to be done to return here."

"It must have been awful," Cotsmur said.

Anne thought back. "It was," she said. "And I was a pretty terrible maid, at least at first."

But part of her suddenly longed for those days in z'Espino. She knew that was absurd. She had been in fear of her life, working like a dog at menial tasks, often missing meals. But still, compared to the times that came later, compared to now, those days seemed simple. And she had had her friends, and they had been working together to survive, which had rewards she'd never imagined while growing up in privilege. She would almost want to have those days back.

But it didn't matter what she wanted, did it?

The girls began chattering among themselves, silly prattle about who was handsome and who was sneaking off to see whom. It made her sad, not least because she had been sillier than most of them not so very long ago.

It was a relief when John came to tell her that the Virgenyan delegation had arrived. Taking Lize and Audry with her, she went to change her dress and receive them.

She chose a black and gold Safnite gown, a light breastplate, and greaves. She had Lize trim her hair back up to her ears and chose a simple circlet for her crown. Then she went to the Red Hall.

As far as Anne knew, the Red Hall never had been used to receive ambassadors. Her father hadn't used it for anything; it was in the oldest part of the castle and not very large. The king had preferred the more imposing chambers to overawe those who came before him.

But that lack of use had made it the perfect place for children to play. Her sister Fastia had held pretend-court there, throwing lavish banquets of cakes and wine or whatever they could pilfer or beg from the kitchens. In those days, more often than not, Anne had pretended to be a knight, since being a princess was—well, what she was. Austra had been her man-at-arms, and they had defended their queen from countless invasions and depredations.

Anne felt comfortable there. It also suited the image of the warrior-queen she had adopted to meet in less formal places, more face to face.

Today the hall seemed a bit large, however, because the number in the Virgenyan delegation was exactly three. The leader she recognized as a frequent visitor to her father's court, the baron of Ifwitch, Ambrose Hynde. The black hair she remembered was grayer now, and his squarish face more lined. She reckoned he was about fifty. He had a vaguely apologetic look in his eyes that worried her. Behind him stood two other men. One was her cousin Edward Dare, the prince of Tremor, a man of some sixty years. His silver hair had been cropped till he was nearly bald, and he had a severe, hawklike look about his face.

The third man, by contrast, was unknown to her and younger, probably no more than thirty. She noticed his eyes first, because something seemed odd about them. After a moment she understood that it was that one was green and the other brown. His face was friendly and intelligent, boyish, really. He had auburn hair and a small mustache and goatee that were redder.

He smiled, and she realized her gaze must have lingered on him while she sorted out his eyes. She frowned and looked away. They were announced by her herald, each in turn kissing her outstretched hand. The phay-eyed man turned out to be the Thames Dorrel, the earl of Cape Chavel.

"Such a large delegation," she said when the immediate formalities were done. "It's good to know our cousin Charles takes our troubles seriously."

"She goes right for it, doesn't she?" Cape Chavel said.

"I haven't spoken to you," Anne snapped. "I'm speaking to the baron."

"Majesty," the baron said, "I understand how this looks, but it wasn't meant as an insult."

"Well, I can't imagine what an *intended* insult must be like, then. But that's not really the point, Baron. The point is that Virgenya and her monarch are subject to the will of their empress. I requested knights and men in arms, not a delegation, and so I can only imagine *you've* been sent to tell me that Virgenya is in open revolution."

"That we are not, Majesty," the baron replied.

"Then you've brought the men with you?"

"They will come, madame," he said.

"I rather need them *now,* not after the ravens are picking our bones."

"It is a long march from Virgenya," Baron Ifwitch said. "And there was difficulty in the levy. Monsters have been swarming out of the Mountains of the Hare, terrorizing the countryside. And since your actions against the Church—"

"What of the Church's actions toward me? Or the good people of Virgenya?"

"Loyalty to z'Irbina has lately become a fashion in Virgenya, Majesty, especially among the nobility. No one actually refused to send men, but they have found ways to . . . delay."

"You're saying that the trouble isn't that my dear cousin is insubordinate but that he cannot command his own nobles?"

"There is some truth in that, yes."

"I see."

"I'm not sure you do, Majesty. The political situation in Virgenya is very complicated at the moment."

"Too complicated for me to sort out, you mean?"

"Nothing of the kind, Majesty. I will be happy to explain it to you."

Anne sat back in her chair. "You will, but not now. Do you have any other bad news for me?"

"No, madame."

"Very well. Have a rest. I would be pleased if you would meet me at my table tonight."

"We would be honored, Majesty."

"Good."

The two older men turned to go, but the younger stood his ground.

"What?" she asked.

"Is that leave to speak, Majesty?"

Despite herself, she smiled a bit. "I suppose it is. Go ahead."

"You asked if we had more bad news. I do not. But I hope you will think I have brought a little good news."

"Delightful if true," Anne said. "Please say on."

Ifwitch took a step toward the earl. "Tam, you shouldn't—"

"Really, Ifwitch, I would like to hear this rumored good news."

He bowed and didn't say anything else.

"It's true, some nobles don't know where their duties lie. I am not one of them. Majesty, I've brought my bodyguard with me, five hundred and fifty of the best horsemen you will ever see. They—and I—are yours."

"King Charles has released you to me?" she asked.

None of them spoke, although Ifwitch reddened.

"I see," she replied. "He hasn't."

"Charles needs the nobles he trusts in Virgenya," the earl said. "It's really that simple. He knows I would never ride against him. But as I am loyal to him, so I am to the empress *he* serves, so I have come directly to petition you."

"I didn't think I would hear much pleasing today," Anne said. "I was wrong. I accept your loyalty."

She shot her gaze back at the other two men. "It is a thing in short supply these days."

CHAPTER TWO

ALONG THE
DEEP RIVER

WITCHLIGHTS LED the way as Stephen, Zemlé, Adhrekh, and twenty Aitivar descended into the roots of the mountain. The ethereal globes of iridescence flitted about, casting the otherwise bleak gray walls in shades of gold, silver, ruby, emerald, and sapphire. Stephen had never seen witchlights before entering the Witchhorn, but Aspar had spoken of them as a fixture of Sefry rewns.

Oddly enough, the Aitivar didn't seem to know anything about them other than what anyone could observe. Were they alive? Creations of shinecraft or some natural product of the tenebres?

No one knew, and no book Stephen could find answered the question. But they were useful, and they were pretty, which was more than could be said about most things.

They were particularly useful just now, as the path they walked was barely a kingsyard wide, bounded on the right hand by the stone of the great central subterrain of the caverns and on the left by the crevasse through which the underground river Nemeneth sought its way through stone and earth to feed deeper streams and eventually, perhaps, the Welph, which flowed in turn to the Warlock and thence to the Lier Sea at Eslen. He could hear the rushing of the Nemeneth, but it was too far below him for the witchlights to reveal.

"Are you sure you're ready?" Zemlé asked him.

"I'm sure I'm not," he replied. "I wasn't ready to walk the first faneway I walked. Then I nearly died—maybe did die—just setting foot on another sedos. But Virgenya Dare wasn't ready, either. She just *did* it. And I'm not going to wait until the Vhelny or whatever it is that's stalking me has its chance."

"Then the journal talks about the faneway?"

"Yes. I was reading an early part, when she was a girl, and the Skasloi took her into the mountains. *This* mountain. She felt the faneway below her. Years later she came back and walked it."

"So she tells where it is."

"Yes. I know where I'm going, if that's what you're asking."

"Is it much farther?"

He smiled. "That's what we used to ask my father on long trips. Have you aged backward to five?"

"No. I don't care how far it is. I'm just curious."

"I reckon it at about half a league. It's in another part of the mountain. Adhrekh, have you ever been this way before?"

"The cavern ends ahead, pathikh."

"You really believe that, or is this just something else you neglected to tell me? Another test to see if I'm really Kauron's heir?"

"It's not a test, pathikh. We've never known where the faneway is."

Stephen stopped. "It's going to stay that way, then. Give me a pack of food and water and return to your rewn."

"Pathikh—"

"Do it. If I even suspect you're following me, I won't go anywhere near the faneway. Do you understand?"

"Pathikh, this place you are going—it is old, very old, and it has been abandoned for a long time. There's no knowing what might lurk there in the dark."

"Stephen, he's right," Zemlé said. "Going alone would be foolish."

"They've just admitted they need me to find the faneway. Maybe that's all they ever needed from me. Maybe once I find it, I'm of no use to them."

"Stephen, Sefry can't walk faneways. Any faneways. Why would they want to know where this one is?"

That drew him to a stop. "What? I've never heard that."

"It's true," Adhrekh said.

Stephen frowned and leafed quickly through his saint-blessed memory. No Sefry had ever joined the Church and walked a faneway; that much was true. But there was something . . .

"As soon have a Sefry walk a faneway as give shiveroot for the gout," he cited.

"What?" Zemlé asked.

"From the Herbal of Phelam Haert. It's the only thing I can think of that supports your claim. Anyway, maybe they have someone in mind to walk it other than me."

"Who? Not Fend, obviously. Hespero? Then why did they fight him?"

You can trust the Aitivar.

Stephen blinked. Everyone was looking at him strangely.

"What did you say?" Zemlé asked.

"What do you mean?"

"You were just babbling in some other tongue."

Stephen sighed and massaged his forehead. "Nothing," he said. "Never mind. All right, Adhrekh. You can come."

Adhrekh acknowledged that by bowing, and they continued the descent. As the Sefry had predicted, the roof of the cave came sloping down to meet them even as the angle of the trail sharpened and finally became stairs. The churning of the river grew louder, and eventually the stairs ended on a bed of gravel and sand at its banks.

Stephen had been trying not to think about this part, but now he was there, and he felt his breath shorten. It wasn't how he had imagined it; it was much worse.

Upstream, where the Aitivar dwelt, the Nemeneth was a relatively placid stream. Here, she came crashing down from a series of shoals and waterfalls to form a great vortex. The cave roof was only two kingsyards above that, and across the river was only stone.

"No," Zemlé said. "Oh, saints, no."

"I'm afraid so," Stephen said. He was trying to sound brave and nonchalant, but his voice quavered. He hoped they couldn't hear that over the steady thrumming of the river-size drain.

"This can't be right," she said, and turned to Adhrekh. "Haven't any of you ever tried this?"

Adhrekh actually coughed out a little laugh, something Stephen had never heard the man do before.

"Why?" he said. "Why would anyone do that? I could live seven hundred years if I'm careful."

Stephen sat on the shingle and tried to take deep, slow breaths. The witchlights seemed slower now, calmer.

"Stephen?"

"I have to," he said. He took a few more breaths, levered himself up, and walked toward the rushing whirlpool. He knew he couldn't pause, and so he leapt in, aiming his feet toward the center of it.

It took him with incredible violence. The power of the water was absolute, and nothing his limbs could do had any effect. All he could do was try to hold on to his air, not scream and let it all out, and he suddenly knew with absolute certainty that he somehow had been tricked. He was a dead man, and knowing that, he lost the power of thought entirely.

When it came back, he remembered being ground against sand and stone and then expulsion and the grip of the flood easing. Now he lay on gravel in utter darkness, coughing out the water that had forced its way into his lungs.

A golden glow rose up in front of him, and then a deep red one. A few heartbeats later the witchlights were all around him again.

He lay on a strand not very different from the one he had just left, but here there was no high-vaulted chamber, only a tunnel two kingsyards higher than the river flowing through it. Water crashed through the roof in a great column on his right, and on his left the passage went on much farther than his luminescent companions could reveal.

He heard violent coughing and saw the silhouette of a head and shoulders rise from the pool: Adhrekh.

"Zemlé!" he gasped. Had she tried to follow him, too?

More Aitivar appeared, but he didn't see her.

"Zemlé!" he repeated, this time at the top of his lungs.

"I have her," someone said. In the stir he couldn't tell where the voice was coming from exactly.

"Who is that?"

Then he made out one of the Aitivar cradling a limp figure. He waded up onto the beach.

"Saints curse me," Stephen snarled. "Is she—"

The fellow shrugged and lay her down. Her head was smeared with black, which Stephen realized was blood rendered dark by the colored lights. For a moment he felt paralyzed, but then she coughed, and water bubbled out of her mouth.

"Bandages," he told Adhrekh. "Get me bandages and whatever unction you might have."

Adhrekh nodded.

"Zemlé," Stephen said, stroking her cheek. "Can you hear me?"

He took the sleeve of his shirt and pressed it to her wound, trying to see how deep it was. Her eyes opened, and she shrieked.

"Sorry," Stephen said. "Can you hear me?"

"I can hear you," she said. "Can you hear me?"

"Yes."

"Good. Because I hate you." She felt toward her brow. "Am I bleeding to death?"

"I think it's a shallow cut," he replied. "There's a lot of blood, but I don't think your skull broke."

Adhrekh returned with linen cloths and some sort of paste with a sulfury smell and set about bandaging Zemlé's head. He seemed to know what he was doing, so Stephen didn't interfere. His pulse finally began slowing down, and he felt unexpected exhilaration flood through him.

Who was he to brave such things? Not the Stephen Darige who had left Ralegh for the monastery d'Ef, what, not even two years ago?

Even Aspar might be proud of him.

"Did we lose anyone?" Stephen asked Adhrekh.

"No, pathikh," the Sefry replied. "All accounted for."

"It's colder down here," Stephen noticed. "You brought the change of clothes I asked for?"

"Yes. And now I understand why you asked for them. But if you had told me more concerning what we were to do, I might have made more effort to *keep* them dry. I can better serve you, pathikh, if you talk to me more."

"The extra clothes are wet? What about the coats?"

"Drier than what we're wearing, pathikh."

"It'll have to do. When Zemlé can walk, we'll move on. Moving will warm us."

"Stephen," Zemlé said. "A small question. Tiny, really."

"Yes?"

"There *is* another way back, yes?"

Stephen glanced at the waterfall. "Right. I guess we can't swim back up that."

"Stephen—"

"Virgenya Dare made it out."

"But you don't know how?"

"She neglected to write about that, I'm afraid. But there must be a way out."

"And we only need find it before we run out of food or freeze to death."

"Don't be a pessimist," Stephen said, his elation starting to fade. "We'll be fine."

"How much farther to the start of the faneway?"

"I'm not sure. Virgenya wasn't sure; it's hard to measure time and distance underground. She reckoned it at several bells but admitted it could have been days."

"What if we get lost?"

"Not much chance of that right now," he said. "We've only one direction to go. Anyway, I can feel the faneway. It's close." He gripped her shoulder. "How are you feeling?"

"A little dizzy, but I can walk."

Adhrekh had dug out the coats from their packs, sturdy elkhide paiden with fur lining. They were hardly wet at all, and once clothed in one, Stephen felt a great deal better even though he was still wet.

Once everything was gathered again, they started out.

The passage bent and turned like the bed of any river and its roof went higher and lower, but it stayed simple in terms of choices. More streams joined it, but they came from above, from fissures too small to accommodate a person. The floor dropped roughly down in places, forcing them to use rope to descend, but was never as dramatic or dangerous as what they already had been through. Not, that is, until they reached the place Virgenya Dare called simply "the valley." Stephen knew they were approaching it because the close echoes of the tunnel began opening up, becoming vastly more hollow, along with the sound of rushing water.

They came to the lip where the river churned and fell far from sight, and a vast black space yawned before them.

"And now?" Zemlé asked.

"There should be stairs here," Stephen said, searching along the ledge. The river must have flooded at times and eaten at the sides of the mouth, creating a shallow, low-roofed cave that went off to the left of the opening. After a moment he found what the Born Queen must have been talking about, and he groaned in dismay.

"What's wrong?" Zemlé asked, trying to see around him.

"Two thousand years," Stephen sighed.

There were indeed stairs cut into the stone of the wall, but the first four yards of them were gone, doubtless eroded by the floods he had just been considering. After that, the steps that remained looked glassy and worn. To reach them meant leaping three yards and falling two and then avoiding slipping upon landing. Or breaking a leg. And once there, he had no assurance there wasn't a similar gap farther on.

Behind him, he heard Adhrekh in a hushed conversation.

"Any ideas?" Stephen asked.

He heard the quick thump of footsteps and air brushed at his locks. Then he saw one of the Aitivar hurl himself into space toward the eroded stairs.

"Saints!" Stephen gasped. He didn't have time to say anything else before the fellow hit the stair, flailed for balance, teetered—and fell. Then he could only stare.

"Who—who was that?" he finally managed.

"Unvhel," Adhrekh said.

"Why—" But then another one was running past him.

"Wait—"

But of course it was too late. The jumper hit the step, and his foot slipped, so that he fell like a tomfool at a traveling show, landing on his prat and sliding. Stephen held his breath, sure the Aitivar would go over, but he somehow caught himself and managed to slip down the waterworn steps to stable footing.

Stephen turned to Adhrekh. "What is wrong with you people?" he asked, trying to contain his anger. "You were just on about how long you could live if you didn't do anything stupid."

"You shamed us at the waterfall, pathikh. If I had known your plan, one of us would have gone in first. We were determined not to let you risk yourself so foolishly again."

"What good would it have done to go into the water before me? I wouldn't have known if you made it or not."

"Begging your pardon, pathikh, but you might have been able to hear us below. You've walked the faneway of Saint Decmanus."

Stephen reluctantly acknowledged that with a tilt of his head. "So you sent them to jump before I could try it?"

"Yes."

"But I wouldn't have jumped."

Adhrekh shrugged. "Very well. But someone had to, unless you know some other way down."

"I don't."

A sharp ringing commenced, and Stephen realized that the Aitivar on the steps was working at the stone with a hammer and chisel, probably trying to create some purchase to tie a rope to. Another Sefry began the same work on their side. After perhaps half a bell, a rope was fixed across the gulf, and Adhrekh went across, hanging upside down, hooking his legs over the cord and using his hands to pull himself along.

Before Stephen went, they tied a second rope around his waist. An Aitivar held it at either end so that if he fell, they had a chance of stopping him. That safeguard made Stephen feel a bit condescended to but infinitely safer, and he insisted that Zemlé be brought across in the same fashion.

Finally, with the exception of a man Stephen hadn't known the name of, they were all on the stairs.

The footing improved after ten or so kingsyards, the steps becoming more defined and the way wider. The witchlights occasionally showed the other side of the crevasse but not the bottom, or the roof, for that matter.

"It's colder still," Zemlé noticed.

"Yes," Stephen agreed. "There is much debate about the nature of the world beneath. Some mountains spew fire and molten rock, so one would imagine there is great heat below. And yet caves tend to be cold."

"Rather that than molten rock," she replied.

"Yes. What was that?"

"I didn't hear anything."

"Up above, at the waterfall: a sort of scraping sound, like something big coming through."

"Something big?"

"Archers," Adhrekh said quietly.

Stephen tried to focus in the direction of the sound, but beyond their luminous companions there was only darkness.

"Is there any way to dampen the witchlights?" Stephen asked. "They make us easy to see."

And then he smelled it, a hot, animal, resiny smell, just like the trace of scent in the aerie.

"He's here," Stephen said, trying to keep his voice from showing his building panic.

A warm breeze blew across them, and Stephen heard the sharp hum of a bowstring.

CHAPTER THREE

THE GEOS

THE BEAST saw Aspar coming and whipped its snake-necked head around, lifting its great batlike wings in challenge.

Aspar rushed to meet it, trying in the few instants he had to see where he should strike.

As on a bat, its wings were its forelimbs. It was crouched down on its hind legs, so he couldn't see much of them. The head was vaguely canine, like some mixture of wolf and snake, and sat atop a kingsyard of sinuous neck.

That long throat seemed the safest bet. The feyknife ought to cut right through it.

But then it beat its wings and jumped, and as its long, sinewy rear legs unfolded, he realized that despite a few details, the thing was grown more like a fighting cock than a bat, as it was suddenly above him, kicking down with wicked claws and dirklong heel spurs. It was *fast*.

Aspar had too much momentum to stop, so he pivoted to his right, but not quickly enough. The spur of one foot struck his chest.

To Aspar's surprise and relief, the thing wasn't as heavy as it looked. Although the claw probably would have laid open his chest if he hadn't been warded, it didn't have the force to cut through the boiled leather cuirass he wore beneath his shirt.

It did stick there, though, and the thing shrieked and yanked, trying to get loose. Then it did the more logical thing and kicked its other set of talons at Aspar's face.

Aspar brought the feyknife up and through the wedged claw and almost couldn't feel the blade cutting. Then he bounded up and slashed at the neck.

Its reflexes were better. It hurled up and back, shrilling—

—and going straight into Winna, who went sprawling on her back.

Aspar started after the beast, but suddenly heard the thrumming of hooves and glanced to see what it was. The monster looked, too, but not in time to dodge the spear that struck it in the ribs and lifted it off the ground, propelling it along with the weight of a bay charger and an armored knight behind it. The knight slammed it into the trunk of an ash, and the spear shivered. The terrible beast crumpled and then started haltingly to get up.

The knight dismounted, drawing his sword.

"Wait," Aspar said. "It might be poison."

He was trying not to think that if it was like the greffyn, Winna was already venomed.

The knight hesitated, then nodded.

Aspar walked over to the creature. Its skin was barely cut, but it was clear that much was broken inside. It watched him come with curiously blank eyes, but when he was close enough, it hopped at him again. It was slower than before.

Aspar sidestepped, caught the leg above the claws with his left hand, and severed the whole limb with the feyknife. Dark, almost purple blood jetted from the stump as the head darted down to bite him. Aspar kept the knife coming up, however, and it went through the serpentine neck as if slicing soft cheese.

He turned away from the bloody work and found Winna hobbling toward him.

"Stay back," he shouted more loudly than he meant to.

She stopped, her eyes widening.

"The blood," he explained. "Every one of these things is different. Its touch may not be so bad, but its blood might."

He noticed she was rubbing her elbow.

"Were you hurt when you fell?"

"It's you," she said feebly. "I should have known. All I had to do was find a monster . . ."

"Yah, it's me," he said more softly, unable to keep his gaze from jumping down to her belly.

"You're—"

"Yah," she said. "Yah." She smiled a wavery little smile. "I knew you couldn't be dead. I told them." He saw that tears were streaming down her face. She reached out her arms, but he took a step back, and she nodded.

"Saints, then," she said, straightening and wiping her cheeks. "Get cleaned up so I can greet you proper. And you can tell me where you've been all this—"

Her gaze went out over his shoulder and became suddenly less tender.

"Oh," she said. "Hello."

"Hello," he heard Leshya say behind him.

Ah, sceat, he thought.

The knight had his helmet off, and he looked familiar.

"There's a spring just over here," he said. "You can leave your clothes and take my cloak. We can be to Ermensdoon in under a bell."

"I know you," Aspar said.

"Auy. I hait Emfrith Ensilson. You saved my life."

Aspar nodded. "You look better than when I saw you last."

"I should think," the greftson said. "How are you feeling?"

Aspar shrugged. "I'm not so easy to poison as some."

"From what I've heard, I'd hardly guess you were human at all," Emfrith said, trying on a little grin that didn't fit and was soon put away. Aspar didn't miss the shy glance at Winna, either.

"Human's not all your mother told you it was," Leshya said.

"He's human enough," Winna said.

"Where's Ehawk?" Aspar asked.

"In the mountains, looking for you."

Aspar had been aware that more horses and men were approaching, and now they were there: twenty-two of them, most in the livery that Aspar remembered from Haemeth.

A couple were dressed more roughly, and he reckoned they were trackers or hunters.

"We've a few extra horses," Emfrith said. "I'd be happy if you and the lady would use them."

"I'll stay on foot till I'm clean," Aspar said. "Where's this spring you were talking about?"

"Just there," the fellow replied, gesturing.

Aspar nodded and headed in that direction.

The spring came cold and clear from the ground and fed a pretty pool edged in moss and ferns. He wearily stripped off his leather chest plate and the gambeson beneath, which was so threadbare that it was worn through in places.

Next to go were the elkskin boots and breeches, and he slipped into water that was almost painfully cold at first but after a few moments felt perfect. He closed his eyes and soaked for a moment, letting the toxic blood flow away from his skin in lazy banners.

Truth to tell, he didn't think that as sedhmhari went the—what, wyver? drake?—was all that poisonous, at least not compared to the woorm or greffyn, whose mere glances were enough to bring death to the weak. But he needed a moment to think, and with Winna in her condition . . .

In her condition. He suddenly remembered the huge sow back in the Sarnwood, the thing within her tearing to be free from its mother's belly, and felt his breath quicken.

"The next human being you meet, you'll take under your protection. And you will take that person to the valley where you found the Briar King sleeping."

That was Winna. Of course it was, Grim damn it all.

Well, he wouldn't do it. To the hanging tree with the Sarnwood witch.

But why would she want him to take her there? Why would she want that?

He heard a twig snap and shifted his gaze. It was Emfrith, coming toward him.

Aspar cast a glance at his armor, a kingsyard away, but

there wasn't any time to get that on. The knife was within arm's reach.

"It's me," Emfrith said unnecessarily.

"Yah," Aspar agreed.

"I've brought my cloak. It's probably best we burn the clothes, don't you think?"

"Probably," Aspar replied.

Emfrith nodded but didn't go toward the abandoned garments.

"Didn't really think I'd see you again," the greftson admitted. "She kept insisting we search, and I did, because, well, I suppose I owe you."

"Was that the reason?"

"Not really. But I did search for you nevertheless, followed the waurm's trail into the Bairghs and lost it there. That still wasn't enough for her. Two days ago she had a dream, she said. Said she saw you coming down through these woods. I reckoned one more look wouldn't hurt."

"But it did."

He shrugged. "I could wish we hadn't found you."

Aspar nodded, trying to take in the whole scene. Were there archers out there? But this boy had taken on the woorm with only a lance and a horse. That was almost the only thing Aspar knew about him, but it suggested he didn't lack courage or conviction. Honor sometimes went with that.

"I never reckoned I could feel this way about someone with common blood," Emfrith went on. "But it's not so unusual in my family. We're not high royalty, after all." His voice lowered. "I can give her a better life than you can, holter. And the child, too."

"I know," Aspar said. "How does Winna feel about all this?"

"What do you think? She's been waiting for you."

"And here we are."

"Here we are," the greftson concurred. Then he started forward, toward Aspar's clothes.

"Maunt you we should destroy the cuirass, too? I can give you another."

Aspar glanced at the worn piece of armor. He'd had it for a long time. He'd already lost Ogre.

Stupid. It was just a thing, a thing nearly used up. And if Emfrith wasn't going to try to kill him now, he probably was telling the truth about replacing it.

"I'm being chased," Aspar said.

"Chased? By whom?"

"A pack of monsters," he said.

"How far behind you?" Emfrith asked. He didn't seem surprised.

"Well, the flying ones are here already, aren't they? The rest could be a day behind or a nineday. I'm not sure about their route or how well they track."

"We can fight them at Ermensdoon."

"No, we can't," Aspar said. "Trust me."

"What, then?"

"I—" Aspar began, but then his throat tickled. What he meant to say was that he and Leshya would continue on, draw Fend and his beasts off someplace.

That was what he meant to say.

"We can keep ahead of them. I know a safe place; it's just a matter of getting her there."

Emfrith frowned. "I understand your feelings for her, but if the monsters are chasing you, wouldn't she be safer if she didn't travel with you?"

Yes!

But Aspar shook his head. "They're after her, too. The wyver was attacking her, yah?"

Emfrith nodded. "Yes," he conceded. "But why?"

Aspar took a deep breath. Could he tell Emfrith about the geos? Then the boy could kill him or imprison him long enough to get Winna away from him.

It was worth a try.

"You remember where I got the berries that cured you from the woorm's poison?"

"The Sarnwood witch, they say."

"Yah." *There was a price for that.* "She told me that Fend was going to kill Winna if I don't stop him."

He wanted to scream, but he couldn't.

"Look," he said desperately. "You said Winna dreamed I would be here?"

Emfrith nodded. "Does she often have premonitions?"

"No!" Aspar replied. "No, she—" But that was all he could manage. He was like a strangpoppet in a children's farce.

"We'll go to Ermensdoon for supplies and the rest of my men," Emfrith said. "And I'll send out a few scouts to see if they can get a better idea of how far behind you they are. You killed the wyver; maybe they've lost you entirely."

"Maybe," Aspar said dubiously.

The ride to Ermensdoon wasn't a comfortable one. Winna rode near him, and Emfrith wasn't far away. Leshya hung back, but that didn't do much good. No one wanted to talk in front of everyone, so they mostly went in silence.

Ermensdoon was an old-fashioned hill castle with a square central tower and a stout wall. It sat on a little stub of a mound surrounded by a moat so old and unused that it had reverted mostly to a marsh of cattails and river grass and was currently home to a number of ducks and coots.

"There's a newer fortress a league south," Emfrith told him. "A full garrison marched up from Eslen last nineday. I reckon the queen thinks Hansa may try a march to the Warlock and then take boats down. My father gave me Ermensdoon when I was little. Before that, it hadn't been lived in for a generation."

Aspar didn't really have anything to say to that, so he didn't speak. Soon enough they were inside, anyhow, and he was in a small chamber in the tower. He was supplied with several cotton shirts, a pair of sturdy riding breeches, and calfskin boots. The thickset fiery-headed fellow who had brought them looked him over.

"What sort of broon you favor?"

"Boiled leather," Aspar said.

"I can come up with a steel one, I think."

"I'm not a knight. Steel doesn't suit me: too heavy. Leather will do."

"I can make one in a couple of days."

"We're in more of a hurry than that, I think," Aspar said.

"I'll start it, but I'll see what else I might have on hand," the redhead replied.

"Thanks," Aspar said.

Then the fellow was gone, leaving him to his worries.

But not for long. The knock came that he had been both hoping for and dreading; when he opened the door, Winna stood there.

"Are you unpoisoned now?" she asked.

"I reckon."

"You'll kiss me, then, or I'll know why."

It seemed like a very long time since he had kissed her, but the taste came right back to him, and he remembered the first time his lips had met hers. He'd just encountered a monster then, too: his first. And the surprise of her kiss had easily matched the shock of seeing a kinderspell beast come to life.

The kiss went on a little longer than its sincerity. Too many questions were behind those lips.

They pulled apart, and Winna smiled.

"So," Aspar said, glancing down at her belly.

Her eyebrows went up. "I hope that's not a question," she said. "Aspar White, I truly hope you're not asking a question."

"No," he said quickly. "But, ah, when?"

"When do you think? In your tree house, back when we first saw the woorm."

Cold crept along his spine. Winna had conceived the same day she'd been poisoned by the woorm. Of course she had.

"That's not the look I was hoping for," she said.

"I'm just—I'm trying to take this all in," Aspar said.

"Yah, well, me too. Where have you been, Aspar? And what, by any damn saint, is *she* doing with you?"

"That's a long story."

"Does it start with you leaving me here?"

Aspar wasn't sure what that was supposed to mean, but he nodded. "Yah."

"Well, tell me."

"Sit down, then."

She took a seat on the bed.

"I went off after the woorm, followed it for a long time up through the Bairghs. Deep up in there I caught up with it, but I wasn't the only one. Hespero had been tracking it, too, somehow."

"The praifec?"

"Yah. He tried to kill me, so I reckon he knows we don't work for him anymore."

"Tried to kill you?"

"Yah. He was in the wrong place to do it, up on a cliff and me below, so I gave him the slip. But Fend was there, too."

"Right. Riding the woorm."

"And there were Sefry in the mountain: Leshya's people. I think they were fighting the praifec. But I was a bit occupied. The Briar King showed up, so only you and Stephen were missing."

"You didn't find Stephen?"

"No. I killed the woorm with the praifec's arrow. Then I had a bit of a fight with one of those Mamres monks. He hurt me pretty bad: broke my leg. If it hadn't been for Ogre, I'd be dead, and that's certain."

"Ogre . . ."

"Died saving me."

"I'm sorry, Aspar."

He shrugged. "I meant to pasture him soon, but the chance just never came up. But he died fighting. Anyway, then Fend, ah, killed the Briar King."

"What?"

"With the same arrow. Turns out it can be used any number of times, not just three. He was about to use it on me when Leshya showed up and got me out."

"Convenient."

"Yah. But I got sick after that, really sick. When I came to my senses, Leshya had found us a hiding place, but I wasn't able to travel for months. Fend found us. He's on my trail again, and he's not alone. We can't stay here, Winna."

"You were alone with her for four months?" Winna asked.

"Yah."

"That must have been awfully cozy."

He felt a flare of anger. "That's kindertalk, Winna. There's nothing there. If anyone's been courting all this time, it seems it was you."

"Emfrith? He's sweet. He's not you. He's not the father of my child." She stood up. "And as for kindertalk, yes, I'm young enough to be your daughter, but that doesn't make me a fool for being jealous. It just means I love you. I was actually beginning to lose hope, to think you were really dead, and then you show up with her? Just don't get all angry and don't dodge my question. You tell me nothing happened between you, and I'll not raise this again, ever."

"Nothing happened."

She let out a deep breath. "Fine," she said.

"We're done with that?"

"Yah."

"Good."

"That's all? Don't you have more to say than that?"

Aspar closed his eyes for a moment. "You know how I feel about you, Winna. But maybe it would be best for you—"

"Stop," she said. "Just stop there, Aspar. There's no best for me. There's only you. You know I never asked anything more than you could give, but you have given me something." She patted her belly. "I never imagined a normal life from you, holter. You never promised it, and I still don't expect it. But whatever happens, this child is ours."

He stared at her belly, remembering the greffyn being born. "Winna."

"What?"

Grim take the Sarnwood witch.

"Let's get you somewhere safe, then. Somewhere you can have this baby without fear."

"You'll go with me?"

"Yah."

She smiled and rushed to hug him, pressing the hardness of her belly into him.

"I've missed you, Aspar White. You've no idea how much I've missed you." She took his hands. "Where shall we go?"

He kissed her hands and answered. He meant to say that they would go to Virgenya or Nazhgave, anyplace that seemed outside the sickness wasting the world.

"To the Mountains of the Hare," he heard himself say instead. "I can protect us there."

And he kissed her again.

CHAPTER FOUR

TWO MAIDS

FASTER WAS thunder beneath Anne as she galloped across the Sleeve. Anne felt a fierce grin pull at her mouth, and she shouted her joy up to whatever saints were listening.

It had been so long since she had ridden for the sheer fun of it. Once she had spent most of her time like this, eluding the pursuers her mother would send to bring her back for lessons or court. Just she and Faster and sometimes Austra.

Austra should be with Cazio by now. She hoped they were happy.

That thought brought her spirits down a bit. She wasn't a carefree girl anymore, was she? The horsemen following her right now weren't chasing her; they were her bodyguard, at her command.

She saw more horsemen up ahead, where the Sleeve began to turn, and slowed down a bit. They wore red, gold, and black over their light armor, and their shields bore a serpent and a wave. She recognized neither the colors nor their emblem. They were practicing some sort of riding formation, wielding compact bows. Targets had been set up, and they were already well feathered.

As she continued to watch, she noticed that one of the riders was quite slight, was indeed a woman. She fastened her gaze on that one, watching as she stood in her stirrups and casually loosed an arrow. It struck, quivering, in the heart of one of the targets. She wheeled her mount, already drawing another shaft from her quiver.

"Whose colors are those?" Anne asked Captain Eltier, the short, balding Craftsman who commanded her horse guard.

"The earl of Cape Chavel, Highness," he replied.

"And Cape Chavel has women warriors?"

"Not that I know of, madame."

A few moments later the horsemen broke off their activity, and two came toward them: the earl and the woman.

They stopped about ten kingsyards away, dismounted, and knelt. Anne saw that the woman was young, probably no more than fifteen.

"Rise," Anne said. "How are you today, Cape Chavel?"

"Very well," he said. "Just riding with my light horse."

"And this is one of your archers?"

His smile broadened. "This is my sister, Emily. Not officially a member of the company, but I can't stop her from practicing with us."

Emily did a curtsy. "Pleased to meet you, Your Majesty."

"You do very well with that bow," Anne told the girl.

"Thank you, Majesty," she said.

An impulse struck her. "Would you two care to ride with me for a bit?" she asked.

"It would be an honor, Highness," the earl said.

They mounted back up and continued along the edge of the Sleeve where it dropped off steeply to the marshy rinns far below.

"That must be Eslen-of-Shadows," Emily said, pointing

to the somber stone structures poking up here and there through the canopy.

"It is," Anne said, feeling the faintest chill. That was another place where she once had spent a lot of time, but unlike the Sleeve, she had no interest in revisiting it.

"It's big," Emily said. "Much grander than the one in Ralegh."

"Well, more people have died here, I suppose," Anne said.

"Oh," the girl said. She sounded uncomfortable, as if suddenly remembering how many of Anne's family had lately gone there.

"Come this way," Anne said. "There are more cheerful things to see on Ynis."

She nudged Faster back to a run, and the others fell easily in with her. The earl and his sister were as used to riding as walking; she could see that right away.

She led them toward the twin hills of Tom Woth and Tom Cast, glancing wistfully at the Snake, the sharp descent she once had used to escape pursuit into the rinns. None of that today. She led them instead up the grassy slope of Tom Cast, switching back and around until they reached its great bald summit, from which vantage the whole island of Ynis was laid out for them.

"It's so beautiful," Emily gasped. "So much to see in every direction."

Anne had been there a hundred times before, but not since returning. She was surprised to discover that it all looked suddenly new to her, too.

East, the city of Eslen rose up in three magnificent tiers topped by the many-towered castle itself. North was the Dew River and the vast lake that was the King's Poel, flooded by her uncle Robert and now colorful with hundreds of ships flying the colors of Liery, Crotheny, and Hornladh. The mist-covered rinns stretched south to where the mighty Warlock River shimmered like fish scales in the midmorning sun and also to the west . . .

"Thornrath," the earl sighed.

"I never could have imagined," Emily murmured.

"The mightiest wall ever built by Mannish hands," Captain Eltier said.

That it was. The island of Ynis was formed in the confluence of the Dew and Warlock rivers where they opened into Foambreaker Bay. Thornrath cut the bay in half, a wall of ivory stone more than three leagues long. It had seven great towers and seven arches each big enough for two men-of-war to sail through safely. It was seven hundred years old; since its building Eslen had never been taken by sea.

"It's all very grand," Emily said. "Thank you for showing me this." Her eyes sparkled.

Anne nodded. "Well, you came a long way to see it."

She turned to her brother. "Why did you bring her here, Cape Chavel? I'm sure she was safer in Virgenya."

"No, I don't think she was," the earl said. "There she might be taken hostage and used to persuade me to return. Here I can keep an eye on her."

"Anyway," Emily said, "I'd rather be here than safe. It's all very exciting."

"What will you do when your brother goes to war?"

"I was hoping for a favor there, Majesty," the earl said.

"What is that, Cape Chavel?"

"If some lady could be found who needs a maid . . ." He trailed off, looking a bit embarrassed.

"What's this?" Emily said. "Why can't I ride with you?" She turned to Anne. "I'm really not much good at sewing."

"I might be able to manage to please you both," Anne said. "I am presently in need of a maid, and your brother, for a time at least, will ride with me. I want to see personally how his men perform."

"Majesty," the earl said, "that is *very* generous."

"It is also very dangerous, Cape Chavel. Any maid of mine is in constant peril."

"I can handle a knife and sword as well as a bow," Emily said.

The earl pursed his lips and shot his sister a look probably meant to silence her.

"It's true," he conceded after a moment. "She can handle herself. There's peril everywhere, Your Majesty. You may attract danger, but from what I've heard, you're also good at repelling it. And to have my sister near me—it really is more than I could have hoped for."

"Well, I promise nothing, but we shall try it out for a few days and see how we get along."

Emily clapped her hands together but did not giggle. That in itself was promising.

A few bells later, in the Warhearth, the fresh air of the sun-lit Sleeve seemed very far away. It wasn't just the lack of windows but the heaviness of the room itself and the massive paintings of her family's martial past. One picture in particular seemed to have singled her out. It depicted from behind the first few ranks of an army on some sort of rise, so near the bottom of the frame of the painting that only the tops of helms were visible, and in the next rank full heads, then down to shoulders. At the crest of the hill stood a woman in armor, also showing her back, but with her head turned back to her men. Her hair was flame, twisting about her in coruscating strands, and her eyes were incandescent, inhuman. Her lips were parted and her neck was taut, as if she were shouting.

Before the warriors loomed a massive, mist-shrouded citadel of dark red stone, and in the mists gigantic shadows seemed to move.

Genya Dare, at that last terrible battle, had fought right here, where Eslen now stood.

Genya Dare, who had let one Skaslos live to be the secret captive of the kings of Crotheny—until Anne let him go.

Follow me, she was saying. *Follow me, daughter-queen.*

"Majesty, if you would like to do this another time—"

Artwair.

"No," she said, shaking herself back to the moment. "I'm fine. I was just wondering how the artist knew what Genya Dare looked like."

"He didn't," Artwair said. "The model was Elyoner Dare."

"Aunt Elyoner?"

"No, your father's grandmother. A Merimoth, originally, but her mother was a Dare from the Minster-on-Sea branch of the family."

"That's her?"

"Well, she didn't look exactly like that when I knew her. She was a good deal older. Why do you ask?"

Because I almost lost my virginity in her crypt.

"No reason," she said.

He shrugged, then pointed at the map he had spread out on the table. "Sir Fail will blockade Copenwis to prevent more reinforcements by sea. They will expect an attack by land because it's the best and quickest way to take the city. The city isn't really built for siege, and the highlands around it make it too easy to bombard with engines. That means they'll try to meet us somewhere on the Maog Vaost plain before we get there."

"And so?"

"And so I propose taking a somewhat indirect route to the city: moving east a bit and then doubling back to attack." His finger described a half arc.

"We can send a smaller mounted force the obvious way and have them camp to provoke the waiting force to settle. They'll have orders to retreat back to Poelscild. By that time we should have the position we want."

Anne nodded. "If you think this is the way to do it."

"We could take a larger force, but that would leave Eslen weakened, and we would still be delayed. If we go heavy on cavalry and light infantry, I think Copenwis might fall quickly."

"We'll try that, then. And if we're taking mostly horse, I've a mind to take Cape Chavel with us."

Artwair frowned a bit. "His reputation is good," he said. "His mounted archers are said to be without equal. But he got those from his father, and the man himself hasn't been tested in battle. Besides that, I worry about his loyalties."

"You think his allegiance to me is feigned?"

"I don't know what to think, Majesty. That's just the problem. I don't know him."

"Aren't we better putting him to the test now rather than later?"

"I suppose. But with you riding along . . ."

"Not that again, I hope."

He looked very much as if he did want to revisit that subject, but instead he shook his head.

"We'll try him," she said.

"As you wish, Majesty. Now, if we can talk about the defenses along the coast . . ."

Another two bells of that, and Anne headed up to her rooms, ready for a rest. She hardly had begun to undress when she heard a soft rap at the door. Throwing on a dressing gown, she went to see who it was.

The knock was from the Sefry guard, of course.

"Forgive me, Majesty," he said, "but someone requests an audience."

"In my rooms?"

"Majesty, it's Mother Uun."

"Ah." She hadn't seen the ancient Sefry for a long while. It wasn't her habit to drop by for no reason.

"Send her up, then," she said. "And find some of that tea she drinks."

"Majesty."

A few moments later, two Sefry women were shown in.

Mother Uun was old even for a Sefry, and Sefry lived for hundreds of years. Even in the dusk light coming through the window, the spider work of veins in her face showed through translucent skin. She had her hair in a braid so long that it was wrapped around her waist three times, like a sash.

The other woman looked very young, but with the Sefry it was hard to know what that meant exactly. Her face was oval, her eyes some dark color, her mouth a bit crooked, as if she were always on the verge of a deprecating smile.

"Majesty," Mother Uun said, bowing. "May I present Nerenai of the House Sern."

The young woman bowed again. "A pleasure, Majesty."

Her voice was pleasantly husky, with a lilting accent Anne did not recognize.

"The pleasure is mine," Anne said. "To what do I owe this visit?"

"Intrusion, I'm sure you mean," Mother Uun said. "I'm sorry for the late hour. I won't keep you long."

"Sit," Anne said. "Please."

The two took their places on a bench, and Anne settled in her armchair.

Mother Uun's gaze seemed to pick through her. "Your power is growing," she said. "I can see it all around you. I can feel you when I close my eyes."

Anne suddenly realized how glad she was the Sefry had come, happy to have someone she could talk to who might not think her merely mad.

"I—things are happening to me. I do things I don't understand sometimes, as if I'm in a dream. I think things . . ." She sighed. "Can you tell me what's happening to me?"

"Not everything, I'm sure, but Nerenai and I have come to offer what knowledge we have."

The tea arrived at that moment, and Anne waited impatiently while the two had a sip.

"There is a woman I see," Anne said. "She burns, and she has power. She helps me, but I don't know if I can trust her."

"A woman? Not one of the Faiths?"

"She killed the Faiths," Anne said.

Mother Uun's eyes widened. "That's interesting," she said. "I don't know what that might mean. Nerenai?"

"The Faiths are advisers," Nerenai said.

"Not very good ones," Anne replied.

The younger Sefry shrugged. "They are limited, it is true. Or were, I suppose. But they see things in the flow of the great powers that others cannot. And they have followers in the temporal world."

"Yes," Anne said. "I've met some of them. They kid-napped me."

Nerenai frowned, and steepled her fingers together.

"The burning woman must be your arilac," Mother Uun said. "It could appear as anything."

"Arilac?"

"In the oldest stories about the thrones, there is a mention of the arilac, a sort of guide who appears to lead those who have the power to claim it toward the throne. She is your ally in that, at least."

"But the question you must ask yourself," Nerenai said, "is what advice the Faiths might have given you that the ar-ilac did not want you to hear."

"I spoke to their ghosts," Anne said. "They didn't tell me anything about why they died."

"They may not have known. It might have been some-thing your arilac feared they would learn later."

"Then she isn't to be trusted?"

"I would question everything she—or, rather, *it*—tells you. It wants you to find and control the sedos throne, and in the most direct manner possible. There may be other, more difficult ways that it withholds the knowledge of. If it asks you to do something you think is wrong, press it for an alternative."

"So if she asks me to cut off my hand—"

"I would question that," Nerenai said. "Follow the arilac, but not blindly. Stay skeptical."

Mother Uun shook her head. "I anticipated the arilac, sus-pected it had already found you the first time we met, but I did not know enough to help you with it. That's why I sent for Nerenai. Her clan holds those secrets. She can help guide you." She smiled. "A guide to help with the guide."

"I am at your service, Majesty," Nerenai said.

Anne studied the two women for a moment. Part of her desperately wanted to believe that Nerenai was sincere, but another part of her feared the woman was a spy. That was the trouble with being queen: She couldn't really trust anyone.

Suddenly, where she had once had friends, she was surrounded by strangers.

But I did that on purpose, didn't I? she thought. Her reasons for it were still good.

"Before I say anything, I'd like to ask you something else," she said.

"I'm at your pleasure, Majesty."

"You know I freed the Kept. Was that a bad thing?"

"Yes."

"How bad?"

"Very bad," Mother Uun said. "Although I can't be more specific than that."

"He promised to mend the law of death and then die himself."

"And he will do both of those things. It's what he does between then and now that is likely to be the problem."

"It's been months."

The ancient Sefry croaked out a laugh, and Nerenai smiled that little smile that had been waiting behind her lips.

"He's been waiting for two thousand years, Your Majesty. A few months are a breath to him."

Anne sighed. "I know you warned me. But I didn't see that I had a choice."

"You didn't," Mother Uun said. "I knew you would do it."

"You *knew* I would do it?"

"Well, I was pretty certain."

"Why didn't you warn me about *that*?"

Mother Uun placed her cup on the small table before her.

"I said it was very bad to have freed him. But things would be worse had you died. You must claim the sedos throne, Anne, not another. Only then can we be redeemed."

"Redeemed?"

"It's an old thing, a Sefry thing. I should not speak of it."

"Is that why you're serving me?"

"While the Kept was prisoner, we were bound to watch him. Now we are free to serve you, and so we do. The moment he was free, our warriors came to find you."

"And saved my life. And helped me win back the castle. And now you want to give me a maid. But I don't understand *why*, Mother Uun."

"Because you can put things right," the old woman replied. "And I won't tell you more than that or it will go to your head and ruin you. Now, do you want Nerenai or not? You are free to refuse; it changes nothing else."

Anne felt a sudden claustrophobic panic, the same sort that she had felt at the gates of the city.

I don't want any of this! I don't want to sit on any sedos throne or save the world. I just want Cazio and Austra back, to be back out on the road . . .

"Majesty?" Mother Uun asked, concern in her voice.

Anne realized she had tears running down her face. She shook back her hair and pulled back her shoulders.

"Nerenai of the House Sern, I would be pleased if you would join my ladies. But you must understand that there is war, and I will be in it, and you will be in danger."

"We are all in danger," Nerenai replied. "I am most honored to accept your invitation."

Anne felt something like a little curl of flame flicker up her spine.

This is a mistake, the woman said.

Maybe. But it's my *mistake. I make my own decisions.*

The only answer to that was a derisive chuckle. Then the heat was gone.

CHAPTER FIVE

✛

A STORM
IN HANSA

NEIL UNBUCKLED his breastplate and, wincing, eased it down to the floor. He gazed at his murky reflection on its untarnished surface and sighed.

A tap came at the door of his tiny room.

"You're welcome in," he said.

The door pushed open, and Alis stood there, looking pretty in a yellow gown.

"Congratulations," she said.

He nodded. "Thank you."

"You don't seem very happy," she noticed. "Let me guess: You're disappointed he ran like a dog."

"He withdrew," Neil replied.

"You were *chasing* him," Alis chortled.

Neil shrugged, which hurt. "I'm sad for him."

"But didn't you mean that to happen? Wasn't it all bluff on your part?"

"I wasn't bluffing," Neil said. "He wouldn't have believed me if I was bluffing. There's nothing more frightening to a man who wants to live than an opponent who doesn't."

"Ah. So you don't want to live?"

"My sword arm is bad, and my other is worse. The skill in my head has no way to my hands, and I won't win a fight again by being the better swordsman. Not caring is the only weapon I have left. I won't kill myself, mind you. But my next foe may not flinch, and that will be that."

"You aren't fully healed yet."

He smiled grimly. "No. But I don't think it will be much better when I am."

"Well, cheer up. Today you've won, and in the best way. Humiliating Sir Alareik is better than killing him. The story is already growing; they say it was your face that broke his will, that your eyes were burning like the sun, that one was as large as a dinner plate and none could gaze straight at you, as if you were Saint Loy made flesh. They say no mere mortal could have stood against you."

"If they couldn't look at me, how did they see that my eye was as big as a dinner plate?"

"Now you're looking for hair on an egg," she said. "Rather than that, you ought to go father a few children; I think you'll find plenty of offers tonight. And since you didn't get any exercise in the fight . . ."

Neil sighed and began working at doffing the rest of the armor.

"I didn't mean *me,* of course," Alis said.

"Is there anything else, Lady Berrye?"

She folded her arms and leaned on the door frame. "Sir Neil, you haven't yet seen your twenty-second winter. It's too early to act the broken old man."

"Thank you for your concern, Lady Berrye," Neil said. "I promise you, I'm fine."

"I'm going," she said. "I tried. And I did come to tell you something: We'll delay here another day and leave at cock's crow tomorrow."

"Thank you. I'll be ready."

The road got a little better as they moved deeper into Hansa, creeping over low hills, along broad fields of wheat guarded by scattered farmers' steadings. Men in the fields watched them go by without much expression, but they passed a pair of little flaxen-haired girls who giggled and waved and then ran off to hide behind an abandoned granary. Muriele could still see them peeking from there until they were out of sight.

"This could almost be the Midenlands," Muriele mused to Alis.

"Farmers are pretty much farmers," Alis said, "whether they speak Hansan or Almannish."

"I wonder if they even care if there is a war or who wins it."

Alis stared at her. "Are you joking?"

"No. You just said farmers are farmers. Their lives will be much the same whoever taxes them."

"Oh, yes, true, but in the meantime—*during* the war— their fields will be plundered and their daughters raped, and it could be either side doing it. Their sons will be pressed into service if they are needed, and they will die bridging moats with their bodies, since they have no skill at arms. They may not care who wages or wins a war, but they will certainly not want one coming through here."

"An army of Crotheny would not behave so," Muriele said.

"It would, I promise you. It has."

Muriele was shocked by the conviction in her voice.

"Tell me," she said.

Alis turned away. "Never mind," she said. "This is a boorish subject. I shouldn't have brought it up."

"You didn't. I did. And as I am the queen and you are my servant, indulge me."

Alis fumbled at her reins and studied her horse's mane.

"It's an old memory," she said. "I was only five. We were poor, you understand. My father couldn't even afford to keep our mansion in repair; some rooms you couldn't even go in, the floors were so rotted. The river had shifted course before I was born, and half of our fields had gone to marsh. We only had five families living on the land. I can't remember any of their names except Sally, because she was my nursemaid. I think she must have been about twelve. I remember she had red hair and her hands were rough. She sang funny songs to me, but I can't really remember them.

"One day a lot of strange men showed up. Some stayed in the house, and some camped in the fields. I remember my father arguing with them, but I just thought it was all very exciting. Then one day when we were at Sally's house, she told me we were going to play a hiding game in the barn. She was acting funny, and it scared me a little. She got me up in the loft and told me not to make any noise. Then some men came in and made her take her clothes off."

"No."

"Oh, yes. I didn't know what was happening, what they were doing, but I could tell it hurt her, and I didn't say anything. After they left, she cried for the rest of the day. I told my father about it. He kissed me and asked if they had touched me, and when I said no, he cried. Then he said there was nothing to be done about it. He said that we were at war."

"The Causy rebellion."

"Yes."

"But Causy's men were brutes."

"The men at our house weren't Causy's men; they were knights and men-at-arms sent from Eslen. I found that out later, of course, and about all the other things those men did when they were living on our land. Not long after that I was taken off to the coven."

"William hadn't been king long when that happened," Muriele said.

"Doesn't matter who the king is. Armies have to eat. The men in them are off to fight and probably die, and it makes them—different."

"You can't be excusing them."

"No. I hope the men who did that to Sally died in agony. I'm making no excuse; I'm just stating it as a fact."

"All men aren't like that."

"Of course not. But one in a hundred is plenty, and there's more than that," Alis replied.

That afternoon, they saw ahead of them towering cloud castles flickering with incandescence. There was no sound, and Muriele felt breathless at the beauty of it. From time to time crooked blue-white lines leaped between the clouds or to the earth, but most of the fire seemed to be in the hearts of the thunderheads. Alis seemed as rapt as she.

So much beauty in the world when one had time to notice it. Why was that almost always on a journey of some sort?

Unperturbed by the fire in the north, the sun went his way toward the wood in the west, but before he reached it, a different sort of spectacle appeared before them. It looked at first like a cloud of dust, but soon enough Muriele could make out the banners and the red glint of evening sun on armor.

She remembered the little girls from that morning and felt spiders on her back.

"How many would you guess, Sir Neil?" she asked the knight as the army drew nearer. They had a good vantage from the top of a hill overlooking a long, shallow valley. Aradal had unfurled his banner, and she could make out an advance party on horse riding to meet them.

Neil pointed to marching men, who walked four abreast in a column that seemed to stretch for a league.

"You see the banners?" he asked.

She did. They were hard to miss, as each of them was several kingsyards square. The nearest depicted a large horned fish. The other two were too far away to quite make out their figuring.

"For each of those banners there are a thousand men, or near. That's an entire harji."

"Harji?"

"The Hansan army isn't organized like ours," Neil explained. "In Crotheny, lords raise their knights, and knights bring retainers, footmen, levy peasants if need be. Men are organized by their natural leaders."

"But not so in Hansa?"

"The horse is arranged that way, but not the marching army. That's divided into units: A hundred men are a wairdu. Ten wairdu make a hansa. Three or four hansa make up a harji, much like a Church legif."

"Sounds organized," Alis remarked.

"It is," Neil replied.

"But if a hansa is a thousand men, why is the country named so?"

"I never wondered about that," Neil answered. "Perhaps Lord Aradal can tell you."

Muriele hailed him, and the Hansan lord trotted his horse over.

"Your Majesty?"

"We were wondering why your country is named after a thousand men."

He looked briefly puzzled, then smiled. "I see. It's got to do with our history. The hansa is more than a thousand men; it is a sacred thing, a brotherhood, a saint-blessed guild. There was a time before the wairdu or the harji, but we always had the hansa. It's the foundation of our kingdom, and it's said that when we first conquered this land, we did it with a single hansa."

"It will take more than that to conquer Crotheny," Muriele informed him.

"Aye. But we *have* more than that, as you see."

The outriders were nearly on them now. The leader was a knight in the livery of the Reiksbaurg, a writhing waurm and a sword. His helm was plumed with horsehair. He had about twenty men with him.

When he drew up, he lifted off his helmet, revealing a young man with high cheekbones, pale golden hair, and eyes as green as moss.

Aradal was already off his horse and going down on his knee.

"Your Highness," he said.

"Rise, please, Aradal, and introduce me," the newcomer said.

Aradal straightened. "Queen Mother Muriele Dare of Crotheny, I am pleased to present to you His Royal Majesty Prince Berimund Fram Reiksbaurg."

"My suitor," Muriele said.

"A most unsuccessful suitor," the young man replied. "It is most unflattering to be rebuffed not once but several times, and now that I look upon you in person, I am doubly, no, triply dismayed. Your beauty may be legendary, but even legend does you no justice."

Muriele tried to look flattered and abashed, but the boy was half her age and the speech sounded practiced rather than sincere.

"With that golden tongue you should have pressed your suit in person rather than through envoys," she replied. "Although to be honest, even Saint Adhen could not have persuaded me out of my mourning."

Berimund smiled briefly. "I hope to marry a woman as steadfast as you, lady. I should like to be mourned."

The prince reddened a little, and a shy look crept across his face. He suddenly looked very young.

"Let's hope no one mourns you for a long time," Muriele said.

He nodded.

"Blood and duty command me to tell you something else, Berimund. This host you lead—I hope it is not bound for my country."

"It is bound for our border," Berimund said, "but I am not leading it. I have been sent here, lady, to escort you to Kaithbaurg."

"That's sweet, but I already have an able escort," Muriele told him.

"The king, my father, was quite adamant about it. Aradal is needed elsewhere."

"Your Majesty—" Aradal began, but the prince interrupted him, his voice suddenly harsher.

"Aradal, if I wish you to speak, I will ask you to. My man Ilvhar will give you instructions. I will escort the queen from here."

He turned back to her. "Your men will be guided back to the border unharmed, I promise you."

"My men? They will stay with me."

He shook his head. "You may keep your maid and a single bodyguard, but the rest of your escort must return home."

"This is outrageous," Muriele said. "I was assured that the old covenant would be maintained."

"Aradal had no right to make such assurances," the prince

said. "Your country has been declared a heretic nation by the holy Church. The old covenants no longer apply."

"Do you really believe that?"

For an instant the uncomfortable boy showed again in his eyes, but then his lips pressed into a thin line.

"I won't argue about this, lady." He nodded at Neil. "And I don't expect an argument from your man, either."

"You're taking me prisoner and you don't expect an argument?"

"You wanted to talk to my father, didn't you?"

"Yes. To try to talk him out of this war."

"Well, the war is begun, and your daughter began it."

"What are you talking about?"

"She slaughtered five hundred holy warriors of the Church, sent by the Fratrex Prismo to keep the peace. The Church is our staunch ally. If it is attacked, so are we. Furthermore, we have news that she is preparing to assault our peacemakers in Copenwis. So we find ourselves in a state of war. You, Your Majesty, represent an invading force, and I would be fully justified in removing all of your men-in-arms from the fray. Instead, I'm doing the honorable thing and allowing them to return to Crotheny."

"And if I wish to return with them?"

Berimund opened his mouth, closed it, and seemed to think for a moment.

"My father told me to intercept your embassy and bring you to him on his terms. If there is no longer an embassy—if you no longer wish to meet with him—then I will take you to the border. He did not expressly tell me to take you prisoner."

"But you imagine that was his intent? That if I do go, I will be hostage?"

Berimund sighed and looked away. "One might imagine that, yes."

Muriele took a long breath, remembering the endless days in the Wolfcoat Tower, where Robert had kept her.

"You have some honor, Prince Berimund," she allowed. "If I go with you, I would ask for your protection."

He paused at that, seemed to study something in his head,

then nodded. "You have it, lady, if that's really what you
want."

"It is."

"Very well. Your knight may keep his harness, for now, if
I have his word he will not attack unprovoked."

He eyed Neil, who looked to her. She nodded.

"I so swear by the saints my people swear by," the knight
said.

"Thank you," Berimund said. He turned to Aradal. "Take
the rest of these men back to the border. They are not to
be harmed or disarmed."

He nodded at Muriele. "When you are ready, lady, we
will ride on to Kaithbaurg."

Muriele felt her hair stir. The wind from the storm had
reached them.

CHAPTER SIX

A HEART
FOUND CHANGED

CAZIO DID NOT have pleasant memories of Castle Dunmrogh. A stone's throw from it he had watched helplessly
as men and women were nailed to posts and disemboweled,
and those doing it had meant to hang him. If it hadn't been
for Anne and her strange powers, he probably would have
died there. He very nearly had, anyway.

Even without that recollection to color things, he still
wouldn't have been happy. What was Anne up to? Was she
being honest with him—did she really need him here—or
was this punishment for opposing her?

He remembered Anne stepping into the clearing that night,
regal and powerful.

Terrifying, actually. And since then he had many times felt that power and terror. It was hard to think of her as the nymph he had met swimming in a pool back in Vitellio.

Maybe she wasn't. Maybe that Anne was gone.

And maybe he didn't care to serve the new Anne anymore.

He sighed, gazing up the hill at the gray walls and three-towered keep.

"What do I know about running a castle, anyway?" he murmured in his native tongue.

"We're here to help you with that, sir," Captain Esley replied in the same language.

Cazio turned to the fellow, the leader of the men Anne had put under his charge. He was short, with a steel-streaked black beard and hairy caterpillar eyebrows shadowing dark eyes.

"A nineday on the road and you don't bother to tell me you speak my language?"

"I don't speak it so well," Esley said. "But I fought for the Meddisso of Curhavia when I was a young man and remember some."

"Listen, if you heard me say anything uncomplimentary about the queen—"

"I wouldn't have been listening to anything like that."

"Good. Good man. *Viro deno.*"

Esley smiled, then jerked his chin toward the castle. "Looks in pretty good shape. Unless the Church sends half a legif to fight us, we ought to be able to hold, depending on the local forces."

"So we'll go introduce ourselves, I suppose," Cazio said.

"I'm sure they remember you, sir."

They didn't, or at least the outer gate guards didn't, so they sent for a member of the household to examine the royal letter before letting him across the moat with a hundred fifty men. Cazio didn't blame them.

After the wait stretched into almost a bell, Cazio rested himself in the shade of a pear tree and closed his eyes.

He woke with Esley tapping his shoulder. "Someone's finally come, sir."

"Ah," Cazio replied, raising himself up against the trunk of the tree. "Who have we here?"

It was an older man in an embroidered saffron doublet and red hose. He had a tuft of gray beard on his chin and a well-weathered face. He wore a floppy little hat the same color as his hose.

"I am Cladhen MaypCladhen de Planth Alnhir, steward of the house of Dunmrogh," he said. "Whom do I have the honor of addressing?"

"Cazio Pachiomadio da Chiovattio the very damn tired of waiting," he replied.

"I am sorry for that," the man said. "I was not presentable when you arrived, and I thought I should muster the men. Considering all the trouble we had here last year, I don't like to take chances. May I see the letter, please?"

Cazio handed it over, and the steward examined it for a moment.

"This all looks good," he said. "I'm happy Her Majesty saw fit to reinforce us. There are all sorts of rumors about armies marching, although it's been mercifully quiet here." He handed the letter back. "Well, if you'll just follow me, we'll find you some quarters and you can start getting to know the place. I'm happy to pass on the responsibility."

"Why?"

The steward paused, seemingly confused by the question.

"I . . . I'm just not cut out for it, I suppose. I'm really more of a scholar. Not much of a politician or a soldier. But Her Majesty purged most everyone else because they were involved in that business in the forest."

He gestured. "Walk with me?"

"What about my men?"

"Yes, of course. We're only half-garrisoned; plenty of room inside."

They followed him into the outer yard, a pleasant green lawn that obviously hadn't seen any fighting in a long time. The flagstone path led to a rather long drawbridge whose lifting cables were affixed to the top of the inner wall some thirty feet up. The bridge did not also function as a door, as in some castles he had seen; the door was to the right of the bridge and was in fact a heavy-looking portcullis banded with iron.

Cazio looked down into the green water of the moat as they thumped hollowly across the span, wondering if there were any dragons or nymphs swimming in its depths.

As he stepped on stone again, he heard a peculiar sound, the hum of something going taut. Then, suddenly, Anne's soldiers were shouting.

He spun quickly, his hand going to the hilt of his sword. He saw that the bridge was lifting, stranding most of the men on the other side of the moat. Those still on the bridge were tumbling toward him or pitching off into the moat. Red-feathered shafts were hurling into them, and cries of surprise became screams of pain.

Cazio drew Acredo but felt something suddenly close about his neck and cut off his wind. He lifted a hand, but it was seized, as was his sword arm. As black spots began dancing in front of his eyes, he felt his weapon stripped from his grasp.

He tried to turn but found himself in the firm grip of three grim-looking men, all Mamres monks. One had some sort of rope snare tightened around Cazio's neck. He couldn't even shout as they dragged him, struggling, toward the portcullis. He saw Captain Esley hollering, running toward him with drawn broadsword, and then the poor fellow was headless.

About then the sun went out.

He came back to his senses, and the only thing he saw at first was a long rectangle of grayish brightness and a thousand tiny lazily drifting motes. It didn't make sense at first, but then he gathered that the rectangle was light on a stone floor, thrown there by a shaft spearing through a window some four pareci above. He blinked, looking away from the light, but it took a few moments for his eyes to adjust. He tried to remember. He'd been ambushed . . .

"Oh, I think he's with us," someone said. The language was Vitellian, but *crefo* was pronounced more like "crewo," the telltale of the aristocratic accent from z'Irbina.

"Wonderful," another voice said. This was also in well-cultured Vitellian, but with a faint foreign lilt to it.

"Let's have a talk with him."

As his eyes adjusted, the faces came into focus, but they were faces he didn't recognize any more than he did the voices. Their clothes, in contrast, he recognized very well. One was clad in the black gown and red mantle of a patir. The other was all in black, with a single red star at the collar. Only one man in the world was allowed to wear that habit.

"Fratrex Prismo," Cazio murmured.

"Oh, a devout," the fratrex said.

"I'm only devout to the saints that love me," Cazio said. "But I'm from Vitellio. Your portrait is everywhere. But it isn't your portrait, is it? You aren't Niro Lucio."

"You're two nirii behind," the man said. "I am Niro Marco."

"You're a long way from z'Irbina, your grace," he observed. "I'm flattered you came so far to see me."

"Cover your teeth!" the patir shouted. "You're speaking to the Voice of the Saints."

"Oh, let him talk," the Fratrex Prismo said. "He seems an interesting fellow—a Vitellian dessrator sent to invest a castle with Crothenic troops? I can really think of only one person he is likely to be."

"Oh, it's him," another voice said from his right. Cazio turned toward the third man. "You I know," he said. "Sir Roger, yes?"

"Yes," the fellow agreed. "I wonder what you're doing here."

"I was just traveling with the soldiers," Cazio lied. "Hoping for a free meal and a bed here tonight."

The highest man of the Church wagged a finger at him as if he were a little boy eating berries in the wrong garden. "Now, that's clumsy. Have you forgotten you were carrying a letter from Anne?"

Right.

"No," he said. "Just taking the chance that you can't read."

The patir started forward, but the fratrex held up a hand, and he stopped in his tracks.

"I really don't understand your hostility," he said.

"Your men attacked me," Cazio said.

"Naturally. You were invading a castle we have occupied in the name of the saints. If you hadn't had an army with you, we might have spoken first, but since you came on unfriendly terms—"

"I offered no terms, unfriendly or otherwise."

"Where servants of the saints are concerned, Crotheny's standard terms seem to be slaughter," the fratrex said.

"We have fought corrupt churchmen, if that is what you mean," Cazio said. "Very near here, in fact."

"That? That was a handful, and that was before Anne Dare made claim to Crotheny. I'm talking about since she usurped her uncle's throne: the military expeditions. I'm talking, for instance, about the butchering of five hundred men at Tarnshead."

"They meant to do the same to us," Cazio said. "Ask Sir Roger there. They believed the odds were in their favor, and they were wrong."

"Their throats were cut as they slept," Sir Roger exploded.

"No, they weren't," Cazio said.

Sir Roger's brow wrinkled, then cleared.

"Oh. You weren't *there,* were you? You never saw what happened to them."

Cazio opened his mouth to retort, but he *hadn't* been there. Anne's Sefry guard had led that attack.

He felt a nasty something in his belly. The Sefry had lost only two men. Maybe the Sefry *had* killed them in their sleep. Anne wouldn't have known about it, but the Sefry might have done it.

"He didn't know," the fratrex said. "I never thought a dessrator would be involved in such a despicable business, especially the son of the Mamercio."

The name struck through Cazio's breast like a sword stroke. "My father? How do you know who my father was?"

"The Church keeps records, you know. But beyond that, I met your father a long time ago. A man of honor."

"You met him? Not with a sword in hand, I suppose?"

The fratrex smiled broadly. "I see. You want to avenge him?"

Cazio felt suddenly very light-headed. "It was you? You killed my father?"

The fratrex snorted. "No. I'm sure it would be convenient for you if I had. Give you good reason to murder me, eh?"

"My father was a fool," Cazio said. "I never pledged to avenge him, only to live better and longer than he did."

"Really? Then I don't understand. You seem to follow the way of the sword, just as he did."

"He fought for honor," Cazio said. "He lost everything he owned and his life in a duel over a ridiculous notion. I fight for food and coin. I fight to survive, and I fight smart, for no other reason. I—"

He stopped. It had been a long time since he had had this conversation with anyone, he realized.

Why had he turned down the chance to walk the faneway of Mamres? Why had he been so disappointed when Acredo had been shot full of arrows?

Ah, no, he thought. *How did it happen?*

He tried to summon up the anger he'd once felt at his father, the outrage, the disdain.

It was gone. When had he changed? How had it happened without his knowing it?

The Fratrex Prismo was still regarding him, apparently waiting for him to go on. When he didn't, the churchman leaned forward.

"So you're just a mercenary, then? Honor means nothing to you?"

"I— Never mind that," Cazio said. "Do you know who killed my father?"

"I've no idea," the man said. "I knew him years before his death. He was on a pilgrimage to the shrine of Uni in

Abrinio, and so was I. He saved our lives when bandits attacked."

For the first time in years, Cazio remembered his father's face and his voice, talking about going to Abrinio on pilgrimage. It was shocking how clear his memory suddenly was, how suddenly full of tears his head seemed to be.

"I don't want to talk about this," he said. His voice felt wet and gritty.

"What shall we talk about, then?" the fratrex asked. "What to do with you?"

"Why not?"

"It's an interesting subject. And it depends so much, you know, on—well, *you.* I'm willing to imagine you've been guided up until now by a personal sense of loyalty to Anne rather than by honest opposition to the Church. But to maintain that viewpoint, I'm going to need some cooperation from you. I'm going to need your help with Anne."

"Suppose," Cazio said after a moment, "I offer you a similar bargain? Just an arrow's flight from here I witnessed men of the Church committing the foulest possible atrocities. At first I was willing to believe that the clergy involved were renegades, but we discovered that the praifec of Crotheny was involved and that the events I witnessed weren't unique. It seems impossible that the rest of the Church fathers knew *nothing* of this, yet I am willing to imagine that you were unaware of these abominations. But to maintain that viewpoint, I'm going to need some cooperation from you. I'm going to need your holy kiss on my bare arse."

The patir was beet-red now, but the fratrex only smiled an odd little smile.

"I see." He leaned forward. "I'm going to give you a bit of time to think about this, my friend." He nodded, and the patir clapped his hands. A door he hadn't noticed opened, and five large monks entered.

Cazio met the man's gaze dead on. "I will tell you one thing: You shouldn't go to Eslen. Anne will crush you."

The Fratrex Prismo shook his head. "No, she won't. I

know something she doesn't. If you help me, she might live. Otherwise I fear for her."

"Fear for yourself," Cazio snarled. "If you threaten Anne, I will have to kill you myself."

"Really?" the fratrex said. "Well, you might as well do it now." He nodded at the guards. "Gentlemen, loan us a pair of swords, won't you."

"Your grace," one of the men said. He removed his heavy cut-and-thrust weapon and walked it over to the fratrex. Another man brought Cazio his own weapon, Acredo.

Cazio took the hilt. Certainly it was a trick of some sort, but at least he would go down fighting, not tortured to death in some dungeon.

He stood, not raising the sword until Niro Marco took the position of guard.

With an amazing quickness that belied his earlier assertion, the man lunged at him. Cazio caught the blade in *perto,* bound it down to *uhtave,* and struck the Fratrex Prismo of the holy Church in the chest.

Except that the point stopped as if he had hit a wall. For an instant he thought the fellow was wearing a breastplate, but then he saw the truth: His point wasn't touching the man; it was stuck in something a fingersbreadth from Niro Marco's chest.

He tried to yank the weapon back for another blow, but all of a sudden his arms and legs went loose and he was on the floor.

"Now," he heard the fratrex say, "these men will take you to a place of contemplation, but I'm going to warn you: I can't allow you to reflect for long. I'm here only for a short time, and then I must go to Eslen, with or without any help you may be able to give me. I would like to save you, but if you don't have anything to tell me by tomorrow, I'm going to have to encourage you any way I can. If that's no use, well, perhaps we can still lustrate your soul before it leaves this world. It's the least I can do for your father."

CHAPTER SEVEN

THE WALK BEGINS

WHEN THE WITCHLIGHTS went out, Stephen shouted and batted at the darkness. Adhrekh hollered orders, and Zemlé screamed. Then something rough struck him, and he heard a deep, ragged gasp of breath. His feet stood suddenly on nothing, and he heard a second shout, this one in that other voice.

Do not trust . . .

Then silence and wind and the wait for the stop at the end.

Something hit him again and knocked all the air out of him. The pain was blinding, but he still could feel, so he figured he wasn't dead.

That wasn't so bad, he thought. *The floor mustn't have been as far as I thought.*

But as he hiccupped air into his lungs, Stephen understood that something had him gripped tightly around the torso, and they were still hurling through the darkness. Was it one of the Aitivar, diving in a vain attempt to save him?

But they weren't moving so much down as *forward.* Whatever had him was flying.

What could fly that was large enough to carry a man? Only something from legend and likely something nasty: a wyver, a dragon . . .

He cried for help but had the feeling the sounds were dying just past his lips. He couldn't struggle. Even if he could, and succeeded, it would mean a long fall.

The smell hit him again, and the creeping sensation of something infinitely malevolent surrounding him, and he suddenly felt stone smack against his feet. Whatever had gripped him had released him, and he fell on his bottom.

He scuttled back, crablike, in terror to escape from the thing. A hard stone wall stopped his retreat.

The darkness remained elementally absolute.

"What do you want?" Stephen gasped. "I—what do you want of me?"

He was answered by a thunder of incomprehensible words that seemed to roll around him, a gibbering no human throat could make. Part of him was fascinated despite the horror. Was this the language of demons?

"I can't—"

"Hush."

It went in his head like a pin through an insect. His mouth froze open.

"Is this the one?" the thing went on. "Are you the one? Are you shadow or substance?"

The voice was burring right in his ear—in both ears, in fact, as if whoever it was somehow was whispering in them both. It didn't sound like a human voice, but he couldn't say exactly why.

Stephen still couldn't move his mouth, so he couldn't answer.

"The smell of you," the voice continued. "Revolting. I don't understand how you don't take your own lives from that alone."

It paused, and Stephen had the sense of something immense slithering around him. But when it spoke again, its voice was still right in his ears.

"You smell of other things, too. You stink of the sedoi. It all rots in you, mayfly. All comes to you to rot. Or will."

Stephen was shivering uncontrollably. He still could move his limbs, and he did—to roll up into a ball.

"Hold still," the voice commanded.

Then he couldn't move at all, although the trembling in his limbs continued.

Suddenly the needle through his mind began to wiggle,

and he was standing in front of the fane of Saint Ciesel in the King's Forest. The forest rose up around him like columns supporting the cloudy sky. The fane was a tidy little structure of gray stone with a low-vaulted roof.

He blinked. He was staring at a different fane, that of Saint Woth.

And then he didn't have time to blink as he flashed from place to place and from time to time. He was nine, looking off the cliffs behind his house and smelling the sea. He was watching Zemlé pull off her shirt. He was relieving himself behind a bush off the Old King's Road. He was watching Aspar kiss Winna.

Part of him understood that these were memories, but it all felt absolutely real: The weight of himself on his feet shifted—sometimes he wasn't on his feet—the scents, the temperature of the air, and it all went faster and faster until his thinking mind suddenly stepped away from it all, watched it flow like a river. Not trying to recognize anything but just watching it ripple and move.

And after a moment he noticed another stream, deep and dark, running alongside him, almost touching, then joining and broadening the river.

What's this?

But then even his ability to form questions disintegrated.

It took him a long time to understand when it was over, that he was back in one place and time, still shivering in the dark and paralyzed. He realized that the thing was talking to him again, and probably had been for some time.

". . . going through it? Nonsense. I feel the bones. The bones are there. And blood in them, yes? In them. Ah, you're back. Listen, mayfly. He doesn't know me, not for sure. I like it that way. I think you will, too. So helpful, isn't he? Do you ever wonder why he wants you to walk the faneway? Do you ever wonder that?"

Yes, Stephen tried to answer.

"Come, tell—ah, wait. I see. It's already working. You may speak in response to my questions."

He felt something like a knot untying in his throat, and he gagged and then vomited. He kept heaving long after there was nothing left in his stomach.

"Answer my question," the darkness snarled.

"Yes," Stephen replied through his gasping. "I've wondered." He wanted desperately to ask who he was speaking to but found he couldn't.

"Do you know *who* it is?"

I won't tell you anything, he thought. "I won't tell you that I think it's the ghost of Kauron."

He suddenly realized that he'd said what he was thinking out loud, and he groaned. What sort of shinecraft was this?

"Kauron?" it said. "That's a name. That doesn't mean anything. Do you know *who* he is?"

"That's all I know," Stephen said, feeling the words rush out of him. "He helped me find the mountain and the faneway."

"Of course he did. No one wants you to walk that path more than he."

Stephen didn't bother trying to ask why.

"Well, walk it you will," the voice purred. "I have no objection."

Stephen felt the beat of wings and a rush of air. He uncoiled like a spring and then went loose, the shaking finally easing out of him.

Stephen lay there for a while, sick at heart, wondering how he ever could have imagined himself brave. It was the same old story: Every time he was close to feeling in command of himself and his world, the saints showed him something to shatter him again.

He opened his eyes and found that the witchlights were back with him. He was still somewhere beneath the earth but no longer in the vast open canyon where he had been abducted; nor was the river anywhere within sight, although he could hear it somewhere, far away.

He couldn't hear anything that might be his companions either, even with his sedos-touched ears. He called experimentally, not expecting a response and not receiving one.

He tried not to think about the very plausible explanation that they were all dead. They couldn't be, because that would mean Zemlé was dead, and she wasn't.

So where was he?

The cavern was very low-roofed, so much so that he couldn't stand, but it went on farther than the witchlights revealed in every direction.

Anne Dare had described a place like this; she had called it the "stooping room." Had his kidnapper actually brought him to the start of the faneway?

Kauron, where are you now?

But there was no answer.

He didn't feel like moving. He didn't feel like doing anything. But after a moment he did, coming up to his hands and knees. He picked the direction where he seemed to feel the faneway most strongly and started toward it.

He didn't have to go far. A column of stone appeared ahead, about as big around as a large oak tree. Scratched into it was the old Virgenyan symbol for "one."

He paused. He had never encountered a sedos underground before. Above ground they usually appeared as small hills, though sometime they were rock outcroppings or depressions. What saint had left his footprint here, and how was he supposed to approach it properly? The faneways of the Church had shrines with depictions of the appropriate saint to help prepare the mind and body to receive his power. Here there was no such clue unless the number was some sort of cipher. But it probably just meant that this was the first place he was supposed to visit.

How had *she* known the order? Her journal didn't say.

Feeling weary, he crawled toward the sedos.

When he reached it, he stayed on his knees and reached toward the stone.

"I don't know what saint you are," he murmured. "Else I would come to you properly."

Maybe it didn't matter. The Revesturi—those renegade clergy who had helped Stephen find this place—claimed that there were no saints, that only the power was real.

He touched the stone.

Something pushed through his fingertips and ran down his arm. He gasped as it clamped around his heart and *squeezed*. He braced himself for the agony, but although everything in him warned him that pain was coming, it didn't.

He rocked back on his haunches as the sensation faded. His skin tingled lightly. An incredible sense of well-being seemed to wash down from his head to his toes.

All his pains—small and large—were gone, and although he remembered that a few moments before he had been on the verge of absolute hopelessness, now he couldn't even imagine feeling like that.

He touched the stone again, but the experience didn't repeat itself.

Neither did it fade. He felt a smile tickle his face.

Why had he put this off? If this was any indication, walking this faneway was going to be a lot better than walking the last one.

He started off for the next station, which he now could sense as clearly as a voice calling him.

The roof dropped lower and lower as he progressed so that eventually he was crawling on his belly, his nose almost on the stone. A distant part of him felt claustrophobic, but it never became overwhelming. He felt too good, too confident that things were going his way now. Besides, at least two people had done this before and survived.

Soon enough his certainty was justified as the floor began dropping away. The walls came in, and soon he was back in a tunnel, albeit one moving downhill in a series of broken steps.

How long since a river had flowed through here? How long had it taken to cut the rock? An unimaginable period of time, surely.

How old was the world?

It wasn't a question he'd thought much about. To be sure, there were scholars who had, and he had read the basic texts in his essentials at the college. There was plenty of speculation, but it fell into essentially two major schemes of thought: The world was created pretty much as it was a few thousand years ago, or it was very, very old.

Then as now, Stephen's love for languages and ancient texts had been his central preoccupation, and the oldest texts in the world were only about two thousand years old. That was when Mannish history had begun. But there had been a Skasloi history before that, one that no one knew much of anything about. How long had the Skasloi kept slaves? How long had the Skasloi civilization existed? What was here before them, if anything?

These suddenly seemed to be very important questions, because it seemed to Stephen that the world had to have been around for a long time for water to dig channels through stone, abandon them, dig new ones, and so on. The saints certainly could have made caverns when they made dry land, but why make them appear as if they had been formed by natural processes that ought to take many thousands of years? They could do so, of course, but why?

And if there were no saints, if the power was just something that *was,* how long had *it* been here? Where had it come from?

How many times since the beginning of the world had someone—or something—walked this faneway, and what had happened?

The thought literally arrested him. So far as he knew, only Virgenya Dare and Kauron had walked this path. Virgenya Dare used the power to conquer and eradicate the Skasloi. Kauron didn't seem to have survived to use his power. If he had, he surely would have stopped the rise of the Damned Saints, the Warlock Wars, and the unholy reign of the Black Jester.

Virgenya Dare had saved the Mannish and Sefry races from slavery. Kauron had died and failed to prevent what was in many ways a rebirth of the Skasloi evil. Now it seemed chaos and night were coming again, and it was his task to walk the fanes, wield the power, and set things right.

Could it really be that simple? Was he really the one? Would he succeed—or fail as Kauron had?

He shook his head. Why hadn't the Skasloi walked the fanes? They must have known about them. How could they not?

"Because the saints love *us*," Stephen said aloud. "They love what is right and good."

But that sounded so silly that he suddenly knew for certain that he didn't believe it anymore.

The next fane was a pool of very cold water. He approached it without hesitation and thrust his hands in, and in an instant he heard a voice. The language was a very ancient form of Thiuda, but before he could cipher it out, it was joined suddenly by ten more voices, then fifty, a thousand, a hundred thousand. He felt his jaw working and then didn't feel much at all as his mind shouted to be heard, to stay different, to not be swept away in the ocean of weeping, pleading, screaming, cajoling. Now it was all one sound, a single voice saying everything and thus nothing, thinning, rising in pitch, gone.

He blinked and yanked his hands from the pool, but he knew it was too late because he could still hear that final tone, itching far in the back of his mind, waiting.

Waiting to swallow him.

And even as he tried to force the voices out, they were starting to emerge again, not from the pool this time but from his own head. And he knew that when they did come back, his mind would be swept away.

All fanes have a limit. All fanes have a demand. They take and they give. If I don't finish this in time, the voices will make me one of them. My body will starve. I'll never see Aspar or Winna or Zemlé again.

He pushed himself up, trying to keep his panic down as the susurrus slowly waxed.

I finish, then. I finish.

CHAPTER EIGHT

⚜

ZO BUSO BRATO

THE GUARDS took Cazio down several halls and through the kitchens, where red-faced women in tan aprons and white head scarves labored about a hearth big enough to walk into without ducking. He wondered briefly if they meant to cook him or at least threaten to, but they pushed him on through the kitchen just as the scent of boiled beef and green vinegar sauce began to waken him to how very hungry he was.

He glanced at a large knife on a cutting table, still red from butchering. If he could get his hands on that—

The guard behind him jabbed him with his sword.

"No," he said. "Don't think about it. They want you alive, but they didn't say anything about hamstringing you."

Cazio half turned. "There are six of you, and you're still scared of me. Come on. Let me have the knife and you can keep your swords. I'll show the ladies what a man really is. If they ever knew, you fellows have made them forget, I'm sure."

He raised his voice a bit more. "What about it, ladies? Would you care to see a little sport?"

"I would at that," one of the women replied. Her face was a little wrinkled, but in the right places.

"Shut that, you," another of the guards said.

"Why?" the woman asked. "What will you do?"

"You'd best not find out."

"Threatening women," Cazio said. "Very, very brave."

"Listen, you Vito scum—"

"Don't be stupid," a third guard said. "He's just trying to goad you. Just keep your head and mind your orders. This is a simple job. Do it."

"Right," the fellow just behind Cazio said, and gave him another push.

"Sorry, ladies, another time," Cazio said.

"Promises, always promises," one of the women shot back as he was forced out of the kitchen and into a cellar, where once more his mouth watered as they moved among amphorae of olive oil, kegs of grain and rock sugar, sausages and hams hanging from the rafters.

"All right," Cazio said. "Lock me in here, then."

"Not quite," the big fellow behind him said. "Dunmrogh doesn't have a proper dungeon, but this will do. Stop."

They were standing in front of a large circular iron plate set in the floor. It had a handhold cut in it, which one of the guards used to lift it up, revealing a dark hole a little less then a pareci wide. Another of the guards then uncoiled a rope and tossed one end into the pit.

"Now be good and climb on down," the fellow said.

"Just let me take a few sausages with me."

"I don't think so. And don't imagine the women from the kitchen will help you. We'll be chaining the lid down. I don't reckon any of them are lock picks."

Cazio already had noticed the six heavy iron eyes protruding from the stone around the trapdoor.

Not seeing any alternative, Cazio took the rope and let himself down into the darkness.

He went slowly, trying to use the light while he had it to see what he was being held in. That didn't take long. The shaft was narrow enough that he could touch opposite walls by stretching out his arms—if he could do that without falling. More interesting were the hundreds of stoneware niches set into the sides of the shaft.

"I hope you left me some wine," he called up.

"Weren't any when we got here," the guard called down. "Worse the luck."

The rope suddenly went slack, and Cazio was falling. He

yelped, but before he could do much else, his boots struck stone. His feet stung and his knees buckled a bit, but otherwise he was fine.

The shaft opened into a dome-shaped chamber about ten paces wide, the entire surface of which was riddled with the bottle-sized niches. He turned, trying to scan every inch of it before they took his light, but he didn't see any way out or any wine.

Why would someone have such a nice cellar and no wine?

The iron lid slammed down, clanging so loudly in the small space that it hurt his ears, and he was in utter darkness. After a moment he heard chains dragging and settling and then nothing.

He stood there for a moment, then sighed and dropped down to sit cross-legged, trying to sort out his options.

The shaft was too high for him to reach, but with some effort he probably could use the wine niches to climb up the dome and get purchase enough to scale it and reach the trapdoor. But what then? He could wait there, hoping to surprise whoever came next, but how long would he have to wait? And would they really be surprised? Only if they were idiots.

Still, he marked that down as a possibility and moved on.

But there wasn't much to move on to. He felt his way around the chamber in the vague hope of finding some hidden exit and rapped on the floor searching for evidence of a hollow but found no sign of either. He hadn't really thought he would.

He searched the niches again, one at a time, on the chance that something useful had been left in one: a bottle of wine, a knife, anything to use as a weapon. Again he found nothing, and an attempt to break one of the ceramic niches to get an edge only hurt first his hand and then his foot.

His stomach was starting to complain, and he hurt all over. With an acquiescent sigh he made himself as comfortable as he could on the floor. Maybe something would present itself tomorrow.

* * *

He awoke from a dream of another wine cellar visited under happier circumstances, unsure whether he had been asleep for an hour or a day. He was distantly aware that something had wakened him but couldn't recall what it was.

He sat up and was wondering whether it was worth his while to stand when he heard a muffled thump.

His first thought was that the trapdoor was being opened, but then the thump repeated itself, and he felt the floor vibrate. His nose itched, and he suddenly found himself sneezing. The air was full of dust.

The sound seemed to be coming from the wall, so he went to it and placed his hands against it. This time, when the impact came, he felt it through the clay and made out a thin shattering sound.

The next was louder still, and the one after that was suddenly sharp and unmuffled, as if he had been underwater listening and suddenly had surfaced. He felt air move against his face and smelled sour wine.

Whatever it was hit again, and he felt clay shards pepper him. He shifted to put himself beside the rapidly growing hole.

Suddenly light came pouring through, so bright that at first he thought it must be the sun, until a lantern poked through the hole and he realized it was just his light-starved eyes playing tricks on him.

"Cazio?"

Oddly, for the first heartbeat he didn't recognize the voice, although in the entire world it was the one most familiar to him.

"Z'Acatto?"

A grizzled face pushed through the opening behind the lantern.

"You're an idiot," the old man said.

"How—"

"Just get through here," the swordmaster snapped. "With your luck, they're on their way to get you now."

"Right," Cazio said. He got down on his hands and knees and pushed the rubble aside until he could crawl through.

What he entered was another underground chamber, and from what he could see of it in the light of z'Acatto's lantern, it was really enormous. A sledgehammer leaning against the wall testified to the method the older man had used to rescue him, and to make matters even odder, on this side of the wall there was a door frame that had been withed and plastered over.

"So there *was* a secret exit," he murmured as he stood.

"Sealed up a long time ago."

Cazio studied his mentor for an instant, then threw his arms around him. He smelled of wine and many days of sweat, and for a moment Cazio thought he was going to cry. He felt z'Acatto stiffen, then soften and return the embrace, albeit tentatively.

"I should have known," Cazio said.

"All right, enough of that," z'Acatto said. "We don't have time to go all weepy. Here, take this."

He handed Cazio Acredo.

"Where did you get that?"

"Some soldiers were fooling around with it and left it in the hall near the kitchen. It wasn't Caspator, but I figured it was probably yours."

"Thanks," Cazio said. Then he smiled. "You stayed."

Z'Acatto's brows collapsed in a frown. "Not on your account," he said, wagging his finger. "I told you I was going back to Vitellio, and that's still my plan."

"You must be healed by now. You could have left months ago. Or has the Church been here this whole time?"

Z'Acatto's eyes lit up with familiar mischief. "No, they only arrived a nineday ago. I found another reason to stay. Do you know who *built* this place?"

"I don't know. The Dunmroghs?"

"The Dunmroghs? They're the last crows to land here. This castle was built two hundred years ago. Back then the land was carved up into petty kingdoms by the knights of Anterstatai. Does that give you a clue?"

"Should it?" Cazio said. "The only thing I remember about the knights of Anterstatai—oh, no. You've got to be joking."

Z'Acatto's smile broadened. "Douco Cherfi daz'Avrii."

Cazio took another look at the room they stood in and realized that all of the wine smell did not come from his old teacher. He was in another cellar, much vaster than the first.

"Impossible."

"Come along," z'Acatto said. "We'll want to be far away when they find you missing."

"You weren't looking for me at all," Cazio accused.

"Not until yesterday, no. But I have to eat, and the kitchen women told me you were imprisoned in the empty cellar."

"Thank the saints for your sotted obsessions."

"Yes," z'Acatto acknowledged as he led Cazio through the vast storeroom. "I was down here when the Fratrex Prismo and his men arrived, so they didn't catch me. I don't think they even know about me."

"They haven't searched here?" he asked.

"They don't know about this place, either," z'Acatto said. "The douco sealed it off before he left."

"Why?"

"To keep his wine safe, I imagine. He left the small cellar as a decoy. I'm sure he expected to come back."

"Then how did you find it?"

Z'Acatto turned on him fiercely, hand on his heart. "I *knew* it had to be here. The douco was the greatest collector of wine in the world. He would never have been without a real cellar." He waved around at the thousands of bottles.

"Aging for a hundred years. Of course most of it is vinegar now, but some is still potable. Enough for me to survive on for several months, at any rate."

Cazio nodded. He had been noticing the piles of opened bottles that littered the floor.

"How many of the douco's reputed cellars have we broken into now?" Cazio asked. "I remember the one in Taurillo when I was sixteen and that one in the house of the Meddisso of Istimma."

"And the one in Ferria," z'Acatto said. "But those were all different. They had all been in use. This one is pristine, and the barbarians living here never thought to look for it. Did you know even the small cellar they had you in was empty? Even before the Church arrived. Nothing they drink here improves with age, so why bother?"

They had reached a small, arched passage, but Cazio stopped in his tracks, incredulous.

"Are you saying you found it? Zo Buso Brato?"

Z'Acatto chuckled. "Four bottles," he said. "And one from the year of the May frost."

"Saints. I can't believe—how was it?"

He frowned. "Well, I haven't tasted it yet."

"What? Why not?"

"Not the right time," the swordsman replied. "Come on."

"But where is it?"

"Safe." He ducked into the passage. "Keep quiet in here. This passes near places where we might be heard."

Cazio still had plenty of questions, but he kept them in.

The passage soon entered a larger and very smelly one littered with trash and filth and prowled by rats. A faint susurrus echoed within it.

Z'Acatto shuttered the lantern, and for a moment they seemed to be in pitch darkness. But after a moment, Cazio began picking out a little light coming from a narrow grate above them.

Z'Acatto, apparently waiting for his own vision to adjust, started off again. As they passed under the grate, the general buzz sharpened into the sound of a pair of women talking, but they weren't speaking the king's tongue or Vitellian, so he couldn't make any sense of it. One of them sounded like the bold kitchen woman.

They passed under a few other grates, and then they traveled in darkness until z'Acatto reopened the lantern.

"We're not under the castle anymore," he explained.

"This leads out?"

"The douco liked escape routes. That's how we got into the one in Taurillo, remember? And that's how I found this one."

Not much later, they emerged through a trapdoor onto a wooded hillside. Below, a wide river flowed lazily by.

"Here we are."

Z'Acatto held up a leather bag. Inside were four bottles carefully wrapped in many layers of linen.

"We'll drink these when we get back home," he said.

"That sounds good," Cazio sighed. He meant it. To be sitting in the sun of the Piato da Fiussa drinking rare wine with z'Acatto, no worries about men who couldn't be killed with swords or what was really going on in Anne's mind or murder dressed up in fine clothes. Some cheese, some pears, a girl who wasn't a queen or handmaid to a queen—

Austra.

Anne was supposed to be sending her to Dunmrogh. How long before she got here? Was she here already?

"I thought you would come around," z'Acatto said. "There's another bag down there with some drinkable but unexceptional wine; food, too. If you'll get that—"

"I can't go back," Cazio interrupted. "Not yet. There are a few things I have to do yet. And I'm going to need your help."

Z'Acatto shook his head. "I told you, I'm going back."

"I'm not asking you to get involved in this war of Anne's," he said. "But Austra is in trouble, and I need to warn Anne about the Fratrex Prismo. After that—"

"Hespero," the swordmaster muttered.

"What?"

"The Fratrex Prismo is Marché Hespero."

"The praifec of Crotheny? The one behind the murders in the woods?"

The older man nodded.

"All the more reason I have to tell her, then."

Z'Acatto's frown deepened. "Don't be a fool."

"Weren't you the one who used to chide me for my lack of honor? For using dessrata as a thing to get money and women? For not being half the man my father was?"

Z'Acatto lifted one eyebrow. "Last time we talked about your father, you called him a fool."

"And now you're calling me one."

Z'Acatto put his face in his palm. "Saints damn you, boy," he said.

Cazio put his hand on his mentor's shoulder. "Thanks," he said.

"Oh, shut up. Let's go steal some horses."

CHAPTER NINE

THE QUEEN RIDES

ANNE REINED Faster to a halt just before the edge of the tree line. Below her the land dropped away in gently rolling hills. Less than half a league away the land started to climb again, a bit more sharply. A little stream wound its way down the bottom of the dale, and near it was the track of North Ratheren Road.

"I see them," Artwair murmured softly. "Majesty, I won't doubt your visions again. We would have been caught between hammer and anvil."

Anne followed the line of his finger, and now she saw them, too, a vast camp in the fold of the hills, easily noticed from here but probably invisible from the road.

"How could they know we were coming? And coming this way of all the ways we might have come?" Artwair wondered. "Even if some traitor flew to them with wings, they would have still had to march here from Copenwis or Suthschild. Look how settled in they are."

"They have a Hellrune," Anne replied. "A strong one."

Artwair cocked his eyebrow. "I've heard those stories," he said. "It's Hansan rubbish, meant to frighten us."

"You've come to believe I can see across leagues and time. Why doubt another could?"

"Your visions have proved true time after time," he replied. "Your Majesty was blessed by the saints."

"If one can be blessed, so can another," Anne said. "I thought he was out there. I can't see him, but sometimes I think I see his shadow." She laughed. "So I did something I've always disliked: I found some books on the matter. It seems some in the Hansan royal line are born with the power, and they raise them from birth on a diet of strange, distilled essences and liquors to make them stronger."

Artwair still seemed skeptical. "If Hansa really has such seers, why would they ever lose a war? Or make a mistake?"

"Even a Hellrune isn't perfect, I guess, and some are stronger than others. And sometimes they are assassinated before the war begins."

"But if they can see the future—"

"Not their own, apparently," she replied.

"Then we should kill this one."

"I'm working on it," Anne told him.

"So he saw us on this road—"

"And I saw the trap they set, *because* of what he saw," Anne replied. "And now we must set a trap of our own."

"We need to know their numbers," he said. "And the composition of their forces."

"I'll send my Sefry tonight," she said. "The moon will be nearly dark. They can discover what we need to know."

Anne thought she saw a brief look of distaste cross Artwair's face, but he nodded.

Anne woke before dawn, shivering although summer hadn't really begun surrendering to autumn yet. She lay there, trying to remember where she was, but the colors and shapes around her didn't make any sense. She closed her eyes and was creeping out of a hole, stretching her eight legs to tick into the sand, smelling the sweet scent of something with blood nearby. She crouched, waiting, feeling the sick power of the earth inside her, feeling the forest stretch out away from her to the great shallow sea and beyond.

She opened her eyes again and sat up, trying not to vomit, pushing at the bedclothes with only four limbs, trying to regain herself.

Quiet yourself. Don't panic.

She was there again, the arilac, a brand in the night, and fear crept away.

But she still didn't know where she was, exactly.

"Mistress?"

She knew that voice. Nerenai.

"Dreaming," she murmured. "Stronger every night. Harder to remember . . ." She shivered again, wondering what she was talking about, because she'd lost it again.

"What is it?" another voice asked. It was Emily, her other maid.

"Majesty has had another bad dream," Nerenai said. "This is what I'm good at. Go back to sleep."

"I'll wait to see she's okay," Emily replied.

Something warm touched Anne's lips, and then she tasted something slightly bitter. She liked it and drank more.

"This will help," the Sefry said. "Was it prophecy?"

"No," Anne replied. "Those are—sharper. No, this—this is different. Like memories so real, I think they're mine. Sometimes not even human memories. I think, just now, I was a spider." She stopped again. "It sounds crazy, but it's getting harder to remember who I am when I wake up."

Nerenai was silent for a moment. She gave Anne another sip of the tea. "Nothing vanishes," she said. "When we die, the river takes it all, but what is in us does not go away."

"I've seen that river," Anne said. "I've seen it take a man."

"Yes. It swallows us, and in time it pulls us apart and we forget everything. But the things we knew are still there, in the waters—but not in *us* anymore, because the thing in us that holds it all together is gone."

She was moving her fingers as if sketching.

"There is another river," she continued, "or perhaps another part of the same one, and there, those with the power to do so can drink and bring those memories and knowledge back into the world, held in new vessels."

"It's more than memories," Anne said. "There is some-thing more there." She took a longer sip of the tea and real-ized she did feel better. "It will drive me mad. What use to have the memories of a spider?"

"It sounds dreadful," Emily said.

"Was it an ordinary spider?" Nerenai asked.

"That's a weird question," Emily opined.

Anne considered that. "No," she said after a moment. "Nerenai is right. I think the spider was like me. I felt power in it, the way I feel when I use Cer's gifts."

"Maybe you are the spider, remembering Anne," the Se-fry said.

"Don't joke," Anne said, feeling sick again, knowing the Sefry wasn't joking.

"Yes, Majesty," she replied.

They sat there for a while in the dark, but Anne didn't feel like going back to sleep. Not much later, word came that the night patrol had come back, so she rose and dressed and went to the war tent.

She found Artwair, the earl of Chavel, and Captain Leafton of her Craftsmen mulling over and marking on a map. They all bowed when she entered.

"Yes, yes," Anne said. "What's the report, Duke Artwair?"

"Heol and his boys make them at about ten thousand," he said. "Half on either side of the road."

"That's only about two thousand more than we have," Anne noticed.

"Auy. But given surprise and their situation—they expect us between them, in the valley, remember—they could have murdered us with fewer men. A few volleys from the archers and a few charges with heavy cavalry to break our center before the men could be decently ready to fight. They could have done it with six thousand."

"And so what do we do?"

"There are just over three thousand foot on this side of the valley and about five hundred horse. If we try to move our whole army up, they'll detect us and have time to bring the other half over and face us with greater numbers."

"So we send the horse now," Anne said. "We have what, three thousand?"

"About that. We've the earl's five hundred and fifty, a thousand heavy lancers with Lord Kenwulf, another thousand of mine, your fifty Craftsmen, two hundred light horse, and your hundred Sefry mounted light infantry. If we take them unawares, we can decimate those on this side. By the time the rest come over, our foot will have arrived and we can fight this battle on our terms."

"It means leaving the foot marching unprotected by cavalry," Leafton pointed out.

"Who do they need to be protected from?"

The Craftsman shrugged.

"Raiht," Artwair said. "Better we should leave a small mounted force here. Perhaps that would suit you, Earl."

"Whatever pleases Her Majesty pleases me," the earl said, "but I would prefer to ride with the attack. I think that my archers might have been practically invented for this situation."

"He has a point," Leafton said. "We've archers in the light cavalry, but they and the Sefry generally dismount to fire. We could use archers experienced at actually shooting from horseback."

Artwair nodded and sent a probing look at Anne.

"Yes, come along with us, Cape Chavel," she said. "It ought to be fun."

Preparations went quickly, and before midday they were riding. Anne was surrounded by her twelve Mamres-gifted Craftsmen and her Sefry guard in their broad-brimmed hats and scarves. Ahead of her was the vanguard, Kenwulf's heavy horse, fifty knights, each with twenty handpicked riders. The light horse and Sefry rode on the right wing, and the earl's men on her left.

Two bells later they were trotting down the hills. Anne
had a brief view of the camp, and her scalp started to tingle.
Had they been noticed yet? The ground must be starting to
tremble from so many hooves.

They breasted a wide ridge, and there was nothing but a
few hundred kingsyards between them and the enemy.

The Hansans were boiling like ants whose hill had just
been kicked, trying to make formations, but as of yet she
didn't see a single pike hedge, although a rickety-looking
shield wall was forming.

"Give the order to charge," she told Leafton.

He nodded, lifted his cornet, and sounded it. The heavy
horse in front of her formed a line five deep and two hundred wide, massed together so closely that an apple thrown
among them wouldn't find its way to the ground. They began the advance slowly but soon began to gather speed.

The air was already thick with the arrows of her men, and
she felt a savage joy as they swept down from the ridge, her
guard forming a wall around her.

Joy mingled with the now familiar sick rage of Cer as she
reached out toward the Hansans, feeling the wet insides of
them. As if with her hands, she softly squeezed.

And as the heavy horse shocked into them, she heard the
vast sob of their despair. Some who had lifted their pikes
dropped them.

The vanguard tore through the half-formed Hansan lines,
and the light horse spread to encircle them. But to her chagrin, the knights around her were drawing to a halt.

"What's this?" she said.

"We're to keep you safe, Majesty," Leafton said. "The
duke's orders. No need for you to be down in there where a
stray arrow or lance might find you."

"Artwair is *my* general," she replied. "His orders weigh
less than mine. Resume the charge, or by the saints, I'll go
down without you."

"Majesty—"

"Your only possible response, Captain Leafton, is 'Yes,
Majesty.'"

"Yes, Majesty," he sighed. Then, in a louder voice: "Resume charge."

They struck what remained of the right flank, but there was little resistance to speak of. In moments the army of Hansa broke and ran, with her knights cutting them down from behind. Anne saw that some of their cavalry had managed to form up and were trying to help cover their fleeing comrades, without much success.

And so she found herself in the center of the camp, the dead and dying spread around her. She felt something swelling inside her, a terrible glee, and realized the woman was there, alive in the power that Anne was funneling through her.

You see? You see what real strength is? And this is only the beginning.

"Good," Anne said, exhilarated.

"Something's wrong," Leafton said.

"How so?"

"This doesn't look like five thousand men, not even half of that."

Wait . . . The arilac sounded suddenly uncertain, something Anne never had sensed from her before.

"What is it?"

The Hellrune! The Hellrune saw this, too! He's a step ahead of you! Anne, flee!

Anne turned to Leafton, but he already had an arrow in his eye, and shafts were falling about them like rain from the north. She knew a sharp rush of pain as one cut along her arm, and then there were shields all around her.

"Someone sound the retreat," she screamed. "We've been tricked. We've got to get back to the infantry."

A moment later the cornet shrilled. Her own guard was already in motion, charging back up the way they had come, but there were horsemen there, charging right down at them. It looked like double their number.

CHAPTER TEN

KAITHBAURG

SINISTER BLACK WALLS beneath dark skies surrounded by leagues of desert rubble: That was what Neil expected of Kaithbaurg. That certainly was how it was in the stories his old neiny Eley had told him when he was a little bern. Kaithbaurg, the city of black towers where evil dwelt.

But the road took them through pleasant fields, woodlands, and bustling little market towns. In the nineday it took to reach the heart of Hansa, they camped only once, resting instead in comfortable inns or castles. His Hanzish sharpened until he almost didn't have to concentrate at all to speak or understand it, even though the country dialects were much softer and less clipped than the coastal vernacular he had learned.

Still, until the road crested a ridge and he actually saw Kaithbaurg, the image of brutal black walls with merlons like shark's teeth was still in his mind.

Well, there were walls and towers, but that was about as close as his old neiny had come to the truth.

He realized they had drawn to a stop.

"You can see it best from here," Berimund said. "It's my favorite view."

"I can see why," the queen mother said. "One can really see most of it, it seems."

It was true. Whereas Eslen was built on a rather dramatic hill, the loftiest point of Kaithbaurg wasn't terribly higher than the lowest, which was the Donau River. The watercourse cut the city into two roughly semicircular parts: a smaller one on their side of the river and a much larger one on the northern side. Three great spans connected them.

Both parts of the city were surrounded by double walls of grayish-white stone. The outer wall was low and towerless. Just inside of it was a broad canal and then an embanked inner wall that looked about six or seven kingsyards high. The inner walls were guarded by a number of elegant, efficient-looking drum towers.

Towers bristled everywhere, in fact: delicate clock belfries with steeped roofs of black slate or green copper, massive cylindrical bastions wherever the walls met the river, sky-reaching gatehouse spires on the bridges.

More surprising was that although houses of all sorts were packed within the walls, Neil also could make out a good bit of green, as if there were fields in there.

The northern side of the city sloped gently up to another wall of darker-looking stone that encircled the hilltop, and the roof of some sort of keep or palace built of white stone could be partly seen.

"That's the castle?" Neil asked, pointing to the last feature.

Berimund smiled. "A warrior's question, eh? That's the palace, yes. Everything inside of those older walls is Hauhhaim; that was the first city, here before everything else. Come down toward the river, and that's Nithirhaim. The part nearest us, with all the green, is Gildgards. The west side of town—you can't see it well from here—that's Niujaim. On our side of the river, that's Suthstath."

"You like your city," Alis commented.

Berimund nodded. "It's the most wonderful city in the world. I'm eager to show it to Her Majesty."

"Let's hope your father allows that, then," Muriele responded.

"You'll see a bit on the way to the palace," Berimund said.

Neil thought he was sidestepping the queen's implied question, which wasn't a good sign.

* * *

They entered through the Suthstath gate and found themselves in a busy market square with a fountain pool in the center and a statue, which by his winged shoes and staff Neil took to be Saint Turm. Across the square stood a massive temple with double clock towers.

The people all stopped what they were doing and bowed as Berimund passed. They continued on as the square narrowed back to a street, and moments later they were crossing one of the bridges, the center one, in fact. The river was active with boats of all sorts but mostly barges and medium craft with triangular sails. Neil wondered what defenses he didn't see in the waters below: chains, probably, or catches that could be raised to hold an enemy to be bombarded from the bridge.

There was nothing like Thornrath or the fastness here, but Neil had to admit that the town was well made. He could only hope the Hansan army hadn't been built by the same architects.

Muriele's chest felt tight as they crossed the Donau. She was well and truly here now. Berimund had been willing to let her return home. Why hadn't she? Once it had been made clear to her that Marcomir had lost any sense of tradition and honor, why had she continued? True, Berimund had promised her protection, but did that really mean anything?

Marcomir must know that keeping her hostage wouldn't deter Anne. Robert had had her hostage, and Anne had attacked Eslen anyway. Everyone knew that story by now.

She was proud of Anne in a way that she had never imagined. Who could have ever foreseen her returning with such strength and character? Who could have imagined her as queen? But the changes in Anne that had made all that possible also made her very little like the daughter Muriele knew. Anne was distant, surrounded by her Sefry and the Vitellian swordsman, by warriors who loved her. She had become strange, inward, always listening to voices no one else could hear. There was even, at times, something a little frightening about her.

"What is it?" Alis asked.

Muriele looked up, realizing that instead of taking in the fresh sights of Kaithbaurg, she had been staring at her reins.

"I was just thinking what a relief it was, at first, to have the crown off my head," she said.

"You mean when Anne took it?"

"No, actually when Robert took it. True, I was a prisoner, but that relieved me of any chance of making bad choices. Nothing was my fault anymore."

"I suppose that's one way of looking at it."

"I'm just wondering if I've done it again."

"You think you came here to be imprisoned?"

Muriele looked up, but Berimund was ahead, explaining his city to Neil, and the other riders were giving the two women plenty of space.

"Anne *sent* me here, Alis."

Alis frowned. "The embassy was your idea."

"So I thought. But when I went to her about it, she already seemed to know. She tried to hide it, but she knew. One of her visions, I suppose. And she was very particular that I bring you and Neil along."

"I would have been with you anyway."

"But not Sir Neil. He should still be recovering."

"Interesting," Alis said. "I wonder what she expects us to do."

"We shouldn't talk about this," Muriele said, remembering that there were monks who could hear a cricket chirp a hundred miles away. Maybe that was why they had been given the space to talk, so that they would. "It's probably nothing."

"Probably," Alis said. "I think you're worried over nothing. It will be much more dangerous to talk in the castle."

"I know. How much do you know about the castle?"

"I know it's called Kunijosrohsn."

"I mean, was it constructed like Eslen? In the particulars of the walls, I mean?"

Alis shook her head slightly, showing that she understood the reference to Eslen's secret passages. "I don't know.

Most of it is much younger than Eslen. I don't think the same, ah, architects were involved. But I can't be certain."

"Well, let's hope we know why we're here when the time comes."

"You came here to try to make peace," Alis said. "Remember?"

"And I will try, earnestly. But I no longer have much hope."

"The war is only just starting. Things will change when one side or the other begins to have an advantage. Then you will be Crotheny's voice here."

"That's true. Of course, the last war with Hansa went on for ten years."

"Well, let's hope the food here is good, then."

The Kunijosrohsn was something of a surprise, and even Muriele who did not have the eye of a military man, could see that it hadn't been built for serious defense. It was rather like a large manse, rectangular in shape, four stories high, and hollowed out by an immense inner courtyard. There were a few towers, but they looked more decorative than useful.

Men took their horses, and Berimund escorted them into the interior, down a series of halls, and up three flights of stairs so that Muriele was certain they were bound for one of the towers. Instead, they were shown into a large suite of rooms with large windows, elegantly appointed.

"Majesty, if this suits you, these will be your rooms."

Muriele peered out the window. She had a beautiful view of the east side of the city, the winding Donau, and the plain beyond.

"It suits me very well," she said. "Thank you, Prince."

"I'll send some servants for you to choose from. I hope after you've had some time to freshen up, you'll join me at my table tonight."

"I accept your invitation," she said. "I wonder if your father will be there."

"I'm going to talk to him now," Berimund replied.

"I would like to speak to him at his earliest convenience."

"Of course, Majesty. I will so inform him."

But when they arrived in Berimund's dining hall a few bells later, Marcomir wasn't there.

Muriele stood politely as she was introduced to a dozen Hansan lords and their ladies standing at the long oaken table. None of them seemed to be above the rank of greft, and they all seemed about the same age as Berimund.

The hall itself was roomy and candle-lit, hung with tapestries of hunting scenes. Two white staghounds prowled hopefully around the table, and beyond all of that she could see the open door of the kitchen and several servants bustling about. Woodsmoke hung in the air, along with delicious odors, familiar and strange.

Mead was brought, which Muriele thought too sweet, followed by some pears and unfamiliar berries that were excellent.

Berimund rose and said something in Hanzish, and all the lords came to their feet. Berimund lifted his goblet and tilted it toward Muriele. Muriele remained seated. She hadn't retained a lot from her childhood tutoring, but the various etiquettes of the civilized nations had remained with her.

"To Queen Muriele of Crotheny, a matchless beauty. The saints keep you hale and happy. *Whairnei!*"

"Whairnei!" they all repeated, and, after drinking, took their seats.

"You are all far too kind," Muriele said, relieved that the toast was short. She wondered how many more she would have to endure.

Fifteen during the first course, as it turned out.

Meat came out next: roasted venison with what she thought was a cherry sauce, suckling pig with leek puree, fried hare in some sort of plum sauce, lamb-and-cheese pie, and a second pie of apples, quinces, and beef.

"Prince Berimund," Muriele asked as she finished cleaning a venison rib and tossed it to one of the hounds, "I wonder if you gave your father my message."

"I did, Majesty."

"And?"

Berimund reddened slightly. "He apologizes that he didn't find it convenient to come tonight."

"But tomorrow?"

"Not tomorrow."

"Is the war keeping him so busy?"

"No, Majesty. He, ah—he's going hunting."

Muriele felt her blood—and the mead mixing in it—rise hot up her neck to her ears. "I see," she said.

"We will find some entertainment for you, I promise."

"I'm sure. What news is there of the war?"

Berimund stopped with a knife full of food halfway to his mouth. "What?"

"The war. You said it's started. What news have you?"

"I really don't think I can make Your Majesty privy—"

"Who would I tell?" Muriele asked. "Is someone here going to carry a letter to my daughter for me? I shouldn't think so. Come, Prince. Tell me of the Hanzish victories."

"Ah, well." He looked around at his retainers. "You're right, I suppose. Well, there's not much really. A fleet from Liery tried to blockade Copenwis, but we met them in open sea with better numbers."

"And?" Muriele asked, trying to stay stone-faced.

"They didn't engage," he replied. "It would have been stupid of them to. Of course, that was five days ago. There's no telling what happened since."

"That was lucky," Alis said, "to find the Lierish fleet in the open sea."

Berimund smiled and said something in Hanzish. Muriele followed enough of it to know that he was repeating Alis' remark.

The reaction was a sort of group smirk.

"Lukka?" one of the nobles said. *"Nei, sa haliurunna."*

"No, no, enough of that," Berimund said. "Enough about the war."

That was interesting. What was a haliurunna? Berimund seemed to have thought it had been a mistake to bring it up.

She would bring it up again when they were all a bit drunker, she thought.

Fish was next: a huge pike stuffed with trout sausage, salmon with grapes and leeks in pastry shaped like a halibut, cold roasted eel in a green sauce, bream in violet sauce.

And the toasts went on, and the mead flowed. Muriele sipped her drink.

By the time the fowl course arrived, the singing had started. A largish fellow who had been introduced as a landrauhtin began it. Berimund tried to wave him down, but the prince was pretty drunk by then, and with a sheepish, apologetic grin at Muriele, he joined in. She didn't know the song, but Sir Neil stiffened.

"What is it?" she asked. "Do you know this song?"

He nodded. "It's a naval song about a great victory at sea. They're celebrating."

She shrugged. "That's hardly a surprise."

"But in front of you? And even without that, this isn't proper behavior in the presence of a queen."

She covered his hand with her own. "Most of William's dinners ended up like this, especially when he had his best men around. I think it's no different in Liery."

"I never dined with a queen in Liery," Neil admitted. "Still, I don't like it."

"Keep calm." Everyone in the room but Neil, Alis, and Muriele was singing loudly now, including the women.

She leaned close. "What's a haliurunna, Sir Neil?"

"It's a sort of shinecrafter, one who can see the future. They say Hansa breeds them."

"Do you believe it?"

"Yes," he said firmly. "That's how they met our ships at sea. They've done it before."

That's it, Muriele thought. *That must be it.*

"We need Berimund's goodwill, Sir Neil. I'll tell you why later."

The song broke off, and somebody tried to start another one, but the prince shouted him down.

"We're being rude to our guests," he said.

Muriele came to her feet, mug in hand. "Forgive my pronunciation," she said. She took a deep breath and sang:

"Wha gaf sa ansu gadrauhta fruma?"

They stared at her for an instant, then exploded out with, *"Sein mahteig arm ya sein hauh-thutsitha!"*

Mead sloshed from tankards.

She knew only the first three questions in Hanzish, but after that they got going again, and it didn't matter.

Berimund made no effort to restrain them, and they drank until they either passed out or went stumbling away to wherever they were quartered.

Berimund himself, impressively, managed to stand up.

"I bid shou guh night, Majesty," he said, his words slow. "You are good, ah, good—I hope you weren't insulted."

"Not at all. In fact, it made me a bit nostalgic."

"Goth. Min shervants will show you home."

"I wonder, Prince, if I could ask a favor."

"Name it, Mashesty."

"I wonder if you would take me hunting tomorrow."

His eyes widened. "With my father?" Then he laughed. "Jah. That will be fun."

Then he bowed and staggered out of the hall. A serving girl led them back to their rooms.

"Well, that was jolly," Alis observed once they were alone. "How did you know a Hansan drinking song?"

"William used to sing it—sort of. It's question and answer. The first question is 'What did the saint give the first Hansan Warrior?' I think the real answer was 'The strength of his arm and courage,' or something like that. William sang, 'His sister to fondle and kiss.' And so on."

"Resourceful," Alis said. "Shall I help Her Majesty with her gown?"

"Please."

Alis stepped very close and began working at the fastenings in the back.

"I heard Sir Neil," she said. "I think I see why we're here."

"Why didn't Anne just tell us?" Muriele wondered.

"Maybe she didn't know. Or maybe the sorcerer would have seen that."

"Find out what you can while I'm away tomorrow."

"Do you really think that sober, Berimund will remember his pledge, much less carry it out?"

"He won't be sober until midday," she answered. "And yes, I think he will." She turned and gripped Alis' hand. "Be very careful. One misstep here—"

"It might not even take that," Alis said. "Marcomir is said to have vicious moods. So you be careful, too."

CHAPTER ELEVEN

THE WOOTHSHAER

ASPAR WOKE with sunlight on his face. He stretched, rolled, and bumped up against something warm.

Winna.

She was still asleep, her face glowing like a saint's in the golden light. He remembered her as a little girl back in Colbaely, full of fire and mischief. He remembered the shock of understanding that he loved her when he thought he couldn't love anyone.

His eyes traced down to her rounded belly. Gently, he stroked his fingers along it.

What's in there? he wondered.

He hadn't given much thought to being a father. Qerla hadn't been able to bear his children; men and Sefry were too different for that. After she'd died, he'd never mont to marry again. And since this thing with Winna had begun, he'd been mostly thinking about keeping them alive.

But a child, a boy or girl, part him, part Winna . . .

He tightened his heart. There was no use thinking like that. Whatever Winna was carrying, it wasn't going to be Mannish.

Should he tell her what he feared? Could he?

It seemed the geos was powerful and canny enough to protect its purpose. Could he jump off a cliff or slit his own throat? Provoke a fight with Emfrith and then lose it?

Probably not. But the thing about a geos, at least he had always heard, was that when its conditions were fulfilled, it was unmade. So when they reached the Briar King's valley, he would be free of it, free to act as he wanted. The witch obviously thought that would be too late, but the witch couldn't know everything.

He just had to keep his head and do what he could do. Test the geos until he found its weakness.

He rose carefully, afraid to wake her.

The sun was higher than he liked. He itched to be gone, keeping Fend as far behind him as he could, but this might be the last good sleep she got for a long time.

He found Emfrith in the inner yard, talking with some of his men. He looked up as Aspar descended the stair.

"Morning, holter," Emfrith said. His tone sounded a bit strained, and Aspar reckoned he knew why.

"Morning," Aspar replied.

"The Woothshaer chasing you wasn't hard to find," he said. "My man Arn spotted it upriver, near Slif Owys but moving this way. They'll be here by tomorrow."

"We'd better get moving, then," Aspar said.

"I think we'll fight them here," Emfrith said.

"Werlic?" Aspar said. "Fine, then; you do that. The three of us will be on our way."

"No, that I *can't* let you do," Emfrith said apologetically.

Aspar's hand went to the feyknife, but he let it drop and balled his fists instead. "First your bloody father, now you," he snapped. "What's wrong with you people?"

"We're just people who do what needs to be done," Emfrith said. "My family guards this march, and I'm not going to let motley monsters and Sefry come strutting in unchallenged."

"Yah, werlic. But what's that to do with us?"

"If I let you go, they'll just follow you. If you're here, they'll be forced to fight, and we'll slaughter them at our walls."

"Didn't you learn anything from your little brawl with the woorm?" Aspar asked.

"Yes," he said, nodding. "Quite a bit. And more since, as we've had occasion to kill a greffyn. They're tough, I'll grant you, but they can die. And there aren't so many of them in the band coming here."

"You've got only fifty men," Aspar pointed out. "They may not be many, but they can do fifty men."

"I've sent for more from my father, and I've alerted Celly Guest—that's the other fort I mentioned, about three leagues north. We'll have more than fifty."

"Maunt, maunt," Aspar said, almost begging. "This is a bad mistake."

Was that the geos talking?

No, this *was* stupid.

"I'd rather have your help than lock you up," Emfrith said, "but we'll do it any way we have to." He sighed. "I'm putting Winna in the tower, under guard, until it's over."

"You're taking her prisoner," Aspar said, his voice flat.

Emfrith strode angrily toward him, and for a moment Aspar thought he might have succeeded in starting the fight he had wondered about earlier. His hand went back to the feyknife.

But Emfrith stopped a kingsyard from him. "I love her, holter. I'm doing what I think is best for her."

"And I'm not?"

"I don't know. But she's not in the best shape to travel, is she? To be chased over hill and stream by this horde? Women die from that sort of thing."

"Yah. But you're still taking her hostage."

"If you want to look at it like that, I can't stop you," Emfrith said. "But this is how it's going to be. Now, you can sulk about it, or you can help me win. You've fought more of these things than any of us. We have a day. What should we do?"

"Run."

"Raiht. Besides that."

Aspar shrugged inwardly, and his mounting anger leveled off. Maybe this was for the best, for them to all die here. Better than waiting to see what the witch had in store for Winna and her child.

"To begin with," he said, "three of the Sefry warriors are something Leshya calls Vaix. They're supposed to be stronger and faster than Mannish warriors. They have swords like my knife and Grimknows what else. Leshya can probably tell us more." He rubbed his chin.

"Some of the beasts aren't that smart," he went on. "Leshya and I killed several of them with pit traps. You might want to dig some of those. And haul heavy things up here to drop on them. Do you have any siege engines?"

"I've got one catapult."

"More would be better."

"We'll make do," Emfrith said. "Why don't we go find Leshya and some beer? I know greffyns, but the other things Arn describes are new to me."

"How did you kill the greffyn?" Aspar asked.

"Eight of us charged it on horseback. Two of us managed to hit it in that sally. That didn't kill it, but it slowed it down. We just kept lancing it."

"You didn't lose any men?"

"We lost two horses, and three of my men got pretty sick, but no one actually touched it. Winna warned us about that."

"Some of these will be harder than that," Aspar said. "I'll help. You've got my word. But you won't keep Winna locked up."

Emfrith held his gaze for a moment then nodded curtly.

Sir Evan of Leanvel had a loose sort of face with several chins and cheeks threatening to join their number. At the moment his bushy eyebrows were pinched together in a frown.

"What's that, then?" he asked, pointing at Fend and his monsters.

"Name it whatever you like," Emfrith replied. "Manticore is what I've been calling it."

"I fancy that," Sir Evan replied. "Like the beast in the story of the Knight-Prince of Albion."

"There's more of them," Leshya said.

Aspar already had noticed that. The number of men and Sefry looked about the same, but Aspar now counted seven utins loping along, four greffyns, and two manticores. There were also a couple of wagons Aspar hadn't seen before, likely because Fend hadn't wanted to bring them over the pass.

"There's something odd about a Woothshaer with a supply train," Emfrith said.

"Yah," Aspar allowed. "But Haergrim's hunt is mostly dead men, alvs, and booygshins. They don't need to eat. The monsters probably eat off the land, but that wouldn't leave much for Fend and his men."

The enemy was still a good ten bowshots away, approaching the Warlock River across a wheat field. Aspar and his companions were watching from a low bluff a bowshot from the river. The land below the rise was clear and flat, a good place for a charge. Better yet, Fend had to cross an old stone bridge that was wide enough for only about three horses to go abreast.

Aspar still didn't feel particularly hopeful.

"Celly Guest would like the honor of the first charge," Sir Evan said.

"It's my duty, sir," Emfrith replied.

"Come along, lad; let us have a go first. We'll save you a greff or two."

"You're the senior," Emfrith said. "If you ask like that . . ."

The knight smiled and reached to slap Emfrith on the back. "Very good. Down we go, then." He raised his voice. "Come along, men."

Celly Guest had spared them not only Sir Evan but fifty heavily armored riders, thirty archers, and thirty pikemen. As Aspar watched, the knight formed his cavalry in a thick column, five abreast and ten deep. He supposed that made sense, as they would only be charging what was coming across the bridge.

The archers fanned out on the bluff, with the pikemen lined up to protect them. Emfrith's men were now the reserve.

Aspar sighed and strung his bow. Leshya did the same. He checked the binding on the spear he'd made from the feyknife one last time, wondering if it would be better to have it in his hand.

Probably not. Emfrith had given him a new throwing ax and dirk, which would be fine against men and Sefry but of less use against the sedhmhari. If he fought one of those, better to keep it at more than arm's length.

Fend was forming his beasts up, too. Aspar wondered how exactly the Sefry communicated with them and how he had learned to do so.

He probably would never know. If he got Fend close enough to talk to, Aspar didn't intend to waste any time asking questions.

Fend didn't seem much interested in getting within bowshot, however. He wasn't in sight. In fact, Aspar still didn't know his old enemy was with the band at all.

Whoever led them, the monsters would be his vanguard.

One of the manticores came first, followed by the pack of greffyns and then the utins.

Have I lost my mind? he wondered. *Am I dying of fever in the Mountains of the Hare? Is any of this real? Because it shouldn't be.*

The archers began firing as the beasts marched onto the bridge. Some of the shafts stuck, but the sedhmhari all had hide like armor, and none of them went down.

He heard the snap and hum of the catapult firing. Emfrith and his men had dragged it down there and found the range that morning.

A stone a little larger than Aspar's head flew to the bridge and struck one of the greffyns just behind the head. It screeched and flopped over with its back plainly broken, and a tremendous cheer went up from the men.

The manticore charged.

Once again Aspar was startled by its speed. Sir Evan and his first and second ranks were trotting now, and as the thing neared the end of the bridge, they went to a gallop, ten lances with the weight of ten horses and ten men behind them.

Oddly, there wasn't much sound as they came together, just a sort of dull thud. The manticore, for all its armor and weight, was driven back. It was hard to tell how hurt it was, though.

The riders wheeled away as the greffyns came leaping across, and the next two rows of horsemen gathered speed.

However Fend controlled them, it was clear that he couldn't make them any smarter or he would have had the catlike beasts avoid the charge and try to flank. They didn't, though, but met the charge head to head, leaping over the downed manticore.

Two of them were actually lifted into the air by the lancers, but the third got through, bowling over one of the horses and ripping into it with its beak and claws. Those riders wheeled away, too, but the beast abandoned its first kill and took down another horse.

The manticore wasn't moving. Two of the four greffyns looked like they were dying, and a third was wounded.

Something was missing.

"Sceat," Aspar said. "Where are the utins?"

But even as he asked it, he saw them swarming out of the river, coming at the cavalry column from the sides.

Utins, unlike greffyns, were pretty smart.

Cursing, Aspar picked the nearest and started shooting at it. His first arrow skipped off. The second stuck but didn't look like it went in deep.

The column already was coming apart as the riders turned their horses to meet the fast-running utins. Aspar watched as the one he was firing at leaped nimbly over the lance aimed at it, danced down it, and struck off the head of the rider with its claws. Aspar sent another arrow at it as it came back to ground and disemboweled another rider's horse.

"Holy saints," he heard Emfrith gasp.

Now the second manticore was starting across the bridge. The archers were pouring arrows onto it because the remaining greffyn and the utins were too mixed up with the horsemen to target well.

With a shout, Emfrith began trotting his horse forward, his men behind him.

The archers shifted their fire again as several of the utins began running toward the bluff. Aspar picked the one coming his way and began letting fly.

His first shot hit it in the eye. It spun and staggered but roared and began speeding toward them again. He saw one of Leshya's white-fletched shafts appear in its thigh. Aspar put another arrow on the string, inhaled, and let it snap. It glanced off the thick scales of its skull.

Then it was up to the pikemen. It grabbed one of the pole arms below the head and flipped itself up and over the first rank, but one of the men in the second rank managed to set his spear, and the monster's weight drove the point into its belly, showering gore all around. Screaming, it grasped at the shaft.

It was five kingsyards from Aspar. He took careful aim and shot it in the other eye, and this time the arrow went all the way to the back of the skull. Its mouth froze open, and it stopped struggling. The pikemen rolled it back down the bluff.

Another one was coming, but fifteen arrows met it. Most either missed or skipped off, but one that found it struck it through the eye.

The archers were beginning to remember his advice concerning the creatures' weak spots.

A glance showed him that the other wing of archers wasn't doing so well. An utin had gotten through the line, and most of the men were in flight.

Things were coming back together on the field below.

Sir Evan and the other nine in his first charge had kept their cohesion and, as he watched, put their lances to the greffyn. Most of the rest had dismounted and were taking on the utins with sword and shield, encircling them with superior numbers. One was already down, being hacked by eight heavily armored men.

Emfrith's group was slowing its charge because the second manticore had stopped advancing and stood just out of catapult range.

In moments, the two remaining utins tore away from their tormentors and ran back across the bridge.

"I don't believe it," Aspar said.

It looked like Sir Evan had lost around fifteen horsemen and probably about that many archers. A few more probably would die of contact with the greffyns. But of his monsters, their enemy had lost all but two utins and a manticore. Suddenly, beating them didn't seem that much trouble at all.

They seemed to know it, too. The wagons were turning.

Sir Evan was forming his men back up, and Emfrith was galloping back up the hill.

"Well," he said as he drew up, "maybe not such a bad idea, after all."

"Maybe not," Aspar agreed. "I never would have believed it, but maybe not."

"We'll dog them for a while, find a good place to attack them, and—"

"Sceat," Aspar said. "I think Sir Evan has other ideas."

Emfrith turned just as the Celly Guest horsemen—what remained of them—went thundering over the bridge, along with about twenty of Emfrith's men. The manticore wasn't there anymore but had moved back up the hill.

"Get back here," Emfrith howled. No one looked back. They probably couldn't even hear him.

The men and Sefry across the river had turned but didn't seem to be readying a countercharge. He couldn't make out their faces from that far away, but something seemed odd about them.

"I don't like this," Leshya said.

Aspar just shook his head, trying to figure it out.

And then, as if struck by a thousand invisible arrows, Sir Evan and all the men with him, along with their horses, fell and did not move again.

Far across the river, Aspar saw something glinting in the back of one of the wagons.

"Turn around!" Leshya screamed. "Close your eyes!"

Aspar felt his own eyes starting to warm and followed her advice. After an instant, so did everyone else.

"What is it?"

"Basil-nix," she said. "If you meet its gaze, you die. I think it's too far away right now, but . . ."

"Get them out of here, Emfrith," Aspar growled. "Get what's left of your men out of here."

"I don't understand," the young man wailed. He sounded as if he'd just been wakened from a deep sleep.

"Sound retreat," Aspar told the man with the horn.

"Sir—"

Aspar took Emfrith's shoulder.

"He'll move up now. We can't fight with our backs turned. We didn't know about this."

"Raiht," the boy said, his face wet with tears. "Sound the retreat."

A black shadow passed over them, and another, and there was a sound of many wings.

CHAPTER TWELVE

KAURON

STEPHEN PAUSED, trembling, staring at his feet, staring at a thousand pairs of feet in shoes, buskins, boots, bare, missing toes, huge, tiny.

It was like what the Vhelny had done to him, except the other memories weren't *his.*

But that distinction wouldn't matter for long. He closed his eyes and stepped, feeling as he did a myriad of other steps, a thousand different swayings of his body.

His stomach couldn't take that, and he doubled over, vomiting, observing with an odd detachment that in that act he somehow felt more solid, more himself.

But he wasn't. That was the greatest lie in the world, the most fundamental illusion. That thing called Stephen was a culling, a mere snip of what really existed. The rest of him was trying to get back in.

Would that end it? Would he be complete if he gave up the fantasy that this tiny Stephen thing was real?

Maybe.

No.

The voice barged through the rest, pushed them back to whispers. It was gentle, strong, confident, and Stephen felt some of the strength from the first fane come back to him.

No, the voice repeated. *That is death. The voices you hear, the visions you experience—those are the dead, those who let go of themselves, who allowed the river to take what was in them. You are stronger because you still have a self. Do you understand? You are still tied together. You are real,*

Stephen Darige. It's totality that is the illusion. Only the finite can be real.

"Kauron?"

Yes. I'm more powerful here. You've passed the fourth fane. There is only one more. Listen to me. What you feel is your mind trying to accept everything in the river. You can't do that without dying, without ceasing to become who you are. Can you understand me?

"I think so."

Then let me help you fight it.

"Aren't you dead, too? Why are you different?"

Because I walked this faneway, too. Because when my body died, I would not permit the river to have me.

"I—" But the voices were coming back, and he couldn't think. "Help me find the last fane," he gasped.

Be strong, Stephen. Hold on to yourself. Hold on to me. It isn't far.

It seemed far, however. He realized at some point that the light and wind weren't illusions, that somewhere along the way he had left the innards of the mountain and was winding up its slopes. Kauron stayed with him, talking to him and not to the other voices, reminding him that he was the real one. It felt as if the ancient monk were walking right beside him, although when he looked, he could not see him.

"The Vhelny," Stephen managed to ask. "What does it want?"

"Vhelny?"

"The thing you warned me against, the thing in the mountain."

"I don't know. I wouldn't think it would be someone else seeking the power of the faneway, not if he already knew where it was. One would think he would have slain you and walked it himself."

"That's what I thought," Stephen said, pausing to make certain that the hand he was using to steady himself was his own.

"So it's someone who *wants* you to have the power."

"But the prophecy says he's my enemy. I'm your heir, and he's my enemy."

"If I had an enemy like that, I don't remember. It's possible, I suppose. Ghosts, even ghosts like me, aren't aware of the things they've forgotten. Anyway, I don't think I would know much about prophecies concerning Kauron's heir, would I? They were all made after my death."

Stephen felt a deep shock of dizziness.

Stephen! The voice was back in his head, fainter, alarmed. *Listen to me, Stephen. Focus on my voice.*

The vertigo eased back. "What happened to you, Kauron?" he asked. "How did you die?"

"I died on this very mountain," the ghost replied.

"Did the faneway kill you?"

"No. It's a long story. I actually returned here to die."

"Why?"

"I'm not sure. I just thought I ought to. It appears I was right."

"But—"

"The fane is just ahead. The path is narrower than in my time."

"I wish—it's hard to think, to ask what I want to ask."

"I know. I remember. Think about who you are. *Tell* me about who you are."

"I—I love languages. You're a thousand years old! There's so much I could learn . . ." He shook his head, trying to focus. Was he still moving?

Yes, inching along. He saw something up ahead, something like a standing stone.

"I, ah—when I'm angry, or frustrated, I make up a little treatise, as if it's going to go into a book."

"Of course you do," Kauron said. "I used to do much the same, especially when I was a novice. I wrote mine down, though, and one of the other brothers—Brother Parsons—found it and showed the others."

"What happened?"

"They made fun of me, of course, and I had to clean the stables for a year."

Stephen had a sudden vivid image of standing ankle-deep in horse muck.

"It's hard to imagine the great Kauron cleaning stables," he said.

"What's so great about me? What did I do?"

"You brought Virgenya Dare's journal here for safekeeping. You must have been important among the Revesturi."

"Like you are, you mean?"

"What are you saying?"

"I was no one. Hardly anyone. I lived in the scriftorium, I found the journal; I found the location of the mountain. My fratrex sent me to bring it here because he reckoned that no one would suspect I was up to anything important, that no one would follow me."

"There are prophecies about you."

"No, it sounds like there are prophecies about *you*, Stephen. I'm just in them, doing what I'm supposed to do: helping you."

The voices were fading now, and his sense of where he was returning. He was on a spit of stone sticking out from the mountain, a triangle four kingsyards at the base and seven long. It slanted up as it narrowed toward its apex, where stood a little spike. The Virgenyan symbol for "five" was barely visible scratched on it.

"It's funny," Stephen said. "You asked me to talk about myself, but it was talking about you that helped."

"I'm your guide."

"I think we must be very much alike," Stephen said.

"It sounds like it. At least in youth."

"When I touch the stone, it's over?"

"Yes. The knowledge and power are in you, but without the blessing of this fane you can't control it."

"What happens to you?"

"It's my sacrifice to make, Stephen."

"What do you mean?"

"Don't worry. All is as it should be. I've guided you this far. Trust me a step farther."

Stephen nodded, walking carefully forward. Sighing, he placed his hand on the upthrust of stone.

The last of the voices faded, replaced by a feeling of vastness. It was as if a great wave had passed over him, spun him in its waters, and set him back on his feet. Everything seemed new and different, as if he were seeing the world with completely novel eyes.

As if he had been reborn.

This is the Alq, he realized. It's not really a place, it's a state of being.

He sank down to his knees, utterly exhausted. He gazed at the beautiful march of mountains before him and felt a sudden, savage joy at the magnificence of it all, at the thunder and lightning that was the world. His body was tired, but inside he felt alive as never before.

But he knew he'd just begun: There was still plenty he had to do. The faneway wasn't the last step. He still had to find the throne, and he had to find it soon.

Stephen stood up, and although his knees were still a bit wobbly, he felt he could walk. He was sure he remembered the way back to the Aitivar city, but it meant going halfway around the mountain, and it wouldn't do to starve to death. Not now, when it was all there before him, when he finally knew what to do.

Something was rushing toward him on the wind, something hot and acrid.

He turned to face the Vhelny.

He still couldn't see it either with his eyes or with the sense that dug beneath the surface of the world. Or maybe it really was nothing more than shadow.

But no, he felt the slow and terrible potency burning in it.

Congratulations, the shadow told him, and opened vast, obfuscate wings. Stephen felt the tickle of command begin. *I can use one like you.*

Stephen didn't hesitate, and that fact in itself was a beautiful thing, almost erotic in its intensity. He flung his will at the Vhelny, drawing from the infinite flood beneath the world.

What met him was raw force of a kind he had never sensed before, and he suddenly felt as if he were wrestling with something of constantly changing form, like the alv-queen's lover in the old tale.

But this was terribly real. He felt suddenly pushed back, surrounded, and it was more and more difficult to keep his focus on the demon, to match his power against it. This was not the power of the sedos; this was ancient night come to life, something that had existed long before the world itself or any of its petty powers.

No. I don't know what it is, but it can be beaten. Take—

A surge of fresh energy filled Stephen's limbs, and he suddenly understood.

Whatever this was sat the Xhes throne. There had been another, years before, who had sat that, a Sefry warlock, and he had been bound, and now he knew how to do it.

He stopped fighting the Vhelny's energies, let them enter him, take hold of his heart and will. And when the demon had committed itself, was in him, he grabbed those energies like the leash of a dog and twisted them, made them his, laid stricture after stricture until the chaos in the monster was hemmed by order and his command.

No, the Vhelny whispered.

"Yes. And thank you for your congratulations, and to paraphrase, I'm sure you will be of use to me."

I will be free. I will grind everything in you.

"I don't think so. Now, what say you fly me back into the mountain and we find my companions."

You will pay.

But something wrapped around him, and in a moment they were soaring through the air, and he laughed in sheer delight.

He couldn't wait to see Zemlé. And Winna. And Aspar. And Queen Anne, especially Queen Anne. The best part was how surprised they would be. He loved it when people were surprised, when they finally got the joke.

Of course he did. That was why they called him the Black Jester.

CHAPTER THIRTEEN

RETREAT

ANNE COULDN'T FEEL the reins anymore. The breeze seemed to spin her around, and then the ground reached for her.

She still could see, but nothing she saw made much sense. Horses' legs were everywhere, and men were reaching for her, and then it was all just noise and color, and finally she was elsewhere, lying in a meadow by a mere. She lifted her hand and saw that there was no shadow. Her side hurt, and when she reached to feel it, there was a stick there. She pushed at it, and agony erupted along her ribs. Her hand felt wet and sticky, and when she looked at it, it was red.

"Shot," she managed. There had been a lot of arrows; she remembered that. And then the horses coming together, a shock like a giant ocean wave that threw everyone around her down until she *drew,* drew down from the sickle moon hanging pale as a cloud in the sky, and struck through them. She remembered seeing their eyes explode in gouts of steam, and the screams . . .

I did that?

"You did it," her arilac confirmed, rising up from the earth. "Even Genya Dare would have been impressed by that."

"Did we win?"

"You broke their charge and killed half of them before you got shot. Beyond that, I don't know."

"I *am* shot."

"Yes."

"Am I dying?"

"I don't know, but you shouldn't stay here in this condition. If *he* should come, you won't be able to fight him."

"I don't—" Black spots were dancing before her eyes.

"I'll help you," the arilac said, and smoothed her forehead
with one burning hand.

A hoof thudded in the earth next to her head, and someone shouted her name. She tried to sit up and gasped.

"She's here!" a man shouted. "Saints know how. We were
looking there—"

"She's shot." A face appeared above her.

"Hello, Cape Chavel," she said.

"You can hear me?"

"Yes."

"I have to get you up. Do you understand? I can't leave
you here; we're in retreat. Unless you can—" He grimaced.

"I'm too weak," she replied.

"You'll ride with me. Your Craftsmen and the heavy
horse have formed a rear guard. My horses are faster. We'll
get you back to camp and to a leic."

Anne searched for a response, but she felt too tired.

It did hurt when he got her up in the saddle with him, and
it hurt more every single time his horse took a stride. Although she tried not to, she cried, wanting nothing more
than for the pain to end.

She woke flat on her back in a small, rumbling room that
she eventually recognized as a wain. She remembered that
Nerenai had given her something bitter to drink, and she
had fallen asleep.

She felt at her side and found the arrow gone. So was her
clothing. She was wrapped loosely in a blanket.

"There, mistress," she heard Nerenai say. "Lie still."

"What's happening?"

Before Nerenai could reply, Emily broke in. "It's very exciting. They say you made their eyes explode. Is it true?"

"I'd rather not talk about that," Anne murmured. "Can
you find Artwair for me?"

"No, Majesty," the girl said. "He's out forming up the lines. You killed a lot of them, but there's plenty left. Like they knew we were coming."

"They did know we were coming."

"How?" the girl asked.

"I was outmagicked," Anne replied. *Pray saints Alis and Neil find this Hellrune and know what to do about him. He's stronger than I.*

A sudden thought occurred to her. "If we're fighting, why is the wain moving?"

"We're retreating," Emily replied. "But orderly, so we don't get slaughtered. Artwair's a smart general."

I led him into a trap, Anne thought. *That will be hard to mend.* Yes, she was queen, but she needed her generals to believe in her, especially Artwair.

"How many have we lost?"

"I don't know. They think around two thousand. They attacked our infantry where we were camped, too."

Two thousand? The number seemed unreal. Had she ever even met two thousand people in her life?

For three more days they fell back toward Poelscild. Losses on both sides were minimal. And then, a day's march from the northernmost dike, the Hansan army stopped following them.

The next day Anne wasn't sleeping in a wagon anymore but in a fine bed in Poelscild's keep.

The count had almost three thousand of her soldiers sleeping in the ground.

"They haven't gone far, Majesty," Artwair told her the next day.

"You look tired, Cousin."

He did. His face looked lined and ten years older than it had a month earlier.

"I'm well, Your Majesty."

"So where have they gone, then?"

"About a league north, in Andemuer. They're building a redoubt there. I expect they'll reinforce it and then come here."

Anne nodded. She'd made Nerenai and Emily sit her up. She couldn't stand, but she didn't want to face Artwair on her back. "And the fleet? Any word?"

"They anticipated us there, too," Artwair said. "Met Liery in open sea. Five ships were lost, and about that on the Hansan side. Sir Fail brought them back to Ter-na-Fath."

"So we're in retreat everywhere," Anne said.

"Everywhere we've ventured."

"Everywhere I've sent us, you mean," Anne said.

"There's no blame to Your Majesty. It seemed like a good plan to me, too. But it wasn't the surprise they thought it would be. And things could have been worse. This Hellrune of theirs isn't perfect, either. He may have managed to trick you, but you fought out of his trap."

"Barely. But I agree that things could have gone worse. I may know little about war, but I know that armies in retreat often fall apart and are destroyed. This could have been a rout. Your leadership prevented that, Duke Artwair."

"I'm not the only one to credit. Lord Kenwulf kept our left flank, and young Cape Chavel our right. If we had ever been encircled, that would have been the end of it."

"I will commend them, too," she said. "What happens now?"

"I've sent for reinforcements, of course. Many of the landwaerden levies are already either here or reinforcing other forts along the edge of Newland."

"Then we're giving them Andemuer and the Maog Voast plain?" Anne asked.

"We're not giving it; they have it. Northwatch fell two days ago, so reinforcements can come along the Vitellian Way without resistance. Copenwis is open to their ports. No, Newland is better fortified than the northern border and always has been. Andemuer has gone back and forth between Hansa and Crotheny for exactly that reason. But they'll have a harder time breaking us here. And if they do, we'll retreat to the next canal and flood these poelen behind us, so they'll have to swim at us."

"You mention the danger of them coming down the Dew. Have you any reports from the east?"

"No report of attack yet, no, but I expect it."

"And the south?"

He nodded. "We've heard that at least three Church legifs are camped along the Teremené River. That news is a few days old, of course. They may have started fighting already."

Anne remembered Teremené.

"The river is in a gorge there," she said. "They'll have to cross at Teremené town or go north into Hornladh . . ." She trailed off.

"Majesty?"

She closed her eyes. *Nothing; just another stupid thing I've done. Cazio, be as smart as I think you are.*

"The Hellrune can't help those in the south. I'll see what my visions can tell me about what the Church is up to. Is there anything else?"

"Not that I know of, Majesty."

"Thank you, Duke. I'd better rest now."

She met her arilac on a heather-covered down overlooking an azure sea. The air was warm and wet and a little dirty-feeling.

The arilac seemed more human each time they met, although she still shone unnaturally at times.

"You were outmaneuvered," the woman said. "With the law of death broken, the Hellrune is stronger than even I suspected."

"You should have warned me," Anne replied.

The arilac raised a fiery eyebrow. "That would have been an insult to your intelligence. If you could see the results of what *he* saw, how could you not imagine it wasn't possible for him to do the same?"

"But when does it end?" Anne asked. "If I had seen the trap, couldn't he have seen me seeing it? And so on, into utter madness?"

"Yes and no. As you've learned, the future isn't a fixed

thing if you can see it. But it has a path and momentum. When the Hellrune saw that your army would march the way it did, and you saw that he had seen that, you might have done a number of things. You might have decided not to go that way, or not march at all, or bring thousands more with you—or what you did: try to turn the trap against itself. The Hellrune would have been shown all these paths, but dimly, and one would have seemed infinitesimally brighter. In turn, his possible reactions—abandon the plan, send more men, and so forth—would be even more contingent, first because your choice was one of dozens, then because his was. That's why you didn't see the reversal of the trap: It was a wispy thing, unnoticeable. For him to see the outcome of his reversal I would call impossible, which is why you managed to escape. So to answer your question, your duel with the Hellrune went as many strokes as it could, and he won. When you are in full mastery of the power, you might see one step farther. Might."

"Then I must guess, you are saying, where Hansa is concerned."

"No, no," the arilac said. "He can't know you've seen something unless you react to it."

"Then what use to see it?"

"It can inform your strategy."

Anne rolled her eyes. "Yes, poorly. Suppose I predict an army coming down the Dew River, and Artwair diverts troops to stop them, and instead the army never marches east but comes here instead?"

"You will find you can rarely see more than a nineday or so when specifics are involved. Visions of the far future are usually vague as to when and how they will happen. The Hellrune's is limited in the same way, and he is not here, Anne. His shadow is still in Hansa. It takes a rider to bring information from him, a rider that may or may not arrive and will always be late. You're closer to where the war is being fought now. And now you know to be cautious."

Anne nodded. "Very well. But first I must see what the

Church is up to on our southern border and what danger I've put Cazio and Austra in." She straightened her spine.

"I'm not afraid of you," she told the arilac.

"I never said you were."

"Oh, I was," she admitted. "But no longer. From now on I expect you to tell me everything I need to know. Do you understand? I don't want to be hit from behind again."

"Very well, Anne."

"Call me 'Majesty.'"

"When you are *my* queen, I shall. But that time is not come. And I'm not afraid of you, either."

She watched the titanic stones of the citadel crack and felt herself like fingers wedged there, tearing at it. The doors were like burning brands, but she pulled, and everything in her seemed next to snapping. In an instant she brimmed with the most profound happiness she had ever known as everything slowed to almost stopping, and the magicked metal rang as it tore, and the power of chaos collapsed before her. She felt the slow burning fire of ten thousand lives bent against her—creatures so much of the master's that even now, when their liberation was at hand, they still fought to remain slaves.

But now they cringed as the citadel lay open and the powers that kept her at bay disintegrated.

She had known the power before, but never like this. Gone were her reservations, gone her fears. She was pure and simple, an arrow already loosed from its string, a storm striking a port, unstoppable, not in need of stopping.

Every weakness purged.

She laughed, and they died, either quenched by her will or gutted by her warriors, her beautiful, lovely warriors. And everything they were and might have been flowed from them and came back, and she knew she finally sat the sedos throne . . .

"It was worse this time, wasn't it?" Emily asked.

Anne held back from throttling the girl over the inanity of

the question, but only barely. Instead she took deep breaths and more of the Sefry tea.

"Is there anything I can do, Majesty?"

Yes, jump out the window, Anne thought.

"Hush, Emily," she said instead. "I'm not myself."

But maybe she was exactly herself. They had wanted her to take on the responsibility? Fine, she had. Now that she was queen, she would be queen, the queen they all deserved.

Emily backed away and didn't say anything.

A bell later Anne no longer felt as if a bed of ants had invaded her head.

"It's getting so easy," she told Nerenai. "I think of what I want to see, and I see it, or something to do with it. But then, the dreams. The clearer my visions come, the worse my Black Marys are. Is that the way it's supposed to be?"

"I think it must just be the price," the Sefry said. "You've separated the visions from the dreams, but they flow from the same source."

"I have to be able to tell them apart."

"True, for now. But when you are strong enough, you won't have to keep them apart. It will all be one."

Anne remembered standing before the gates as they shattered, the liberation of it, the joy.

"I hope so," she sighed. "Send Emily back in, will you? I want to apologize to her."

"She's just outside," Nerenai said. "With her brother. He's come to see you."

"All right," Anne said. "I'll see him."

The earl stepped through a moment later, Emily tugging at his hand. He was in a new-looking deep red doublet and black hose.

"Good of you to come, Cape Chavel," she said.

"Majesty," he said, bowing.

"Emily, my apologies for earlier."

"It's nothing, Majesty," Emily said. "It's your dreams, I know. I'm just here to serve you."

Anne nodded. "Cape Chavel, I don't think I've thanked you for saving my life."

"I'm glad you haven't," he replied. "It would only embarrass me. Especially as it was your saint gifts that got most of us out of there alive."

"Well, you'll have to be embarrassed. Thank you."

He actually blushed. He was a funny fellow, a bit like Sir Neil but a bit like Cazio as well.

Cazio. She had seen him free, with z'Acatto, but Dunmrogh fallen. And Hespero—but that part had been unclear. In fact, any vision concerning the praifec was unclear.

"How are you feeling?" the earl asked.

"Better. The leic will let me walk in a day or two. Nothing too badly hurt inside, I suppose."

"I'm relieved," the young man said. "Very relieved, in fact. I've seen such wounds before, and they are usually, ah, worse."

That gave her a bit of a pause. It had been rather bad, hadn't it? The shaft had been half in her. She had seen bodies cut open before. How could it have missed all of that? She should have died, shouldn't she?

She remembered the knight who wouldn't die, the one Cazio had been able to stop only by hacking the body into individual pieces. She remembered the other one in the wood near Dunmrogh.

And her uncle Robert, whose blood was no longer quick but who walked and did his evil anyway.

Oh, saints, she thought. *What have I become?*

CHAPTER FOURTEEN

✛

THE SINGING
DEAD

LEOFF STARED at the blank parchment, terrified.

It was not the sort of thing that usually frightened him.

Since childhood he had been able to hear music in his head: not just music he had experienced but music he imagined. Not only melodies but harmony lines, counterpoint, chords. He could compose a sinfonia for fifty instruments and hear each individual voice. Writing it down was an afterthought, a convenience, a way to share his music with the less fortunate.

But now he feared the music lurking in his skull. Every time he tried to think about the forbidden modes he had rediscovered while he was Robert's captive, he felt ill. How could he find an antidote when he couldn't face the disease?

"I saw my mother last night," a soft voice behind him said.

Startled, he turned to find Mery watching him from a few paces away.

"Did you?" he asked. Mery's mother was dead, of course, but one saw the dead now and then.

"In the well," she confirmed. "The old well in the back garden."

"You shouldn't be playing around there," he said. "It's dangerous."

"I wasn't playing," the girl said softly.

Of course you weren't, he thought sadly. *You never play anymore.*

Not that she ever had, much, but there once had been something of a little girl about her.

"Did your mother say anything?"

"She said she was sorry," Mery said. "She said she's been forgetting things."

"She must have loved you very much to come see you," he said.

"It's easier for them now," she said. "The music makes it easier."

"The music we made together? For Prince Robert?"

She nodded. "But they're singing it now, over there."

"The dead?"

"They sing and sing and don't even know they're doing it."

Leoff rubbed his mess of a hand against his forehead. "They're singing it," he muttered. "What is happening?"

"Why does it make you sad that the ghosts are singing?"

"It doesn't," he said gently. "Not in and of itself. But the song is bad, I think." He held up his hands. "Do you remember when I could play hammarharp with these?"

"Yes," she said. "The praifec had your hands broken."

"Right," Leoff said, shying from the memory of that pain. "And for a long time they didn't heal, but now they have. Something in the world is broken: The thing that separates life from death. Our song made it worse, and I think *their* song—what you hear them singing—is *keeping* it worse. Preventing things from healing."

"Your hands didn't heal right," she said. "You still can't play hammarharp."

"That's true," he conceded.

"What if the world heals, but not right?"

"I don't know," Leoff sighed.

She looked at the blank paper. "Is that what you're trying to do? Make music that will heal things?"

"Yes," he said.

"Will it heal me?"

"I hope so."

She walked over and leaned against him. "I'm sad, Leoff," she confided. "I'm always sad."

"I know," he replied.

"I wish I could help you, but every time I try to play something, I hurt people."

"I know."

"I sing for the ghosts, though, and sometimes play for them very quietly, when no one is around. Like at the well."

"Does that make you happy?"

"No. But it makes me feel a better kind of sad."

Rain had washed Haundwarpen that morning and left it smelling new, as if its cobbles and bricks had been laid that morning. It was a neat little town anyway, but today it almost looked like something that had been painted, so fresh were the yellow and rust trims on the houses, the blue sky held in street puddles, the copper roof of the clock tower. Artwair's estate was only a short walk from town, and Leoff enjoyed going there, especially with Areana, who despite having grown up five leagues away in Wistbirm, seemed to know everyone. He liked to watch her haggle for fruit, fish, and meat and knew by the curve and tautness of her neck when she was about to settle.

He enjoyed the details of the place, the door knockers in the shapes of fish and flowers and especially hands, the weather vanes on the rooftops, some shaped like banners, others like cranes or dragons, but especially hands.

And he loved the Rauthhat, the lively beer hall in the center of town. It was always alive with both locals and travelers, and there was usually a minstrel or two trying to get by to learn new melodies from.

He needed the quiet of the estate, but he needed this, too—life. Especially after his talk with Mery that morning.

So the three of them found an empty table at the Rauthhat, and Jen, the barmaid with red hair and a wide grin, brought them the brown beer the place served, mussels cooked in wine and butter, and some thick, crusty bread to sop up the liquid with. Not surprisingly, Leoff felt a little more cheerful. Areana sparkled like a jewel as she said her hellos, and Mery at least ate some of the mussels and sipped at the wine.

But that went only so far, and even in the Rauthhat things were a bit subdued. No one was talking about it, but everyone knew there was an army from Hansa just a few leagues away. Haundwarpen had a garrisoned keep and respectable walls, but determined armies had taken them before.

But for this night at least, Leoff joined everyone in the place in pretending nothing bad was afoot, and he let himself develop a bit of a glow. That all ended quite healthily in the arms of his young wife that night, when, as they lay damp and sleepy in the sheets, she kissed his ear and whispered, "I'm with child."

He cried with happiness and fear, and they fell asleep holding each other.

The next day found him staring at the blank sheet again, with—finally—the glimmer of an idea.

What if he could give the dead something else to sing?

A number of questions came around at that. Why were they singing the deadly music he had written? Would they sing anything using the forbidden modes?

Was Mery lying or deluded? That was an important one.

The old music had progressed in stages, coaxing and finally seducing the living toward death. Those who had died seemed to have expired by some act of sheer will, their hearts stopping because they—with all the strength and purpose in them—*wanted* their hearts to stop.

He remembered wanting it, too. He had almost surrendered everything.

Was it possible to write a backward progression? One that would make the dead yearn toward life? And if so, would that be the right thing to do? He pictured hordes of corpses rising, walking to the Rauthhat for beer, seeking the beds of their widows and widowers . . .

But at least he was thinking now.

He made beginnings, musical vignettes and fancies on the themes of life and death. He wrote melodies and countermelodies stripped of the modal accompaniments that would give them real power, able now to sense something of what they might do in his head.

It was with a start that he realized it was after midday and someone was calling—no, screaming—for him.

He flung open his door and hurried out of the house. Areana was running toward him across the clover, her long lace-trimmed blue skirt billowing. Her face was red from crying, and she was so hysterical, hiccups kept any sense from her words. But she was pointing, and he finally made it out: "Mery."

The girl was lying in the well, facedown. His first thought was that it wasn't Mery at all but just a little doll someone had dropped down there.

When the servants fished her out, he couldn't pretend that any longer. She wasn't breathing, and water poured from her mouth and nose.

The next few bells were a blur. He held Areana and tried to say comforting things while the servants changed the girl, cleaned her up, and put her on her bed.

"She was so unhappy," Areana said when things starting coming back into focus. "Do you think . . ."

"I don't know," he said. "She told me yesterday that she heard the dead singing at the well, that she saw her mother. I told her not to go there anymore, but I should have—I should have stopped her."

"It's not your fault."

"It's all my fault," he replied. "If I had never written that cursed music. If I had watched her more carefully . . ."

"You loved her," Areana said. "You gave her more than anyone else in her life. You showed her a little of what she was capable of."

He just shook his head, and she took him by the temples and kissed his forehead.

"Why are you crying?" Mery asked. She was standing in the doorway in the fresh dress they had put on her. Her hair was still wet.

PART III

✣

FEALTY AND FIDELITY

To pledge fealty, one must first know what it is, my lord. Thus, although a dog might be loyal in an unreflective fashion, it can never give you fealty. You are surrounded by dogs, my lord, and I am not one.
— THE TESTIMONY OF SAINT ANEMLEN AT THE COURT OF THE BLACK JESTER

I see. Well, dogs must eat.
— THE BLACK JESTER, IN RESPONSE

Decios mei com pid ammoltos et decio pis tiu ess
Tell me who you walk with, and I'll tell you who you are.
— VITELLIAN PROVERB

CHAPTER ONE

THE HELLRUNE

DAWN HADN'T yet shown her rosy hair when Alis gently woke Muriele.

"Berimund remembered his promise, apparently," she said. "A lady has come to fit you into a riding habit."

"Really," Muriele said, rubbing her eyes. "They hunt at night here?"

"No, but early. You'll want to look your best, won't you?"

"Doubtless. Very well. Give me a moment and let her in."

She went to the window. The air was cool, and most of the city below was a dark mystery, with only a few pin-pricks of light. The stars were diamonds and sapphires still. There was that faint smell of differentness in the air, or she might have been looking out of the Wolfcoat Tower at sleeping Eslen.

What was happening there? Was Anne well?

An image flashed through her mind of Anne at four, her hair in long red braids, scrunched up in the window of the chamber of Saint Terwing, dressed in boy's clothing, singing a little song to herself as she fiddled with a toy sword. Muriele hadn't meant to spy on her, but the girl hadn't seen her in the darkened hall, and she had watched her daughter for long minutes without knowing why.

She remembered Fastia with her long dark hair and prim humor and Elseny, never too bright but so sweet, so full of life.

Gone now. She'd once thought she heard Fastia whisper "mother" in Eslen-of-Shadows, but that had faded, and nothing remained of her beautiful girls but those things in their coffins.

But Anne had survived. Anne whose mischief often had crossed the line into caprice, who'd never thought herself pretty, who had tried to keep out of the way of the family and its affairs her whole childhood.

Anne, who had seemed at times to hate her. Anne, who probably needed her now more than she ever had.

Why had she left her only remaining daughter?

Maybe she couldn't bear not to.

A throat cleared softly behind her.

"I'm ready, thank you," she said.

The sun was a hand above the horizon when she met Berimund in the courtyard. The young man's face was flushed, and his eyes a bit glassy.

"I hardly believe you can walk," Muriele said. "I'm impressed."

"Practice," Berimund said. "Long practice from childhood."

"Well, I thank you for remembering your promise."

"About that," he said. "There's still time to change your mind."

"Why would I? I'm looking forward to meeting your father."

He nodded, looking as if he wanted to say something but not saying it.

"You make that riding habit look very nice," he said finally.

"Thank you," she replied. "It's an interesting dress."

The overskirt was cut rather like a knee-length hauberk, split up the front and back and made of wool felted into myriad patterns of serpents, falcons, and horsemen in muted golds, reds, and browns. It was sleeveless, so she wore a darker brown shirt beneath and numerous underskirts to protect modesty. Her calf-high buskins fastened at the top with a wolf's head and were laced over woolen stockings. It seemed silly and barbaric, and she had thought at first that the dress was an attempt to humiliate her.

But Berimund was attired in equally outlandish pants and a robelike coat.

"Interesting," he repeated, grinning. "I sense an understatement."

"I'm not familiar with the fashion, that's all."

"It's a recent one. My father has an interest in the ancient times, and his scholars have determined that our mountain tribes are more like our revered ancestors than we folk of the cities. We have therefore adopted some aspects of their dress."

"I see. I had no idea the mountain tribesmen wore Safnian silk shirts."

"Well, there have been a few adaptations, I'll allow."

"When I first came to Eslen, the men were favoring floppy woolen caps like the ones the Cresson brothers wore at the battle of Ravenmark Wold. It seems silly now."

"I wouldn't make that comparison," Berimund said stiffly. "Or call our fashions silly. Is it a bad thing to remember the virtues of our forefathers?"

"Not at all," Muriele said. "I wish you and your father were more reminded of them, as a matter of fact, since your forefathers helped in originating the ancient covenant of embassy."

Berimund actually seemed to wince slightly, but he didn't reply.

"Shall we go to the hunt?" he asked instead.

The horses were clad in similarly strange harness, and her mount was provided with a quiver of arrows and a spear with a broad leaf-shaped head.

So caparisoned, she and Berimund and six of his retainers rode out of Hauhhaim through Gildgards, a tidy neighborhood with so many gardens that it seemed almost like countryside. She asked Berimund about it.

"The merchant guilds are given land within the walls for farming," he explained. "In good times, they sell their surplus and profit from it. When Kaithbaurg comes under siege, their produce reverts to the king. Anyway, it makes the city more pleasant, don't you think?"

Muriele agreed, and not much later they passed through the Gildgards gate and into a countryside of vast barley fields and small villages. After perhaps a bell, their path took them into the lowlands around the river and finally into Thiuzanswalthu, Marcomir's hunting preserve, a vast, park-like evergreen wood. Soon they came upon a bustling camp sprawled out around a large tent. A group of horsemen and horsewomen were mustering like a small army, and they were all dressed much as Berimund and she were.

Berimund dismounted, took the reins of her horse, and led her over to the group.

Marcomir was a bit of a shock. She had met him once when she was fourteen and he had come to the Lierish court. At that time he had been in his fifties, but she still had been struck by the physical power that seemed to animate him, and she'd been a bit infatuated, taking every excuse to hover around while he was visiting.

Even now, she had a clear image of him in her mind.

That image was no longer accurate, however. Time had so shrunken and bent the monarch that she didn't recognize him until she was introduced. The color had been bleached from him. If she didn't know better, she would think him an albino. He trembled constantly.

But when she met his gaze, she glimpsed that old strength. It had been drained from his body and fermented, distilled, bittered there behind his eyes. As those pale orbs fastened on her, she felt as small as a barleycorn, and less significant.

"Father," Berimund said. "I introduce to you Muriele Dare, queen of Crotheny, queen mother to Empress Anne I."

Marcomir continued to stare at her.

"I've invited her to hunt with us."

"What do you want here, witch?" the old man asked. His speaking broke the spell; his watery, quavering voice could not match his gaze. "Have you come here to murder me? Is that your intention?"

Muriele sat straighter but did not see any reason to answer such a question.

"Father!" Berimund said. "Do not be so ill-mannered. This lady—"

"Hush, whelp," the king snarled. "I told you I would not see her. Why have you brought her here?"

"You said I could not present her in court," Berimund replied. "You said nothing about hunting."

"That's a hair in my beard," Marcomir snapped. "You understood my intent."

He swung back to Muriele. "But since you are here, let me spell clearly for you. Your shinecrafting daughter is not and will never be queen. She has unleashed horrors that no man should ever see and tilted the world toward doom. I will not be guiled with words; I will not be won with gifts or favors. This is the battle foretold, the great war against evil, the ansuswurth itself, and we—with the holy Church—will stand against your dark lady and your unhulthadiusen, and we will send you all back to the abyss."

As she watched the spittle drip down his chin, Muriele found that she had had enough.

"If I had known," she began, "that Your Majesty was a despicable liar who clothes himself in holy raiment to disguise the greedy, covetous ambition he has nursed for decades, I certainly would never have come here in hopes of a conversation. You are a loathsome thing, Marcomir. A better man would simply admit his avarice for power and control, but like a little child you make up stories to disguise your disgusting nature and in doing so become even more abhorrent. You dress your lords and ladies in homage to your beloved ancestors, but there is more honor in a single one of their rotting bones than in your entire body. Sing your churchish songs and play the harp of saintliness, but I know what you are, and so do you, and nothing you say or do, no host you muster, no war you win, will change that. I traveled to Hansa in hope of finding a man. Instead I find *this*. How sad and repulsive."

Marcomir had found color for his face somewhere. He trembled more violently than ever.

"My dear sister-in-law," a voice said behind her. "You still have that turn of phrase that so wins the hearts of men."

Only Muriele's anger kept her from screaming as she turned and saw Robert Dare sitting casually on a spotted mare, grinning from ear to ear.

Neil glanced up at the vast ceiling of the chapel and shook his head.

"What's that for, Sir Neil?" Alis asked.

"Why is it so big?"

"You don't find it beautiful?"

Neil traced his gaze up a narrow buttress that must have been twenty kingsyards high. Light colored its lean length, suffused through a dome pierced by a myriad of crystal portals that also illuminated statues of the winged saints, the lords of sky, wind, thunder, the sun, moon, stars, and planets. Many looked as if they actually were flying.

"It is. But it's also distracting. How can one pray properly among so much . . . so *much*?"

"The chapel in Eslen is easily as large and ornate."

"I know. I didn't understand that, either."

"It's not so in the islands?"

"No. The chapels are very plain and no bigger than necessary to kneel or be lustrated. I feel lost in a place this big."

"Well, I, for one, feel the need to pray. Will you wait for me?"

"Should we separate?"

"I don't see why not," she said. "If our escort wanted to do us harm, I don't imagine that would be a problem."

"I'll try to find Lier's fane in all of this, then," Neil said. "I'll meet you back here in the center."

Alis nodded and walked off, the *whisk-whisk* of her skirts echoing in the cavernous place.

Neil strolled past the saints of law and war, wondering if he ought to stop there, but the real need he felt was to find Lier, and so he continued to search, wondering what the saints thought of such ostentation. He supposed it depended on the saint. Some of them might be flattered.

It took a bit of time for him to realize the consistency
of the groupings. The saints of sky were above, those of the
qualities and affairs of men at eye level. That meant logi-
cally that he ought to look for a staircase down.

Once he knew what to search for, it wasn't hard to find.
Soon he was in a darker, quieter part of what was rightly a
temple rather than a chapel.

There he found the saints beneath the earth and there, at
last, the altar of Lier. The saint was carved from marble and
shown as a man rising up from a wave, his long hair and beard
blending with the foam.

The chapel on Skern had a rough image whittled from an
old piece of mast found as driftwood.

Neil knelt, placed two silver coins in the box, and began
to sing his prayer:

Foam Father, Wave Strider
You feel our keels and hear our prayers
Grant us passage on your broad back,
Bring us to shore when the storm's upon us,
I beg you now
Grant passage to my song.

It echoed weirdly through the halls, coming back to him
to form odd harmonies. He tried to focus beyond that, to fill
his mind with the presence of the saint, with the wild salt
spray, with the great eternal thing that was the ocean. And at
last he did, as the rhythm of his prayer ebbed and flowed,
and he felt the deeps beneath him once again. He prayed for
Alis and Muriele, for Queen Anne and his friends, for the
dead and the living.

When he was done, he felt better, and humbled. Who was
he to disparage what sort of chapel someone chose to build?

Before Muriele could find any words to meet Robert with,
Marcomir's voice began rattling in such rapid Hansan that
she couldn't have understood him if she was trying to,
which she wasn't. She was vaguely aware that Berimund

also was shouting. Robert's grin became somehow more wicked.

Marcomir's tone dropped, and he finally switched back to the king's tongue.

"You do not speak to me like that," he said very coldly. "It is a mistake you will regret."

Muriele kept her gaze on Robert as she replied.

"Here is the proof of your hypocrisy," she said. "You claim my daughter to be a witch, and yet you harbor this—this *thing* at your court. He is a fratricide and an abomination of nature. Cut him; see if he bleeds. Feel his heart; see if it beats. You will find it does not. But then, you already know that, don't you?"

"Oh, dear," Robert began. "I know we've had a bit of a tiff, Muriele, but really—"

"*Swiya!* Silence!" Marcomir snapped at Robert before turning his full fury on Muriele.

"I ought to kill you like a rabid bitch, right here and now," the king said very quietly. "You twist words, but I know the truth. You speak for *her.*" He came closer. "There will be no truce with evil, no compromise, and no peace. We will destroy your daughter and the heretics who follow her, or we will perish trying. In either case, no peace will ever be made, so I need never explain what happened to you."

"You would not," Muriele said.

"He wouldn't," Berimund replied.

"What do you know, whelp? What makes you so compliant? Have you lain with this mother of witches?"

"I have not," Berimund replied.

"Haven't you?"

"I just said that I have not," Berimund gritted out.

The old king straightened a bit. "Very well," he said. "Then you take her to Wothensaiw and strike off her head for me."

Berimund went pale. "Father, no."

"You are my son and my subject," Marcomir said. "As neither can you refuse me."

She actually heard him swallow. "Father, you're angry now. Take some time—"

"Berimund, before the Ansus and all my men, do this or you are not my son."

"It's not right, and you know it."

"I am king. What I say is right."

Muriele felt the tightness in her chest and realized her breath had been caught there for a while. As she let it out, she seemed to be drifting away with it, watching it all from above.

Berimund's head bent and then nodded.

When he looked up, his eyes were brimming. "I'm sorry," he said.

"Berimund—"

"Hush, Majesty."

As they led her off, she saw Robert moving his lips, perhaps taunting her, perhaps trying to tell her something. Either way, the glee on his face was obvious.

Neil and Alis were escorted back to Berimund's "rooms," where they were free to wander in what amounted to a small mansion. He walked about restlessly, learning the floor plan, finding the ways in and out.

Worrying about Muriele.

Alis had managed to charm one of the retainers into giving her an extended tour of the castle. He would rather remain here, where he could greet the queen when she returned.

Of course, it might be days. He wished he could have gone.

He found a window facing east and watched the Donau flow toward the sea.

Night came, and he reluctantly took to his bed.

As the door burst open, Neil was already on his feet and reaching for Battlehound. He shook back the Queryen webs from his eyes, trying to remember where he was and who might be coming at him with blinding lanterns.

"Lay your arms down," a voice commanded. "In the name of Marcomir, king of Hansa, give up that sword."

Neil hesitated. There were a lot of them. He had slept in his gambeson, which would afford a little protection, but he couldn't see how they were armored.

"I am Queen Muriele's man," he said. "I am here on embassy and claim the rights that come with that."

"You've no such rights, not anymore," the man behind the lanterns said. "Give up that weapon and come with us."

"I will see my queen first."

"She isn't here," the man replied.

Neil charged.

Something heavy came from behind the light and smacked him on the side of the head. He stumbled, and hands gripped his sword arm. He swung his left fist and connected with someone and was rewarded by a grunt. Then they were all over him, punching, pummeling, kicking. His hands were lashed behind his back, a blindfold was tied on his face, and they dragged him from the room and through the castle for what seemed like an infinity. Then they were out of doors for a while, then back inside, in a place where the air felt very heavy. He was finally pushed roughly to the ground and heard the slamming of a metal gate. The floor smelled like urine.

He lay there for a bit and then started working at the bonds. It didn't take much. They had gone on quickly and sloppily, and he'd kept tense as possible while they had tied them. Once they were off, he removed the blindfold.

It didn't help much. It was still utterly dark.

By feel he discovered that he was in a stone cell barely large enough to lie down in and not quite tall enough to stand in.

His heart picked up a bit. He'd grown up on the moors and mountains and open sea. Even spacious rooms with no windows made him feel trapped.

This—this would drive him mad right quickly.

He lay back down so that he couldn't feel any of the walls and tried to imagine he was on the deck of a ship, with the clouds rolling overhead.

He wasn't sure how long it was before he heard footsteps.

He both fastened on them and tried not to hope. What hope was there? That Alis had followed, killed whatever guards there were, and was ready to spirit him to safety?

Then he heard a feminine voice, and the ridiculous hope suddenly found roots.

It wasn't Alis, of course, but a large gray-haired woman dressed in a peculiar black robe. Four other women in similar habit and a large man who stank as much as the floor accompanied her.

"I am Walzamerka Gautisdautar, the king's inquisitor," she said. "You will not struggle. You will answer my questions. If you want any answers at all, if you want to live until tomorrow, you will hang on my every word, as if I were the mother who gave you life, for I am surely the one who can take it away."

"I'm at your mercy," Neil said. "Only tell me how my queen is."

"Your queen has been kidnapped," the woman said. "We are searching for her now."

"Kidnapped?"

"Yes, by Prince Berimund, if you can believe it."

"They were going hunting—"

"Indeed. Instead he abducted her. Do you have any idea why?"

"None. It makes no sense to me."

"To me, either." She paused. "You should know we've captured your little coven-trained spy, as well."

Neil didn't say anything to that.

"Very well," Walzamerka said. "Come along and mind your manners."

The inquisitor led him down past a line of cells like his, up some stairs, and into a long, narrow hallway. Then they went up two minor staircases and finally ascended a long winding one, so he reckoned he was in one of the towers.

They emerged at last into a room lit with gentle candlelight. He blinked, and for a moment he felt a strange movement of time, as if he had gone back months and was waking on a certain ship. The chamber was warm, wood-paneled, and close, the light dim and golden.

A woman stood there, clothed in a black gown. She wore an ivory mask that did not cover her mouth. Her hands were alabaster; her white hair was fine and came only as low as her throat.

And he knew her.

"Sir Neil," the woman said in her familiar, throaty voice.

"Take a knee, Sir Neil," the inquisitor said. "Take a knee before Her Highness, the Princess Brinna Marcomirsdautar Fram Reiksbaurg."

CHAPTER TWO

THE ANGEL

ROMMER ENSGRIFT backed away from Mery, who watched him go without much expression.

"A word outside," the thin, almost skeletal leic muttered to Leoff.

He followed obediently. Once on the stoop, Ensgrift mopped his forehead with a rag.

"I've heard stories," he said, his voice quivering. "Maryspellen. But I never thought there could be any truth."

Leoff couldn't think of anything to say or do until the leic composed himself, which he did in a moment.

"She's half-alive," he said.

"Half-alive," Leoff said, repeating the nonsensical phrase.

"Auy. Her heart beats, but very slowly. Her blood crawls through her veins. She should never be able to walk or talk like that, but she does, and I can only think that is because she is half-animated by something else, something other than breath."

"Something else?"

"I don't know. I set bones and give herbs for the gout; I don't deal with things like this. A demon? A ghost? This is for a sacritor, not me."

Leoff flinched. For years he hadn't had much interest in the organized Church. Since being tortured by one of its praifecs, he hadn't had any use for it at all. Even if he did, given the present climate in the holy institution, they more likely than not would burn her immediately. If he could even find a sacritor, which in Crotheny wasn't an easy thing these days, given the queen's ban on them.

"Isn't there anything you can suggest?" he asked.

The old fellow shook his head. "There's nothing natural about this. I can't see that anything good can come from it."

"Thank you, then, for your time," Leoff said.

The leic left in a fuss of relief, and Leoff reentered the house. Mery still was sitting where he had left her.

"I'm sorry if I frighten you," the girl said in a small voice.

"Do you know what happened to you, Mery?" he asked.

She nodded. "I was at the well. I thought I might see my mother again, but I didn't. There was an angel there instead."

"An angel." It was an old word, one that people didn't hear much outside of Virgenya. It was a sort of keeper of the dead, a servant of Saint Dun or Under.

"Mery, what did it look like?"

"I didn't see anything. I felt him all around me, though, and he talked to me. He told me I was on my way over anyway, that if I crossed to where the singing was, I could hear it better and even sing with them. He said I would be able to help you better, too."

"Help me?"

"Write your music. To heal the law of death."

"And then?"

"It hurt at first, when I first breathed in, but then it was all right. And then I went to sleep and woke up in my room."

That she spoke so matter-of-factly about the whole thing was the most awful part, the thing that was hardest for him to accept.

Was she like Robert, then? But the queen said that Robert had no heartbeat, that when stabbed he didn't bleed. How many varieties of the walking dead were there?

But the leic had said that Mery *wasn't* dead. She just wasn't fully alive, whatever that meant.

He was a composer. All he had wanted to do was write music, hear it played, live a decent life. His hiring by the court at Eslen had been a proud moment, the opportunity of a lifetime. But he had walked straight into a Black Mary of terror and death, and now this. Why had the saints put this on him?

But then Areana laid her hand on his, saying nothing, and he remembered that if he hadn't come to Eslen, he wouldn't have met her. And although he had written the most hideous thing of his life, he also had written the most sublime.

And he had befriended Mery and come to love her. Mending the law of death was an awfully big thing, too big for him to comprehend. The angel—whether it was real or Mery's own genius coming out again—knew that. The saints had given him something smaller to do, something real to him. They had suggested a way to save Mery or at least to make a start at it.

"Mery," he said. "Go find your thaurnharp. You and I are going to play."

And for the first time in a long while, she smiled at him.

CHAPTER THREE

✢

SUITOR

ANNE STOOD on the battlements, gazing across the Great Canal down on the fires of the enemy camps. They went to the horizon, it seemed, a bloody mirror of the clear, starry sky above.

The wind had a lot of autumn in it. The unseasonably long summer had relinquished its hold on the world in a nineday, and now winter was looking for a home.

Winter that might freeze flooded poelen and let armies walk across them. Had the Hellrune foreseen an early hard freeze? Was that what the Hansans were waiting for?

She had been out of bed in a nineday; the wound was completely healed, and she was feeling fine. For another ten days she had been watching the army growing below her. Artwair had it numbered at fifty thousand, with more marching from the north every day.

Her own forces were swelling, too, as the landwaerden sent her the cream of their men and the knights from the Midenlands arrived.

A glance around showed her she was alone.

I shouldn't feel bad about this, she thought. *They'll only kill my men, invade my kingdom. And I need the practice.*

Still, it felt odd. It was one thing when someone had a lance pointed at you; it was another—

No, she thought. *No, it isn't. It's the same.*

So she reached through the night and spread her senses out, feeling the flow of the twin rivers and the terrible beauty of the moon, concentrating, breathing deeply, holding herself together as the poles of the world sought to pull her apart and past and future melted into a single unmoving moment.

Then she was done, her heart faltering in her chest. She was drenched in sweat despite the chill in the air.

"There," she whispered. "Only forty-nine thousand of you now. Did you foresee *that*, Hellrune?"

Then she went down to her chambers and had Emily fetch her some wine.

Duke Artwair spread butter and soft cheese on a slab of brown bread and took a healthy bite of it. Anne dolloped clotted cream on a spongy slice of sweet mulklaif and nibbled at it. With the morning sun peeking in through the eastern window and a pleasant coolness in the air, Anne was enjoying breakfast for the first time in a long while.

"Your Majesty looks well," Artwair commented. "You must have slept better last night."

"I slept all night," she said. "I can't remember the last time that happened."

"And the nightmares?"

"None."

He nodded. "I'm glad to hear that."

"Thank you for your concern," she replied.

She tried one of the rather large blackberries on her plate and was surprised at the tart, sweet flavor. Had it been so long since she had had a blackberry?

"Something happened in the Hansan camp last night," Artwair said.

She thought it rather abrupt. "I'm sure a great many somethings happened," she said.

"A particular something happened to a great many people," Artwair said. "About a thousand men died."

"Well, that's good, isn't it?"

"Your Majesty—" He stopped and looked uncomfortable.

Anne reached for another berry. "If you had a siege engine that could reach them across the Dew, would you use it? Would you be bombarding them even now?"

"Yes."

"Well, then," she said, and popped the fruit in her mouth.

His frown was small but obvious. "Why not just kill them *all* in their sleep, then?"

"I can't yet. It takes too much out of me. But I think I can kill another thousand tonight. I'll try for more, in fact."

"Majesty, the Hansans claim their cause is a holy one and say you are a shinecrafter and all manner of things. This sort of thing only gives that weight."

"My power comes from the saints," Anne said. "That is why the Church fears me, and that is why they spread these lies about me. Was Virgenya Dare a shinecrafter? She was not, and neither am I. My people know that. The Hansans choose not to believe it, but so what? They made this war long before they had me as an excuse, and you know that as well as anyone else."

"I do, but it's our allies I'm thinking of."

"Allies? You mean Virgenya. Everyone else is pretty much off the fence by now, I think."

He tilted his head in agreement.

"You're a warrior, Artwair. Killing for you comes from a sword or spear. It seems natural to you. What I do does not, and that bothers you. But the dead, in the end, are still dead. Do you think I want to kill anyone? I hate the idea. But I don't intend to lose this war. Hansa may have started off with the upper hand, but that's not going to last. If a thousand or more of them die every day before the first arrow of this siege is even loosed, how long will they remain squatting on our property?"

"It may incite them to attack sooner."

"Before they're ready."

"Madame, they are ready."

"No. They have a flotilla coming down the Warlock. It's about three days away. Forty barges, maybe ten thousand men, and a lot of supplies. They will disembark at Bloen and cut us off from Eslen. Or at least that is their plan."

"Why didn't you tell me this?"

"I just saw it this morning."

"I thought you said you didn't dream last night."

"I didn't," Anne said. "I don't dream my visions any-more. I'm in better control of them."

"So, then these new forces played no role in your decision to exterminate a thousand men."

"No," she said, unable to prevent a little grin, "but it might still have that effect."

"Might?"

"They'll try to cross the river tomorrow morning," she said.

"You saw that, too?"

She nodded and pushed the bowl toward him. "Try these blackberries. They're very good."

Artwair looked more than anything, puzzled.

"What's the matter?" she asked.

"You just seem . . . Are you really well? You don't seem yourself."

"Why do people keep saying that?" Anne asked. "You re-ally want the old me back, the girl who was too selfish to look past her own nose? I've feared this power of mine for too long, only using it when I absolutely had to, out of fear or anger. But the saints *want* me to use it. Do you think it's an accident that I didn't have nightmares last night? It's keeping it inside that's made me ill. Now I feel fine. I'm still Anne, Cousin. I haven't been gobbled up from the inside by some booygshin or ghost. I know; I worried about that my-self. I even thought I might be a walking dead, like Uncle Robert, until last night. I'm not. I heal fast because the saints will it, but my heart beats and my blood flows. I get hungry and thirsty. I eliminate, sweat, cough. No, all that's happened is that I've learned to accept what I am rather than be afraid of it. And that is good for Crotheny, I promise you."

Artwair took another bite of his bread. "Thank you for your candor, Your Majesty. And now I suppose I had better see to that river crossing."

He lifted himself from the chair, bowed, and left. When he was gone, she signaled for Nerenai and Emily to enter.

"Do either of *you* think there's something wrong with me?"

Nerenai shook her head. "No. As you said, you're starting to come to terms with your power. You rely less and less upon the arilac, yes?"

"I see less of her," Anne said. "And when I do see her, she seems . . . faded."

"Did you—" Emily began, but then stopped and put her hands in her lap.

"What, Emily?"

The girl looked back up. "Did you *really* kill a thousand men?"

Anne nodded. "Does that bother you?"

"Bother me? It's amazing. The saints really have touched you. It's like you're Genya Dare reborn, come to lead her heroes against the Scaosen, to tear the doors off their palaces and grind them into the dust."

"I don't quite have *her* power," Anne said.

"No, but you will," Nerenai said.

"My uncle Charles is so stupid," Emily said. "He said you were just a silly girl. If he could see—"

"Wait," Anne said. "Your *uncle* Charles? Do you mean Charles IV?"

Emily's hand flew to her mouth, and she reddened.

"I see," Anne said. "This is what I get for not learning those tedious royal lineages, I suppose."

"I shouldn't have said that," Emily said.

"On the contrary," Anne said, "you should have told me that long ago. And so I think now you should tell me anything else you might have failed to mention, or I might become very, very cross. Do you understand?"

"Yes, Majesty."

Anne stood on the battlements of the south tower again the next morning, clad in a suit of black plate trimmed with gold. She left the helm off so that she could see better.

The view was wonderful. Directly below her was the Yaner Gravigh, the northernmost canal of Newland, hewing from east to west. A wall four kingsyards high stood on the southern birm and went off beyond sight in either direction.

Beyond were the vast downs of Andemuer, gently rolling hills tilled and terraced by a hundred generations of plowmen.

The host of Hansa was a bit of an eyesore, but at the moment, even that was beautiful to her because for almost a league the canal was clogged with their wrecked and burning boats.

They had come before dawn, dragging light watercraft from behind the hills. In a few places they had tried to float bridges, but those had fared no better. Artwair reckoned that more than three thousand Hansans had been slaughtered in the attempt, falling to siege engines and archers massed upon the birm wall.

The cost to Crotheny could be counted on a pair of hands.

"You sent for me, Majesty?"

Anne didn't turn, but she nodded. "Good morning, Cape Chavel."

"A glorious victory," he ventured.

"I'm very pleased," Anne said. "Of course, they'll try again tomorrow, two leagues upstream."

"Why not farther?" he asked. "I understand they need to reduce Poelscild, but why try to cross here, under our engines?"

"More than two leagues upstream the ground around the river gets low and swampy, or so they tell me," Anne replied, "and beyond that they would have the Dew to reckon with. South, we've flooded the poelen nearest the canal, so they would cross it only to find a lake."

"But the force coming on the Warlock—"

"You'll meet them," Anne said. "You, Kenwulf, and Cathond and his light horse. You'll stop them, won't you?"

"Yes, Majesty."

"Cape Chavel?"

"Yes, Majesty?"

"Why didn't you tell me you're third in line for the Virgenyan throne?"

For a moment he just stood stupidly. Then he clasped his hands behind his back.

"Ah," he said. "You've been checking up on me."

"No," Anne replied. "Emily let slip that your uncle is Charles. Once that was out, I made her tell me everything. She mentioned, for instance, that you actually came here to propose marriage."

She leveled her gaze on him.

"Yes," he replied, looking abashed. "Yes, that is the case."

"I don't like being deceived," Anne said. "Explain yourself, please."

The earl tilted his head apologetically. "My uncle sent that insulting delegation as a negotiation," he said. "He reckoned you would be desperate, and his lack of respect would make you more so. My role was to offer a marriage in return for the troops you've requested."

"So you've lied about several things. You didn't come here to fight for me."

"No," he said, "but I decided to the moment you spoke. You were right, and my uncle was wrong. I was too ashamed of my original mission to mention it to you, and the only deception I've engaged in has been to prevent that shame from being exposed. I can't tell you how sorry I am, Your Majesty."

Anne nodded, not quite sure what she should feel.

"If you had made the proposal—and if I had accepted— would your uncle have sent troops?"

He shrugged. "I don't know, to tell you the truth."

"Well, let's find out," Anne said. "Send word that you've made your proposal and I received it favorably. Court me, and I will discover what sort of man your uncle really is."

"You're going to answer one lie with another?" the earl asked.

"It's the same lie," Anne said. "I just want to expose the whole thing. Anyway, would it be so difficult for you to feign interest? I know I'm not the most beautiful of women, but I am the queen."

Cape Chavel's eyebrows went up. "I have no need to feign interest, Majesty. I've never met a woman like you, and I'm sure I never will again. And it's only because you *are* queen that I haven't told you that. I'm dead in love with you, Queen Anne."

As he spoke, an odd warmth suddenly spread down her limbs.

"You needn't overdo it," she said, suddenly not so sure of herself. "No one is listening."

"I'm telling you the truth," he said.

"Be careful, Cape Chavel," Anne said. "I've been badly betrayed by someone who claimed to love me. I found out he was merely using me for political gain. I won't feel like that again, ever. So be honest."

He stepped closer, and suddenly he seemed to enclose her, blotting out everything else around her.

"I am honest," he said. "I refused to court you for political reasons, remember? And I won't pretend to court you now when you so plainly have no interest in me. So let us keep things as they are: you my queen and I one of your knights."

Anne thought she had a reply, but she lost it somehow. She had believed she'd hit on a clever political ploy, but it was suddenly very much out of control. The earl sounded *hurt*. Was he really serious?

"May I go, Majesty?" Cape Chavel said stiffly.

"Yes, go," she said.

She heard his footsteps start off. "Wait," she said.

The footfalls stopped, and she felt a giddy sort of fear.

"I never said I didn't care for you," she said softly.

"Do you?"

She turned slowly. "Since we've met, I've been very . . . busy," she said. "I've had a lot on my mind."

"I know," he said.

"And as I've told you, I've been hurt before." She paused. "Not just once. And there is—was—someone else. I admire you, Cape Chavel. I like you very much."

"That isn't love."

"I've no idea what love is," Anne said. "But you're judging me too quickly. You're guessing. You will never know if I can love you unless you court me, and neither will I."

He held her gaze well past the point Anne found comfortable, which amounted to around three heartbeats.

"Majesty, now I have to ask if you are serious."

She suddenly wanted to make a joke out of the whole thing, explode the moment as she had done with Cazio and back away.

And what about Cazio? She was sure he had feelings for her. If something happened to Austra—

No, she couldn't think like that.

And so she nodded in response to his question.

"Then I will court you," he said softly. "And hope I do not regret it. How should I start?"

"Ideally? Long walks in the gardens, riding, picnics, flowers and poetry. But as we're in the middle of a war and I'm sending you off to fight this afternoon, I think a kiss might be nice."

And so there was a kiss, and it *was* nice, and another, which was *very* nice, and so they spent the rest of the morning as the boats finished burning.

CHAPTER FOUR

FEND MAKES
AN OFFER

ONE OF THE WYVERS folded its wings and dropped, hitting the man riding ahead of Aspar in the middle of the back with its wicked spurs. The fellow went flying over his mount's neck, and the horse reared in terror. So did Aspar's mount, and he cursed the loss of Ogre one more time. Ogre would rear only to attack.

Trying to control the beast with one hand, he jabbed his

spear at the wyver with the other. To his satisfaction, he poked a hole right through its wing.

It screeched, hopped out of reach, and leaped skyward. The wounded wing still caught plenty of air, and in heart-beats it was up with its four brethren.

The attack had come as a surprise, because for bells the things had just been circling, following them. Fend's eyes in the heavens.

When they reached Ermensdoon, the flying creatures broke off their attack and went even higher in their coiling paths.

"We don't have long," Aspar said. "They'll be coming."

"We almost beat them," Emfrith muttered. His face was still tear-streaked. "If we could just find some way to kill the basil-nix. I hear Duke Artwair killed one down in Broogh, with fire."

"Maunt they may have another fox behind their ears," Aspar pointed out.

Emfrith nodded. "I won't argue with you again. We'll form up here only as long as it takes to evacuate the castle. Then we're off, wherever you say."

Aspar felt happier than he ought to at Emfrith's capitulation. It was the geos again.

Aspar knelt in the brush and looked down across the fields, gritting his teeth against the ache in his leg.

Leshya sighed almost silently and shook her head from side to side.

"I could have scouted alone," she whispered.

Aspar didn't answer. Fend and his monsters were just appearing over a low hill about ten bowshots away. He glanced at the sky, but he and the Sefry seemed to have been successful in sneaking away from the larger party without a winged escort.

There were more sedhmhari than ever. At this distance he couldn't make out what all of them were, but it looked as if there were at least twenty.

"Well, that's that," Aspar said.

They made their way back over the ridge to their mounts and turned them south.

"That should convince Emfrith not to fight again," Aspar said.

"Aspar, where are we going?" Leshya asked.

"A place in the Mountains of the Hare."

"The Vhenkherdh?"

He nodded curtly.

"But you'll lead Fend right to it."

"If it's really Fend back there. Anyway, Fend's been there. He nearly murdered me there. It's no secret to him." He glanced over at her. "That's where you wanted to go, isn't it?"

"Yes. But . . ."

"What?"

"The child Winna carries is yours, yes?"

"Yah."

"And Winna was waurm-poisoned. She nearly died of it, as I understand."

"Yah."

"Then you must know that what she carries probably isn't human."

"I cann that, too," he snapped.

"But she doesn't, does she? She doesn't know what we know, and you haven't told her."

"No."

"Why?"

"Because I can't."

Leshya's eyes thinned to violet slits. "Can't or won't?"

"Can't," he replied, hoping she would get it.

But she just blinked and took her horse to a trot. "We'd better catch them," she said.

They caught up with Winna and the rest a few bells later.

"They're half a day behind us," Aspar told them. "They've also got reinforcements: twice as many beasties as before the bridge fight."

"Sceat," Emfrith said. "Where do they come from?"

"They're everywhere now," Leshya said. "He calls, and they come."

"Why don't we leave the road?" Emfrith suggested. "With those wagons of his, he'd have a hard time following us."

"He's already slower with the wagons," Aspar said. "When we leave the road, he'll abandon them, and then they'll be a lot faster. So I think we stay between the ruts as long as we can."

"Why hasn't he already done that?" Winna asked. "The greffyns could catch us, murder us all, and be back at the wagons in a bell."

Yes, but Fend doesn't want all of us dead, Aspar thought. *Me, maybe, but not you. If he sent the greffyns, they'd slaughter everyone.*

"I can't say what's in Fend's mind," he said. "For whatever reason, he doesn't seem to be in a big hurry. I reckon he doesn't think we can get away."

"My concern isn't just for us," Emfrith said. "There's a village less than a league up ahead, Len-an-Wolth. We can't lead an army of monsters through there."

"He's right, Aspar," Winna said.

"Werlic," he agreed. "We'll go around, then. I'll ride ahead and warn them, though. Fend's booygshins will want to feed, and they'll probably find the town, anyway."

"Aspar," Winna pleaded, "let Emfrith send someone. You just got back."

"I'd better do it myself," Aspar said, and kicked his horse into motion.

Every moment he spent away from Winna was a moment he didn't have to lie to her.

As it turned out, they needn't have worried about Len-an-Wolth; the little market town was already empty of human life, although he saw plenty of bones scattered about. What had killed them? Slinders, bandits, monsters? It didn't matter to them, did it?

It had never been a big place. There was a smallish church, thirty or so houses, and a little tavern whose clapboard proclaimed it "Sa Plinseth Gaet." Underneath the lettering was a picture of a goat dancing on its hind legs and holding a beer in one forehoof.

He looked inside and in a few of the houses, calling out as he did so, but there was no answer. The buildings were all fine except that a few of the roofs needed to be rethatched.

He was just getting ready to go when a familiar voice called his name.

Fend.

He put an arrow on the string and peered around the corner. It was Fend, all right, with one of his Sefry companions and three beasts that would have looked something like a combination of wolf, horse, and man if they hadn't been scaly.

Well, sceat, he thought. *I should have kissed Winna goodbye.*

"There you are," Fend said brightly. "Somehow I just knew you would have to warn the villagers. I'm glad I was right. Bareback on a wairwulf is fast, but a little rough."

Aspar drew back for the shot, but then he felt something sharp prick him in the back.

"No," a soft voice said.

Aspar lowered the weapon, then dropped it. In the same motion he let his palm hit the hilt of the feyknife.

It was only half-drawn before another hand caught his, and then an arm came around his neck. Snarling, he stomped back with his heel, hoping to break an ankle or knee, but he was suddenly on the ground with his face pressed in the dirt, one arm twisted behind his back, and a shin on his neck. He felt the dagger slide out of its sheath and then the ax come out of his belt. Then his arm was released, and the pressure vanished.

He came back to his feet, but the fellow had backed away, carrying his arms.

"I'm not here to kill you, Aspar," Fend said. "At least not right away. We need to talk, you and I."

"Everyone wants to talk to me today," Aspar said, trying

to keep his rage bottled so that he could think. What was Fend playing at?

"Yes, but I have to manage to talk to you without one of us killing the other, which is quite a trick."

"I don't see what we have to talk about," Aspar said.

"About this whole thing," Fend replied. "There's no reason for us to fight."

"Really? What about that business back at the bridge?"

"Not much of a chance for talking, was there? Your friends just charged us. Didn't you expect us to fight back?"

"You've been chasing me."

"Yes and no. After the battle at the Witchhorn, I sent some of my servants out to hunt you. I wasn't with them until just before the fight at the bridge the other day. Things have changed. I no longer mean you any harm."

"Last time we met, you tried to bloody execute me. If it hadn't been for Leshya, you would have. Now you expect me to trust you?"

"You and I have taken turns trying to kill each other for twenty years, Aspar. I'm sure neither of us really remembers why."

"Sceating saints, Fend; you killed my wife."

"Fine, I guess you do remember. But it wasn't anything personal; I didn't do it to spite *you*. I always rather liked you, Dirt."

Aspar flinched at the old nickname but tried not to let it show.

"What do you want, Fend?" he asked.

"The same thing you want."

"And what is that?"

"To find the Vhenkherdh and restore life to the world. To make a new Briar King."

That was so ridiculous that Aspar felt as if he were choking. The words wouldn't come out for a moment.

"You murdered the Briar King, you sceat!" he finally managed.

"Well, yes—but he was quite mad. He was going to bring

back the forest, sure, but he was also going to kill us all. He wasn't the Briar King we needed."

"Oh, I wat not. What sort do we need, then?"

"Your child, Aspar. Your child can be the new Briar King—or Queen, I suppose, if it's a girl. You're already geosed to take her there; I'm just here to help."

"My child?"

"I know Winna's carrying your baby, Aspar. The witch knew it when you met her. Your child can heal the world; isn't that what you want? To fix your precious forest?"

"I do. I just don't believe *you* do. And I don't trust the Sarnwood witch. I know where the monsters come from, Fend. I know they're born from normal animals touched by the poison in the world, the poison your beasts spread around. Winna was sick from the woorm. Grim's balls, the woorm *you* were riding. That means there's a monster in there. Now, why would the Sarnwood witch want one of her monsters to be the new lord-o'-the-forest?"

"To heal the world. To take the poison out of it, to make it so her children are born without venom. She's old, Aspar, very old. She kept this world a garden until the Skasloi betrayed her. It was the old Briar King that kept things this way, divided, one nature fighting against another. Your child can bring it all together, make it whole again. It won't be a monster; it'll be a saint, the greatest saint of all."

"If all that's so, why did your wyver attack Winna?"

"Wyvers are stupid," Fend replied. "It didn't know who it was attacking!"

"What about all that business with the fanes, the murders at Cal Azroth? How does that all work in?"

"That was something else," he said. "Hespero hired me for that. That was just murder for money, really. But then he sent me to get the woorm from the Sarnwood. Don't know what he wanted, don't care. The witch showed me the truth, my destiny—to be the Blood Knight."

"Yah. Then why did you try to kill me?"

"The witch didn't tell me we would need you. Maybe she didn't even know at the time; she's strange like that. And, well, I hate you. You hate me. If I don't kill you, you'll kill me. But I'm willing to set that aside for now, and you should be, too."

"You're mad."

"I feel better than I ever have in my life," Fend said. "I've actually got a cause, something to fight for other than my own greed and desires. You ought to be able to understand that."

"You're a liar, Fend. I don't believe anything you've said, and I certainly won't ride with you."

"That's too bad," Fend said. "It'll make it harder."

"Harder to do what?"

"To protect you. There are those who will try to stop you."

"Who?"

"I'm not sure about that. But you'll need my help. I reckoned it would be easier if we worked this out now. I see we can't. But the geos will take you there anyway, and I'll follow and help you whether you like it or not."

Fend mounted the wairwulf, which bristled but let him on. His companions got up on their beasts.

"See you soon," Fend said, taking hold of a rope that necklaced the monster.

Then they bounded off, long legs reaching with incredible swiftness, much faster than a horse. The Sefry who had Aspar's weapons dropped them to the ground. Aspar rushed toward them, scooping up the bow and his quiver, but before he could put missile to string, they were out of sight. He limped to a stuttering run to get to where his horse was wandering, mounted, and gave her his heels, screaming at the top of his lungs as red rage tinted everything.

Whipping around one of the houses, he nearly collided with another rider and for one savage instant thought he would get his fight. But before he let the shaft fly, he realized it was Leshya.

"Fend," he told her, trying to get his skittish mount back under control.

Leshya's eyes were wide and her mouth was scrunched up as if she had just tasted something sour.

"You're alive," she said.

"Yah. Surprised?"

"I just saw Fend and two of the Vaix riding hellhounds or something, so yes."

The horse was over its panic now, and he started off again.

"You won't catch them," Leshya yelled after him. "And you don't want to."

"Oh, yah, I do," he muttered.

Leshya was right, of course. The wairwulves were much faster than horses, and besides, his mount kept shying from their scent.

When he finally gave up, Leshya came trotting up alongside him.

"Why did you come, anyway?" he asked.

"I had a bad feeling," she said. "I get them sometimes, and when I do, I'm usually right. What were they doing, Fend and the Vaix?"

"They were looking for me."

"Good thing they didn't find you."

"Oh, they found me," he said. "Fend offered to escort us through the King's Forest. He thinks we'll need his help."

"His help with what?" Leshya asked, her tone larded with incredulity.

"I don't know," he replied. This time he wasn't sure the lie wasn't his own. It felt awfully natural.

"Really?" she asked, the tone deepening. "He was trying to *kill* you last time you saw him."

"That's true. I pointed that out to him."

"Well?"

"He said things had changed."

"What things?"

"It's just another of his tricks," Aspar said. "I'm not sure what he's up to, but it's nothing good."

"Well, he wants you alive for something, or you wouldn't be, right?"

"Werlic."

She shook her head. "Why would the Blood Knight want you alive?"

"He didn't really say."

"Curious."

How long was she there? he suddenly wondered. *Did she hear the whole conversation? Is she testing me?*

Or was she, after all, with Fend?

Either way, he should probably kill her. He reached for the feyknife casually, as if he were just going to take the reins.

CHAPTER FIVE

✦

AUSTRA

"THAT'S LIKELY IT," Cazio breathed, gesturing with his nose toward the long coil of the Old King's Road they could see from the cobbled-together treehouse z'Acatto referred to as their "mansion." There, a carriage with an armed escort was making its way along the ruts. The driver, Cazio could make out, wore the gold, black, and green livery of the duchess of Rovy, which was Anne's household title.

"So it'll be a fight," z'Acatto sighed.

Cazio was starting to ask what the old man meant when the scene suddenly shifted into finer focus.

The escort wore the orange and dark blue of the knights of Lord Gravio, one of the Church's military orders.

"She's already been captured," he murmured.

"There's no proof she's even in there," z'Acatto said. "It may be some fat sacritor or a half dozen soldiers."

"It might be," Cazio agreed, "but I only *see* five. I'll worry about any in the carriage later."

"Five men in full armor mounted on war steeds," z'Acatto pointed out. "One or two would be plenty."

"Yes, I've learned my lesson there," Cazio said.

"I doubt that."

"No, I have. One doesn't fence such men; one hits them with something heavy, yes? So what do we have that's heavy?"

He searched for an answer to that. The mansion was nothing more than a sort of blind they had constructed where the branches of two large trees came together. It was about ten pareci off the ground. They had some empty wine carafes and a few sticks. That was about it. Given the distance, they still had a little time, but not more than a quarter of a bell.

Z'Acatto took another drink of their last bottle of Matir Mensir, and for a moment Cazio thought he was going to sleep. Instead, he sighed and wiped the back of his hand across his stubbled mouth.

"I have an idea," he said.

As Cazio stepped into the road in front of the small cavalcade, he was still not certain that z'Acatto's idea was a good one, but it was the only one they had.

"Halt there," he shouted.

The knights lifted their visors, and he could see their astonishment.

"What's the matter with you?" one of them, a fellow with a reddish mustache, asked.

"I heard knights of Lord Gravio were on this road," he said. "I said to myself, 'Has the knight of Gravio ever been born that I couldn't beat wearing nothing more than my skin and a sword?' And the answer, of course, was no. But then I wondered, 'What if there were two or three of them? I might break a sweat.' But I'm thinking four of you might have a chance."

"Get out of the road, you naked idiot," another of the knights said. "By that popinjay's sword you wield, you're no knight."

"Let me get this perfectly clear," Cazio said, leaning on

Acredo. "You're afraid to fight a naked man. You understand I was saying you can all come at me at once, right?"

"Knights of Gravio only battle knights, you slack-jawed pig sodomizer," the mustached man said. "All others have two simple choices: stand aside or be cut down like honorless dogs."

"I heard that about you brave, brave fellows," Cazio said. "Heard you mostly kill women because headless lovers can't complain of your impotence."

"Leave him be," one of the fellows in the back said. "He's clearly mad."

"There's only so much I can hear before I must act," Mustache gritted. "But I make allowances. Stand aside."

Cazio stepped a little closer. "If it's my words that are the problem, let me use a language more apt to you fellows."

He sent an arc of urine in their direction.

That did it. Mustache howled, and two of his fellows broke after him, all drawing broadswords.

Cazio turned and ran as fast as he could. That wasn't as fast as a horse could run, of course, but he could reach his top pace first.

As he dashed around the bend that took the road into the forest, he glanced back and saw they were gathering speed, their swords held low and cocked, ready to decapitate him.

He ran another three pareci, hurtling around another curve, and then turned to get on his guard.

The three horsemen thundered around the bend. Mustache had on a fierce smirk and started to shout something, but at about that time, he and his brothers hit the rope Cazio had strung between two trees. It caught Mustache right across the face and one of his companions at the gorget. The third had seen the trap and tried to bring his sword up to cut it, so he was caught by the forearm. All three went flipping backward off their mounts.

Only one of them got back up, and that was the man who had brought his arm up. Cazio didn't wait for him to find his feet but walked up to him quickly, opened the visor that had snapped shut when he fell, and smashed Acredo into his nose. As the man screeched, Cazio lifted the helm off completely and hit him again. He went sprawling back.

"I gave you cowards a chance to fight with honor," Cazio said. "It was more than you deserved, more than you offered me, and so here we are, with you forcing me to this."

Then he turned and sped back toward the carriage, where he found z'Acatto standing over the fourth knight, who was prone on the ground.

"Are they dead?" z'Acatto asked.

"One of them, maybe. I didn't stay to find out."

"We should finish them," the old man said.

Cazio shook his head. "I don't murder men who can't fight back. You know that. You taught me that."

"That's in a duel. In war there are times you do what you have to."

"I'm not at war," Cazio said. "I'm only trying to save my friends."

"You have to be practical."

"I've been plenty practical enough for today," Cazio said. "Let's just get on with it."

"Have it your way, then," z'Acatto said. "I'll just walk over and see if they have anything useful on them."

"Oh, let's do that together," Cazio replied.

"You don't trust me?"

"On the contrary, I trust you to be you. Anyway, what if there *are* fifteen soldiers in the carriage? I'll need your help."

Z'Acatto shrugged and wiped his sword on the dead knight's tabard. Then the two of them approached the carriage. The driver was gone, apparently having run off.

Each door had a little barred window, but Cazio didn't see anyone peering through it, and his heart sank. What if they already had done away with her?

He grasped the handle and pulled, but the door remained fast.

"There's no lock out here," z'Acatto observed. "But there *is* someone in there."

"Austra?" Cazio asked, rapping on the door. "It's me, Cazio."

There wasn't any answer. He rapped again, harder. Cursing now, he started to pound on the door.

"Step back," z'Acatto said.

Cazio did so and saw that the swordmaster had the dead knight's heavy blade.

"Careful," Cazio cautioned.

The first swing shattered the glossy varnish, the second sent splinters flying, and the next caved in the panel. Using the tip of the weapon, z'Acatto pushed the cracked wood aside so that they could see in.

Austra was there, pale, unmoving, and gagged. A fiftyish man with faded blond hair slumped next to her, eyes open but unfocused. His nose and mouth had drooled blood onto his chin.

"Austra!" Cazio shouted, reaching through the hole to locate the bolt on the inside. He found it, drew it, and yanked the door open.

He touched her face and found it warm. An angry red mark on her cheek and left eye told of a bruise to come in the next day or so. Her dark saffron gown was slashed and bloody, revealing red-smeared thighs.

"Austra!"

He put his ear to her heart and to his relief felt it beat.

"We need to go," z'Acatto said. "The Church is all over these roads. We'll take the carriage and hide someplace."

"Right," Cazio muttered, still trying to get some sort of response from Austra.

"Help me get the man out."

Reluctantly, Cazio reached over and opened the bolt on the other door. When z'Acatto started pulling, he began to shove.

The fellow coughed, and blood spewed from his nose.

"Diuvo!" Cazio swore. "He's alive."

"So he is," z'Acatto said.

Snarling, Cazio reached for Acredo.

"No," z'Acatto said, holding up his hand. "I'll drag him over in the woods, see if he has anything useful on him. Yes?"

Cazio balanced on his rage for a moment. He looked back at Austra. The blood on her was coming mostly from a series of shallow cuts on her thighs.

"Why don't you do that," he said softly.

Cazio dressed quickly and found several skins of white wine liberally mixed with water. As they bumped along in the carriage, their own horses on trotters behind them, he washed Austra's cuts as best he could. None were particularly deep, but it looked as if the fellow had been cutting a methodical diamond pattern on her. He made another search for any deeper wounds but couldn't find any.

He was starting on her second leg when she suddenly sucked in a huge breath, then screamed, her eyes wide open and brimming with terror.

"Austra, Austra *mia errentera*."

She beat at him with her hands, still screaming, probably unable to hear him over her panic. He let her flail away until she had to pause for breath.

"Austra, it's Cazio!" he said urgently.

The look in her eyes shifted to dazed puzzlement.

"Cazio?"

"It's me, *errentera, min loof*. Porcupine."

"Cazio!" she gasped. Then she looked down at her bare legs, and a huge sob heaved out of her, and then another. She kept gesturing at her wounds and trying to talk, but she half strangled on whatever she meant to say.

Cazio wrapped his arms around her and pulled her face onto his shoulder.

"It's not bad," he whispered in her ear. "It's not bad. Just a few little cuts, that's all. You're going to be fine."

He held her like that for a long time before she could talk.

He got the story out of her in drabs. Her carriage and guard had been set upon by knights, many more of them than Cazio and z'Acatto had dealt with. They had slain her guard to a man.

"There were two leaders," she said. "The . . . the man you found in the carriage and a younger fellow with a little beard. They seemed to know who I was, or— I think they thought I was Anne."

"Why do you say that?" Cazio asked gently.

"I don't know. Something one of them said. Cazio, it's hard to remember. But they had some sort of fight, and the younger man said something about the Fratrex Prismo, and that's—" She shuddered and closed her eyes.

"What?"

"The man you found me with stabbed him in the side of the throat and laughed while he died. The other knights laughed, too. Then he got in the carriage with me, closed the door, and tied my hands behind my back. The way he looked at me. I've thought I was going to be raped before, and I've seen the look in the eyes of men when they're thinking about it, but this was more than that."

"How? What do you mean?"

"*More.* He wanted more than just to rape me; he wanted something worse. He pulled up my dress, and I didn't do anything. I thought that if I was quiet, he wouldn't hurt me. But then he said something about the 'blood telling,' and he started to cut me, and then I—" She coughed off into crying again, and he waited, stroking her hair.

"We can talk about it later."

She shook her head. "If I wait, I won't be able to. I know I won't."

"Go on, then. When you're ready."

"I fainted, and when I woke up, he was still cutting me. Blood was all over. I was so scared, Cazio. Everything we've been through, everything we've seen. I couldn't take it. I couldn't take it."

"What happened?"

"I wanted to hurt him," she said. "I wanted to reach inside of him and tear him up. I wanted it so bad, and then he screamed, and there was blood, and I don't remember anything until you were here."

"It's over," he soothed. "The cuts will heal, and everything will be fine."

"It doesn't feel that way."

"I know," he said, although he reckoned he probably didn't.

"Now I know how Anne felt," she said softly. "I should have understood."

"You mean when she was nearly raped?"

"No."

Something about the timbre of the word sent a little witch shot through his chest. It was as if an infant in its crib had just looked straight at him and said something no child that age could possibly say.

But quietly, almost in passing. Not showing off, not even trying to be noticed.

She looked up at him and tried to smile. "What are you doing here, anyway?"

"Looking for you, of course."

"Why?"

"I got to Dunmrogh and found it full up with churchmen who wanted to skin me. I knew Anne was sending you to me, and I figured you were in danger, so z'Acatto and I hid along the road, planning to waylay every carriage until we found yours."

"How many did you waylay?"

"Only the one, really. There aren't many casual travelers on the road these days."

"I'm glad," Austra said. "I was afraid I wouldn't see you again. I knew I wouldn't. But I should have known. You always manage to save me somehow, even if it's just because you saved Anne."

"It's all for you this time," he said.

The carriage bumped along without any talking for a little while.

"Why did she do it, Cazio?" Austra asked finally. "Why did she send you out here?"

"I don't know. She asked me to do something I didn't want to do, and I don't think it sat well with her."

Austra attempted a chuckle. "Everyone thinks she's so different now. It's funny."

"What do you mean?"

"Well, I mean she used to be frivolous, and now she's

taken responsibility. She never even thought about being queen, and now she is."

"It does sound like she's changed."

"Sort of. I love her, you have to understand, more than anyone. But I know her, too. She's always been impossibly selfish, so selfish she didn't even have a clue she was selfish. You know what I mean?"

"I think so," Cazio replied.

"She always had to have her way, whoever had to pay the cost. Did you know that when we were on our way to the coven, she decided to run away? She would have if I hadn't caught her. Actually, she still would have done it, but I broke my leg trying to catch her. She hadn't given a single thought to what would become of me if she went missing.

"It wasn't that she *wanted* to hurt me or get me in trouble; it just never occurred to her to *think* about whether her actions would have repercussions for others. A stablejack back in Eslen was beaten and sent away for letting her take her horse out when her mother had forbidden it. I could go on, but the fact of the matter is, the rest of us are shadows to her, some more real than others maybe, but still shadows."

"But I think I've seen some change even since I've known her," Cazio said.

"Yes," Austra agreed. "Some, yes. But then she became queen."

"Which you say she never wanted."

"Right. Because she never *thought* about being queen. When we were girls, there was no chance of that ever happening. Her father didn't get the Comven to legitimize his daughters as heirs until just before this whole mess started, and even so there were still Fastia and Elseny ahead of her." She pushed back a little and regarded him seriously. "Now, though, she's talked herself into believing she was forced into this new role, and true, there is something to that. But here's the thing, Cazio: She *loves* it. Now she *always* gets her way, even if what she wants is stupid and even if everyone knows it. What queen gallivants about playing knight-errant when a serious war is threatening?"

Austra's voice was rising as she got angrier.

"You're right. When we were out on the road, running for our lives, she was starting to get the idea, to think about the rest of us now and then, to understand that the world wasn't all about her, with the eyes of every foocned saint on her. But now it *is* all about her, isn't it?"

"She cares about you, Austra."

"Yes, and you. You and I are more real to her than anyone else. But it's what we mean to her that matters: what we can do for *her,* how we make *her* feel. When we cross her, when we don't want to do what she wants, she can't understand it. It doesn't make sense to her, and rather than figuring we have our own wants and reasons, she thinks we're attacking her. You see? That's how she sees things: Everything *we* do is about her."

"It can't be that bad," Cazio said.

"You just said she sent you away because you wouldn't do something she wanted."

"Well, that's not what she said. She said she needed someone she could trust in Dunmrogh."

"What did she ask you to do?"

"Ah, walk the faneway of Mamres."

Austra's tear-reddened eyes went bigger. "Oh, saints, Cazio." She lay back. "You see?" she sighed. "As much as she ought to know you, she doesn't. How could she think you would sacrifice your art as a dessrator to become one of those—things?"

Cazio blinked and suddenly realized he was on the verge of tears himself.

"Ted amao," he said, completely lost in emotion. *"Edio ted amao.* I love you."

"Ecco," she said, her voice·faint but firm. "I love you too."

He took her hand.

"Anne loves us, too, in her way," Austra said. "I think she

sent us away because we know her. We remind her that she has been better, could be better."

The pace of the carriage suddenly picked up, and z'Acatto was shouting something up front.

"A moment," Cazio said, and kissed Austra on the forehead. He stood and opened the little door in the ceiling and pulled himself up.

"We have friends," z'Acatto shouted.

Cazio looked behind and saw six mounted knights, all in the colors of Lord Gravio.

Swearing, he drew Acredo, but there was nothing much to be done until the riders caught up with them, which wouldn't be long. Then there wouldn't be any time for tricks, just two against six.

Well, that wasn't so bad. He had beaten more than that below the palace in Eslen. Of course, they hadn't been as heavily armored, but the odds had been worse.

If he could reach the same state, *chiado sivo,* they had a chance.

So he paused, clearing his mind, trying not to think about the fight ahead, only about the symmetries of arm, foot, body, point, edge, and grip.

A moment later they passed into a wood, and Cazio began humming, because that was even better: Their horses would be less useful here, their armor more of an encumbrance. He was just about to jump to the ground and start the fight when z'Acatto cursed a saint whose name itself was a curse.

He turned to find out why in time to see footmen pouring into the road from the trees and the trap well and truly closed.

Chiado sivo. Entirely sword.

He leaped from the carriage toward the lead rider, blade straight out like a spear.

CHAPTER SIX

✛

BRINNA

NEIL KNELT to the masked woman.

"Majesty," he said, trying to keep his mind still.

"Pleased to meet you, Sir Neil," she said with a slight emphasis on "meet" that he thought he understood.

Neil heard a little gasp behind him and saw that Alis had been brought in. Her eyes were founts of incredulity.

"Ah, Sister Alis," Brinna said. "Did you know who I was?"

"Lady, I did not know," Alis said. She seemed completely off her footing, something Neil hadn't ever seen before. Of course, he was having a hard time keeping his own face composed.

"And now you do," the woman he had known as both Brinna and Swanmay said. She took a step toward Alis and raised a cup of wine. "Would you like a drink?"

"No, Highness, I would rather not."

"You admit it, then," the inquisitor snarled. "You admit the attempt at murder."

Alis held her head high. "My queen and this knight knew nothing of my intentions. You cannot hold them accountable."

"Oh, it was all your idea, then?" the masked woman said.

"I'm telling the truth," Alis said.

"I'm sure you are," Brinna replied. "You just haven't mentioned who actually put you up to it."

Alis didn't reply, but Brinna's gaze turned languidly to Neil. "That would be your Queen Anne, Sir Neil."

"I don't believe that, Highness," Neil said.

"Because it is untrue," Alis added.

"Well, we shall see. Inquisitor, take Lady Berrye to the room of the waters. Don't do anything permanent to her, do you hear? I want to talk to her myself later."

"Very good, Highness. And the knight?"

"I wish to converse with him alone," she replied.

The matron frowned. "That is unwise."

"I do not think so, inquisitor. Every exit from this place is guarded, and he is unarmed. But from what I've heard of this man, that wouldn't stop him any more than your continued presence would if his intention was to strangle me. What will stop him is his word. Sir Neil, will you behave yourself if left alone with me? Will you promise to make no assault on me or attempt to escape?"

"I promise not to harm your person in any way, Highness, and I won't try to escape during our conversation. After I leave this room, I can't make any such promise."

"That seems fair enough to me, inquisitor."

"Lady, it is still not appropriate."

"I say what's appropriate in my own house," Brinna purred. "And there will be no gossip of it, or I will know where it came from."

"I serve your father, not you," Walzamerka said.

"But unless my father gives a very specific command to disobey, you will do my will."

"Why do you want to be alone with him?"

"Because I believe you can torture Sir Neil for a thousand days and learn nothing. But a candid conversation held in private might yield some . . . insights."

The inquisitor's mouth parted, and a look very like fear passed across her features. "I see, Highness," she said. "I didn't understand."

"Good."

When she was gone and the chamber door had closed, Brinna smiled.

"Walzamerka thinks I'm going to tear your soul out."

"Are you?"

She gestured toward a chair. "Sit, Sir Neil."

He did so, and she stared at him for several moments with those eyes of hers, so deep blue that in any light other than sunlight they appeared almost black.

"Did you also come here to kill me, Sir Neil?"

"I swear by the saints my people swear by that I did not, Princess Brinna."

Her lip quirked, and she poured two goblets of wine.

"This is not poisoned," she said. "Would you have some?"

"I would."

She handed him the goblet. He took it with numb hands.

"You're Marcomir's daughter," he said at last.

"Yes," she said. She reached up and removed the mask, revealing the strong cheekbones and contours he remembered so well. Only her gaze was different; it looked slightly unfocused.

"I don't understand," he said, unable to look away from her dark eyes. "When I met you—"

"Fancy a game of Fiedchese?" she interrupted.

"Fiedchese?"

"Yes."

She rang a bell, and a moment later a young girl in braids brought a board and pieces. The board had squares of rust and bone. The girl left again through a cleverly placed door Neil was unable to see once it had closed.

"It's the same board," he said. "From the ship."

"Yes, of course." She placed the pieces in their starting positions. "This set is rather dear to me." Her eyes shifted up. "King or raiders?"

"Raiders, I suppose," Neil replied.

Her melancholy little smile broadened, and she made her first move. He saw now it was more than her gaze. There seemed to be something *slower* about her, dreamier. Not stupid, but calculating and diffident.

"I'll answer all of your questions, Sir Neil," she said. "I've nothing to hide from you anymore."

Neil made his own move mechanically, unable to concentrate on the game.

She *tsk*ed softly. "You're better than that," she said.

"I'm distracted."

"As am I. I didn't know I would be so nervous at this meeting. I've thought about it often." She shifted the king a few spaces.

He remembered their kiss months before. It had been soft, inexperienced, tentative, and at the same time frighteningly sincere. It was more real at the moment than anything else in his recollection.

"No," he said, moving another raider. "It's not silly."

"Now you know what tower I was trying to escape from and why I couldn't tell you at the time."

"Yes," Neil replied, watching her capture a double-headed ogre. "And no. Why were you fleeing your own father?"

She studied the board. "It wasn't just my father I was running from," she said. "It was everything. Look around you, Sir Neil. This tower has five floors. I live in the top three. Everything I need is provided for me. Attentive servants surround me. I once had friends, but since my escape, many of them are now out of my reach."

"I'm sorry," Neil said. "I know it was because of me. But I still don't understand why." He sent a lizardish monster down the board.

"I was born in this tower, Sir Neil. I have lived all of my life here except for the few months of freedom in which we met. I will die here, in this place with one window."

"What about the rest of the castle? The city? The countryside?"

"All denied me," she said.

"Then you *are* a prisoner."

"I suppose so," she said, moving another of the kingsmen to block Neil's weak stratagem.

"Again, why?"

A frown pinched her brow. "I've been watching you, Sir Neil."

He had the sudden feeling of the very sky growing heavy and fragile above them, a huge plate of glass pressing on the tower, crushing them and breaking under its weight.

"At the battle of the waerd," he said. "I thought—"

"I was there," she said. "I saw you fall. I did what I could."

And then he knew.

"You're the Hellrune," he said.

"What a funny way of saying it," she replied.

"Wait," Neil said, closing his eyes, trying to put it all together. Anne's insistence on his coming, Alis' many questions about the Hansan seers.

Brinna was the *enemy,* the beating heart of the Hansan war beast.

"Don't look at me like that," Brinna said softly.

"How long have you been doing this?" he asked.

"Don't," she said. "Please."

"How long?"

"They knew when I was born. They started giving me the drugs when I was two, but I was nine before I was of much use. Move, please."

He did so, a reckless attack that she swiftly crushed.

"And how old are you now?" he asked.

She paused. "That's an unfriendly question," she said. Then, more softly: "I had nothing to do with your father's death, Sir Neil. I have twenty-three winters, but you don't imagine I was *seeing* for a band of Weihands."

"And yet you know—"

"I have seen it *now,*" she said, "The death of your father, your first hard wounding. As I said, I have been watching you, past and present."

"Nevertheless, in these years you have caused the deaths of many friends," he said. "The fleet at Jeir—"

"Yes, that I was responsible for," she replied. "You understand? I will not lie to you."

"I lost an uncle there."

"How many uncles did you slaughter, Sir Neil? How many children did you leave fatherless? It was war. You cannot be so squeamish or judgmental."

"This is hard, Brinna," he managed.

"For me as well."

"And now you're waging war on my queen and country."

"Yes. Because it is my duty. We discussed duty, didn't we? You approve of it if I remember correctly."

"I did not know what your duty was then."

"Really? And would you have advised me differently if you had? Is my duty less relevant when it conflicts with your own?"

He looked at the game he'd just lost, trying to find something to say.

"Or would you have sacrificed yourself and killed me?" she asked very softly.

"No," he managed. "Never that."

"Then you still consider yourself obligated to me."

"I consider myself more than obligated," Neil replied. "But that puts me in an impossible situation."

"I had escaped," she said. "Do you know that? Even after the delay taking you to Paldh, we sailed through the straits of Rusimi. My father would never have found me."

"What happened then?"

She sighed. "You."

"What do you mean?"

"Sir Neil, I found you nearly dead, hurt to the heart by betrayal, yet still steadfast in your duty even to those who betrayed you. That grew in me. It was because of you that I returned. You and a vision."

"A vision?"

"I'll tell you more about that later. May I tell you why I left in the first place?"

"Of course."

"You're beaten in two moves," she said.

"I know. Why did you leave?"

"I have two roles in this life, Sir Neil, two obligations deeper than birth. I enjoy neither of them. One obligation is to be my father's haliurunna. I dream and send men to death. I take drugs that allow me to see better, but days of my life vanish sometimes. There are whole months I have no recollection of. I know too much and too little all at once. But I did what I was told, dreaming one day of freedom, knowing in my heart I would never have it. I fastened myself on duty and pride in defending my father's throne—and especially on my higher calling—and hoped that would be enough. And it might have been, but my father asked me to do something . . . wrong. Worse, I did it, and it ruined something in me. Soon it wrecked far more than that."

"What was that thing?"

"I broke the law of death."

For a moment Neil was speechless. "My queen, Muriele. She believes she did that, with a curse."

"Oh, she did the worst of the damage. But my brother Alharyi was dying, and my father always loved him best. He commanded me to stop his death, and I managed it before understanding what I had really done. Once I knew, I tried to mend the law, and I think I might have done it, because I only stopped him from his rightful death, I didn't bring him back from it. But then Muriele made her curse and brought Robert back, and the law was well and truly breached."

"What about your brother?"

"He went to Vitellio after Anne. His men found him chopped into many pieces—by your friend Cazio, I think. The parts were still alive. There is a ritual. The power was passed on to my cousin Hrothwulf, whom *you* cut into pieces." She shrugged. "Anyway, after making my brother a nauschalk I no longer wanted any part of it. I made my escape."

"And willingly returned. Because of me. Because of duty to Hansa."

"Because of duty to the world," she replied. "I am in part responsible for what is coming. I must do what I can to stop it, although I don't think there's much hope."

"Stop what?"

"Your queen, Anne."

"Why? I know your father wants Crotheny."

"Oh, yes, he does," Brinna said. "But I wouldn't have returned here to feed his ambition. I wouldn't be a part of a war waged because of an old man's vanity."

"Then why?"

"Because if she isn't stopped, Anne will destroy us all."

* * *

The forest smelled fresh, of evergreen and rain. Muriele tried to focus on that, on seeing beauty at the end of her life, trying to not have fear be her last feeling.

Everyone dies, she thought. *If not now, later. There is no escape.*

But that was not what her gut told her. She wanted to beg, and every moment brought it closer to the surface.

How far was it, this bog? How long did she have to live?

Berimund was resolved; she could see that. The boy in him was hidden again, replaced by the hard man he was becoming.

She wished she could see Anne once more. There were things she should have told her when she had the chance.

Had Anne foreseen this? Part of her wondered. Had her own daughter sent her to her death? Was some greater purpose being served?

She had to be brave a little while longer.

"Berimund," she murmured. "One thing, please."

"What's that?"

"Let Sir Neil and Alis take my body to Liery. Give me that, at least: a resting place with my ancestors."

Berimund's response was to look at her as if she were crazy, and her heart sank.

"You don't think I'm actually going to *kill* you, do you?" he exploded.

She was afraid to understand that at first.

"But Marcomir—"

"That's Father. He's old, near to losing his mind. I won't execute you on his whim. It goes against all honor and all common decency. My brothers may do his every bidding, but I will not."

Muriele felt relief, but it was guarded. "Where are we going, then?"

"A place only my wulfbrothars and I know about," he said. "A place we found during our roving days. You'll be safe there until I can either calm him down or arrange passage for you back to Eslen."

"You would do that?"

Berimund nodded grimly. "I am no traitor," he said. "Our war with Crotheny is just, holy, and right. But that means our *actions* have to be just, holy, and right. I will not become evil to fight evil."

"My daughter isn't evil," Muriele said.

"I wouldn't expect you to believe so," Berimund replied. "Do you think I am evil?"

He shook his head. "I think you are in every way honorable." He smiled. "And I've never heard anyone talk like that to my father. For that alone, I would spare you."

"Then how can you imagine I would serve an evil cause?"

"Without knowing you do so," he said.

"Couldn't the same be said for you? Mightn't you be serving the wrong master?"

"My father might well be the wrong master," Berimund said. "But the holy Church is behind us."

"You think you can trust the Church?"

"Yes. But even if I couldn't, there is someone I do trust. Someone very dear to me. And I know we have to fight your daughter."

"Then we are enemies, Berimund."

"Yes, we are. But we shall be civil ones, yes? We shall behave honorably."

"You're still hung over," Muriele said.

"Indeed. And as soon as possible I shall cure that by being drunk."

"And your men?"

"My wulfbrothars. I've known them all since childhood. Our first oaths are all to one another. None of them will betray me."

Muriele nodded, but in her mind's eye she saw Robert watching her being led off and the words he had mouthed at her. She hadn't caught them then, but now with sudden clarity she knew what he had been saying:

I'll see you soon.

CHAPTER SEVEN

THE COMMANDER

ACREDO'S POINT struck the knight just below the gorget and slipped up beneath the helm. Helped by the man's reflex of throwing his head back, the weapon lodged in his throat. Cazio let his elbow bend as the blade struck home, but the shock was still terrific. The knight flipped back out of the saddle, and Cazio, helpless to control his flight, followed him to the ground.

He hit hard on his off-weapon hand and used it to tumble head over heels, but he had too much momentum and ended up rolling four times before he could come back up on his feet. When he did, he turned unsteadily to meet his fate, Acredo still in his hand.

But the other knights weren't paying much attention to him. The men swarming out of the woods were filling them full of arrows or stabbing at them with pikes, and that seemed to have distracted them.

He recognized them then. They were what remained of the troops Anne had given him to invest Dunmrogh.

He checked the fellow he had hit and found him without breath, then watched Anne's soldiers finish off the knights. He rubbed his shoulder, which hurt as if Lord Aita were racking it in his halls of punishment. He wondered if it was dislocated.

Z'Acatto peered up from the front of the carriage.

"What are you doing back there?" he asked.

"A lot more than I needed to, it appears," he replied.

"Nothing new there."

A few moments later, one of the men came over and doffed his helm, revealing a seamed face with a long white scar across the forehead and a nose that looked like it had been broken a few times. Cazio recognized him as a fellow named Jan something or other.

"That was timely," Cazio said. "Many thanks."

"It was at that," Jan said, his tone cool. "We reckoned you dead, Sir Cazio."

"I'm not a knight," he pointed out.

"No? I reckon you're not, are you? But we were put in your charge."

"Yes, and look how well I did for you," Cazio said. "I led you straight into a trap."

Jan nodded. Some more of the men were walking up.

"Yeah, you did, didn't you?" another of them agreed, an older, nearly bald fellow with thick features. "Near half of us are dead or missing. Playing sausage with Her Majesty don't make you a commander, does it?"

Cazio's hand twitched on Acredo's hilt. "I'll agree I'm no commander, but you'll take that back about Queen Anne, and you'll do it now."

The man spit. "Pig guts, I will," he snarled. "If you want—"

"Easy, Hemm," Jan said. "No good dragging the queen into this."

"She put us here as much as he did," Hemm said.

Cazio lifted his weapon toward the guard. "Take it back."

The men had surrounded him.

"You'll take us all, then, with your fancy little sword?" Hemm asked.

"I'll certainly kill *you*," Cazio promised.

"And I'll help him kill the rest of you," z'Acatto's voice said sharply from outside the circle. "Are you pigs or soldiers?"

Hemm looked puzzled. "Pigs or soldiers?" he repeated. Then his face lit up oddly, and he spun toward the old man. *"Emrature? Cassro dachi Purcii?"*

"Ah, *zmierda*," z'Acatto swore.

"It *is* you," Hemm said.

"Sodding saints, it is!" another gray-haired soldier agreed. "Older and uglier than ever."

"You're still just as stupid, Piro," z'Acatto bit back. He pointed his sword at Hemm. "You want to fight the son of Mamercio, go right ahead, but it'll be a fair fight, just you and him."

Hemm glanced back at Cazio. "That's Mamercio's pup?" He rubbed his bearded jaw. "Yeah, I see it now."

He turned fully back to the swordmaster. "No harm meant," he said. "I just, well, the rumor is—"

"Is wrong," Cazio said firmly.

Hemm held his palms up and out. "Then it's wrong. I stepped in it."

That sounded enough like an apology, so Cazio lowered his sword.

"There's a good lad," Hemm said, clapping his hand on Cazio's shoulder. "Me and your father and that old man there, we saw some times. I was sorry to hear about your papa." He pointed at z'Acatto. "He was the finest leader a band of *probucutorii* ever had. He used to call us his *purcii*, his pigs."

"It wasn't a term of affection," z'Acatto said. "It's what you smelled like."

"Sure," Hemm agreed. "And the worst— Whatever happened to that old sow Ospero?"

"He went into business in z'Espino," z'Acatto said. "I saw him a few months ago."

"Business, eh? I can imagine what kind. That's what I should have done. Now see where I am. But it's good to have you here, Cassro. Me and the boys here are about at our wit's end."

"You couldn't have started far from there," z'Acatto said.

"He was your leader?" Cazio asked Hemm.

"Just me and old Piro there fought in the twenty-year war," Hemm said. "The rest of these are too young."

"Right, but I've heard of him," Jan said.

"Who hasn't?" someone else piped up. "The battle at Cummachio Bridge? Everyone knows that story."

"I don't," Cazio said, sending a sharp look z'Acatto's way.

The men just laughed and seemed to think he was kidding.

"What exactly are you men doing out here?" z'Acatto asked.

"Ask him," Piro said, gesturing at Cazio. "The queen gave us to him to play with, and he fair broke us. The horsemen that didn't die at Dunmrogh rode off and left us, so it's just us infantry left. We've been hounded for days. Gave 'em the slip for a bit, but they've found us again. They're forming up down the road to finish us off. I thought we were dog meat, but with you here I see a chance."

"There's nothing I can do for you that you can't do yourselves," z'Acatto said.

"Gone all humble on us, have you, Cassro?" Hemm asked. "Come on. We need you."

"No, you don't."

"We've got good men here," Piro said, "but no leader. Now the queen put the young Pachiomadio there in charge of us, didn't she? And he got us in a bad spot. The way we see it, he should get us out of it."

"Right," Jan said. "Help us get back to Eslen."

"It's where we're going, anyway," Cazio said.

"I only agreed to help you find Austra," the old man said. "You're on your own getting back to Anne. But either way, we'll have an easier time slipping out of here alone."

"I see how it is," Piro said. "Can't say I don't understand, even though I hardly believe it coming from you, Cassro. You were never one to protect your own *stang* when there were them around needed you."

"That was then," z'Acatto said.

"Leave him be," Hemm said. "He was man enough back then for four lifetimes. I owe him my life six times over, so when I die tomorrow, I'll still owe him five."

"After all, z'Acatto," Cazio said, "you've got wine to drink. What's more important?"

"Dog's piss on the lot of you," z'Acatto snapped. "And

Cazio, you cover your fester hole when you don't know what you're talking about."

"Right," Cazio said. "I've no idea what these fellows are talking about, and whose fault is that? But it doesn't matter. I wish Anne had never put these men in my charge. I wish I had refused her. I'm a swordsman, a good one, but I'm not a soldier and certainly not a leader. But if they're going to fight tomorrow, I have to fight with them."

"Now," Piro said, "*that's* Mamercio's son."

"What about Austra?"

"What about me?" a voice said from behind. He turned to find her leaning against the carriage. "I wouldn't have him do anything else. And I'll be here with him, z'Acatto, and you will, too, because as much as you don't want it in you, as much as you try to drink it away, you have a noble soul."

Z'Acatto heaved a sigh and looked around.

"Now, that was a pretty speech, lady," Piro said.

Then all eyes turned to z'Acatto. For a moment he had the look of a caged animal, but then Cazio saw something firm up in him.

"All right, *purcii,*" he said. "We're wasting time. Somebody tell me what we're facing."

"There's ninety of us. Our scout's last count of them was seventy horse, sixty heavy foot, twenty archers."

Z'Acatto looked around at the men. "I make you at about half and half heavy and light. Does that get it?"

"Yes."

"We need a narrow field," he said. "Forest or cliff on our flanks. Anything like that around here?"

"I'll find it," a young rusty-haired fellow said.

"Do it, then," z'Acatto said. "Now, someone talk to me about supplies."

Cazio stayed with z'Acatto, trying to absorb what the old man was doing, to be what help he could, but in the end he felt rather useless. Z'Acatto and the soldiers spoke a language he didn't understand, and it wasn't the patois of the king's tongue, Vitellian, and Almannish but something deeper, rooted in common experience. He said as much to Austra that night when he went to check on her.

"You've marched with soldiers before," she pointed out.

"We marched alongside them," he said. "But I never fought as a soldier. In fact, tomorrow I've no idea what I'll do. I'm not a pikeman, I can't shoot a bow, and a rapier isn't much use in a battle formation."

"Did you have any idea? About z'Acatto?"

"There were hints, I guess. Ospero called him 'Emrature' once, and I knew my father and he fought in the wars, but he wouldn't talk about it. I never imagined that soldiers somewhere were still telling stories about him."

"Well, it sounds like they trust him to lead them," Austra said. "And they know more about what we're up against than we do."

"They have no choice, though. You remember the army we fought at Langraeth? They were all infantry, like these men. Anne's horse destroyed them. It's hard to fight cavalry."

Austra leaned up and kissed him. "We've been in a lot tighter spots than this."

"True," Cazio said. "But those were situations where being a swordsman counted for something."

"You'll always count, Cazio," Austra said. "The saints love you as much as I do."

He smiled. "Errenda gave me you, so I know she loves me. I'm pretty sure Fiussa has a soft spot for me."

"Courting two female saints? That could lead to trouble."

He felt a guilty little start and then another at the novel feeling of guilt.

"I don't think I'll be courting any other women, saints or no," he said, suddenly feeling very out of sorts.

"I was just joking, Cazio."

"I'm not," he heard himself say. "In fact, I hope that you'll agree to marry me."

She frowned. "Look, don't joke," she said.

"I'm not. I can't offer you much more than you see, but I'll give you that."

She just stared at him. "You really do think we're about to be killed, don't you?"

"That's not it," he said. "I love you, Austra. I've just figured out how much, and I feel foolish for not knowing it earlier, for not marrying you the day we set foot in Eslen. I hope you'll forgive me for that."

"I really do," she said, her eyes watering. She kissed him, and it lasted a long time.

"Just another reason we have to go to Eslen," he said, stroking her hair. "I have to ask Anne's permission to steal you away."

"She's already given it," Austra said. "She told me before she sent me away. She said she's going to create you a duke or something and give me leave to marry you."

"Duke?" Cazio said.

"Or some title. Lord Dunmrogh, maybe."

"I have a title already," he said. "It's not much of one, but I was born with it."

"You can have more than one, you know."

"Hmm. Duke Cazio. *Duoco Cazio.* That doesn't sound half-bad."

Something rustled outside, and then there was a tap on the carriage door. He opened it, and found Jan standing there.

"Aeken found a place," the soldier informed them. "The Emrature wants us there before sunup, so gangen we now."

The march took them about a league east to an old levee on the Saint Sephod River, and once there they went to work quickly, cutting stakes and digging trenches. The latter was easy, because the field the embankment looked down on had been plowed that spring and the soil was loose, without roots or other hindrances to the spade.

Z'Acatto paced about with more sustained energy than Cazio had ever seen in him. He wasn't even sure if the old man was drunk.

Taking a break from digging, Cazio went up on the levee to see how things were forming up.

On his right the field gave way to low, swampy forest, but

on the left it was relatively unbounded. The carriage and the two remaining wagons of their supply train were drawn up as barriers there, but Cazio didn't imagine they would offer much protection. The dirt in front of the levee now had three wide toothy grins of stakes and trenches.

Z'Acatto joined him.

"Had enough of digging?" he asked.

"I'll go back to it in a moment," Cazio said. He gestured at the field. "Why have you backed us against a river? We can't retreat."

"That's a funny thing for you to say," z'Acatto replied. "I've never heard you talk about retreating before."

"It's not just me here."

The old man nodded. "Right. That's what I hate about it. You see?"

"I'm starting to," Cazio said. "But I wish you had told me more."

"I've just been trying to forget all that," the old man said. "I never meant for you to have anything to do with this sort of business."

"It's not your fault. My own choices led me here."

"I'm not disputing that," z'Acatto replied.

"So why no retreat?"

Z'Acatto shrugged. "They have greater numbers, and we don't have enough pikes to make an effective battle square. We need our backs and flanks safe."

"The left flank looks pretty open."

"It'll slow a cavalry charge," z'Acatto said. "It's the best we can do, given the time we have. Anyway, retreat isn't an option. We have to win. If we don't, we're done."

"What if they bring more men than we think?"

"Our scouts are pretty good. They might pick up another man or two, but for some reason the bulk of Hespero's forces seem to be going east."

"East? What's east?"

"I've no idea, nor do I care. We've problems enough here."

"Can we win?"

Z'Acatto lifted his hands but didn't answer in words.

"What's my part in all of this?"

"I'm putting half the archers on the field and half strung through the forest, there. They won't send horse at the forest, but they will probably detach infantry. You'll protect the archers."

Cazio nodded, relieved. He'd imagined himself in the press, holding a pike, and didn't care for the image.

Z'Acatto's gaze shifted.

"There they are," he said.

The horsemen formed a block in the center, and the footmen were lined up behind them with archers on their wings. Cazio had seen the formation before; it was essentially a cavalry hammer, ready to smash them. When the smashing was done, the foot would come in and clean up.

What he had never seen before, however, was the formation in which z'Acatto had put his men.

They stood tightly packed in columns five deep, with the ten columns arranged in a sort of hollow wedge open to the river. Z'Acatto called it a "hedgehog," and with their pikes bristling out, it resembled one. The men had the pikes braced at their feet and set at various angles from low to high so that anyone charging in had to deal with at least five wicked levels of sharpness.

The bowmen who weren't with Cazio in the woods had formed in ranks, too, out in front of the hedgehog.

No one had come out to offer terms, and it didn't look like they would. They just kept coming closer, the horses and the metal-clad men on them looking bigger and bigger.

The archers began firing into the horsemen both from the field and from the trees. The enemy archers returned fire, targeting those visible on the field, but after a moment, as predicted, a line of about thirty spearmen with large, heavy shields broke away from the enemy foot and started plodding toward them.

Concentrating on their progress, Cazio missed the start of the charge, but he heard the shouts and turned to see it begin.

Ignoring the approaching spearmen, the archers around

him concentrated their fire on the cavalry, as did those on the field, and the effect was astonishing. Five or six of the lead horses and their riders went down, followed immediately by another ten or so tripping over the fallen. The hedgehog archers poured shafts into the confusion, creating further havoc. The charge slowed to a crawl under the deadly rain, but the forty or so horsemen who remained mounted quickly re-formed and charged at the archers. They were slowed by the stakes, however, and several dismounted and began uprooting them, giving the archers plenty of time to retreat behind the battle wedge and take their places on the levee, where they could send more darts down on the enemy line.

While half the bowmen in the woods were still helping to riddle the cavalry, the other half had begun firing at the approaching infantrymen, who were now only about thirty kingsyards away, moving their shield wall along with good discipline.

There had been sporadic fire from the enemy archers, but Cazio didn't see any more of them.

"Move back," Cazio said, echoing z'Acatto's orders. "They won't be able to keep that shield wall in the woods."

As ordered, the bowmen started backing into the swamp, continuing to fire at the infantry, whose shields were now pretty well feathered. Seven of them had already dropped out of formation, either dead or too gravely wounded to keep on, but that left the numbers pretty even, and although the archers had swords with them, they didn't have shields or spears.

The cavalry was charging again, and this time there was nothing between them and the hedgehog. The massed horsemen looked unstoppable.

Mirroring the horse, the infantry advancing on Cazio's archers sent up a hoarse cry and charged.

Cazio drew Acredo.

"Run," he told the archers. "Back to the wedge."

Although, glancing that way, he wondered if there would be anything to retreat to.

CHAPTER EIGHT

✠

THE WAY
OF POWER

THE GRASS RIPPLED, shifting to trees and hills as Anne unraveled herself and moved like a cloud. She had been afraid at first of discorporation, but in the sedos realm, the body was more illusion than anything else. Once that deception was put behind, there was much fun to be had. She could twine like grapevines through massive forests or flow like rainwater down a hillside. She could choose another illusory body. She had played at being a horse, an eagle, a porpoise, a spider, a creeping lizard. They felt more welcome in her thoughts now, too, more easy. The more she used her power, the more secure her identity seemed to become.

She had to remind herself sometimes that she wasn't there just for simple enjoyment. She never wanted to leave and returned more and more often whether or not there was anything particular she was looking for.

In fact, sometimes she forgot what she *was* looking for.

But not today. Today she drifted back days and toward the south.

She saw the army of the Church massed in the thousands at Teremené. That was nothing new, and already half of her army was marching to meet them. Looking at them now, she felt a coldness in her belly. Crotheny was caught in a vise; the Hansans were being held at Poelscild, but to attack with enough force to drive them back would mean letting the Church come to her gates, and the south was poorly defended. She had seen, too, a new fleet of strange copper-skinned men sailing down from the north, from Rakh Fadh, in the company of tow-headed Weihand raiders. That sailing hadn't happened yet, and the results of it seemed inaugurable.

And in the south the future was also unclear. Sometimes she saw massive carnage, sometimes an unhindered march, sometimes nothing.

None of this was new, nor did it long hold her attention. She was looking for her friends.

She already had seen Cazio, captured by the Church. She knew there was something missing, someone he had talked to that she could not focus on. But she also knew he and z'Acatto were free again.

Austra had been the hardest to find.

She imagined her friend's face, her laugh, and the chagrined pucker of her forehead when she was afraid Anne was about to get them both into trouble.

And there was something, a reflection, a flicker in the distance of leagues and also time. But as Anne moved toward it to peek up from the sedos like a groundhog from the earth, a current of sickening power caught and twisted her misty form, a massive flow against which she could not struggle. It slammed her into something, submerged her in pain and horror, and congealed her back into human form.

Someone was cutting her. She smelled the blood, felt the pain. His stinking breath was in her ear, and she saw her legs all exposed and smeared red. She felt the fear, sheer panic, the certain horrible knowledge that she was going to die, the animal need to tear away and run and the impossibility of doing so. She couldn't even think. She couldn't scream. She could only watch as the knife peeled her white skin.

Fight! she tried to scream. *Stop him!*

When the echo came back, she suddenly understood that this wasn't happening to *her*. The body being tortured was Austra's.

Fight, Austra, for the love of the saints! I can't lose you!

Something turned then, and Anne was yanked back out into the currents. For the first time she saw Austra's face, her empty, horrified gaze, and then she was dwindling away, gone.

Anne went frantically back, racing up and down, back and forth, but there was no longer any trace of her friend, and now she couldn't locate Cazio again. But she didn't give up; she had to find them. She had the power to find them, to bring them back from the dead if need be, and by all the saints, she would do so.

She woke shivering and shaking, wondering who she was, where she was, the sense of losing herself as bad as ever. She was weeping helplessly, and although she eventually understood that it was Emily who had awakened her, she wasn't able to respond. Only after Nerenai brought some of her tea was she able to muster the coherence to listen.

"Again, Emily," she murmured.

"Majesty," Emily said. "The army of Hansa."

She opened her eyes and saw the girl kneeling next to her.

"What about them?"

"You've been . . . gone for two days. We could not rouse you."

"What's happened?"

"Fifteen thousand more of the enemy arrived two nights ago. They attacked yesterday morning. They've just breached the canal and are surrounding the keep."

The keep surrounded. Austra and Cazio dead. The Church, the fleet from the north . . .

Too much. Too much.

"Where's Artwair?"

"Outside."

"Get my dressing gown."

She heard a lot of clattering in the hall. When she emerged to meet Artwair, she saw that it was filled with her Craftsmen and Sefry.

"What's all this?" she asked.

"Just a precaution, Majesty," he said. "There is a chance the keep will fall. We'll want to get you out of it."

She nodded. *Let Artwair take over. Get Faster, ride away, and never look back. Find Cazio; he may still live . . .*

She felt everything in her buckling. She didn't want this. She thought of Austra, of the horror of her torture, of how someone could *do* that to her friend, and was sickened. Was Austra dead? Probably. And now death was coming for her.

But where would she ride? Where would she be safe?

"No," she said. "Wait."

"There isn't much time, Majesty. They're already in the city."

"I said *wait*."

"Majesty," he replied stiffly.

She fought down the claustrophobia seeking to swallow her. "Take me where I can see what's going on and explain it as we go."

"Majesty—"

But he saw her glance and cut himself off.

So they made their way to the now-familiar tower.

The sun was just a hemisphere in the east, and mist lay heavy on the earth. The air had the cool scent of autumn that brought feelings of nostalgia even when one was ten years old.

The keep was indeed surrounded except for the area around the southern gates, where a wall of pikes kept the Hansans back. It looked like an island in a stormy sea.

"That's where I'm supposed to make my great escape?" she asked.

"It's your best chance," Artwair replied.

"So the keep will fall."

"If we can hold out for two days, reinforcements will arrive."

"Two days. Can we do it?"

"I don't think so."

It seemed to Anne there was a bit of a reproof in his tone. *I was trying to find my friends,* she wanted to protest. But she knew what his answer to that would be, whether he had the nerve to say it out loud or not.

"I can't see *everything* in advance, you know," she told him. "There is so much to keep my eye on."

But her negligence was all around her now, and she knew that if Hansa won, she would never live to claim the sedos throne. She could never set things right, free Crotheny from terror, avenge Austra, extinguish the Hansan threat for all time.

Her hubris had doomed her.

No.

"Step away from me," she said. "Get below, all of you but Nerenai."

When they were all gone but the Sefry, Anne closed her eyes.

"You can do it, Majesty," Nerenai said.

"If I don't, we'll all die."

"That's not how to think, Majesty. Fear and worry will only hinder you. You must be confident. You must be strong for strength's sake, not to achieve an end."

"I'll try," Anne replied, swallowing. Her mouth was bone dry.

She felt at the moment very much the girl. Why was this *her* burden? Why had the saints laid this on her when all she wanted was to ride her horse, drink wine, gossip with Austra, maybe fall in love? Why was she denied all of that?

I miss you, Austra. I'm so sorry.

Thinking that brought the anger she needed, and Anne slipped into otherwhere.

Arilac.

At first no answer came, but then a shadow lifted from the green and wavered like smoke before her, grudgingly forming into the pale image of a woman.

"I need your help," Anne said.

"I'm nearly consumed," the arilac replied in dissipated tones. "I may not be of much help."

"What's consuming you?"

"You are," the arilac replied. "This is how it is."

"Who are you?" Anne demanded.

"You've asked that before."

"Yes, and you've never answered. Who are you?"

"What was. What will be. I was never merely a living person. I was born here, created here."

"Who created you?"

The arilac smiled wanly. "You did."

And with those two words, Anne suddenly understood, and everything fell into place, and she was ready.

"Good-bye," she said.

And the arilac was gone, and her limbs pulsed with power, and the power remembered itself in her.

She stepped halfway so that otherwhere shimmered around her, but so did Newland and Andemuer, the keep and the host of Hansa.

She looked over the teeming thousands bent on her destruction, the enemies who had ripped her out of the life she wanted and made her *this,* and felt a cold, determined hatred rise up in her that she never had known before.

She liked it, and the power in her had felt that hatred before many times, and it knew what to do.

Artwair was still pale bells later when he came to see her.

"You're not going to vomit again, are you?" she asked.

"No, Majesty," he replied. "I've nothing left in my stomach."

"I'm surprised at you," she replied. "With all you've seen."

He closed his eyes and nodded. She saw the apple in his throat bob a few times.

"There were a few survivors," he said. "What will Your Majesty have done with them?"

She thought about it for a moment. "How many?"

"About a thousand."

"So many," she said.

"There were fifty thousand this morning, Majesty."

"Well, kill them, I suppose. I want Hansa to understand that if they attack us, they can expect no quarter."

"May I remind you that your mother is their hostage?"

"Yes, and Marcomir has given the order for her execution.

What more can I do but show him the price he pays for affronting us? How else can I save her?"

"May I make a suggestion, Majesty?"

"Of course."

"Show mercy. Let them return to Hansa and tell what they saw here. What army will attack us when they know what could happen to them?"

There was something in his tone that it took her a moment to understand.

"You feel sorry for them," she accused.

"Saints, yes," Artwair said.

"They would have killed all of us," she pointed out.

"Auy." His face was as if cast in iron.

"I don't want to be cruel," she finally said. It seemed the thing to say. "Do you really think letting them go is the right thing? Or is this just sentiment talking?"

"Majesty, for me this morning was all confusion. But the Hansan survivors speak of the sun blotting out, of blood and serpents raining from the sky. They saw their comrades' steaming entrails writhe out of their bellies like boiling eels. I think that story from a thousand lips will be more valuable than their deaths."

"Very well," she sighed. "See to it, then. And now that we're done here, I should like Copenwis back."

"That shouldn't be a problem now," Artwair said. "Will Your Majesty be accompanying us?"

"No," she said. "I think you might do this with the army, Artwair. I should like to return to Eslen for a time. But rest assured that when we march on Hansa, I will be with you."

"March on Hansa, Majesty?"

"I don't see any reason to let them try this again, ever. Do you?"

"I—no, Majesty,"

"Right. Tell my bodyguard I'll ride to Eslen in two bells. And send word to Cape Chavel that I want him to join me there when he's done with the army coming down the Dew."

"There's still the army of the Church in the south," Artwair said.

"They have already withdrawn," Anne said. "I'm not sure why. But send a few of the Hansan captives to them. Tell them that if they cross our border again, I'll come do the same to them."

Artwair nodded, bowed, and left.

Riding to Eslen, she met cheering crowds, but in the first few leagues it seemed to her there was an uneasiness in their plaudits, as if they feared she would kill them if they did not cheer. The nearer she got to Eslen, however, and the farther she got from the charnel fields around Poelscild, the less ambiguous the applause seemed. By the time she entered the city, she felt their joy and enthusiasm as absolutely genuine. Some were shouting "Saint Queen Anne," and others were calling her "Virgenya II."

She bathed and rested and the next morning took her breakfast with John in her solar, where he rattled off various household matters and gave her a sheaf of documents for her seal. He then sat back, looking a bit uncomfortable.

"What is it, John?" she asked.

"You've received a number of letters, Majesty, some important, most not. But there is one that I believe needs your immediate attention."

"Really? Who is it from?"

"Our former praifec, Marché Hespero."

She stopped with a scone halfway to her mouth. "You're kidding," she said.

"I'm afraid not."

"Let me see it, then."

He handed her the folded paper with the seal of Crotheny's praifectur.

"Took it with him, I see," she said. Then she opened the letter. It was written in a beautiful flowing hand.

To Your Majesty Anne I, Queen of Crotheny,
I hope this letter finds you well and in good keeping with the saints.
Time is pressing, so I must be blunt. I know I have

*been implicated in certain matters and that a general
order for my arrest has been issued. I will not here argue
the charges against me—I will save that for a later time.
What I will tell you is that I have information you need.
It concerns the power you no doubt feel growing in you,
and most particularly it has to do with the emergence
of a certain throne you may have heard of.*

*I also believe that it is important that there be peace
between the Church and Crotheny, and healing. By the
time you read this, you will find Church forces have all
withdrawn beyond the Teremené. I await the pleasure
of meeting with you personally. I am prepared to come
to Eslen with as few companions as you name, or
alone if that is your command.*

Marché Hespero

Anne fingered the page, wondering if it might be impreg-
nated with poison. But no, John had handled it before her.

"When did this arrive?" she asked.

"Yesterday, else I would have had it sent to you."

She studied the words again, trying to figure out what was
going on.

She had trusted Hespero growing up, had gone to him for
lustration and advice. He had seemed wise, not particularly
kind but not unkind, either. Even when her father had gone
against him in naming Anne and her sisters heirs to the
throne, he had remained polite and nice to her.

But then she had learned things. She had seen a letter from
him that made him responsible for the unholy slaughter in
Dunmrogh. He had colluded with Robert against her mother
and tortured Cavaor Ackenzal, the court composwer, nearly
to death. He'd left Eslen before Anne's forces had recap-
tured it and hadn't been seen or heard from since.

And now he wanted to talk. It didn't make sense. The
Church had turned its bloody resacaratum into a holy war
against her, and now suddenly Hespero wanted to be friends
and help her claim the power the Church so vehemently
named shinecraft?

She closed her eyes and tried to find Hespero out in the sedos realm, to see where he was and what he was about, to find some inkling of the consequences of meeting him.

But as with the Hellrune, all she found was a quiet, dark place.

And then she knew.

"It's him," she told Nerenai later that day. The Sefry was weaving a shawl, and Anne was pacing in her quarters.

"The man who attacked me in the wood of the Faiths, the one who threatens me. It was Hespero all along."

"How can you be sure?"

"He has power like me, like the Hellrune. Only someone with art like that can go within the sedos unsummoned. Who else could it be? I thought once it might be the Briar King, but from everything I've heard about him, I no longer believe so."

"What will you do? Will you see him?"

"He tried to attack me," Anne said. "I'm certain he was at least partly responsible for the murders of my sisters and father and the other attempts on me. Yes, I will see him, and I will find out what he knows, and then he will pay."

CHAPTER NINE

TWO REASONS

NEIL STARED at Brinna for a long few breaths before responding. He felt as if he were somehow outside of the world, looking in from a great distance away.

"Why would you say that?" he finally managed.

"The world is poisoned, Sir Neil," she said. "Poisoned by two thousand years of unchecked use of the sedoi. That's what ultimately made breaking the law of death possible. Were the world in better health . . ." She looked away. "But it wasn't. The monsters—the greffyns and such—those are all symptoms of that coming death, of a very ancient being trying to reclaim the world, but without the power to heal it. Then there is—was—the Briar King, who did have the power to restore it but who is now dead. That leaves your queen and two others to fight over the sedos power, to take it when it reaches its peak. But that power, you see, can't be used to *mend* anything. It can only corrupt. And in this moment coming very soon, the sedos power will be so strong that all other puissance in the world will fail before it. Life and death will cease to have meaning, as will chaos and order. It will all become the dream—the Black Mary—of the one who takes the power."

"Anne won't misuse it."

"She does so already. She drains the life from our warriors. She boils them in their skins. Soon she will do far worse. And of the three who seek the sedos throne, she is favored to win. And so my people fight and die, and I use my visions as best I can to help them. But I am too far away now, and she has become too strong. To be of any use I need to leave here, but that isn't allowed. It's never been allowed, and after my earlier escape, my father is doubly committed to the ancient way. He doesn't really understand what's going on. He twists what I tell him and tells his men that Anne is evil, that our war is just and holy."

"Isn't that what you just told me?"

"No. I chose to take the fight to Anne because I know where she is. The others I cannot find. But they must seek her out, too, and they will, because they cannot see each other. Anne is queen of Crotheny—she is in Crotheny. Prescience can't find her, but spies can. She's visible every day."

"But if Anne *knew*," Neil said. "If she *knew*, she would not do—not seize this throne you speak of."

"She won't have a choice when the time comes. She will have to take the power or die. I do not think she will choose to die. Nonetheless, I have tried to contact her. I've sent coven-trained, first to tell her these things, later to assassinate her. None ever made it near her. She has a great many protectors who have no wish to see her refuse this power."

"The Sefry."

"Them, yes. But there are others, with different goals."

"But you must have sent your brother to Saint Cer. He and his men tried to murder Anne *then*."

She shook her head. "I had nothing to do with that. The Dunmrogh boy betrayed her there to your uncle, who was in fact working with my father."

"Is Robert here?"

"Yes."

He digested that for a moment. "Is my queen safe?"

"You mean Muriele now. Yes and no. Safe for the moment. But safe here, in Hansa? Not remotely."

She held Neil's gaze so long that his scalp began to prickle, but she finally looked away again.

"We've spoken enough for now," she said. "A longer talk will raise suspicions, and to be frank, I haven't decided what to do with you." She picked up her mask. "I'm sorry I can't offer you better accommodations, but that, too, would attract attention."

"I have to try to help my queen," he said. "You know that."

"I do," she said softly. "I'll do what I can to help Muriele."

"And Anne?"

But Brinna didn't reply. She just replaced the mask on her face.

"Why do you wear that?" he asked.

"I spoke of a higher calling," she murmured. "Perhaps I will tell you about that one day."

She turned and left through the same concealed panel, and a few moments later guards appeared and returned him to his cell.

Muriele sipped wine and leaned on the timeworn balustrade of a stone balcony. Below her, a stream coursed noisily through a narrow whitewalled gorge very pleasantly grown in hemlock, spruce, and everic. The balcony supporting her was carved from the living rock of the ravine.

"Who made this place?" she asked Berimund as he joined her.

"I don't know," he replied. "I'm told that the style of the carving resembles that of the *Unselthiuzangardis,* the, ah, 'Wicked Kingdoms.'"

"That was during what we called the Warlock Wars."

"That's right," he said. "Anyway, I believe it was probably the refuge of a sorcerer or perhaps the secret dwelling of his mistress. My wulfbrothars and I found it when we were in farunya."

"Farunya? That's this province?"

He looked at her blankly a minute, then laughed. "No," he said. "Farunya—that's when boys who are almost old enough to be men band together and wander, hunt outlaws, pick fights with hill tribes. My wulfbrothars and I went out for years, went all the way into Zhuzhturi. When we returned—those of us who returned—we were made men and warriors. Any boy who hopes to fight in a hansa must go in farunya first."

"You lost friends?"

"There were forty of us to start with. Thirty-two came back. Not bad considering some of the fights we got into." He grinned. "Those were good times. And that's how I know my brothers won't betray me. We were forged into men together. It's a strong bond."

The thing about betrayal, Muriele thought, *is that only someone you trust can really betray you.*

She didn't say it, though. If Berimund was wrong, he was wrong. Her saying something wouldn't serve any purpose.

"So, this place," the prince went on. "We spotted it from down there. Took us five days to find the entrance above. We came back later and furnished it. We swore to keep its location secret."

"That's why you blindfolded me."

"Jah. Even then, I had to put it to a vote with my men."

"I'm flattered they allowed it." She let her gaze drift back down to the river. "So what now?"

"We wait for my father to calm down," he said.

"And if he doesn't?"

"In that case, we'll have to wait until he dies, I think."

"Well," Muriele said, "at least there's wine."

Neil lay in the dark, wondering if he was going mad, wondering how long he had been there. He thought he probably slept a lot, but the distinction between sleep and waking was starting to blur. His only indication of the time was when they brought his food, but he was always a little hungry, so he wasn't sure if he was being fed twice a day, once a day, or once every two days.

He tried to think about mountain pasture and wide blue sky, but instead his mind kept replaying just a few things.

Had the entire embassy really been a sham, a disguise for assassination? Would Anne really have ordered that? Would Muriele have been part of it?

Maybe, maybe. Queens were forced to do that sometimes, weren't they? It was childish to think otherwise.

But Anne had insisted *he* go along. Did she know? Know that he knew Brinna? Did she think that he would kill her if Alis failed?

Should he, if he got the chance? *Could* he, if it was his queen's wish? After all, it was his fault that Hansa even had a Hellrune.

And the thing that kept burning up through everything else was the memory of his kiss with her out in the marshes around Paldh, the touch of her lips and the sweet gift of her against him.

Someone was humming a weird little song. Fingers traced along Neil's bare spine, up to his shoulder, along his ruined sword arm, back up around the edge of his ear. He smiled and rolled that way.

Hazel eyes gazed down from a delicate face framed in dark tresses. She had a sad little smile on her lips.

"Fastia," he gasped, his heart thundering.

"I know you," the ghost sighed. "I remember you."

Neil tried to sit up but found that he couldn't. His body seemed impossibly tired and heavy.

"I kissed you once, too."

"I'm sorry, Fastia," he whispered.

"Why? For kissing?"

"No."

"I'm almost gone," she said. "The river is taking me. Whoever you are, I've almost forgotten you. If you ever wronged me, it's in the water now."

"I love you."

"You love *her*."

"Yes," he said, miserably.

She stroked his cheek. "No need for that," she said.

"Did she bring you here?" he asked.

"No. She's like a doorway, and through her I saw you. You drew me here."

"I do love you."

"I'm glad I was loved," she said. She closed her eyes. "Something is coming," she said. "You need to go back. I wanted to tell you that."

She bent and brought her lips to his, and he felt a tickle. Then she began singing in a language he didn't know. He found himself wanting to sing it as well, to leave his flesh and join Fastia. But the song faded, and her with it, until she was gone.

He started and was awake.

Footsteps. Someone was coming. It didn't sound like the jailer.

It wasn't; it was four guards. They didn't say anything, and he didn't ask them anything; he just let them lead him out of the hole and back up into the halls. They took him back to the chamber where he'd seen Brinna and left him there alone.

He was wondering what to do, when the small door opened and the girl came in with a pitcher and filled an alabaster washbasin.

"My lady asks that you bathe yourself," she said in

Hanzish. Her eyes were darting, fearful, not like the last time.

"I'm to leave you alone while you do so. Fresh clothes are there." She pointed to some garments folded on the chair he'd sat in before, then exited the way she had come.

He stripped off his filthy weeds and scrubbed himself from head to toe. A bath would have been better, but when he was done, he felt so much more human that it was shocking. When he was dry, he slipped on the hose, breeches, and shirt that had been provided and stood waiting, enjoying the ability to straighten his limbs, back, and neck all at the same time.

The girl stuck her head in a bit later, and a few moments after that Brinna entered, wearing the same, or an identical, black gown. She did not, however, have the mask with her.

Her expression didn't tell him much, and for a little while that was all he got. Then she walked over and took her place in her armchair.

"Please sit," she said.

He complied.

"Things are complicated," she said. "I wouldn't have had you stay in that place if they weren't."

"I appreciate the sentiment," he muttered.

"I doubt that, but that's not this discussion."

She looked down and cleared her throat softly.

"There are three reasons you're here and not dead or still imprisoned," she said. "The first is that I believe you are not an assassin. The second is that I think we can help each other without you breaching your *real* duty."

She paused and settled her shoulders. "The third isn't important right now."

"I'm glad you don't believe I'm an assassin," he said.

She nodded and placed her hands on her knees. "I want you to help me escape again."

"What?"

"Anne has destroyed a third of our army," she said.

"This *is* war," he said gently.

"You needn't condescend to me, sir," she said. "I know what war is."

"Sorry."

"Understand, it was not the army of Crotheny that killed our men. It was Anne herself."

"Oh," he said, frowning, trying to understand. He'd been with Anne a few times when she had used her gifts. But even on the march to Eslen, she had never been able to affect more than a dozen or so people and never actually had killed more than one or two. Even so, it had made him a little sick.

"How many?" he asked.

"Forty-eight thousand."

"Forty . . ." It didn't make any sense.

"It has begun, Sir Neil. She is coming into her strength. My father will keep sending his men against her, and they will continue to die."

"What do you intend to do?" he asked.

"Anne is beyond me. There is nothing I can do directly. But I think I might undo the damage I myself did. I might help mend the law of death, and if that is done, everything changes. All visions of the future, all prophecy becomes moot. On that, if nothing else, I ask you to trust me."

"But why must I help you escape?"

"I have to reach Newland," she said. "That's where I must be, and in a short time."

"It's impossible for me to promise that," Neil said.

"I realize that," she replied. "I just wanted you to know what I'm about. I need to talk to Queen Muriele, clearly. Only she can make the decision to take me to Newland. I just want your permission first, since she is in your charge."

"That means having her brought up here?"

"If I could do that, I would have already done so," she replied.

"What do you mean?"

"She went hunting with Berimund, yes?"

"Yes, the day after we arrived. Just before I was seized."

"My father isn't a stable man. He condemned your lady to death and ordered my brother to carry out that charge."

Neil stood so violently that the chair went clattering to the floor. "You saw this?"

She sucked in a breath and flinched back.

"Did you?" he asked more softly.

"No. I have spies, as well. But I have seen where my brother took her."

"To murder her, you mean?"

Her eyes focused outward and seemed to glaze. "Berimund won't do that," she said, her voice a bit singsong. "He's taken her someplace to hide. He doesn't know he's been followed."

"Followed? By your father?"

She shook her head. "No. Robert Dare."

Without thinking, Neil put his hand up to his head, where the usurper had struck him with a bottle.

"I have to get to her," he said. "Can you help me do that?"

"I need her, too, and I need her alive," Brinna said. "Alis has agreed to aid me, but I need you, too."

He took a deep breath. "I'll help you escape," he said. "But after we find the queen, I must obey *her* orders."

"Even if they are to slay me?"

"Any order but that," he said.

Something bright flitted behind her face but quickly vanished.

"Well," Brinna said. "Are we agreed?"

"Yes."

"That's good," she said. "Because we've already begun, I'm afraid. The interrogator insisted on being with me in this interview, and she got my father to put it in writing that she would be."

"Where is she, then?"

"In the next room, dead. I poisoned her. The men who brought you have also been dealt with. Or at least I hope so."

"They've been dealt with," a quiet voice said.

Neil started and found Alis standing behind him, clad in a dark blue gown. She held something bundled in a cloak.

"I think this hauberk will fit you, Sir Neil," she said. "And you've your pick of these swords."

"I'm sure you would prefer your own," Brinna said. "But those are beyond my reach. I hope one of these is suitable. You're going to need it very soon."

CHAPTER TEN

✢

AN OLD FRIEND

ASPAR HAD begun to draw the knife before he realized he was losing his mind, that the geos had taken his sense without him even knowing it.

Leshya saw his expression and raised her eyebrows.

Fighting down the paranoia, Aspar pushed the eldritch blade back in, unhooked the scabbard, and held it out toward her.

"This is yours," he said. "I should have given it back to you days ago."

"You make better use of it than I would," she said.

"I don't like it," he said.

"Neither do I," the Sefry replied. "It's a sedos thing."

Aspar proffered it for another few breaths, but she didn't reach for it, so he hooked the sheath back on his belt.

"Let's keep Fend's offer to help us quiet for now," Aspar said. "Until we cann what he's up to."

"It could confuse things more than they already are," she said.

He couldn't tell if it was a question. "Yah."

They found Emfrith's bunch setting up camp in a field not too far from the road. Winna came running up as they passed the watchmen. She was flushed, and though she seemed

excited, it was hard to tell if it was from a good or a bad
cause.

"He found us," she said. That sounded happy.

"Stephen?"

Her expression fell, and then she shook her head.

"Ehawk."

Aspar felt a slight lift of his shoulders. "Really? Where
is he?"

"Sleeping. He was nearly falling out of his saddle. I don't
think he's rested in days."

"Well, I reckon I'll talk to him later, then."

"That's all you have to say?"

"I'm glad the lad's alive," he said. "But I reckoned wherever he was, he was all right. Ehawk can take care of himself. Not like—" He stopped.

"Not like Stephen," she said softly.

"Stephen's fine, too," he said gruffly. "Probably holed up
in a scriftorium someplace."

"Right," Winna agreed. "Probably."

Early the next morning, Aspar found Ehawk crouched
around the coals of the fire. The young Watau grinned when
he saw Aspar.

"You were hard to find," he said. "Like tracking a ghost.
Lost you before the cold river up there."

"The Welph."

"I don't like those trees. It's like always being at the snow
line in the mountains."

"Yah," Aspar said. "Different. Anyway, you should have
just waited like Winna. I would have just come to you."

"I couldn't do that," the Watau boy replied. "Winna
didn't wait, either. She made Emfrith look for you, but once
her belly started swelling, he wouldn't go far." He stirred
the embers with a stick. "He didn't want to find you, anyway."

"Yah, I conth that," he said.

Ehawk nodded and pushed back his pitch-dark hair. His

face looked leaner, older. His body was catching up with
the man inside.

"So where are we going?" he asked.

"Mountains of the Hare. The western ranges, near Sa
Ceth ag Sa'Nem."

"Ah." The boy shook his head. "You're seeking the
Segachau, then."

"What?"

"The reed-water-place," the young man said. "The well
of life. The hole everything came out of at the beginning of
time."

"Grim's eye," Aspar swore. "You know something
about it?"

"My people have lived in the mountains for a long time,"
the Watau replied. "That's a real old legend."

"What do they say?" Aspar asked.

"It gets pretty complicated," Ehawk said. "Lots of tribes
and clan names. But really, when you simple it, the story
spells that in the ancient times everything lived beneath the
earth: people, animals, plants. There was also a race of
demons under there that kept everything penned up. They
ate us. So one day a certain man got out of his pen and found
a reed that went up into the sky. He climbed it and came out
here, in this world. He went back down and led everyone else
up here, too. That man became the Etthoroam, the Mosslord—
him you call the Briar King. He stopped the demons from
following, and he made the sacred forest. When he was
done, he went to sleep, and he told the people to worship the
forest and keep it from harm or he would wake and take his
revenge. And the place where he came up is called Segachau.
They say you can't always find it."

Aspar scratched his chin, wondering what Stephen would
make of that story. The Watau didn't have writing or li-
braries. They didn't follow the ways of the Church any
more than his father's Ingorn people did.

And yet in two ways at least, Ehawk's story agreed with
Leshya's tale of the Vhenkherdh. Both said the Briar King
came from it, and both agreed it was the source of life.

Other than that, though, the Watau story was very different from the Sefry's, and that made him feel suddenly better about the whole thing. He'd learned from Stephen just how twisted time could make the truth; maybe no one, not even the Sarnwood witch, had all the facts. Maybe when he got there, Aspar could find some way to surprise everyone. Come to think of it, he probably knew at least one thing no one except maybe Winna did.

"It's good to have you back, Ehawk," he said, patting him on the shoulder.

" 'Tis good to be back, master holter."

Aspar's improved mood didn't last long.

Another two days brought them to the Then River, and the land was starting to warn Aspar what to expect on the road ahead.

Green fields gave way to sickly yellow weeds, and the only birds they saw were high overhead. At the banks of the Then, some tough marsh grass still clung to life, just barely.

But across the stream what once had been rich prairie was brittle and brown, dead for a month or more. There was no birdsong, no buzz of crickets, nothing. It was wasteland.

The villages were dead, too. They found no one alive, and the bones that remained were gnawed and crushed as no natural beast could manage.

The next day, the edge of the King's Forest appeared, and Aspar prepared himself for the worst.

Winna, who hadn't been talking much to him lately, rode up beside him.

"It'll be bad, won't it?" she said.

"Yah." He already could see how wrong the tree line was.

"I'm sorry," she said. "I know how it hurts you."

"I'm the holter," he said. "I'm supposed to protect it."

"You've done your best," she said.

"No," he replied harshly. "No, I haven't."

"Aspar," she said gently, "you have to talk to me. I need to know why we're coming here, where everything is dead except for monsters. I trust you, but you usually tell me what's going on. Fend's not even trying to catch us, and Emfrith is starting to question our direction, too. He's wondering what happens when we run out of supplies."

"Emfrith can ask me himself," Aspar snapped.

"I don't think this is about taking me someplace safe," Winna said.

The geos stung him, but he held his ground against it, because now the only way to convince Winna that they should be doing this entailed telling her part of the truth.

It was such a relief, he almost felt like crying.

"Listen," he said softly. "I learned some things from the Sarnwood witch, from my trip into the Bairghs. What you see here—what we'll see ahead—it's not stopping with the King's Forest. It'll keep spreading until everything is dead, until there are no woods or fields anywhere. There's nowhere I can take you where you and the child will be safe, not for long."

"What are you telling me?"

"I'm spellin' that our only chance is to stop this somehow."

"Stop it?"

He explained in brief about the Vhenkherdh and the possibility of "summoning" a new Briar King. He didn't tell her how Leshya had come by her knowledge, and of course he made no mention of Fend's assertion that her unborn child was to be the sacrifice that would save the world. He still wasn't sure he believed that himself. When he was done, she looked at him strangely.

"What?"

"There's still something I don't understand," she said. "I accept it's true that there's no place where this rot won't eventually reach me. But there are places that will be safe from it for a while longer. The Aspar I know wouldn't have wanted me along for this . . . attempt, not in my condition. He would have had Emfrith take me as far from the King's Forest as possible while he went to fight and maybe die. Now, don't get me wrong. I'm glad you didn't do that."

"I think Fend's after you, too," he said.

"Then why doesn't he send an utin for me?"

"The wyver attacked you, remember?"

She nodded uneasily. "Is that the only reason?"

"When I saw Fend last, he told me as much," Aspar said.

"But why?"

"You were his captive for nearly a month. What do you think? Fend hates me, he's barking mad, I love you. How much reason do you maunt he needs?"

"Right," she said. "Right. It's just—something doesn't feel right."

"Nothing *is* right," Aspar replied.

"I know," she said calmly. "But we're going to fix it, werlic. So our child can grow up."

"Yah," he said, his voice tight.

"I've thought of names," she said.

"The Ingorn don't name children until they're two years old," Aspar said roughly.

"Why not?"

"Because most don't live," he said. "If you don't name them, they can try to be born again. Them with names die true deaths."

"That's stupid," Winna said. "Why name anyone, ever?"

"Because eventually our names find us, just like our deaths."

"This child isn't going to die, Aspar. I know that in my heart. I don't know why you would try to—" Her voice cracked.

They rode along for a moment.

"What names?" he asked.

"Never mind," she answered.

He glanced over at her. "I always thought Armann was a good name," he said.

She frowned, and at first he thought the conversation really was over. But then she nodded. "Yes," she allowed. "My father would like that."

"And if it's a girl?"

"I like Emmer," she said. "Or Sally."

* * *

A bell later the wind shifted to blow from the woods, and the scent of corruption was so strong that Aspar gagged and lost his breakfast, then lay over his horse's neck dry-heaving.

"For the saints, Asp, what's wrong?" Winna asked.

"The smell."

"Smell?" She sniffed at the air. "I smell something a little rotten," she said. "Nothing to be sick over. Are you all right?"

"Yah," he said.

But he wasn't. When they got nearer, he saw some others wrinkling their noses, but to him the stench was so overpowering that he could hardly think. He wanted anger to hold him up, get him through it, but mostly he felt sick, tired, and sad. Something deep in his chest told him it was time to lie down and die, along with the forest he had known.

Because it was gone.

Every natural tree had rotted into viscous black slime, and growing from their putrefied corpses were the triumphant black thorns he first had seen growing from the footprints of the Briar King.

But it wasn't just the vines now. They had been joined by trees with long saw-toothed leaves, barrel-shaped plants that resembled giant club moss, leafless, scaly bushes. He recognized some of them as being like those he had seen in the Sarnwood, but although unnatural, those had seemed healthy. These were not; like the ironoak, yew, poplar, and pine they had sprung from, these plants were dying, too.

So were the beasts. They came across the corpses of a greffyn and an utin. It looked like the first had killed the second, started to eat it, and then died of its own wounds.

Later they came across other sedhmhari that appeared simply to have dropped dead, perhaps of hunger.

There were no birds at all, no sounds except those they and their horses made. And for Aspar the smell only got worse and worse as they climbed up into the Lean Gable Hills and then back down along the edge of what once had been the

Foxing Marshes but were now noisome meres infested with the giant scabby mosslike plants. There were things still moving in the water, big things, but none came close enough to see.

"This is insane," Emfrith said as darkness started to settle in and Aspar hunted for a campsite. "What could have done this?"

Aspar didn't feel like answering and didn't, but the knight persisted.

"And what refuge do you hope to find in this desert? And where will we find supplies? We don't have that much food or wine left, and I wouldn't drink from any of the springs we've seen. There's nothing to hunt."

"I know a place where we might find supplies," Aspar said. "We can be there by tomorrow."

"And then what?"

"Then we head into the mountains."

"You think they won't be like this?"

No, Aspar thought. *They'll be worse.*

They reached the White Warlock the next morning, crossing the ancient Brew Bridge, a narrow span of pitted black stone. The river was no longer the clear stream that had inspired its name but ran black as tar.

When they were halfway across, something exploded out of it.

As his horse reared, Aspar had the impression of something that married snake and frog. Its immense greenish-black bulk rose up above them and showed a mouth topful of yellow needles that was reared to strike down toward them.

But it stopped suddenly, swaying there. Aspar saw that its eyes had pupils like a toad's, and weird gills opened and closed on the sides of its massy neck. He saw no limbs; the sinuous neck—or body—continued deep into the water.

He started to put an arrow to his bow, but the beast suddenly turned its head, looked back the way Aspar and his companions had come, and vented a forlorn croak. Then it withdrew into the river as quickly as it had risen.

"Sceat," Aspar breathed.

"It didn't attack us," Emfrith wondered.

"No," Aspar agreed. *Fend told it not to.*

After the lowlands around the river, they again began to climb up into the Brogh y Stradh, where wild cattle once grazed in pleasant meadows and periwinkle finches came to breed and lay their eggs. Traveling through the forest wasn't the discovery of a loved one lost; it was a fresh loss around every corner, a new corpse every league.

Toward dusk they reached Tor Scath.

Unlike the forest around it, Tor Scath was unchanged. The last time he'd been there had been with Stephen Darige. He'd just rescued the lad from bandits, and he remembered with muffled amusement the way the boy had gone on and on about things that at the time seemed absurd.

But time told, and in the end he had been more of a fool than Stephen, hadn't he? Stephen, with his knowledge of the ancient past, had been more ready to face what was coming than Aspar, despite the lad's sheltered upbringing.

"That's an odd-looking place," Emfrith said, breaking Aspar's chain of thought.

Aspar nodded, taking the place in once again. It was as if someone had taken a small, perfectly reasonable keep and tried to cram as many weird towers onto it as possible. There was actually one tower that had another one starting from it halfway up.

"Yah," he agreed. "They say it was built by a madman."

"Does anyone live here? It hardly seems defensible."

"It's lately a royal hunting lodge," Aspar replied. "Kept by a knight named Sir Symen Rookswald. I doubt that anyone is here now."

"Surely Sir Symen left in time," Winna murmured.

"I'm sure he did," Aspar said. "He was onto the danger before I was."

He said it, but he didn't really believe it. Sir Symen took his duty seriously despite his morose character.

Human bones lay in a thick scatter outside the walls.

"The people of the keep?" Emfrith asked.

Aspar shook his head. "I maun Tor Scath is more defensible than you think. These died trying to get in."

"Slinders," Winna reckoned.

"Yah."

"So Sir Symen stayed and fought."

"For a while, anyway."

"What are slinders?" Emfrith asked.

"Tribespeople from the hills, driven mad by the Briar King. They were like locusts. They would pull down and eat anything before them."

"Eat?" the knight asked incredulously. "I heard rumors like that, but I never believed 'em."

"No, they ate people, all right," Aspar said. "Without salt, even. Now keep aware. We don't know what lives in here now."

The keep's entrance was as odd as the rest of it, a smallish gate at the base of a narrow tower. Aspar tested it and found it barred from the other side, but that triggered a sudden baying and barking from within.

"There are dogs in there," Emfrith said. "How is that possible?"

A few moments later the gate opened, revealing a hulk of a man on the other side.

"Isarn?" Aspar said, not believing it.

"Master White," the fellow replied. "It's good to see you."

But Aspar was looking around, astonished. There were not only dogs in the yard but chickens and geese. There were even a few green weeds and what looked like a plot of turnips.

"Sir Symen? Is he here?" Aspar asked.

The giant nodded. "In the hall. He'll be glad to see you. Let me show you where to put the horses."

* * *

Symen's long hair and beard were more unkempt than ever, lending him the appearance of an old lion on the verge of starvation, but he smiled and came shakily to his feet when Aspar entered. Winna rushed to him and gave him a hug.

"Aspar," the old man said. "What a pretty gift you bring me." He frowned. "Is this little Winna?"

"It's me, Sir Symen," she confirmed.

"Oh, sweet girl, how you've grown. It's been too long since I went to Colbaely." He glanced at her belly but politely didn't say anything.

"Have you heard anything about the town?"

"Your father left, I know that; headed over the mountains toward Virgenya. Most others fled or died when the slinders came."

He turned to clasp Aspar's arm. He felt no more substantial than a straw.

"I told you, didn't I, Aspar? Hardheaded man you are."

He nodded. "You were more right than wrong," he admitted. "What happened here?"

"Sit," Sir Symen said. "I still have wine. We'll have a drink."

He signed, and a young boy who had been sitting on a stool in the corner got up and went off down the hall.

"Anfalthy?" Aspar asked.

"I sent her to relatives in Hornladh," he replied. "Along with the other women. This is no place for them now."

The boy returned with a jug of wine. Mazers were already scattered about the table, and he set about filling them.

Symen took a long quaff. "It's good to have visitors to drink with," he said. "We don't have much company these days."

"You never did," Aspar replied.

"No, that's true," the knight allowed. He trailed a glance at Emfrith and his men. "Who are your friends?"

Aspar made the introductions, trying not to let his impatience show. When that was all settled, Symen finally got around to the holter's question.

"The slinders came," he said. "But they couldn't breach the walls, and they soon left. They came several times, but it was always the same. They were terrifying if you met them in the forest, but against a keep—even such a poor keep as this one—they had no weapons. They couldn't chew their way through stone, could they? So we stayed put, and when they were distant, I sent men to help the villagers and to lay up meat for a siege.

"Then the monsters started to show, but it seems mad King Gault wasn't so mad after all. He built this place to keep the alvs and booyghs out, and damned if it doesn't."

"What do you mean?"

"They can't or won't come in. I can only imagine some enchantment keeps them out."

"Grim," Aspar murmured. "That's a turn of weird."

"But a fortunate one for us," Symen replied.

"Yah."

"So they came and went, and then the forest began to die. Then slinders returned, hundreds of them, and greffyns and manticores and all manner of beasts, and they killed each other outside the walls, and what was left starved. We waited inside here, and now here you are."

"But that's wonderful," Emfrith said. "Holter, this is the place. This is where Winna can have her child."

The geos was still finding a lie for Aspar to tell when Isarn suddenly burst into the hall.

"Sir Symen," he shouted. "There's an army coming, not two leagues away. Henne saw it."

"From the north?" Aspar said. "Yah, that'll be Fend."

"And he'll be helpless," Emfrith said. "His beasts can't harm us here. They'll starve like the others."

"He still has men," Aspar pointed out. "They can come in, and probably the Sefry, too."

"This army is marching from the west," Isarn replied. "Men and horses, maybe five hundred."

"Not Fend, then," Winna said.

"Relief from Eslen, perhaps?"

"Perhaps," Aspar said. But he remembered what Fend had told him, and in his heart he didn't think there was any relief in sight.

CHAPTER ELEVEN

✛

DRINKING WITH WARRIORS

THE ARROW felt like liquid fire in Cazio's arm, and he went all knee-weak.

Dodging arrows, he had decided, was not his forte. That was too bad, because he could see that the man who had shot him was drawing back another shaft as another fellow with ax and shield was bearing down on him hard.

He stepped to put the axman between him and the archer and raised Acredo, glad he'd been hit in the left arm. The arrow was still there, like a little tree sprouting from his bicep. His balance felt off.

He speared at the axman's face, but the fellow lifted his shield, turned his blade with it, and stepped in with a hard cut. Cazio jerked his blade to parry in a high *prismo,* with his hand above his head and the blade slanting from right to left across his body. It met the ax just below the hilt, deflecting it a fingersbreadth from hitting him.

With his point down and standing belly to shield with the other man, Cazio did the only thing he could think of: He sprang straight up, tilting his hand out so that the earth-pointing blade came down on the other side of the enemy's shield and stabbed him in the neck just above the breastbone. Encountering no bone, Acredo slipped right down into the man's lungs.

When Cazio's feet hit the ground again, his legs wouldn't

hear of standing, so he went on down while the axman stumbled off, trying for a little while to pull Acredo back out of his body before fetching against a tree.

That left the archer, who was advancing cautiously toward him. Desperately, Cazio began crawling for cover, glancing back often. The man looked grim now and stepped up his pace. Cazio wondered if the axman had been his friend.

But then the fellow sat down hard and dropped his bow. Cazio saw that he had an arrow in his belly.

"Ah, sceat," he heard the man say. "I *knew* it." He sat that way for a moment and then used his bow to push himself to his feet. He looked around, then cast another glance at Cazio.

"Sceat on this," he said, and began hobbling off into the woods.

"Good luck," Cazio called after him.

"Fooce-thu, coonten," the man called back.

"Right," Cazio breathed, trying to stand. It was absolutely astonishing how much blood was on him. Should he try to get the arrow out?

He took hold of it, the sun exploded, and the next thing he knew, someone was looking down at him. He hoped it was a friend.

"This is going to hurt," z'Acatto said later that evening.

"You've never lied to me before," Cazio said sarcastically. "I—" But he forgot whatever he meant to say as his vision went white with pain and his capacity for speech was reduced to a series of ragged gasps.

"Told you," the old man said.

"Yes," was the cleverest response Cazio could manage.

"You'll be fine if the fever doesn't get you."

"What a relief," Cazio replied, wiping tears of pain from his eyes with his good hand.

A glance at Austra's concerned face, and he felt suddenly a bit ashamed. He'd only had an arrow in the meat of his arm. What had been done to her was far worse.

He drank something z'Acatto handed him. It tasted like fire stirred with the sweat of a drunk.

He took another drink, and as z'Acatto plugged and bandaged the wound, he got the broad strokes of what had happened. Shortly put, they had won. The hedgehog had held back the attackers so that the archers could keep putting arrows in them.

"Then the Cassro orders us forward," Jan told him. "Against what's left of the horse. At first they can't believe it; they reckon we're a defensive formation. But we advance with pike a step at a time, braced together like old times, and they got their infantry behind 'em. Even charging they couldn't break us, and now we're startin' to tickle 'em with our pikes, and they've no room to charge. Before you can say Jaq Longwick, they turn and cut their way through their own infantry."

He jerked his chin toward the swordmaster. "That's a man who knows a thing or two about fighting," Jan said.

"I'm sorry I missed it," Cazio said.

"Ah, you did your part. Here, have another drink with me."

"Pleased to," Cazio said.

"One more," Austra said from behind him. "Then he's mine, boys. The sun's going down."

They'd set up a tent for her, and once inside, he took her gently by the shoulders and kissed her. She had alcohol on her breath, too, and her eyes were troubled, showing more need than desire.

He pulled her closer, and need suddenly was replaced by what looked like panic. He felt her go rigid and released his grip.

"I'm sorry," she said.

"No need for that," he replied, stroking her head. "You've been through a lot."

She kissed the shoulder of his wounded arm. "So have you."

He bussed her forehead, then sidled around behind her.

This time when he pulled her close, she didn't tense up. He kissed the back of her neck, and she sighed.

Gently, gently, he undressed her, and soon they were spooned flesh to flesh. He reached around and stroked her forehead, then down her ribs and hip.

"Is this enough for this evening?" she asked softly.

"More than enough," he replied. "Kingdoms more. Empires more."

"Thank you."

"You'll heal," he told her. "I'll heal, and we'll both be better. But we're fine now. We're alive, and we have each other."

"That's true, isn't it?" she murmured.

He woke a few bells later. It was cold, and he made sure Austra was well covered in her blanket. Then he pulled on his pants and shirt and went outside. His arm throbbed as if a demon were in it, and the liquor had gone thin as milk in his veins.

About half the men were still awake, singing and laughing by the fire.

He found z'Acatto alone, up on the wagon.

"Is it time for the wine yet, old man?" he asked.

He could just make out his mestro's face in the distant firelight. It looked like he was smiling a little.

"No, not yet."

"Why didn't you tell me any of this? I mean, I know we have our quarrèls, but you're almost my father."

"I'm *not* your father," z'Acatto snapped. Then, more softly: "I could never be that."

"No? But you took on the role. Why?"

"I couldn't think of anything better to do," he said.

"You haven't answered my question."

"Doesn't look like I'm going to, does it?"

Cazio sighed. "Don't you ever get bored with this bickering?"

Z'Acatto was silent for a moment, and then he chuckled. "Easier than talking," he said.

"Exactly. For me, too."

"Fine," z'Acatto said. "I never wanted you involved in this sort of thing. Your father made me promise to teach you the sword, but he never asked me to make you a soldier. I don't think he wanted that for you, and I damned sure didn't. So I didn't fill your head with tales of our exploits."

"Maybe if you had, I wouldn't be involved in all of this now."

Z'Acatto laughed again. "Right, that's funny. No matter how bad I made it out to be, it would have sounded exciting to you. And because your father did it, and maybe because I did—"

"You were both *famous*."

"Yes. All the more reason you would have wanted to follow in our footsteps."

Cazio nodded. "You're probably right. I was a little hard-headed when I was younger."

"When you were younger? Your head gets harder every day. And a good thing, because you get hit on it more often all the time."

He handed a bottle down. It was a not very good wine. Cazio took a swallow.

"What now?" he asked.

"You seem to have that worked out," z'Acatto said.

"You're the Emrature," Cazio replied.

Z'Acatto took the bottle and had another drink.

"I guess I am," he finally said. "Most of these fellows want to go back to Eslen and fight for Anne. I've never seen the place, and I guess I should."

"Well, it's something to see," Cazio said, yawning.

They finished the bottle and started another one before exhaustion overcame the ache in his arm.

"Back to bed for me," he said, clapping his mentor on the back.

"We move early," z'Acatto told him.

"Yes, sir, Cassro," Cazio replied.

He went back to the wagon and found Austra just as he'd

left her. He lay against her, relaxing against the warmth of
her body.

He woke the next morning in exactly the same position.
Austra was still quiet, so he thought to rise and help break
camp without waking her.

But as he sat up, he noticed that her eyes were open.

"Morning, love," he said, and kissed her on the cheek.

She didn't move, and her eyes were glassy. He shook her,
and she didn't respond. He shook her harder.

CHAPTER TWELVE

DEPOSITIONS

ANNE STRETCHED her limbs and closed her eyes as a
cool zephyr ruffled the grass. Faster snuffled nearby, and
a lute sounded in the distance.

Something tickled against her lips, and with a smile she
parted them and gently bit down, filling her mouth with the
tart juice of a grape.

"You didn't peel it," she murmured.

"Oh, I see where I stand now," the earl of Cape Chavel
said. "One day a suitor, the next a Hadamish serving girl."

"You can be both," Anne said, lazily opening her eyes.

Gulls fluttered overhead in the sea breeze.

"This is a nice place," the earl said.

"One of my favorites, Cape Chavel," she replied.

"Really?" he said. "Can't you see your way clear to call
me Tam?"

"Can you see your way clear to peeling a grape?"

He tugged at the sleeve of her dress. "If that's a manner
of speaking."

"You're too bold, sir," she said.

"I wonder if your legs are freckled," he replied.

"Huh. I wonder if they are."

"There you go." He pressed another grape to her lips. This time it was peeled.

"Very good, Cape Chavel," she said. "You're learning."

"But we still aren't on a first-name basis?"

"I think we should be after a few more years of courting. Are you in a rush?"

"No," he said. His voice became a bit more serious. "It hardly seems necessary now."

"What do you mean?"

"You've beaten back the army of Hansa. The Church has withdrawn and is suing for peace."

"Who told you that?" she asked, pushing up on her elbows.

"I guess—well, that's the word going around."

"I've no idea what Hespero wants," she said, "but I doubt very much that it is peace. He's foolish even to come here, given the crimes he's implicated in."

"I stand corrected, then."

"Continue to recline instead," Anne said.

"As you wish."

"Are you saying you no longer wish to court me?"

"I'm not saying that at all. But if our courting is pretense to encourage Virgenya to send troops, well, you don't seem to need them."

"I don't, do I?" Anne replied. "But I'm going to get them anyway. And not by any pretense."

"What do you mean?"

"Charles slighted me, and he slighted the empire. What sort of empress would I be if I allowed my subject kings to treat me like that? No, I think we will change the head beneath *that* crown." She cocked an eye at him and reached to stroke his hair. "I think it would sit well right here," she told him.

The earl blinked, and his mouth opened. Then he smiled as if he'd just understood a joke.

"Your Majesty is in a jesting mood."

"No," she said. "I'm quite serious."

A troubled look turned his features.

"What's the matter?" she asked.

"I hope Your Majesty doesn't think— You can't imagine I had this aim when we began our friendship."

She shrugged. "I don't care if you did. Loyalty is good, but so is intelligence. When you cast your lot with me, I wasn't the dog favored to win this fight. You took a risk with me, and I won't forget that."

"I'm not sure what to say, Majesty."

"I don't require you to say anything," she said. "Just don't pass the news around. I expect your uncle may put up a bit of a fight when you go to claim his hat, and right now we still need our army here. It's not over yet. Even now Hansa is sending another army, larger than the first."

"You'll crush it as easily."

"It will be easier," she agreed, "now that I know how to do it."

"I think you overestimate my uncle's bravery," he said. "When he really comes to understand your power, he won't stand against you. I doubt that any army from anywhere would."

"Well," Anne said in a speculative tone, "I was very ill treated in Vitellio and Tero Gallé. I've half a mind to add them to the empire. Certainly z'Irbina must be taught a lesson."

He was staring at her again.

"Don't be so serious," she said. "Let's just come back to this. Our courting is now pretense only for you to kiss me, and I would prefer you start on that now."

And so he did. His lips were familiar with her neck and shoulder, her hands, the hollow beneath her throat. His hands were acquainted with the broader territory of her body and made themselves languidly busy there. He was not sneaky or apologetic, as Roderick had been. He didn't pretend to have brushed her breast accidentally but went there with confident deliberation.

And if he explored where he was not allowed, he could

tell, and he accepted it, and that was that. It didn't seem to bother him or hurt his feelings or make him seem weak.

But by the saints he kindled her, found the slow fire in her belly and stroked it out to every inch of her, until all she wanted was for more of her flesh to press his, to feel what two unclothed bodies were like together.

But not here, where anyone could see. They could go back to the castle, though . . .

"Enough," she said faintly. "Enough, Cape Chavel."

"Is something wrong?" he whispered.

"Yes," she replied. "I want you. That's what's wrong."

"Nothing wrong with that," he replied. "I want you, too. You've no idea."

"No," she said. "I think I have some idea. But we can't. *I* can't. I'm queen. I have to be responsible. What if I got pregnant, for saints' sake?"

She was surprised to hear herself say it, but there it was.

"I understand," he said. "It doesn't make me want you any less."

She stroked his face. "You're dangerous," she said. "Another few moments and you might have convinced me."

He smiled halfheartedly. "I'm sorry," he said. "I would not make a mistress of you."

She nodded.

"I would make you wife, though, if you would say yes."

She started to make a joke of that, but then, with a bit of a shock, she understood the look in his eyes.

"Let's not get in a hurry, Cape Chavel," she said.

"I love you."

"There's no need to say that," she whispered. "Just hush."

He nodded but looked a little hurt.

Saints, he's serious, she realized.

Things felt turned around all of a sudden. She hadn't understood until this moment that *she* was the one in control of the situation.

"I'm not closing the door," she said. "When I was younger, it was my dream to marry for love. My mother, my sister—everyone—tried to make me understand that a princess didn't have that option, but I refused to believe it. Now I am queen, and I begin to understand. Marriage isn't something I can choose because my heart or body wants it. You have become dear to me in a very short time, and I am tempted to rush. I can't. Please bear with me, court me, be my friend. I never took you for a man easily discouraged. I hope I wasn't wrong about that."

He smiled, and this time it looked more sincere. "You weren't."

"Good." She kissed him again, lightly this time. "And now I'm afraid I must return to the castle. Thank you for a pleasant morning. And welcome back. I'm very well pleased you didn't get yourself killed."

The morning left her with a pleasant tingle that lasted well into the evening. Emily seemed to be grinning a lot, and Anne was pretty certain the girl had made it her business to watch at least a little of what was going on through the hedges. Anne couldn't really bring herself to care.

That afternoon she prepared to meet Hespero. After a little consideration, she chose to wear the habit and wimple of a sister of Saint Cer. Then she went to the Red Hall. They were to meet late, after the dinner hour, around ninth bell.

She made him wait until the eleventh.

He didn't seem particularly disturbed when she entered alone. He was dressed in the simple black robe and square hat she was accustomed to seeing him in as praifec. He still had the mustache and barb, too.

"Majesty," he said, bowing.

"I didn't know your grace accepted me as queen," Anne said. Her heart was beating a little too fast, and she realized that now that he was here, she was nervous.

She couldn't let that show.

"It has been difficult for me, I admit," he said. "But I thought to start on a note of conciliation."

"Well, that's promising," Anne said. "Speak on."

"News has spread of your rather impressive powers. Would you be surprised to learn that it was not unexpected?"

"No," Anne said. "I believe you expected it. I believe you did your level best to stop it—stop me—before I realized the extent of them."

"You can't mean that," Hespero replied. "Why would you think that?"

Anne waved aside his protest. "Never mind that now. Why have you come here?"

"To make an offer."

"And that offer is . . . ?"

"Your Majesty, I can train you. I can school you in the use of energies which, I assure you, are not done revealing themselves. You will soon face others whose gifts are a match for yours, who also wish to control the emerging sedos throne. Do you know what I mean?"

"I do," Anne said. "And the fact that I cannot seek you out in vision suggests to me that you are one of them."

"I have power," he admitted. "I am the Fratrex Prismo of the holy Church, and the faneway one walks to ascend to that position carries . . . authority. But it isn't me you should be concerned about. It's the other. The one they used to call the Black Jester."

"The Black Jester? You mean from the histories?"

"Yes—and no. It's complicated. Suffice to say that he wouldn't be the most pleasant fellow to sit the sedos throne."

"You'd rather have me, then."

He pursed his lips. "When I was quite a young man, I had an attish in the Bairghs, and there I discovered some very ancient prophecies that led me to very strange places. One of the strangest was here, below Eslen castle, where a certain prisoner was once kept. I think you know which one I mean."

"Yes."

"Those of us steeped in the sedos power have difficulty seeing one another, as you mentioned. But the Kept has no such constraints; the source of his power is not the same. And I extracted a vision or visions from him. He showed me, in effect, some of the results of what will soon happen. Now, as you also know, the future feeds back to the present.

The thing each of us is to become beckons us to become it. You had a guide, a tutor, did you not?"

"Yes," she said.

"She is in part what was you in the past, but she is also Anne Dare after taking the sedos throne."

"That's absurd," Anne said, knowing as she said it that it wasn't.

"Not at all."

"So you're saying I *will* take the throne, then?"

"Maybe. Or maybe *he* will."

"And that would be bad."

"I'm not sure. That's not what I saw, but I imagine that yes, it would be bad. But what I've seen is you."

"Really? And what did you see?"

"A demon queen, bruising the world beneath her heel for the thousand years it will take it to utterly die."

Anne had a sudden, vivid vision of her arilac, the first time she had seen her, a demon without mercy, a thing of pure malevolence. Was that *her*? What she would become?

No.

"That's the most insane thing I've ever heard," she said.

"Without my help, that's what will happen."

"And what sort of help are you prepared to give me? The kind you gave my father and sisters? The kind you gave the sisters of Saint Cer? Will you help me as you helped those at the sedos in Dunmrogh? Be aware I have a letter in your own hand implicating you."

"Anne," Hespero said, his voice tinged with desperation. "The world teeters at the edge of collapse. Almost all futures lead to ruin. I can help you. Do you understand?"

"No," she snapped. "No, I don't. I can't imagine what is behind your contemptible lie or why you chose to deliver yourself to me, but hear me now: Fratrex Prismo or not, you will answer for your crimes."

"Do not make an unwise decision here," Hespero said. "Don't you understand? We must mend matters between us and move forward."

"I'll hear no more of this. You're a murderer, a torturer, and worse." She nodded at her guards.

"Take him."

"I'm sorry," Hespero said. "Sleep, everyone."

Anne felt something warm brush her face. The guards collapsed in midstep.

"What are you doing?" Anne said.

"What I must," he replied. "What I probably would have had to do in the end, anyway." He stepped toward her.

"Stop," she said.

He shook his head.

Her fury boiled up, and she sent her will at him. His step faltered, but he came on. She couldn't quite *feel* him, couldn't boil his blood. Anxiously she pushed deeper, finally sensing something softer, something she could attack. And at least his gifts didn't seem to affect her; she could feel them flailing uselessly about her like butterfly wings.

But he was standing right next to her. She felt a sharp blow just under her ribs.

"No!" she said, pushing away, staring at her habit and the dark stain spreading there, at the knife in Hespero's hand.

Then he caught her by the hair, and she felt it draw across her throat. She felt air blow through her head. She had to *do* something, stop him, stop him before it was too late . . .

But she couldn't think or feel him at all anymore.

Or anything.

Hespero knew he had to work quickly, while Anne's blood was still pumping. Holding his hand to her head, he closed his eyes, opened himself to otherwhere, and searched for her life to catch hold of it before the dark river took it away. There he would find the attunements he needed to use her gifts. He would need them to face the Black Jester alone. To win the throne.

But there was nothing draining from her, no memories or sensations, no power—no gifts.

He opened his eyes. The blood still was pulsing from her

carotid, which meant her heart was still beating. She was still alive despite her empty gaze.

He'd killed her too fast, knocked the life out of her instead of draining it. He'd been in too much of a hurry. But she'd almost had him. Another few seconds would have been enough, and it would have been him, not her, lying there dead.

The blood stopped. With a sigh, he stood and looked down at her pale corpse.

"You were always foolish," he said. "You never minded your lessons."

He hesitated, looking around at the sleeping courtiers. Could he keep them all thus until his army arrived and he could rule safely here?

Not without Anne's gifts. He was going to have to leave, come back, and fight his way in. How annoying, when he was already here.

Ever pragmatic, Hespero turned and left the room, the castle, and Eslen. Time was short, and he had leagues to travel and much to do.

CHAPTER THIRTEEN

LEAVING

MURIELE LIFTED pen from paper and turned her head; she'd thought she'd heard a distant strain of music. She went to the balcony but didn't hear anything other than birdsong in the valley. She glanced at what she'd been writing and found she wasn't in a hurry to get it done. It was just something she was doing to pass the time.

There was a lot of time. Berimund had left men to serve and protect her, but he had departed more than a nineday ago. Her Hanzish wasn't really good enough to have a decent conversation with any of her guards, not that any of them seemed all that interesting.

She wished she had Alis with her, but she had to face the fact that Alis and Neil were probably dead or at least imprisoned. It wasn't a pleasant thought, but she thought it best that she keep her feet on the ground from here on.

So she spent her time playing card games with herself, writing letters to Anne that she had no way to deliver, trying to puzzle through the few books available—all in Hanzish except one, a book of meditations on Saint Uni, which was in Church Vitellian.

She was still shocked at how wrong it had all gone. Was it her fault? Was it her own mouth that had condemned her? Maybe, but it seemed to her that Marcomir would have found an excuse even if she'd stayed as quiet as a mouse. No, it was the embassy itself that had been the mistake.

But the man at the table always knows what the cook should have done, and there was no going back.

Maybe Alis had at least had time to find the Hellrune and do whatever Anne intended. That seemed to have been the actual point of the delegation, for Anne, at least. But even that seemed terribly unlikely. It was true the girl had gifts—she could even render herself unseen in the right circumstances—but to make her way through an unknown castle to find an opponent who could see the future seemed as dubious as her own mission of peace.

She sighed and patted her belly, thinking it needed filling. Someone eventually would bring her something, she knew, but she had a taste for cheese and wine. She had the run of the pantry and nothing better to do, especially treading the same regrets and worries over and over again.

She went to the stairs and started up, as the balcony room was the lowest in the underearth structure.

She found the pantry and cellar and cut a slice of hard white cheese, poured herself some wine, and sat alone in the kitchen, eating and idly studying the hearth, marveling again at the craft involved in building this place. The kitchen was still some ten kingsyards beneath the surface, which meant a chimney must have been cut down to the fireplace, which drew perfectly.

That led her to muse about the possibility of cooking something for the evening meal. She hadn't cooked in twenty years, but once she had rather enjoyed the alchemy of it.

She got up and started going through the pantry and was imagining what she might make from pork confit, pickled radishes, spelt flour, dried cod, and prunes, when she heard voices. She ignored them at first but noticed eventually that the language didn't have the cadence of Hanzish. It sounded more like the king's tongue.

She abandoned her exploration of dried goods and made her way down a short corridor that brought her to the great hall, a lovely chamber that must have been partly natural, for it had stone teeth depending from the ceiling, as she had heard existed in caves.

But the chamber didn't hold her attention at the moment.

The many dead men on the floor did.

And Robert, talking to a fellow in a black jerkin. Robert, who now waved at her and smiled.

"We were just wondering where you were," he said.

In the gray of almost dawn, Neil gauged the distance and wasn't happy with what he thought.

"Is this the only way?" he asked.

"The only other way is down," Brinna said. "There are twenty guardsmen between us and freedom there, and even at the peak of your fighting ability, I doubt you could manage that much killing."

He nodded absently. He was standing on the casement of the only window in Brinna's suite, which faced another tower and another window. The second building was perhaps three kingsyards away, the window around a yard lower than the one on which he stood. He was being asked to jump from one to the other.

Other towers jutted up all around, a virtual forest of them.

"Where are we?" he asked. "This doesn't look like any-place I saw in the city."

"This is Kaithbaurg-of-Shadows," she said.

"You live in the city of the dead?"

"I get my visions from the dead," she said, "so it is conve-nient. Besides, haliurunnae are considered to be more dead than alive. Many people feel polluted by our presence."

"That's terrible," he said.

"Can you jump that far?" she asked, passing the issue back into wherever seldom spoken of things belonged.

"Why not just lower us down to the ground?"

"The rope isn't that long," she said. "I took it from the boat, thinking I might have need of it one day, but I was only able to manage so much without it being noticed in my things."

"Well," Neil said, "I'll jump it, then."

He tossed the hauberk and sword first, worried at the echoing sound of their impact, and then flexed his knees.

He knew he wouldn't manage to land on his feet, and he didn't. He hit the bottom of the window with his breast-bone and caught his arms over the edge. His left arm cramped up in a ball, and the right went weak, but he managed to get one elbow up, then the other, so that he could squirm through.

Alis tossed him the rope, and he tied his end on a roof beam above the window.

He waited impatiently as Alis tied off their end, then showed Brinna how to hang on the rope by her hands and knees. Even though it was a downward slope, he could see the princess was having trouble. Although she didn't make a sound, tears were running from her eyes by the time Neil received her on his end.

He was astonished at the lightness of her body as he drew her in, at the feel of her. For an instant their gazes locked, and he wanted to brush the water that had collected on her cheeks.

He set her down instead and followed her gaze as she

looked at her hands. They were bleeding, and he suddenly
understood that she almost hadn't made it, that what he
thought of as a minor physical effort was at the further limits of her ability. Living one's life in a tower didn't do much
to toughen the body.

Courage, he reflected, was a relative thing.

Alis came across as quickly and surely as a spider while
Neil armed and armored himself.

They had no choice but to untie their end of the rope and
let it dangle on the other side to inform pursuers of where
they had gone. Not that there was anywhere else to go, really.

Alis had brought a lantern, which she unshuttered to reveal
three rickety chairs and rotting tapestries on the walls.

"Down," Brinna said.

They had to cross the next room to continue, and there
they were greeted by a skeleton in a rotted gown looking
very relaxed in an armchair.

"My great-grandmother," Brinna informed them. "When
we die, our rooms are sealed off, and we remain in them."

That seal was their next obstacle; a wall obstructed the
stairs; fortunately, it was of rather desiccated wood rather
than brick or stone. Neil was able to smash through it with
the hilt of the broadsword he had chosen, and they continued down through the crypt until they reached the lowest
level, which was sealed by an iron portal that, also fortunately, was not locked.

The northern wall of Kaithbaurg loomed a few kingsyards
away, casting a permanent shadow on the bases of the clus-
ter of fifteen towers that formed the heart of the shadow
city. Moss was thick and springy underfoot, jeweled with
colorful mushrooms.

"Quickly," Brinna whispered.

They set off north on a path paved in lead brick, through
the mansions of the dead that crowded up to the Hellrune towers, into the meaner dwellings beyond, and finally to the
tombs of the poor, mass graves with nothing more than di-
lapidated wooden huts to act as shrines. It began to rain, and
the path, no longer paved, quickly turned to viscous mud.

They came at last to a large iron gate flanked by stone towers in a wall that enclosed the necropolis and went around to join the one guarding Kaithbaurg.

A man in lord's plate stepped from the gatehouse, raising his visor so that Neil could see the aged features within. His breastplate bore the hammer of Saint Under, marking him as a Scathoman, a guardian of the dead.

"Majesty," the knight said, his voice formal and quavered by the rain. "What brings you here?"

"Sir Safrax," Brinna said. "It's raining. I'm cold. Open the gate."

"You know I can't do that," he said apologetically.

"I know you will," she replied.

He shook his head. "Princess you may be, but my holy task is to see to the dead and keep you where you belong."

Neil drew his sword. It was heavier than Battlehound.

He didn't insult the older knight by saying anything. He just took a stance.

"Alarm!" the knight shouted, then drew his weapon and came at Neil.

They circled for a moment before Neil took the first swing, stepping in and cutting hard toward the juncture of neck and shoulder. Safrax turned so that the blow glanced from his armored shoulder and cut back. Neil ducked that and went under his arm and behind him. His arms already were aching, so he spun and hammered the blade into the back of the other knight's helm, sending him down to his knees. Two more strokes ended it.

But by then three more knights had come clattering out of the tower, and he heard a horn blowing to broaden the alarm.

Robert smiled and gestured toward an armchair.

"Have a seat, my dear," he said. "We should chat, you and I."

Muriele took a step back, then another.

"I don't believe I will," she said. Every fiber of her wanted to run, but she knew that she would only sacrifice her dignity if she did so. Robert would catch her.

She tightened her belly and stood her ground.

"I don't know how Hansa has put up with you this long," she said, "but now you've killed your host's men. I think you've worn out your welcome."

"I'm going to sit," Robert said. "Join me if you wish."

He folded his lean frame into a second armchair. "There are a few things wrong with your supposition," he said. "The first is that anyone will ever find these bodies. The whole point of this place is that it is secret, yes? And if Berimund returns—and that is itself a very large if because his father is quite mad with rage at him—there is no reason for him to suspect my hand in this. But a much more profound trouble with your reasoning is the fact that I'm leaving Hansa anyway. It proved a useful haven, but I'm not so foolish as to believe that Marcomir would put me on the throne."

"What are you up to, then? Where could you possibly go?"

"Crotheny. I have one small thing in Newland to tidy up, and then I'll be on to Eslen."

"Anne will execute you."

"You know I can't die. You tested it with my own knife."

"True. So your head will live after it's struck off. Perhaps Anne will keep it in a cage as an amusement."

"She might, but I don't think so. Obviously, or I wouldn't go back there. It's all about to happen, Muriele. I've no idea how things will turn out, but I have nothing to lose and everything to gain."

"What's happening?" Muriele asked. "What do you mean?"

"Nothing for you to worry about," he said. "I didn't really come here to drag you back into politics. I'm here to bring you a gift."

"A gift?"

"A musical gift from your own court composer."

Music started then, a soft chord growing louder, and she saw that Robert's companion was playing a small thaurn-harp.

* * *

Neil sighed and backed toward the gate, hoping to keep from being surrounded.

"Lady Berrye," he said softly. "I can only hold them for a moment. Do what you can."

"I will, Sir Neil," she said.

"Do not die cheaply, Sir Neil," Brinna said. "A little time should help."

"It will be very little," Neil said.

Alis laid her arm on the princess, and they suddenly became difficult to look at. He couldn't put his gaze on them, but that was just as well, because he had a lot to pay attention to.

The lead knight cut at him, and Neil dodged to the side so that the weapon scraped through the metal bars of the gate. Neil hit the outstretched arm with his off-weapon hand, forcing him to lose his grip on the sword. With his weapon hand he cut at the knee of the knight to his right and felt it shear through the joint, setting the man—quite understandably—to screaming. Neil suppressed a shriek of his own as his arm shot with the pain of the blow, and his fingers loosened their grip. Gasping, he lunged at the third knight, wrapped his arms around the knight's knees, lifted him and dumped him on his head. He fell, too, rolled, and came back up. The first man had recovered his sword and was advancing on him.

He heard horses blowing behind him and the thump of hooves.

He hoped that Alis had gotten Brinna away.

But then something odd happened. The knight straightened and looked past him.

"Put that away," a voice said. "I command here."

Neil turned and found Prince Berimund and about ten riders behind him. The gate was being raised.

"But my Prince, this man was—"

"My sister is in my care now," Berimund said. "And so is that woman and this man."

"The king—"

"You may take this up with me now or with my father later. You will not have the chance to do both."

The knight hesitated and then bowed. "Yes, Majesty."

"Come along, Sir Neil," Berimund said. "Your queen has been asking after you."

They rode west into country that quickly became rugged and verdant. Berimund and his men seemed to know their way, moving through the dense forest as if they had been born there. Neil reflected that he never would have imagined this Berimund from the one he'd met on the road. This Hansan prince was more in his element, freed of the fetters of court and the restraints upon honor they created. He and his men seemed almost to be able to hear one another's thoughts, to be the band of brothers they claimed to be in name.

Kaithbaurg wasn't a black fortress, and the prince of Hansa was a man with a history, friends, and scruples. He was still, of course, an enemy, but an enemy Neil would gladly call a friend if the times changed, and one he could kill or die by the hand of with a warrior's dignity.

Brinna he was having trouble even thinking about. She was still very much the woman he had met on the Lier Sea whose voice and expression had haunted him since he'd first opened his eyes to her. But there was something cold in her center he'd only sensed then, the thing that allowed her to poison someone and speak of it as if she had put a cat out the door.

But if she was cold, why did she seem like white fire from the corner of his eye? Why could he still feel the heat on his hands from touching her, even through the steady drizzle of rain?

He glanced at her and found her studying him, or thought he did. It was too dark to see her eyes beneath the eaves of the hat her brother had given her to keep the rain off.

They rode through the day as the rain grew steadily colder and more miserable. Mists lay heavy in the trees, dying dragons dragging themselves off to watery graveyards. Berimund's men lit torches that hissed and sputtered and trailed noxious, oily fumes but still burned, until at last they reached a stone face concealed by a sort of wickerwork grown over with vines, which Berimund shifted to reveal a stout wooden door. He stood looking at it for several long moments.

"What's wrong?" Neil asked.

"It ought to be locked," he said. "It isn't even closed."

Neil was off his horse before the thought to dismount was even conscious. He drew his stolen weapon and stalked toward the door.

"You'll follow us, Sir Neil," Berimund insisted. "We know this place, and you do not."

Two of his scouts went ahead, and then they all dismounted, tying the horses near the entrance. Stairs carved in living rock took them down.

Not much later they debouched into a large chamber carved in antique style but furnished much like Berimund's hall in Kaithbaurg.

The floor was littered with the dead. He heard a sudden, sharp sob from Berimund, who flung himself at the corpses, lifting their heads, kissing them, moving from one to the next in the vain hope that one still breathed.

Then Alis pushed past him and flew across the floor, the muddy hem of her dress dragging a snail's trail behind her.

Neil saw then, too, and ran after her, knowing his heart would fail.

Muriele did not look like she was sleeping. Her lips were almost black, and even in torchlight he could make out the bluish tinge of her skin. Alis had the queen's head cradled in her arms. Her eyes were open, her features twisted into a look of utter and desolate despair such as he had never seen.

Something lay on the floor beside her. In a daze he reached for it and found that it was a half-withered rose.

He rose up, choking back tears but letting the rage rise up, each breath filling him with red light. He stepped toward Berimund, who still knelt with his own, and stepped again, nearly treading on a dead man staring up at him with the same forsaken expression as Muriele.

Berimund hadn't done this. Berimund hadn't known about it. But Berimund was the only enemy before him, and by the saints, the floor was going to be red.

"No," Brinna said. "Stop there, Neil."

It arrested him. He hadn't seen her enter the chamber or follow him to Muriele's body. Her tear-jeweled eyes caught him like iron bands.

"Why would you cry for my queen?" he snapped.

"I'm not," she said. "I'm crying for you."

His hand trembled on the sword. "Why didn't you see *this*?" he asked. "You said Robert was coming . . ."

"I didn't see this part," she said. "I was occupied with other things."

"Like your own escape? You knew Berimund would be at the gate."

"There was nothing eldritch about that," she said. "I heard he was in the city. I sent a message telling him of my plans. Besides you, Berimund is the only one I trust."

"Was it Robert?"

"I can see your queen," she said, her voice suddenly dreamier. "I see a man, hear a music . . ." She trailed off, her breath quickening, her eyes rolling back.

"Make her stop," Alis said. "Sir Neil, make her stop."

Brinna was trembling now as if an invisible giant had taken her in his hand and was shaking her.

He gripped her by the shoulders.

"Brinna," he said. "Wake up. Stop seeing."

She didn't appear to hear him, so he shook her harder.

"Brinna!"

"What are you doing to my sister?" Berimund's raging voice shouted from across the room.

"Brinna!"

Blood began running from her nose.

"Swanmay," Neil cried in desperation. "Swanmay, return!"

She went rigid and suddenly sighed, collapsing against him, her heart beating weakly.

He felt the tip of a sword prick his neck.

"Put her down," the prince commanded.

Neil cut his eye toward the prince but kept Brinna bundled against him, feeling her heart strengthen.

"Do as I say!" Berimund exploded, pushing hard enough that Neil felt blood start on his neck.

"No." Brinna's hand came up and rested on the blade. "He saved me, Baur." She gently pushed down on the weapon and then reached for her brother. He tugged her away from Neil and wrapped her in both arms.

Neil just stood there, his knees feeling weak.

Alis took his elbow and got under his arm to support him.

"Robert did this," she said. "I'm certain of it."

Neil walked back to Muriele and sank slowly to his knees, understanding finally reaching his grieving brain.

She's gone. He couldn't protect her anymore. There was nothing else he could do.

Except find Robert and cut him into so many pieces that it wouldn't matter if he was alive or not.

PART IV
✣
THE
BORN QUEEN

When walks again the Born Queen, the bones of men will clatter within them; the wombs of their women will fill with venom; every rider of the night will take her lash with hideous joy. And when at last the bones shake off their flesh, and the wombs consume their bearers, and the lash murders; when finally it is only her single voice screaming in the night—when she lacks any man or beast or ghostly thing to harrow and she must at last turn on herself—then all will be still.

But ten times a hundred years will first pass.

—Translated from the Tafles Taceis or Book of Murmurs

CHAPTER ONE

⊹

OCCUPIED

LEOFF CLOSED his eyes and let the form build in the ensemble of his mind. The first bass line began, a male voice, rising and falling: the roots in the soil, the long slow dreams of trees. Then, after a few measures, a second line entered as deep in pitch but in uneasy harmony with the first: leaves rotting into soil, bones decaying into dust, and in the lowest registers the meandering of rivers and weathering of mountains.

Now the middle voice came in: Birth and growth, joy and tragedy, suffering and learning met with forgetting, the loss of senses, discorporation, disintegration . . .

It wasn't until Joven, the gardener, started shouting that Leoff understood that someone had been pounding on the outside door, probably for some time. His first reaction was impatience, but then he recalled that Joven rarely got excited and never to the point of shouting.

He sighed and set down the quill. He was at a standstill anyway. He had the form; the instruments were his problem.

When he answered the door, Joven proved to be more than excited; he seemed to be on the verge of panic.

"What is it, fralet?" Leoff asked. "Come in, have some wine."

"It's the enemy, Cavaor," Joven said. "He's here."

"The enemy?"

"Hansa. They've besieged Haundwarpen, and about a hundred of them just rode into the estate. The duke didn't leave many men here to guard it; I think they surrendered."

"I don't understand," Leoff said. "I thought Hansa was beaten at Poelscild."

"Auy. But they say Queen Anne is dead, and without her sainted power to hold them back, they've taken Poelscild and crossed the canal. All of Newland is in their grasp."

"The queen is dead? Queen Anne?"

"Murdered, they say."

"That's terrible news," Leoff said. He hadn't known Anne very well, but he owed her mother, Muriele, a lot. She had lost all but one of her children now. He couldn't imagine how she must be feeling.

Nor did he want to learn, at least not by direct experience.

"Where are Areana and Mery?" he asked, trying to keep calm.

"Lys went to find them. She thinks they're in the garden."

Leoff nodded and took up his cane. "Get them to the cottage and stay there with them, please."

"Yes, Cavaor," the old fellow said, and sprinted off as fast as he could on his aged legs.

Leoff pushed himself up and went out to stand on the stoop. Dogs were barking everywhere, but other than that it seemed a normal day, pleasant even.

He didn't have to wait long. Within a bell, a knight with a red-plumed helm came riding through the gate, followed by ten horsemen and about twice that number on foot.

The knight turned his head this way and that and, apparently satisfied he hadn't ridden into a trap, doffed the headgear, discovering an oval-faced man of twenty-something years with auburn hair and a lighter red mustache.

"I hait Sir Ilzereik af Aldamarka," he said in accented but good king's tongue. "I declare this house and its grounds spoils of war in the name of Marcomir, king of Hansa."

"I hait Leovigild Ackenzal," he replied. "I'm a guest here, by leave of Duke Artwair Dare."

"You live alone, Fralet Ackenzal?"

"No."

"Bring the others, then."

"I can't do that until I have your word they will be well treated."

"Why do you think you're in a position to bargain?" Ilzereik asked. "Who are you protecting? Your wife and daughters, perhaps? I could find them easily enough and do whatever I liked with them. But I am a knight of Hansa, not some thrall of your dead witch-queen. You need not beg me to behave properly in the eyes of the saints."

"I'm not begging," Leoff said. He'd been afraid of men like this once. He wasn't anymore, not for himself, anyway.

"Your house is mine," the knight said. "My men will sleep in the yard. You and whoever else is here will see to our needs. Do that and no harm will come to you. Is that understood?"

"It's understood," Leoff said. "If that is your word as a knight of Hansa."

"It is," the knight said. "Now, my man Aizmeki will go with you to find the others."

Aizmeki wasn't a big man, but he looked to be made of muscle and scars and not much else. He followed Leoff wordlessly out to the garden and the little cabin there.

Areana rushed out and hugged him. Mery just peered at the warrior as if he were some strange insect and took Leoff's hand in her little cold one.

The knight's word proved good, at least for that afternoon. Although many of the Hansan warriors leered openly at Areana and some at Mery, which was disgusting, none dared do more than make a few probably crude comments in their own language, and they returned to the house in peace.

He found Ilzereik looking through his music.

"Who wrote this?" he asked.

"I did."

"You did?" The knight peered at him a little more intently. "You're a composer?"

"I am."

"Ackenzal," the knight mused. "I don't recall the name."

"You know music?"

"I studied a little. My father thought I should, so he kept an instructor in our hall and sent me each autumn to study at the Liuthgildrohsn."

"Ah. With Mestro Evensun."

A little smile played on the knight's face. "You know the mestro?"

"I do. He lectured at the college when I was apprenticed to Mestro DaPeica."

The smile broadened. "I have a book of DaPeica's short works for hammarharp."

Leoff nodded.

"Well," the knight said, gesturing toward the hammarharp, "play me something of yours."

"I'm afraid I can't," Leoff said.

"You shouldn't fear my criticism," the Hansan said. "I'm not a snob. The great composers and the small, I like them all."

"That isn't it," Leoff said, holding up his hands.

"Schithundes," the man swore. "What happened?"

"He was tortured," Areana interrupted in a brittle voice. "He's suffered much."

"I'm sorry to hear that," the knight said. "And I understand you, Frauja Ackenzal. Your husband will not suffer at my hands, not if you all behave."

"I can play for you," Mery said softly. "Areana can sing."

"Really?" Ilzereik looked pleased. "I would like that, *barnila.*"

Leoff squeezed Mery's hand. "Play the Poelen Suite," Leoff said. "I think he'll like that. And play it as written, Mery. Do you understand?"

She nodded and went to sit at the instrument. Areana went hesitantly to join her.

Mery put her fingers on the keys and struck down. The chord rang a little wrong, and Leoff bit his lip and prayed to the saints that she could hold back the darkness in her.

But the second chord was pure, and from there everything proceeded smoothly. Areana's voice was lovely, as always, and when they finished, the knight applauded.

"I never expected to find such wonderful accommodations," he said. "Sir, let's have some wine. You and I will talk, fralet. For quite some time now I've been working a little here and there at a sort of musical telling of the *Shiyikunisliuth*, an epic about the tribe my family arose from. If I could play you a little of it, perhaps you might have some ideas of how I might go about fleshing it out."

And so their first night under occupation passed if not pleasantly, at least without disaster. When they took to their beds that night on the floor in the kitchen, Leoff prayed that the Hansan continued to be entertained enough by them to keep his men in check.

He was breathing a little more freely three days later. Some of the men, notably a stout fellow they called Haukun, continued their leering, but Ilzereik seemed to have them under control.

On the third afternoon, he was pretending to work on the knight's "epic" but instead was going back over the third section of the work he was beginning to think of as a kind of requiem; he heard the door burst open and Areana shout. He tried to get up too fast, toppled his stool, and fell. He grabbed his cane and pushed himself up to find himself facing the point of a sword held by a man with closely cropped sandy hair and a missing ear. He didn't know the fellow's name, but it was one of Ilzereik's men.

"Easy, now," the man said. *"Qimeth jus hiri."* He jerked his head toward the common room.

Leoff went with the sword at his back. Black clouds boiled in his peripheral vision.

Haukun and three other men were there, along with Areana and Mery.

"There we go," Haukun said. "Every one here now."

"What is this?" Leoff said, feeling stones in his gut. "Sir Ilzereik—"

"He is gone," Haukun said bluntly. "Called to siege. He comined back not too soon. I in charge this place now."

"He won't be pleased if you hurt us."

"I care little for his pleasing," the soldier said. "Stingy man, not understanding how to keep his men happy, you know? Sit in here every night while pretty girls make pretty music." He pushed Mery toward the hammarharp. "You play, jah? And this one will sing. Maybe not hurt you too much. Maybe women even like it."

Areana slapped him hard. "If you touch Mery—" But Haukun cut her off with a fist to the chin. Areana slammed against the wall and slid down, stunned, crying but making no sound.

Leoff lunged and swung his cane at the man, but something hit him hard on the back of the head, and for a while he couldn't focus beyond that.

When he could, he realized that Mery was playing. He looked up, feeling nauseated, and saw that Haukun had forced Areana to her feet and had her pressed against the wall. Her dress had been pushed up.

"Sing," he said, starting to take down his breeches.

Areana slitted her eyes, and the purest malice Leoff had ever seen in her peered from there. And then she did sing, and Leoff realized what Mery was playing.

"Remember," he called hoarsely. "Remember, for saints' sake."

Then they were past the point of no return, and the song took them all to its end.

When it was over, Areana was huddled in a corner and Leoff couldn't get up; every time he tried to move, his stomach started heaving again. It had been worse this time, harder to sing the counterpoint that had preserved their lives at Lord Respell's castle.

Mery looked no worse for wear, though. She hopped down from her stool and sat with him, stroking his neck.

Haukun and the others, of course, hadn't been so fortunate. Only Haukun was still alive, probably because he had been near enough to Areana to hear her countercant. He wasn't well, though. He was sprawled on the floor, twitching, whining with each breath like a sick old dog.

Still trying to rise, he saw Areana come unsteadily to her feet and leave the room. She returned a moment later with a kitchen knife.

"Look away, Mery," she said.

"Go in my study," Leoff told the girl. "Get everything we've been working on. Do you understand? Then go get your thaurnharp. Don't leave the house."

When he could walk again, Leoff peered out the front door. He didn't see anyone. Then he went back to look at the bodies. Areana had cleaned up the blood from Haukun, and the others had died without a mark on them.

"What now?" Areana said.

He stepped to embrace her, but she flinched back, and he stopped, feeling a lump in his throat. He didn't feel like much of a man.

"I think we have to leave," he said. "If more soldiers come, the same thing will happen. If Ilzereik returns, he'll probably have us burned as shinecrafters."

"Not if we get rid of the bodies," Areana said. "Then he'll reckon they just deserted. There's no way he'll imagine we managed to do away with all these." She prodded one of the corpses with her toe.

"True," he said. "But as I said, it might not be Ilzereik. It could be a knight more like Haukun, or worse."

"Where will we go?" she asked. "All of Newland is probably occupied. For all we know, Eslen has already fallen."

He was trying to think of an answer to that when they heard a whinny in the yard. Leoff charged to the door and saw it was Ilzereik and the rest of his men.

"Well," he sighed. "It's moot now."

"Taste," the knight said, proffering a bite of barley mush to Mery. She blinked and took a bit.

"I told you we didn't poison them," Leoff said.

"I'm starting to believe you," the knight replied. "I'm

starting to think this is an entire nation of witches. I
befriended you, composer. I treated you well."

"Yes, but you left your men to rape my wife while you
were gone," he said. "We were just defending ourselves."

"Jah, but how—by what means?"

Leoff firmed his jaw and didn't answer.

The knight sat back.

"You'll tell," he said. "I've sent for the sacritor of our
hansa. He should be here within a bell, and he will know
what happened here. He will know what to do."

"Shall I play you a tune in the meantime?" Mery asked.

"No," the Hansan said. "There will be no music. If I hear
anything that resembles a cantation, I'll kill whoever starts
it. Do you understand?"

"Be still, Mery," Leoff said.

Ilzereik went back to the bodies. "Haukun was stabbed,"
he mused. "The others just fell dead. Whatever you did,
Haukun wasn't affected. A puzzle."

He went to the music Mery had packed and began pulling
it out.

Someone in the yard called the knight's name.

"Ah," he said. "That will be the sacritor, won't it? Are you
sure you wouldn't rather tell me? You'll still be lustrated, but
at least you won't be questioned."

"I've been 'questioned' by the Church before," Leoff said,
holding up his hands.

"I see. There's a history, then. Well, it's a shame. I was
really enjoying your company. I can't believe I was so deceived."

He rose and went to the door. Leoff closed his eyes, trying
to think of something, *anything,* to do.

Nothing came to mind.

CHAPTER TWO

✚

A FINAL MEETING

FRATREX PELL turned quickly when he heard Stephen sigh.

"You!" he gasped. Beneath his graying brows, his eyes glimmered with disbelief.

Stephen wagged a finger at him. "You've been a bad little boy," he said. "You and your Revesturi playmates."

Pell drew himself taller. "Brother Stephen, there is much you don't know, but even so you should not presume to talk to me in that fashion." He cocked his head. "How did you get here? This tower is twenty kingsyards high."

"I *know*," Stephen replied. "It's wonderful. Like a wizard spire from the phay stories. And so well hidden! You Revesturi are so clever-clever. *Really* clever. You couldn't walk last time I saw you, Fratrex Pell."

"I healed."

"Oh, you *healed*. That's impressive. Not as impressive as surviving the explosion at d'Ef, though. My ears are still ringing from that."

"We were trying to stop the waurm."

"You didn't, though. It chased me right up into the mountains, like it was supposed to. Died like it was supposed to. And I—I found everything I was supposed to find. I came here, I suppose, to tell your superiors about your tragic and heroic end—and see what I discover."

"I have no superiors," Pell said. "I am the Fratrex Prismo of the Revesturi."

Stephen crossed his arms and leaned his shoulder against

the wall. "Well, I see that now," he said. "I can feel your power. Desmond was really lucky to get you from behind."

"I'm stronger now than I was then."

"Right," Stephen said. "As the sedos power waxes. Feels good, doesn't it?"

"Brother Stephen, time is short. Did you find the answers? Did you discover how Virgenya Dare healed the world?"

Stephen laughed.

Pell watched him impassively. That seemed even funnier than the question, and Stephen's laughter became uncontrollable. Tears sprang into his eyes, and his ribs hurt.

"Come now," Pell said after a moment.

But that just made it harder to stop.

When, some time later, he was able to talk again, he wiped his eyes. "She didn't heal it, you old idiot," he said, fighting the hiccups. "She poisoned it by drawing on the sedos power. When she realized what was happening, she abandoned the high throne of its power and hid it away to try to control the damage."

"Are you saying there's nothing to be done? Did Kauron discover nothing?"

"Of course there is something to be done," Stephen said. "And Choron discovered the best thing of all: himself."

"I'm afraid I don't follow."

"That's wonderful," Stephen said. "Because I *love* to explain things. It's my forte, as you must remember from our first meeting. Such a funny trick you played on me, that bit with you pretending to be a simple fratir cutting wood. I didn't really appreciate it then. I assure you, now I do."

Pell's expression grew even more guarded. "What do you have to report, Brother Stephen?"

"Well, first of all, you were completely right about that business about there being no saints, about power being the only reality. It's true. The sedos power is what holds the world together. It tames and orders the other energies of existence. It keeps everything from rotting into unchecked chaos. And anyone who walks a faneway takes some gift for using that force with him and becomes the conscious agent of that particular energy. But any given faneway allows only limited access to the total possibilities of the sedos—even the greatest ones, such as the one I've walked and the one the Fratrex Prismo walks in z'Irbina. And the one *you* walked in the Iutin Mountains, the faneway of Diuvo."

"How did you know—?"

"Oh, I can see them all now, like constellations in the sky. That's one of the particular gifts of Virgenya Dare's secret faneway."

"Then you can walk them all?"

"I tried walking one near the Witchhorn," Stephen said. "It's not enough. Take my analogy that the faneways are like constellations. Now imagine the night sky is a black board with thousands of small holes drilled in it, and the light shining through those holes from behind is the real source of the sedos power. It's not all the little holes you want to control; it's the one light behind them. What we call the Alwalder, I suppose. That's what I'm after."

"But why?"

"To save the world. To bring order and balance to its eldritch principalities."

"I thought you just said the sedos power was the source of all of our problems."

"The source and the solution. Virgenya Dare never saw that. She imagined the problem would just go away, but it was already too late. Still, she must have had an inkling. She made a shortcut for her descendants."

"What?"

"Never mind that. See, it's the lack of control and imprecise vision that's led us to where we are. If someone—one person, not two, or three, or fifty, but *one*—could control the source of the sedos power, one person with a clear vision, all of this could be fixed. I'm sure of it."

"And who will do this fixing? You?"

"Right," Stephen said. "Without the mistakes of last time. I think I just got frustrated back then. Ruffled some feathers."

"What *are* you talking about?" Fratrex Pell asked. "What other time?"

"I told you, already. Choron found himself. I found myself. Me."

"You're Choron?" Pell asked incredulously.

"Yes. Or yes and no. Like everything, it's a little complicated. See, time is a funny thing in the Not World. The man you called Choron and the man you call Stephen are each echo and source of the other, and both were always working toward the promise of the one who will rise when we find the throne. As Choron I never found it. As Stephen I will."

"Are you saying you are Choron reborn?"

"No. Imagine a plucked lute string. It vibrates side to side, a blur that appears wider than the string, and in doing so produces a tone. Let's say Stephen is the farthest reach of that vibration on the left and Choron is the farthest reach of it on the right. But it's the same string, the same tone. We're one and always have been, even before the string was plucked."

"This is a lot to ask me to take on faith."

"Oh, I don't care if you believe me. After all, you're Revesturi, always questioning. That's fine. And I won't say there wasn't some fiddling with things to bring them along. As Choron, I broke the law of death and made myself immortal, hoping to survive long enough to find the throne. Of course, my enemies found a way to destroy my body, but I already understood about my echoes in the past and future, and at some point they all understood about me, so together we managed—this. It's all really very interesting."

"So you aren't Stephen anymore."

"You really aren't listening, are you?"

The fratrex frowned. "When you talk about Choron becoming immortal, breaking the law of death, being defeated—"

"Yes!" Stephen cried. "I was wondering how long it would take you. This is every bit as much fun as I imagined it would be."

"You're the Black Jester."

"I never called myself that, you know. I think it was suppose to be a bit of an insult."

"Saints," the fratrex breathed.

"Phoodo-oglies!" Stephen breathed in imitation. "I just made that up," he confided. "They aren't real, either."

"You can't be the Black Jester and at the same time Stephen Darige," he said. "Fratir Stephen is good, incapable of the evil things the Jester did. If you are whom you claim to be, I believe you have possessed Brother Darige. Either that or you are merely Brother Stephen gone mad."

"That's disappointing," Stephen said. "You talked so fine about the intellectual purity of the Revesturi, about how your method of reasoning sets you apart from your rivals, and yet here you start with good and evil. It's sad, really. Was Choron a good man? And yet I promise you, I walked into the mountains as Choron, and a few years later I was the Black Jester. The difference is in power; him you call Stephen is merely the Black Jester without it. But at our center we are the same. Good and evil are judgments, and in this case judgments made without understanding."

"The Black Jester strapped razors on children's heels and elbows and made them fight like cocks," Fratrex Pell said.

"I told you, I was frustrated," Stephen said. "Maybe to the point of being a little mad."

"A little?"

"It doesn't matter. Things have changed, and I see the way clearly now."

"And what do you see?"

"The sedos throne is emerging again, as it never did in Choron's time. In fact, it has already emerged in a sense—the waxing of the power has reached its peak. But the complete claim of it by any one person isn't possible yet. I control a lot of it. The *other* Fratrex Prismo, whoever he is, also has a strong claim. The strongest is that of Anne Dare, because Virgenya left a shortcut to the power that privileges her heir—and founded a secret organization dedicated to making certain that heir would be led to it if the time ever came."

"Why?"

"I don't know. Perhaps she thought a descendant of hers

would follow in her footsteps, deny the power, hide the throne for another two thousand years."

"Maybe she would."

"In the first place, that's not enough this time. The law of death is broken. The Briar King is dead, and the forests of the world are dying, and when they are dead, we will certainly follow. But do you never *see*? Don't you have visions?"

"Of course, at times."

"But you haven't seen what the world will become if Anne sits the sedos throne?"

"No. I've not sought such a vision, and none has come to me."

"A three-thousand-year reign of terror that makes my small epoch look like a child's party. And at the end of it, the world passes into nothingness."

Pell looked troubled but shrugged. "I have only your word for that," he said. "And visions do not necessarily come to pass."

"That's true. And that's why I'm here."

"Why?"

"Well, two reasons, really. Like the others who have walked one of the greater faneways, I can see you, at best, in a cloudy fashion."

"You just said you saw Anne."

"Only after a fashion. I can see the world she will make. Were you always this obtuse?"

"I—"

"Rhetorical question," Stephen said, waving him down. "It's you I'm talking about now. I wasn't sure who you were, how much you knew, who you are allied with. So I came to discover all of those *fascinating* answers."

"And the other reason?"

"To strike a bargain. You don't control enough of the se-dos power to challenge Anne. Neither do I. But if I had your gifts, I would have a fair chance."

"Walk the faneway of Diuvo, then."

"It doesn't really work that way, and I think you know it. The power is finite. With minor faneways like that of

Mamres or Decmanus, tens or hundreds might have gifts at once and never be diminished. But those such as we have walked are different. For me to gain strength, you must relinquish your gifts to me—a simple process that won't do you any real damage—or I can take them from you, which will unfortunately involve your discorporation."

"I can either give you, who claim to be the Black Jester, the power you need to seize the greatest power in the world or die? Are those my only two choices?"

"I'm afraid so," Stephen said apologetically.

"I see," Fratrex Pell said, brows lowering.

It wasn't a long fight, and when it was over, Stephen felt the new gifts settle under his skin. Then he called his captive demon and made it fly from the tower and for several leagues to the south. As he had expected, Pell had unleashed the same explosive power on him that he had on the waurm, and although he could protect himself from that, he didn't want to risk Zemlé or his faithful Aitivar.

When he came to ground, Zemlé rushed to meet him.

"I heard the sound," she said. "The sky was full of strange colors. I feared the worst."

He kissed her and smiled. "I'm glad you worry about me," he said. "But here there was no need for that. This isn't where my real test will come."

"You'll win there, too," she said.

Later that night, in their tent, she seemed less certain.

"Are you sure about this?" she asked. "Is this really your task, to challenge the queen of Crotheny?"

He rolled back a bit and propped himself on his elbows. "I'm not sure I understand," he said. "We went through this back in the mountain. It was you and the Aitivar who were so convinced I was Kauron's heir, back when I believed it was mere insanity. Well, you were right. Where is this sudden doubt coming from? Are your allegiances still mixed? Do you still think Anne is a savior?"

She gave him a tentative smile. "No. I suppose it's that I never quite believed it. But I believed in the shy, smart man

I met in Demsted. I thought he would find a way to help somehow."

"Am I so different?"

"No. Stronger. Bolder. All of the things you were becoming anyway, now that I look back. It just happened so quickly."

"Well, do you still believe in me?"

"Yes," she said.

"Good, then. Do you still want to help me?"

"I don't see what help I can be," she said.

He smiled. "You just said it. You believed in me. You still do. That is a strength I can always use."

"And I love you," she said.

"And I love you, too," he said.

He knew she would be a lovely queen. Or mistress, depending on how things went.

CHAPTER THREE

✣

SIR HARRIOT'S TASK

"YOU'RE GIVING us too much," Aspar said, lashing a pack onto one of the spare horses. "You'll starve."

"No," Symen said. "Like as I won't, since I'm going with you. There's not much sense in staying at Tor Scath anymore."

"You can't be sure what the Church's army intends," Aspar said.

"That's true," Symen replied. "But even if they leave us be, what will we eat in a year? Two? And who's going to hunt here, anyway? No, I'll give you whatever I can. This world is lost, and the only thing or person in it I have any trust in is you, holter. So pack quickly, and let's be on."

Aspar nodded and resumed packing.

A moment later he heard someone cough softly behind him. It was Emfrith.

Sceat, Aspar thought. *And again.*

"I don't understand why we're leaving," the young man said. "This is the perfect place to keep Winna safe."

"Keeps monsters out, not men, and we'll never hold off five hundred."

"It's an army of the Church," Emfrith said.

"That's the same Church that has been hanging every other villager from here to Brogswell, yah?"

"They didn't hang anyone in Haemeth," Emfrith pointed out. "We follow the saints there."

"Good for you. But we've had some experiences to make us skittish of anyone under saintly armor. Ask Winna. It's not worth the chance. We've this one moment to escape, and here it is—werlic?"

"Raiht," Emfrith agreed, sounding reluctant. Then he sighed. "Look, why don't I just go talk to them? See what they want? If you're right and they mean no good, we can still flee. But if you're wrong, then we can stay here, where the monsters can't get in, until Winna has the baby."

"There's not enough food for five months."

"Me and my men can ride out and get some when it's needed."

"From where? The blight is moving outward."

"Yes, but we're riding straight *into* it."

"I thought you weren't going to question me anymore."

"That was when I thought *this* was the safe place you meant."

"There's a safer one," Aspar said.

"Is there?"

"Yes."

"Very well," he said after a moment. Then he walked away.

You really love her, don't you? Aspar thought. *Grim, but I wish I could speak my mind.*

His leg was throbbing as he mounted the horse he'd begun calling Grimla in hopes that a stout name would make the beast stronger.

They started southwest, off the Old King's Road, fording the shallows of the Little Moon River before the end of the first day, then starting up into the Walham foothills. He and Winna hadn't come this way the last time, because they had been along the Slaghish River, following the trail of the first greffyn. That had led them to Rewn Aluth and the strange, possibly dead Sefry who called herself Mother Gastya. She had sent them into the Mountains of the Hare to find a hidden valley that Aspar knew for a fact couldn't be there.

But as with so many things, he'd been wrong. The valley had been there, and the Briar King, and Fend, and for him and Winna it had all very nearly ended there, as well. But it hadn't, and Stephen had had a large hand in that.

He tried not to wonder where Stephen was, and he didn't like to talk to Winna about it, because the simple fact was that the boy was most probably dead. Even if the slinders hadn't killed him, the woorm probably had, and if not the woorm, the explosion of monastery d'Ef or one of a thousand other things. Stephen was smart and a good fellow, but surviving on his own even before the world went mad was not exactly his strongest talent.

He'd done all he could to help Stephen, hadn't he? Followed the slinders, chased the woorm. He'd found no sign whatever of the lad.

He shifted his gaze to Winna and Ehawk. At least Ehawk had found them again. It was good to know the Watau wasn't a lonely ghost wandering in the Bairghs.

The foothills rose and fell in ever-sharper undulating folds and ridges. It had always been easy to get turned around in the Walhams, but now, without the usual reference points, it was more difficult than ever to keep a true path. He could see that there had been a lot of rain in the last several months and much flooding. The invading growth didn't have the same deep roots as the natural flora, and many of the ways he knew were closed by massive mud slides. Most of the ridges had washed down to bedrock, and the valleys were filled with viscous muck.

But in those low-lying places the eldritch vegetation was very strong. It was starting to sicken, but it wasn't nearly as far gone as what he'd seen back in the Lean Gables. They had to cut their way through it in places.

They progressed very slowly. Aspar reckoned that in three days they'd managed only five leagues as the raven wings toward their destination.

And that evening, Henne, Sir Symen's tracker, turned up with bad news.

"The churchmen are boxing you in," he said. "Don't know how. It's like they know where you're going."

"Where are they exactly?" Aspar asked him.

Henne sketched a map on the ground, and when he was done, Aspar cursed Grim and ground his teeth.

I reckon Fend was telling the truth about this at least.

Because it looked like they *were* going to need some help.

The knight woke when Aspar's dirk pricked his neck. To his credit, he didn't scream or wet himself; in fact, he hardly flinched. His eyes registered first shock, then chagrin, and finally, as he understood he wasn't dead already, curiosity.

"That's a good man," Aspar whispered.

"You must be Holter White."

"Ah, I'm famous," Aspar replied. "But I've not your name in my word horde."

"That would be Roger Harriot. Sir Roger Harriot."

"Virgenyan?"

"Yes, from St. Clement Danes."

"But you're not just on your way home."

"Regrettably, no. I have several tasks to accomplish, and none involves returning to my home."

"And these tasks?"

"Well, one would be to bring to heel a certain renegade holter, should I run across him."

"By whose order?"

"The Fratrex Prismo of the holy Church."

"And for what reason?"

Sir Roger seemed to wonder how to answer that for a moment. "There are many I could give," he finally replied. "But I've heard a lot about you, and I think I'll tell you the truth. My primary task isn't to find you; it's to find the valley where you first discovered the Briar King. I'm to go there and hold it against all invaders until Niro Marco sends word."

"Why?"

"I don't rightly know. I don't care. But as you seem to be going there, I thought I would best discharge my mission by stopping you here in the foothills."

"How do you even know where you're going?"

"You made a report to the praifec of Crotheny, and he dispatched scouts to find the place. It's on our maps now."

Hespero, Aspar thought darkly.

"Well," Aspar said, "I reckon you ought to turn back."

"Why? Because you've got a knife to my throat? Everything I know about you says you won't kill me."

"You don't know everything, though, do you?" Aspar asked.

"Well, we all have our secrets."

His eyes shifted the barest bit, and Aspar suddenly found himself airborne, then pinned by two fantastically strong monks.

Stupid, he thought. Was it the geos making him an idiot or just old age?

It didn't matter now. Had they caught Leshya, too?

"Are you here alone, holter?" the knight asked, answering that question.

"Yah."

"Well, I'll try to have someone keep you company, at least until we've detained your friends. Do you think they will fight? It would be foolish."

"They might not," Aspar said. "Take me there. I'll talk them out of it."

Harriot shrugged. "It doesn't make *that* much difference to me. Anyway, my men have already started closing. I expect this to be over before sunrise."

Aspar relaxed his muscles and sighed, then put everything he had into breaking loose from the monks.

It was like trying to snap iron bands.

"You've no chance, holter," Harriot said.

"You have to let me go," Aspar said. "You've no idea what you're doing. You said it yourself. Unless I get to that valley, everything will die."

"That's very dramatic," Sir Roger replied. "In fact, the Fratrex Prismo makes similar claims about what will happen if you *do* reach the valley. Imagine who I believe. Now, if you'll excuse me, I need to oversee this. I promise you, I will spare whoever I can."

"Harm any of them and I'll send you straight to Grim," Aspar said.

"Grim? How quaint. A mountain heretic."

"I'm serious," Aspar said. "I'll kill you."

"Well that is as may be," the knight replied. "I'll trust you to think about the method."

They tied him up and put him under guard, leaving him to continue contemplating his mistake. He knew that there were monks who could hear a butterfly's wing against the breeze; Stephen had been one such. But when he'd been able to slip into camp, apparently unnoticed, he'd reckoned this bunch didn't have any of those.

And maybe they didn't. Leshya seemed to have escaped without being seen.

Maybe part of him wanted to be caught. This way, at least, the Sarnwood witch wouldn't get her way.

But what if Fend was right?

It was hard to even consider that. It was also moot; it no longer mattered what he thought.

A bell or so before dawn, the monks broke down the tent and lashed him over the back of a horse, then set off at a fast trot. There was a lot of shouting about formations and such, so Aspar figured that Emfrith must be giving better than Harriot had imagined he would. He wished they would set him upright so that he could see.

They reached a ridge top, and the horsemen started forming ranks.

Aspar smelled autumn leaves.

A sudden marrow-scraping scream went up, and he tried to lift his head higher. Then something knocked the horse out from under him. Blood came down like hot rain, and he had to blink it out of his eyes to see.

Gasping, he tucked his legs up and brought his bound hands from behind, cursing at the pain, eyes searching wildly for the source of the horse's disembowelment. But all he saw were the stamping hooves of other horses, and all he heard were screams of pain, terror, and defiance.

He got his hands under his boots and pulled forward, then started working at the knots keeping his feet together.

As he did that, the fighting moved away from him. By the time he could stand up, it was well down the ridge, leaving only carnage behind. Almost twenty horses were down, and nearly as many men. He took a dirk from one of the corpses and whittled through what remained of his bonds. He found a throwing ax on a headless body and stuck it in his belt.

From his vantage, he could see two battles being fought. One was up on the ridge with him, albeit farther down. He could see only part of it, but he could make out a couple of greffyns and an utin tearing at what remained of Harriot's rear guard.

Most of the rest of the army of the Church lay dead in the valley below, sprawled side by side with dozens of dead and dying sedhmhari. Only a few dozen men remained, and he recognized some of them as Emfrith's horsemen.

That was his fight, then. He started down the slope as quickly as he dared and as his legs allowed him.

He picked his way through the corpses, and by the time he reached the knot of men, only half a dozen of Emfrith's men were still on their feet. They faced about ten church-men, three of them still mounted. Of Winna there was no sign.

One of the knights saw him and wheeled his way but was unable to come to a full charge because of the heaped bodies. Aspar took the ax out of his belt and hurled it from four kingsyards away. It smacked into the knight's visor, and his head popped back. Aspar followed close behind the missile, grabbing the man's arm, hauling him out of the saddle, and slamming him to the ground. Then he stabbed the dirk up under the helm and through his neck.

With bleak purpose he turned to the next man, and then the next . . .

When it was over, Aspar, Emfrith, and two of his warriors were all that remained.

But Emfrith didn't have long. He had been stabbed through the lungs, and blood was choking out with his breath.

"Holter," he managed to gasp. "You have a berry for this?" He was trying to sound brave, but Aspar could see the terror on his face.

He shook his head. "I'm afraid not, lad," he said. "Do you know what happened to Winna?"

"Leshya took her before the fighting started. Said you had sent for her."

"I sent for her?"

Emfrith nodded. "Some of the knights broke off and went north. I think they may have gone after them."

"Maybe. I'll find her."

"I wish I could help."

"You've helped plenty," Aspar said.

"Be good to her," Emfrith said. "You don't deserve her. You're a damned fine man, but you don't deserve her."

"I know," Aspar said.

"It's a good death, isn't it?"

"It's a good death," Aspar agreed. "I'm proud of you. Your father will be, too."

"Don't *you* tell him. He'll hang you."

Aspar nodded. "I've got to go," he said. "You understand?"

"Yes."

Aspar rose and collected the ax. He found a bow and a few arrows, a dirk, then a horse. Emfrith's men stayed with him.

He wondered where Ehawk was. He hoped he was with Leshya but didn't have time to search the dead.

The battle on the ridge seemed to be over, too. At least he didn't see anything moving up there anymore.

He rode south, along the valley bottom.

Fend was waiting for him.

CHAPTER FOUR

✛

OVER BLUFF AND DOWN SLOUGH

NEIL'S STEED stumbled, tried to catch her stride, then stopped and tossed her head, blowing. Her coat was slick with foam, and her withers trembled. Neil leaned forward and stroked her neck, speaking to her in his native language.

"It'll be fine, girl," he told her. "The prince says we'll be giving you a rest in less than a league. But I need you to go now, yes? Let's do it."

He gave her a gentle nudge, and she started gamely forward, finally working up to match the canter of the others.

"It's a beautiful evening," he told the mare. "Look at the sun there, on the water."

Three days of hard riding had brought them to an old coastal trail that wound over bluff and down slough. The sun was going home, and Saltmark Sound was skinned copper.

Part of him yearned toward that water, those islands, to be adrift in those terrible and familiar waters. He had been too long landlocked.

But he had things to do, didn't he? What his heart wanted was no matter at all.

That sent him glancing ahead to where Brinna rode behind her brother, looking paler and less well than he had ever seen her. She had never ridden a horse, much less endured the tortures of a hard ride of many days. He was sore to the bone; he couldn't imagine how she must feel. To even remain mounted she had to be belted to Berimund. He feared in his bones she wouldn't survive.

As the sun touched the water, they came to an old castle on a little spit of stone sticking out into the sea. Barnacles up its walls showed that during the highest tides it must be cut off entirely from land. The tide was rising now but was far from high enough to cover the causeway, so they rode in to change their horses, the third time they had done so since starting their push for Crotheny. Berimund was being careful. The first of his friends he had visited had told him his father had put a price on his head and on the head of every man who aided him.

So they traveled ways less straight and warded than the great Vitellian Way.

They didn't stop for long. Neil kissed the mare on her soaking forehead as they led her away and met his new mount, Friufahs, a roan gelding. He was introducing himself when he heard Brinna say something he couldn't make out.

"It's not seemly," he heard Berimund answer.

"Nevertheless," Brinna replied, "it is my wish."

His gaze attracted by the conversation, Neil saw Berimund looking at him.

The Hansan walked over. "You have been alone with my sister on more than one occasion."

"That's true," Neil said.

"Have you been improper with her?"

Neil straightened. "I understand you might doubt me, but why would you cast such aspersions on your sister, sir?"

"My sister is both very wise and very naïve. She has not known many men, Sir Neil. I'm only asking you for the truth."

"Nothing inappropriate happened," Neil said. "Not when we were alone. When she set me off her ship in Paldh, I did kiss her. I did not mean to dishonor her in any way."

"She told me about that. She told me she asked you to kiss her."

He nodded.

"You did not think that part worth telling, although not doing so would put you in my ill graces?"

"It is her business," Neil said, "and not my place to make excuses."

"You admit, then, that you should have refused her?"

"I should have. I can't say I'm sorry I didn't."

"I see."

He looked out at the half-vanished sun. "She wants to ride with you for a while," he said. "I don't think it's right, but she is my sister, and I love her. Do not take undue advantage, sir."

He returned to Brinna and helped her over and up behind Neil. He felt her there, taut as a cord, as Berimund strapped them together. Her arms went awkwardly around his waist, as if she were trying somehow to hold on to him without touching him.

Resupplied and rehorsed, they continued on along the coast. Small, scallop-winged silhouettes appeared and fluttered against the bedimmed sky, and a chill breeze came off the waves. Far out at sea he made out the lantern on the prow of a lonely ship. Inland, a nightjar churred.

"I'm sorry about your queen," Brinna said. "I wish I could have met her."

"I wish you could have, too," Neil replied. "I wish I could have saved her."

"You're thinking if you hadn't been in our prison, you might have."

"Maybe."

"I can't say. But I couldn't act until Berimund came, and

I wouldn't have been able to find where she was without him. Neither could you have."

He nodded but didn't answer.

"He thought she was safe. He intended to keep her safe."

"I know," Neil said. "I don't blame you."

"You blame yourself."

"I shouldn't have let her come."

"How would you have stopped her?"

He didn't have anything to reply to that, so they rode on tacitly for a bit.

"It sounds so easy in the stories, riding a horse," Brinna finally ventured.

"It's not so bad when you're used to it," he said. "How are you doing?"

"Parts of me are on fire, and others feel dead," she said.

"Then let's rest for a day or so," he urged. "Let's get you out of the saddle."

"We can't," she murmured. "We have to reach her before Robert does."

"Anne?"

"Not Anne. A little girl. She's in Haundwarpen with a man and a woman. There is music all around them, some terrible, some beautiful, some both."

"That sounds familiar," Neil said.

"The man and woman are newly wed. The child is not theirs."

"There was a composer named Ackenzal," Neil said. "A favorite of—of the queen's. She attended the wedding, and I went with her. He and his wife have a girl in their care: Mery, the daughter of Lady Gramme."

"Yes. And half sister to Anne, yes?"

"So they say."

"You can guide us when we're near?"

"What has this to do with mending the law of death?" Neil asked.

"Everything," she replied. "And if Robert knows that, she is in terrible danger."

"How should Robert know it?"

"I don't know. But I see him there." She paused for a moment. "I know what killed Queen Muriele and Berimund's wulfbrothars."

"It nearly killed you, too."

"Yes. It's music, horrible and yet somehow lovely. Once you begin listening, it is very difficult to stop. If you hadn't stopped me, if you hadn't called that other name, I would be gone now."

"The name from the ship."

"Yes," she whispered. He wished he could turn and see her face. "The ship, when I wasn't me and you weren't you."

"But now we are who we are."

"Yes," she replied. "We are who we are."

He thought she paused, as if meaning to go on, but she didn't, at least following from that thought.

"I told you I had a higher purpose," she finally said.

"You did."

Again she seemed to feud with herself for a moment before going on.

"I once had three sisters," she said. "We were called by many names, but in Crotheny and Liery we were most often known as the Faiths."

"As in the stories? The four queens of Tier na Seid?"

"Yes and no. There are many stories. I am what is real."

"I don't understand."

"There were Faiths before me who wore my masks. Many of them, going back to the hard days after Virgenya Dare vanished. We were known as Vhatii then. Time changes tongues and twists names. We have lived, some of us hiding in the open, others secluded in distant places. We're not real sisters, you understand, but women born with the gift. When we grow old, when our powers fail and even the drugs no longer open our vision, we find our replacements."

"But what do you do?"

"It's hard to explain. We are very much creatures of two natures. Here, we are human; we eat and breathe, live and die. But in the Ambhitus, the Not World, we are the sum of all who have gone before us—more and less than human. And we see need. Until recently our visions were rarely specific; we reacted as plants bend toward the sun. But since the law of death has been broken, our visions have become more like true prescience. My sisters and I worked for years to assure that Anne would take the throne, and in one terrible, clear moment I saw how mistaken we were to do so.

"My sisters would not believe me, and so they died, along with the order we founded, or at least most of them. Your Alis was once one of ours."

"She knew who you were."

"When she saw me, yes. Not before."

"How did your sisters die?"

"That's complicated, too. Anne killed them, in a way— the Anne that was and will be, not the one you know. The one she is becoming."

"How did you escape?"

"I withdrew from the Ambhitus and hid. I abandoned my role as a Faith and dedicated myself to correcting our mistake."

"And now?"

"As I said, Anne is beyond me. But I have a chance to mend the law of death. The girl, Mery—we've been watching her. She has a strange and wonderful power—like mine in ways but also unlike anything that has ever been. Before she died, one of my sisters planted the seed in the composer so that he and Mery could undo the damage to the law. I must now see that to fruition."

"If the law of death is mended—"

"Yes. Robert will die."

"Let's do that, then," he muttered.

The moon set, and stars jeweled the sky. They moved from canter to trot and back to delay wearing out their mounts.

Brinna, shivering from fatigue, sagged into him and then straightened.

"Hold on or you'll fall off," he said.

"I wish . . ." she sighed.

"What?" He managed to croak, though he knew he shouldn't.

She didn't answer, and behind him she felt even more rigid than when she first had been placed there.

"I said there were three reasons I risked having you brought up from the dungeons," she murmured.

"Yes. You said the third didn't matter."

"I said it didn't matter then," she said. "I never meant it didn't matter. Do you remember the first two reasons?"

"You said that you didn't believe I could be an assassin and that you thought we could help each other."

"You have to understand my world," she said. "The way I lived. Four attempts that I know of were made on my life; one was by one of my own cousins, who was afraid I would see that he was cuckolding my father. A coven-trained assassin sent from Crotheny when I was ten. I don't know who sent her. A Black Talon killer from the dark forests of Vestrana came closest. He actually had the dagger to my throat. I want you to understand all of that because although I didn't *want* to think you would kill me, part of me still thought you might."

"Then why? What was the third reason?"

"The third reason was that I was willing to risk death to touch you again."

The horse thunked along in silence as a great bloody moon sank toward the dark sea.

"I love you," he said.

He felt her soften, then mold against his back, and her arms were suddenly comfortable and familiar around his waist. He couldn't, didn't dare turn around to kiss her, but it didn't matter. It was the best thing he had ever felt in his life, and for the next few bells nothing, not his failure, not his grief, not even his thirst for revenge, could distract him from the woman who had her arms around him, from the mystery and wonder of her.

CHAPTER FIVE

ACMEMENO

CAZIO STROKED Austra's face, then gently prized open her lips and dribbled some watered wine between them. After a moment her throat worked, and the liquid went down.

He regarded her still features, trying not to let the strange panic rise.

She's still alive, and so there's hope, he thought.

"Anne will have chirgeons who can cure you," he assured the sleeping girl. "This always turns out well in the stories, doesn't it? Although there it's usually the kiss of the handsome prince. Am I not handsome or princely enough?"

The carriage rumbled on for a moment.

"We might not even have to go all the way to Eslen," he told her. "We'll be at Glenchest by this afternoon. Probably the duchess can help us."

Austra, of course, said nothing.

They ran into a knight and his retainers about half a league from Glenchest, one Sir William, a servant of the duchess. He escorted them back to the rather baroque and defenseless mansion. The duchess did not meet them, which was rather uncharacteristic, but after the men were settled in quarters in the village, Cazio received an invitation to dine with her. He took z'Acatto and Austra in the carriage.

Elyoner Dare was a petite woman whose demure composure gave little immediate hint of her deep satisfaction in the pursuit of vice. One usually discovered her pleasantly wicked nature early in conversation, but this day she was very different from the last time he had seen her. She wore a black dress and a black net on her hair, and her courtiers and servants, usually quite colorfully attired, were also dressed in muted tones.

When they entered, she rose and offered her hand. Once they all had kissed it, she bent and kissed Cazio on the cheeks.

"It's good to see you, *mi dello*," the duchess said. "All is dark, but you are still a light to these eyes."

"Duchess Elyoner, I would be pleased to present my swordmaster and mentor—" He realized he did not know the old man's real name. Z'Acatto was the family nickname and simply meant "the cursed."

"Acmemeno d'Eriestia dachi Vesseriatii," z'Acatto said. "At your service, Duchess."

Cazio blinked, trying not to show his surprise. The duochi of the Vesseriatii were some of the richest, most powerful men in Vitellio.

Elyoner kissed him on the cheeks as well.

"Austra is with us," Cazio said. "She isn't well. I was hoping your chirgeons could help her."

"Austra? Ill? Of course we shall do what we can." Her forehead puckered in a small frown. "How is it you were not with Anne when . . ." She didn't finish, but her eyes seemed to glisten a bit.

"She sent us away, to Dunmrogh," Cazio replied, then caught Elyoner's tone.

"When *what*?" he grated.

Cazio sat on the very bench where he first had kissed Austra and took a deep pull from the carafe of harsh red wine. He glanced at z'Acatto as the old man came up and then handed him the stoneware jug.

Oddly, the older man hesitated, then took a drink.

"Anything else you have to tell me?" Cazio asked, trying to work up some anger and finding he couldn't. "Are you actually a duoco? Or perhaps meddicio of z'Irbina?"

"My brother is duoco," z'Acatto said. "I assume he is. I haven't seen or heard from him in years."

"Why? Why did you live in my house as if you were my father's servant? Some vagabond soldier he dragged back from the wars?"

Z'Acatto took another drink, then another.

"I always told you I did not know the face of the man who killed your father," he said.

"Yes."

"I lied."

Cazio stared at the old man, and his life seemed to stretch out behind him like a rope he was trying—and failing—to balance on. Was anything he knew true?

"Who killed him?" he demanded.

Z'Acatto squinted off into the middle distance. "We were in a little town called Fierra, in the Uvadro Mountains. They make a fortified wine there called uchapira. We were drinking a lot of it, your father and I. There was a man; I don't even remember his name. Turned out I had slept with his woman the night before, and he called me to steel. Only I was too drunk. When I got up to fight, my legs failed me. When I awoke, your father was out in the street with him. I was only out for a few moments, so I was still drunk and mean. I only meant to fight my own duel, but when I came screaming out of the tavern, Mamercio was distracted, and the man stabbed him right through the spleen." He looked back at Cazio. "I killed your father, Cazio. My drunken stupidity killed him. Do you understand?"

Cazio stood jerkily. "All this time—"

"I did the only thing I knew to do," he said. "I took his place, raised you."

"The man he fought?"

"I killed him, of course."

"You could have told me. You could have told me a lot of things."

"I could have. I was a coward."

Cazio felt his heart constrict as he looked at this man he did not know, had never known.

"This is worse, knowing now," Cazio said. "Now, when everything is all coming apart."

"What will you do?"

"Now that Anne is dead? Kill Hespero. Find a cure for Austra. Go home. *Why didn't you tell me*?" he shouted.

"I can only apologize so much," z'Acatto grunted.

"You haven't apologized," Cazio said.

"Cazio . . ."

"Go away," he said, suddenly very tired. "Just leave me alone, whoever you are."

Z'Acatto got up slowly and stood there, arms hanging at his sides, for a long moment. Then he walked off.

Cazio continued drinking.

He woke the next morning, still on the bench, with one of Elyoner's pages tapping him apologetically. He groggily levered himself up to a sitting position.

"What?" he said.

"My lady would have you come to her chambers at third bell."

"What bell is it now?"

"Second, sir,"

"Fine," Cazio said. "I'll be there."

It was only as he found his room and was bathing as best he could from the basin that he began to worry about the place assigned for the meeting.

When he arrived to find the duchess in bed and Austra on an adjacent bed, his worries intensified.

"Don't look like that," Elyoner said with more than a hint of her old self. "Every man wants a go with two women."

"Duchess—"

"Hush and sit on the foot of the bed," she said, sitting up against enormous pillows. She was clad in a dressing gown of black-and-gold brocade.

As Cazio sat gingerly on the bed, two serving girls came in bearing trays of food. One was placed in front of the duchess, another next to Cazio. A third servant, a slight girl with large eyes, entered with what looked like porridge and began to feed Austra.

"Greyna is very good," the duchess said, nodding at the girl. "Her brother was injured in the head at a joust and was unable to feed himself. He lived two years, so she's had plenty of practice. She has a large soul."

"Thank you for all of your kindnesses, Duchess."

Elyoner glanced over at Austra. "That girl is as dear to me as Anne was," she said. "She was as much my niece as Fastia or Elseny." She shook her head. "I am hardly thirty, Cazio. I hope when you are my age you have not lost so many dear ones."

"Austra isn't dead," he said.

"No," the duchess replied. "She isn't. Break your fast."

He looked down at the tray, thinking he wasn't hungry, but the cream fritters, sausage, and dewberries invited him to try a few bites, anyway.

"Unlike Greyna's brother, Austra doesn't seem to have an injury to her head or any wounds at all except those cuts on her legs. You said it was done by a churchman. Do you know what he was up to?"

"No. She said he said something about the 'blood telling' but nothing about what that meant."

"Curious," Elyoner said. "In any event, whatever has happened to the dear girl, I think we must suspect some eldritch cause—something I, unfortunately, know very little about."

"Do you know anyone who knows more?"

"I assume you mean outside of the Church?"

"That's probably best."

"No, not really. But surely you do."

He nodded. "Yes, there's an old Sefry woman in Eslen that Anne consulted."

"Eslen won't be easy to get into," Elyoner said. "The city is under siege, with Hespero's army camped on the south and Hansa on the north. The fleets have met in Foambreaker Bay, but I haven't heard much more than that."

"Who rules?"

"Artwair had declared himself regent," she said. "The logical heir is Charles, but no one wants that charade again. After him it gets complicated; there's Gramme's bastard, Robert, any number of cousins."

"You," Cazio pointed out.

"Oh, yes," she said. "Yes, that's out of the question. I simply won't do it. Buts it's actually rather moot, because I suspect Eslen is going to fall, and Marcomir and Hespero will decide the matter."

Cazio shrugged. "I don't care who rules. They can put a pig on the throne as far as I'm concerned. But I'll have Austra back, and I need to kill Hespero."

"Kill the Fratrex Prismo of the Church? I'll be interested to see how you do that."

"I've met them that seemed immortal and unbeatable before," Cazio said. "Most of them are dead now, or might as well be."

"That's it, then? You're really going to Eslen?"

He nodded. "If I can impose on you for a few horses."

"Of course," she replied. "Do you have a plan for getting into the city?"

"No," he said. "But I'll have one when I need one."

He rode out the next day with Austra in the carriage and three spare horses. He didn't bother to find z'Acatto to say good-bye.

The road took him west across the flat yellowing grass of the Mey Ghorn plain. Clouds scudded across the sky like fast ships until near sundown they piled up and blotted out the stars. The air was wet and cool and smelled like rain when he went to where Austra lay and fed her some porridge and watered wine. She seemed thinner.

"The Sefry will know what to do," he assured her. "Mother Uun will have a cure."

The rain came gently enough, and he lay there listening to it on the canvas until sleep at last folded him into her blanket.

He woke to the morning songs of birds and realized that the sun was well up and he had lost time. He felt guilty for sleeping at all when every bell counted. He gave Austra her morning meal and ate a bit of dried meat. He found the horses grazing and brought them back to the harness. He settled onto the seat and started out.

It had been a long time, he realized, since he had been alone, his time in the wine cellar at Dunmrogh aside. He wasn't technically alone now, but for all intents and purposes he was. He'd once spent a good deal of his time solitary, and he understood now how much he missed it.

What sort of man am I? he wondered. Anne was dead. Austra was well on her way to joining her. And yet, somehow, part of him was excited to be in the quiet of his own thoughts, with no one questioning him, with nothing to do but watch the road.

"Anne is dead," he murmured aloud. He remembered his first sight of her, bathing in a pool in the wilds around the Coven St. Cer. She had become so completely a part of his life, that the thought that he would never see her again seemed not only wrong but fundamentally impossible. They had survived so much together, and for what? For her to die now? Had any of it been worth it?

But of course, no matter what one survived, death was always coming. There was no winning that game.

By noon the road was winding gently downhill, and the occasional malend could be seen turning its sails in the distance. He stopped to feed and wash Austra and let the horses go to water. He was just about to start off again when riders appeared on the road ahead.

He looked about, but it was all open fields. If they were enemies, there wasn't much he could do.

Oddly enough, the impression he had was that the horses he saw were mounted by giant mushrooms, but as they drew nearer, he saw that they were Sefry, wearing their customary broad-brimmed hats to keep the sun from their dainty skins.

When they were even nearer, he recognized their colors as those of Anne's Sefry bodyguard.

He watched them come, wondering what they could possibly be up to. Having failed their mistress, were they now on their way to cast themselves into the eastern sea?

He counted forty of them and wondered why he bothered to do that. Weren't these friends? If they were, why did he have such a strange feeling in his belly's abyss?

And why were they flanking him?

He drew the horses to a halt. One of the riders came forward and pulled down the gauze that hid most of his face, revealing Cauth Versial, the leader of Anne's guard.

"Cazio," Cauth said. "Fancy meeting you here."

"Yes," Cazio replied. "Fancy it."

"You've heard the news?"

Cazio nodded, noting from the corner of his eye that the Sefry were continuing to surround him.

"It was a terrible shock."

"I would imagine," Cazio said. "To have the person you were supposed to be protecting murdered in plain sight with you all around her. How could that happen?"

"I'm sure if you had been there, things would have gone differently," Cauth said.

"I'm sure of that, too," Cazio said.

"Austra is in the wagon, I take it."

"Why would you think that?"

Cauth sighed. "Time is short," he said. "I won't waste it bantering with you. I've seen you fight, and I imagine you'll probably kill a few of us if you choose to, but there's no reason it should come to that."

"Why should it come to that?"

"It shouldn't. We've come to escort you to Eslen."

"How nice. I was going there anyway. But why do I need an escort?"

"The city is under siege. You'll need our help to get in."

"But why are you interested in helping? I suppose is my real question."

"We're not," Cauth said. "Austra is our concern. Whether you're there or not is immaterial."

"What do you want with Austra?"

"That's nothing to concern yourself about."

"Oh, I'm very much concerned."

Cauth started to say something, but then he peered beyond Cazio, and his face wrinkled in what seemed to be chagrin.

"Not traveling alone, after all," he said.

Cazio turned and saw, on the hill, a line of pikemen forming up.

"Z'Acatto," he murmured.

"Come along," Cauth said, drawing his sword. Cazio drew Acredo, noticing as he did so that six archers had arrows aimed at him.

"We'll go up the hill and talk to your friends," Cauth said. "We'll explain that there's no need for a fight, yes?"

"If you insist," Cazio said.

"Don't forget that Austra will be here, with my men."

"I won't."

He marched up the hill with the Sefry. Z'Acatto watched them come, sitting a gray stallion in front of his men.

"I didn't ask for your help," Cazio shouted once they were in earshot.

"No, you didn't," the old man said. "And I wasn't planning to give it. I told the men I would get them to Eslen, that's all."

"Good, then."

"Who are your friends?"

"Anne's old guard," he replied. "They've kindly offered to escort me to the castle."

"Well, good," z'Acatto said. "Then you're well off my hands."

Cazio nodded. "How was the wine? Did you drink it yet?"

"Not yet," z'Acatto said. "It's not the right time."

"I'm not sure there's going to be a better one."

"You just want a taste of it."

"I won't deny that," Cazio said. Then he spun and punched Cauth in the jaw, drew Acredo, and threw himself flat as arrows whirred overhead.

They want Austra alive, he thought, praying he was right, knowing in his bones this was the best choice.

With a roar the pikemen started down the hill.

CHAPTER SIX

✛

BRACKEN HOPE

FEND DIDN'T HAVE much of his army left, either. One of the Vaix stood behind him, favoring an injured leg. Of monsters, Aspar saw only a greffyn, a wairwulf, and two utins.

That was still likely to be more than he could kill, but he was ready to try.

"I told you you were going to need my help," the Sefry said.

"Yah, thanks," he said, nocking an arrow to the string of the unfamiliar bow.

The wairwulf and the utins were fast, though, moving in front of Fend before he could aim.

"Aspar," Fend called. "If you manage to kill me here or, more likely, if I kill you, what happens to Winna, to your child, to your precious forest? I'll tell you. That knight of Gravio and his twenty men are going to catch her. Probably they'll kill her. Whoever sent them—and I'll bet my other eye that it was Hespero—doesn't have any interest in bringing a new Briar King into the world, not until they've taken the sedos throne and hold sway over everything. You and I have the same interest, Aspar."

"I doubt that."

"Doubt it if you want; my offer to help still stands. I can find the Vhenkherdh; you know I don't need you for that. And yes, I'd love to kill you now, but then I would have one less man—or monster, which is more what you are—to go up against this knight with. We need each other. We can settle our differences afterward, don't you think?"

Aspar stared into Fend's single eye, remembering the sight of Qerla's dead body, remembering the last time they had been in the valley of the Briar King.

He had never hated the Sefry more, but the geos wouldn't let him fire.

"Let's stop bloody talking, then," he snarled, lowering the bow. "Let's go."

Stephen and Zemlé floated in the grip of the Vhelny, which, now that Stephen had gentled it, was soft, firm, almost velvety. He had determined that the demon's limbs were more like tentacles than arms. It was still obfuscated from the examination of Stephen's senses; no power he had or command he could give would lift that apparently ancient magic and reveal the creature's true appearance. It was a subtle thing that would take time and perhaps more power to overcome.

He was happy that the cloud that concealed the Vhelny had no effect on his own vision, however, as they drifted through the delicate layers of clouds and the vista below revealed itself.

Directly beneath his feet Eslen castle pointed towers up at him like whimsical lances. About that were the tiers of the city and the long, green island of Ynis, held all around by the two mighty rivers and a thousand neat canals stretching off toward the horizon.

And along the banks of those rivers, beside those canals, were fires, tents, and tens of thousands of men.

West across a great bay, beyond an awesome many-toothed wall, the Lier Sea was thickly jeweled with ships for as far as he could see.

"Eslen," Zemlé breathed.

"Have you been here before?" he asked.

"Never."

"Nor have I."

That wasn't exactly true. He had never been to *this* Eslen, but he remembered an earlier, much smaller one, little more than a hill fort, really, a tiny place trying not to be crushed by giants, its little leaders capering to his will.

Now it was quite splendid, though. He could hardly wait to see the royal scriftorium. Who knew what precious texts it might hold, unappreciated for millennia?

But first things first.

He had the Vhelny set them down on a pretty little hill on the island, where they had a good view of the surrounds, then set the demon to guard them from anyone approaching. They picnicked on salty ham, pears, and a sweet red wine. Zemlé was nervous at first, but when no one bothered them, she eventually relaxed and even drowsed.

He noticed the Vhelny drifting near.

"I smell the throne," it said.

"Yes," Stephen said. "So do I. It's not here, but it will be soon, down there in the shadow city. That must be where Virgenya put her shortcut."

"You're speaking nonsense, wormling."

He shook his head. "No. She left the power, but she left a key to it in the blood of her line and a place for that key to unlock. She made a faneway, a brief one containing only two fanes—but separated by a hundred leagues. But once one of her heirs visited the one, it was inevitable that they should visit the other and inherit much of her power. That's what happened to Anne. But Anne isn't Virgenya. She won't use the power and then give it up."

"That's why you seek the throne? To save the world?" the Vhelny sounded dubious.

"To make it what it should be."

"Then why not go now to the city of shadows and wait?"

Stephen plucked a straw of grass and placed it between his teeth. "Because I can't make out even the faintest shadow of Anne anymore. Even after I walked the faneway, I couldn't see anything about her, but I knew where she was. Now it's as if she's gone completely. She might be a thousand leagues from here or right there, waiting for me. I can still see Hespero, and I should probably challenge him first, garner his strength before attempting Anne."

"Coward."

"Ah, you want me to rush into this and lose. You'd like to be free again. You won't be, I promise."

"Man-worm, you know so little." Stephen felt the prick of a thousand ghostly needles against his flesh. He rolled his eyes and dismissed the attack with a wave of his hand.

"Hush. I'm going to try to find her again. Maybe being closer will help."

The Vhelny said nothing, but he felt it coil in upon itself, sulking.

He sent his senses drifting, expanding away from him like ripples in a pond. There was the throbbing sickness that was the emerging throne; there was the contained puissance of the man whom he once had known as Praifec Hespero but who lately had risen in the world. He would be difficult. Should he make an alliance with him against Anne? That might be the safest course; he could strike the Fratrex Prismo once they had won.

But then, Hespero would nurse the same plan.

He was almost ready to give up when something caught his attention, a sort of glimmer in the corner of his eye. It was a few leagues from the city, and like Eslen-of-Shadows, it reeked of Cer.

At first he didn't understand, but after a moment he smiled in delight and clapped his hands together.

"I should have guessed," he said. "This is really wonderful. And no one else knows."

"What do you babble about?" the Vhelny asked.

"We'll just go and see," Stephen said, rubbing his hands together. "At worst it will help pass the time. But I don't think it will be worst. The first thing is to find a safe place for Zemlé."

The last time Aspar had seen the Sa Ceth ag Sa'Nem, the "Shoulders of Heaven," he had been in the bloom of early and unexpected love. They—and everything else he saw—had appeared beautiful beyond imagining.

He supposed they still were, those mammoth peaks whose

summits were so high that they faded into the sky like the moon at midday. But he wasn't giddy with love this time, far from it. No, he was thinking mostly about killing.

The geos wouldn't let him, not yet, not until he actually had gotten Winna to the Vhenkherdh or, presumably, when she got there with Leshya. Until then, he couldn't slit Fend crotch to breastbone because then Fend's monsters would kill him, and the geos didn't want that.

That was how things were. When they reached the valley, they would change.

He no longer held much hope that anything useful could be done there. He didn't doubt that Fend would cut open Winna and offer whatever was growing in her in some grizzly and pointless sacrifice dreamt up by the diseased mind of the Sarnwood witch. But heal the forest, bring it back? It didn't seem possible. It also didn't seem very likely that he and Winna were going to get out of the valley alive once they got there. It might be that the best he could do was give her an easy death, then slaughter Fend and as many of the others as he could before they took him down. The thought of dying didn't bother him much; without the forest and without Winna, there wasn't anything keeping him in the lands of fate.

He was still in that bleak mood a few bells later, when the unexpected walked up and slapped it right out of him.

They were switchbacking up to the top of a long ridge of hills when a stream crossed their path. And there, just where the water ran off the hill, grew a little green fern. Not a black spider tree or dragon-tongue thing but a simple honest bracken.

Farther along the trail they found more, and by day's end they were in almost natural woodland again. For the first time since entering the King's Forest his chest relaxed a bit, and the stench of putrefaction was almost gone.

So the heart of it is still alive, he thought. Leshya was right about that, at least. Maybe she was right about more.

Leshya had taken Winna, which suggested the Sefry also thought that the child she carried might be the solution to the problem. But had she thought that all along, or had she heard his conversation with Fend?

And Leshya and Winna weren't alone. There was a third set of tracks: Ehawk's. Leshya was taking them to the valley the same way Aspar had the last time, a long way around that required climbing down a deep gorge of briar trees.

They'd left their trail a day before; Fend was going by a more direct route that would allow horses in. That was how the knight was going, too. With any luck at all, they would actually beat Leshya, Winna, and Ehawk. When Winna entered the valley, the geos ought to lift, and then Aspar could do as he pleased.

By nightfall, with the sound of whippoorwills around him, he no longer was so certain what that would be.

Because he had hope again, as frail and as obstinate as a bracken.

CHAPTER SEVEN

THE PROOF OF
THE VINTAGE

CAZIO FOUGHT in a bloody blur, all sense of time lost. His arm was so tired that he'd had no choice but to switch to his left, and when that failed him, he went back to the right, but the rest hadn't helped it much. His lungs flamed in his chest, and his legs wobbled beneath him. As he clumsily drew Acredo from his latest opponent, he saw another coming. He spun to face the foe and kept spinning, toppling to the bloody earth. The Sefry slashed at him with a curved sword, but Cazio kept rolling, then reversed direction and thrust Acredo out hopefully. The Sefry, probably nearly as tired as he was, obligingly ran onto the point. He slid down the blade and onto Cazio, gasping strange curses before setting off west.

Grunting, Cazio tried to push the dead weight off, but his body didn't want to cooperate. He summoned the image of Austra, helpless in the carriage, and finally managed to roll the man off and stagger back to his feet, leaning on Acredo just in time to meet five more of the Sefry, who were spreading to surround him.

He heard someone behind him.

"It's me," z'Acatto's voice said.

Cazio couldn't help a tired grin as the old man's back came against his.

"We'll hold each other up," the mestro said.

From that simple touch, Cazio felt a rush of strength he had no notion still lived in him. Acredo came up, fluid, almost with a life of its own. Steel rang behind him, and Cazio shouted hoarsely, parrying an attack and drilling his rapier through a yellow-eyed warrior.

"Glad I came?" z'Acatto grunted.

"I had the upper hand anyway," Cazio said. "But I don't mind the company."

"That's not the impression I had."

Cazio thrust, parried a counter to his arm, and sent his enemy dancing back from his point.

"I sometimes speak too quickly," Cazio admitted.

The two Sefry he faced came at him together. He bound the blade of the first to strike and ran through the other, then let go of the blade and punched the first man in the face. He reeled back, during which time Cazio withdrew Acredo and set it back to guard.

He heard z'Acatto grunt, and something stung Cazio's back. He dispatched the staggering Sefry, then turned in time to parry a blow aimed at z'Acatto. The old man thrust into the foe's belly, and suddenly they were alone. Around them the battle was nearly over, with z'Acatto's men surrounding a small knot of the remaining Sefry.

Z'Acatto sat down hard, holding his side. Cazio saw blood spurting through his fingers, very dark, nearly black.

"I think," z'Acatto grunted, "it's time we drank that wine."

"Let's bind you up first," Cazio said.

"No need for that."

Cazio got a knife, cut a broad strip from a Sefry shirt, and started wrapping it tightly around z'Acatto's torso. The wound was a puncture, very deep.

"Just get the damned wine," the mestro said.

"Where is it?" Cazio asked, feeling the apple in his throat.

"In my saddle pack," z'Acatto wheezed.

It took Cazio a while to find the horse, which wisely had moved away from the fighting.

He dug one of the bottles of Zo Buso Brato out and then raced back to where his swordmaster still sat waiting. His head was down, and for a moment Cazio thought he was too late, but then the old man lifted his arm, proffering a corkscrew.

"It might be vinegar," Cazio cautioned, flopping down next to his mentor.

"Might be," z'Acatto agreed. "I was saving it for when we got back to Vitellio, back to your house."

"We can still wait."

"We'll have the other bottle there."

"Fair enough," Cazio agreed.

The cork came out in one piece, which was astonishing, considering its age. Cazio handed it to z'Acatto. The older man took it weakly and smelled it.

"Needs to breathe," he said. "Ah, well." He tilted it back and took a sip, eyes closed, and smiled.

"That's not too bad," he murmured. "Try it."

Cazio took the bottle and then hesitantly took a drink.

In an instant the battlefield was gone, and he felt the warm sun of Vitellio, smelled hay and rosemary, wild fennel, black cherry—but underneath that something enigmatic, as indescribable as an ideal sunset. Tears sprang in his eyes, unbidden.

"It's perfect," he said. "Perfect. Now I understand why you've been trying to find it for so long."

Z'Acatto's only answer was the faint smile that remained on his face.

"I'll tell them I did it," Mery said. "I'll tell them you weren't even here."

Leoff shook his head and squeezed her shoulder. "No, Mery," he said. "Don't do that. It wouldn't work, anyway."

"I don't want them to hurt you again," she explained.

"They're not going to hurt him," Areana promised in a hushed and strained voice.

Yes they are, he thought. *And they'll hurt you, too. But if we can keep them from examining Mery, from noticing the wrongness about her, she might have a chance.*

"Listen," he began, but then the door opened.

It wasn't a sacritor standing there or even Sir Ilzereik.

It was Neil MeqVren, Queen Muriele's bodyguard.

It was like waking up in a strange room and not knowing how you got there. Leoff just stared, rubbing the bent fingers of his right hand on his opposite arm.

"You're all right?" Neil asked.

Leoff plucked his voice from somewhere. "Sir Neil," he said cautiously. "There are Hansan knights and warriors about. All over."

"I know." The young knight walked over to Areana and cut her bonds, then Leoff's, and helped him up.

He only glanced at the dead men on the floor, then at Areana's swollen face.

"Did anyone still living do that, lady?" he softly asked her.

"No," Areana said.

"And your head, Cavaor?" he asked Leoff.

Leoff gestured at the dead. "It was one of them," he said. The knight nodded and seemed satisfied.

"What are you doing here?" Areana asked.

The answer came from an apparition near the door. Her hair was as white as milk, and she was so pale and handsome that at first Leoff thought she might be Saint Wyndoseibh herself, come drifting down from the moon on cobwebs to see them.

"We've come to meet Mery," the White Lady said.

* * *

Neil watched the stars appear and listened as the hum and whirr of night sounds rose around him. He sat beneath an arbor, half an arrow shot from the composwer's cottage.

Muriele was there, too, still wrapped in the linens from Berimund's hideaway. She'd made most of the trip unceremoniously tied to the back of a horse, but once in Newland, they'd found a small wain for her to lie in state on.

She needed to be buried soon. They hadn't had any salt to pack her in, and the scent of rot was starting to remark itself.

He noticed a slim shadow approaching.

"May I?" Alis' voice inquired from the darkness.

He gestured toward a second bench.

"I've not much idea what they're talking about in there," she said. "But I got us this." She held up a bottle of something. "Shall we have the wake?"

He searched for something to say, but there was too much in him to let anything come out right. He saw her tilt the bottle up, then down. She dabbed her lips and reached it toward him. He took it and pressed the glass lip against his own, held his breath, and took a mouthful. He almost didn't manage to swallow it; his mouth told him it was poison and wanted it out.

When he swallowed it, however, his body began to thank him almost immediately.

He took another swallow—it was easier this time—and passed it back to her.

"Do you think it's true?" he asked. "About Anne?"

"Which? That she slew forty thousand men with shinecraft or that she's dead?"

"That she's dead."

"From what I can tell," she said, "the news came from Eslen, not from Hansa. I don't see what anyone there would have to gain from letting such a rumor circulate."

"Well, that's a full ship, then," he said, taking the again proffered bottle and drinking more of the horrible stuff.

"Don't start that," Alis chided.

"I was guard to both of them."

"And you did an amazing job. Without you they would have both been dead months ago."

"Months ago, now. What's the difference?"

"I don't know. Does it make a difference if you live one year or eighty? Most people seem to think so." She took the bottle and tugged at it hard. "Anyway, if anyone is to blame for Muriele's death, it's me. You weren't her only bodyguard, you know."

He nodded, starting to feel the tide come up.

"So the question," Alis said, "is what do you and I do now? I don't think we'll be much help to the princess and the composer and Mery in whatever it is they're doing."

"I reckon we find Robert," Neil said.

"And that is *excellent* thinking," Alis agreed. "How do we do that?"

"Brinna might be able to tell us where he is."

"Ah, Brinna." Alis' voice became more sultry. "Now there's an interesting subject. You have acquaintances in very interesting places. How is it you two grew so fond of each other so quickly?"

"Fond?"

"Oh, stop it. You don't seem the woman conqueror on the face of it, but first Fastia, now the princess of Hansa who is also, ne'er you mind, one of the Faiths. That is quite a record."

"I met her—we had met before," Neil tried to explain.

"You said you had never been to Kaithbaurg before."

"And I hadn't. We met on a ship, in Vitellio. This isn't the first time she's run away from Hansa."

"I don't blame her," Alis said. "Why did she go back?"

"She said she had a vision of Anne bringing ruin to the whole world."

"Well, she was wrong about that, at least."

"I suppose."

"Well, if Anne is dead . . ." She sighed and handed him the bottle. "She was supposed to *save* us, or so I thought before I quit caring. The Faiths told us that."

"Your order?"

"Yes. The Order of Saint Dare. There's no point in keeping it secret now."

"Brinna said that she and the other Faiths had been wrong. That's all I know."

He took two drinks.

"Did you know Anne well?" Alis asked.

He took another pull. "I knew her. I wouldn't say we were friends, exactly."

"I barely knew her. I hardly knew Muriele until last year."

"I don't suppose mistresses and wives socialize that much."

"No. But—" She closed her eyes. "Strong stuff."

"Yes."

"She helped me, Sir Neil. She took me in despite what I had been. I try not to love, because there's nothing but heartbreak in it. But I loved her. I did."

Her voice only barely quavered, but her face was wet in the moonlight.

"I know," he said.

She sat that way a moment, staring at the bottle. Then she raised it. "To Robert," she said. "He killed my king and lover, he killed my queen and friend. So to him, and his legs severed at the hip, and his arms cut from his shoulders, and all buried in different places—" She choked off into a sob.

He took the bottle. "To Robert," he said, and drank.

The White Lady—Brinna, her name was—looked up from Leoff's music. "Will this do it?" she asked.

Leoff regarded the strange woman for a moment. He was tired, his head hurt, and what he mostly wanted was to go to bed.

"I don't know," he finally said.

"Yes, he does," Mery said.

He shot the girl a warning glance, but she just smiled at him.

"You don't trust me?" Brinna asked.

"Milady, I don't know you. I've been deceived before— often. It's been a very long day, and I'm finding it hard to understand why you're here. We had another visitor, you know, pretending to be a relative of Mery's, and you remind me a lot of her."

"That was one of my sisters," Brinna said. "She might have dissembled about who she was, but everything else she told you is true. Like me, she was a seer. Like me, she knew that if anyone can mend the law of death, it's you two. I've come to help."

"How can you help?"

"I don't know, but I felt called here."

"That's not too useful," Leoff said.

Brinna leaned forward a bit. "I broke the law of death," she said quietly. "I am responsible. Do you understand?"

Leoff exhaled and pushed his hand through his hair, wincing as he touched the sore spot. "No," he said. "I don't really understand any of it."

"It will work," Mery insisted.

Leoff nodded. "I compose more with my heart than with my head, and my heart says it would work if it could be performed, which it can't. That's the problem, you see."

"I don't understand," she said.

"You read music, yes?"

"Yes," she said. "I can play the harp and lute. I can sing."

"Then you notice that there are three voices, yes? The low, the middle, and the high."

"Not unusual," she said.

"No. Quite the norm. Except that if you look closely, you'll see that there are two distinct lines in each voice."

"I noticed that, too. But I've seen that before, too, in the *Armaio* of Roger Hlaivensen, for instance."

"Very good," Leoff said. "But here's the difference. The second lines—the one with the strokes turned down—those have to be sung by . . . ah, well—by the dead."

When she didn't even blink at that, he went on. "The up-turned lines are to be sung by the living, and for the piece to be done properly, all the singers must be able to *hear* one another. I can't imagine any way for that to happen."

But Mery and Brinna were looking at each other, both with the same odd smile on their faces.

"That's no problem, is it, Mery?" Brinna said.

"No," the girl replied.

"How soon can we perform it?" Brinna asked.

"Wait," Leoff said. "What are you two talking about?"

"The dead can hear us through Mery," Brinna explained. "You can hear the dead through me. You see? I am the last piece of your puzzle. Now I know why I'm here."

"Mery?" Leoff turned his gaze on the girl, who merely nodded.

"Fine," he said, trying to resist the sudden dizzying hope. "If you say so."

"How soon?"

"I can sing the middle part," he said. "Areana can sing the upper. We need someone for the low."

"Edwyn Mylton," Areana said.

"Of course," Leoff said cautiously. "He could do it. If he's still in Haundwarpen and if we could get to him."

"Haundwarpen is under siege," Areana explained.

"No," Brinna said. "Haundwarpen is fallen. But that's actually good for us."

"How so?"

"My brother is a prince of Hansa. They won't stop him entering or leaving the city, and they won't ask him questions. Not yet."

"A pri—" He stopped. "Then you're a princess of Hansa?"

She nodded.

"Then I really don't understand," he said.

"My brother and I are here at our peril," she said. "Understand, it doesn't matter who wins the war. If the barrier between life and death deteriorates further, all of our empires will be dust."

"What do you mean," Areana asked, "at your peril?"

"My brother tried to help your queen, and I am run away," she said. "If we're caught, we may well both be executed.

That's why we need to move quickly. At the moment, the army here recognizes my brother as their prince. But word from my father will reach here very soon, and we will be found, so all must go quickly."

We'll do the piece, his thoughts rushed. *We'll cure Mery.*

He clung to that thought and shied from the next: Brinna was prepared to die, perhaps expected it, perhaps had *seen* it. That did not bode well for the rest of them.

"Well," he said, "we'd best find Mylton, then, and get on with this."

CHAPTER EIGHT

REUNIONS STRANGE AND NATURAL

"WHAT NOW, sir?" Jan asked Cazio.

Cazio stared at the freshly turned earth and took a few deep breaths. The morning smelled clean despite the carnage.

"I don't know," he said. If Anne's Sefry guards were traitors, Mother Uun probably was, too. If he took Austra to her, they might be walking right into the spider's web.

But what else was there to do? Only in Eslen was he likely to find anyone who could help Austra.

"I'm still going on to Eslen," he said. "Nothing's changed about that."

"I reckon we'll be going with you, then," the soldier said. "The empire is a month behind on our salary, and we've worked hard enough for it."

Cazio shook his head. "From what I hear, you'll only walk into slaughter. Go back and keep the duchess safe. I know she'll pay you."

"Can't let you walk into slaughter alone," the soldier replied.

"I won't get in by fighting," Cazio said, "with or without your help. I'll have to use my wits somehow."

"That's a bloody shame," Jan said. "You're bound to come to a bad end that way."

"Thanks for the confidence," Cazio replied. "I think it's for the best. You fellows will just draw a fight we can't win. The two of us might be able to slip in the back way."

Jan held his gaze for a moment, then nodded and stuck out his hand. Cazio took it.

"The Cassro was a good man," the soldier said.

"He was," Cazio agreed.

"He raised a good man, too."

They broke camp a bell later. The soldiers headed back to Glenchest, and Cazio and Austra were alone again.

It was along about midday that Cazio felt a strange, hot wind carrying an acrid scent he had smelled before, deep in the tunnels below Eslen. He drew Acredo and turned on the board, searching. There wasn't much to see; the road was bounded on both sides by hedges and had been for nearly a league. Until now he'd been enjoying the change from open landscape; he could almost pretend he was back in Vitellio, taking a tour of one of the grand trivii with z'Acatto, working up an appetite for pigeon with white beans and garlic and a thirst for a light *vino verio*.

Now he suddenly felt claustrophobic. The last time he'd come this way, it had been with an army, and they hadn't much feared bandits; now he realized this would be a perfect place for them to hide, say, just around one of these bends, and wondered if he hadn't dismissed Jan and the others too quickly.

Of course, that had nothing to do with what he had smelled, which he was beginning to think was an illusion, anyway, just a stray memory of one of the many horrible things he had experienced in the last two years or so.

He kept Acredo in hand as they went around the curve.

There was someone there, all right. It wasn't a bandit.

"Fratir Stephen?" He drew back on the reins and brought the carriage to a halt.

"Casnar!" Stephen replied. "You're a coachman now."

Cazio was momentarily at a loss for words. He didn't know the fellow well, but he did know him, and the odds seemed against a chance meeting. And there was that other thing . . .

"Everyone thinks you're dead, you know," he said.

"I expect so," Stephen replied. "The slinders did make off with me. But here I am, fit and well."

He did look well, Cazio thought, not dead at all. Although there was something about the way he spoke and carried himself that seemed very different.

"Well," he said for lack of something better, "I'm glad you're well. Did Aspar and Winna find you?"

"Were they trying?"

"Yes. They went after you. That was the last I saw or heard of them."

Stephen nodded, and his eyebrows pinched together for an instant. Then he smiled again.

"It's good to have friends," he said. "Where are you off to, Cazio?"

"Eslen," he said, feeling guarded. The whole encounter seemed stranger every moment.

"You're looking for help for Austra."

Cazio shifted Acredo to a better grip. "Who are you?" he demanded.

"What are you talking about? You know me."

"I knew Fratir Stephen. I'm not sure that's who you are."

"Oh, it's me more or less," the man said. "But like you, I've been through a lot. Walked a new faneway, gained new gifts. So yes, things are revealed to me that are denied most. I can put my gaze far from me. But I'm not an espetureno or estrigo if that's your fear."

"But you aren't here by coincidence."

"No, I'm not."

"What do you want, then?"

"To help you. To help Austra now and Anne later on."

"Anne?" Cazio said. "How can you know where to find me and not know?"

"Know what?"

"Anne is dead."

Stephen's eyes widened with what appeared to be genuine disbelief, and for the first time his new cockiness seemed to fail him.

"How is that possible?" he said, speaking so low that Cazio could barely hear him. "There's something going on here I'm missing. But if Anne is dead . . ."

He raised his voice. "We'll sort that out later. Cazio, I can help Austra. But you have to come with me."

"Come with you?"

"Get her," Stephen said. "Him, too."

Cazio jerked his head around to see who the fratir was talking to, but all he saw was a weird wavering, like the air above hot stones. Then something wrapped itself firmly around his waist and lifted him into the air. He shrieked involuntarily and stabbed his blade into the invisible thing, but then something grabbed Acredo and wrenched the blade from his grasp.

Then they were hurtling through the air, all three of them, born by the Kept, and there was nothing Cazio could do about it but curse and imagine what he was going to do to Stephen when he could get to him.

After a while, Cazio finally had to give in to the fact that he was enjoying himself, at least a little. He had wondered often what it might be like to fly, and once the initial terror had worn off, it was exciting. They were whisked over the poelen and canals, covering in a bell what would have taken him days in the carriage. Eslen appeared in the distance, a toy castle far below them.

"Hubris," Stephen said. "It's always the death of me. But I can't turn my eye in every direction at once, can I? Especially with the others interfering."

"What are you talking about?"

They plunged suddenly not toward Eslen but toward the dark necropolis south of it.

"But he doesn't know about Austra," Stephen went on. "That'll be his undoing. He killed Anne for her power and didn't find it because it all went to Austra. She walked the same faneway as Anne—*after* her. I would have *known* that if I had thought about it for six breaths."

Cazio tried to catch that thought. Austra *did* seem to have some of the same gifts as Anne. And the churchman—had he known somehow? Was his strange cutting of her connected to that? And did that have anything to do with what was wrong with Austra?

It had to, didn't it?

"See," Stephen whispered. "Hespero moves."

Cazio's attention was suddenly drawn to the several hundreds of men fighting in front of the gates of Eslen-of-Shadows, but he only had a glimpse of that before they rushed down into the city itself, over the lead streets and into a mausoleum as large as some mansions. The Kept settled them in front of it. The two guards at the door started toward him, but then their eyes glazed over, and they sat down rather suddenly.

Cazio suddenly found himself free. He started toward Stephen.

"Don't," Stephen said. "If you want Austra alive and well, don't."

With that he swung open the doors.

Inside, on a large table, lay Anne. She was dressed in a black satin gown set with pearls, placed with her hands folded across her chest. Two women—one very young, the other a Sefry—and a man Cazio did not recognize were sitting with the body. The man stood as they entered and drew a broadsword.

"I need my blade," Cazio told Stephen.

"Pick it up, then," Stephen said.

Cazio turned and found it lying on the ground. Austra was still in the Kept's invisible grip.

"By the saints, what is this?" the man shouted. "Demons!"

* * *

Stephen held up his hand. "Wait," he said. "There's no need for that."

This wasn't what he had expected. This was where he had sensed the throne, not Anne, although it made perfect sense that she was down here, too.

He could feel the sedos force pulsing just where she was.

"How did she die?" he asked, a suspicion suddenly born in his mind.

"Stabbed," the girl said, her eyes red from crying. "The Fratrex Prismo murdered her. There was so much blood . . ."

"Stabbed where?"

"Under the ribs, up into her heart," the Sefry woman said. "Then her throat was cut."

Stephen stepped forward.

"No, by the saints," the man shouted. "Who *are* you?"

Stephen silenced him as he had the guards. It wouldn't hurt him permanently, but his thoughts would be too disordered to allow him to, say, move his limbs.

He saw the line where Anne's throat had been cut, but it was puckered and white.

Stephen felt a sort of coldness ringing in his ears.

It was a scar.

"Oh, screaming damned saints," Stephen sighed.

Austra gave a sudden gasp behind him, and he felt a tremendous surge around him as the throne exploded into being.

On the throne, Anne Dare rose up, shining with unnatural light, her face so beautiful and terrible that Stephen couldn't look on it.

It was the face from his Black Marys.

"Hespero," she whispered, and then, at the top of her lungs, screamed the name.

She didn't even glance at him, or Cazio, or any other person in the room.

"Qexqaneh," she said, and Stephen suddenly felt his control of the Vhelny utterly dissolve and heard the demon laughter in his ears. All the hair on his body suddenly stood up, and then Anne was in the demon's grip, flying, gone out of the crypt and into the darkling sky.

Aspar still could feel the geos in him when they entered the high valley where he first had seen the Briar King. He reckoned that meant Winna wasn't there yet.

Maybe Leshya wasn't bringing her there at all.

Sir Roger and his men *were* there, however, camped and entrenched around what appeared to be a lodge of some sort, though Aspar knew it had been formed from living trees. He'd been in it; it was where he had found the Briar King sleeping.

"I count seventeen," Fend said. "Four of them Mamres knights."

Aspar nodded. "That's what I see."

"I don't see your three friends."

"No."

"Always the conversationalist," Fend said. "Well, let's get this over with."

"We're not in a hurry," Aspar said. "You just pointed out that Winna isn't here yet. Why should we charge down to their defended positions?"

"You have a plan, then?"

"What happened to your basil-nix?"

"They're really quite fragile creatures once you get past their gaze. That's why I used it from a distance. Harriot's troops figured out what it was and poured arrows on it."

Aspar nodded.

"Was that your plan, to use the nix?"

"If we had it, sure."

"What now, then?"

For answer, Aspar studied the distance and the play of the almost nonexistent breeze on the grass. Then he set a shaft to string and let it loose.

One of the churchmen pitched back, grasping at the arrow in his throat.

"Buggering saints!" Fend swore. "You've still got the eye, Aspar."

"Now there are sixteen," he said as the men below scrambled for cover behind the crude barriers they had erected.

"When they get tired of this," Aspar said, "they'll come up after us, fight on our ground. If Winna shows up before we're finished, we can always make your mad charge."

"We can't take too long. The beasts will get hungry."

"Send one or two down to hunt when it gets dark."

"I like the way your mind works, Aspar," Fend said.

We'll soon change that, Aspar thought.

Fend sent an utin down that night. It didn't come back, but the next morning Aspar counted two fewer men below. The Mamres monks were all still there, though, so it wasn't as good a trade as might have been hoped for. Aspar watched through the day from the cover of the trees, looking for another opportunity to skewer someone, but the knight was being very cautious now.

Toward sundown, he felt it all starting to catch up with him and found himself almost dozing, his eyes unwilling to keep open.

He'd just closed them for a moment when he felt an odd turning. He looked down to see what was going on and realized that two of the Mamres monks and three mounted men were racing across the field toward the other entrance to the valley.

"They're here!" Aspar shouted. He stood, took aim, and let go. One of the horsemen pitched off.

Something went streaking by him. He saw it was Fend on the wairwulf. The remaining utin loped along behind him.

Aspar fired again, missing a Mamres monk, but his third arrow found its mark in the man's leg, and he went rolling down. He had one more shot before they were out of range, and that hit another horseman.

Grim, let Fend and his be enough, he thought. But Winna had Leshya and Ehawk, too.

The other nine men were charging up the hill. Seven knights and two Mamres monks against him, the Vaix, and a greffyn.

Aspar gritted his teeth and drew the cord, wishing he had more than five arrows left. But if wishes weighed anything, he'd have a heavy pack right now.

The first one hit a knight and skipped off his armor, but the second one punched right through his breastplate, and now they were eight.

From the corner of his eye he saw the greffyn bounding down the hill. Three of the knights turned their lances against it. The Mamres monks came on, dodging his next two arrows, but then the strange Sefry met them with his glistering feysword, and things went too quickly for him to follow even if he had had time to, which he didn't, because three armored mounted men were coming up on him fast.

Aspar shot his last arrow from four kingsyards away at the knight on his far left, and it went through the fellow's armor as if it were cambric. He dropped his spear and slumped forward, and Aspar let fall the bow and ran as hard and fast as he could, putting the now masterless horse between himself and the other two mounted men. He grasped the spear as one of his pursuers dropped his lance, drew sword, and wheeled to meet the holter.

Aspar caught him in midturn, ramming the sharp point into the armpit joint. The fellow hollered and went windmilling off his horse. The other fellow had ridden out a little farther and was turning for a proper charge. Aspar just then recognized that it was Harriot himself.

Aspar grasped for the reins of the horse, but it galloped off, leaving him no mount or cover.

The fellow he had just knocked off was moving feebly, but it looked like it would take him a bit to get up, if he did at all.

Aspar reminded himself that most men on foot killed by knights died with holes in the back of the skull, and it was a good thing, because his legs were telling him to run as Harriot's charger hurtled at him. Grimly, he set the butt of the lance on his foot, pointed the spear tip at the horse's breast, and braced for the impact.

Harriot shifted his grip and threw the lance, turning his mount an instant later. It thunked into the earth two handsbreadths from Aspar. Aspar wheeled, keeping the spear ready for the next pass.

The knight drew his sword, dismounted, took down a shield, and came on.

That's smart, Aspar thought. *All he needs to do is get past my point, and I'm no real spearman.*

He caught a blur at the edge of his vision and saw it was one of the Mamres monks.

Well, good try, he thought.

But suddenly the greffyn was there, too, barreling at the monk from his right. They went off in a tangle.

Harriot charged during the distraction.

Aspar thrust the spear into the shield so hard that it stuck and then ran to the side, turning the fellow half around before he let go of the shaft and drew his ax and dirk. Put off balance by the unwieldy weapon lodged in his shield and by Aspar's maneuver, the knight had to fight to get his sword arm back around.

He didn't make it before Aspar smashed into the shield at waist level so that Harriot went back and down, landing with a muffled clang.

Aspar hit his helmet with the blunt side of his ax, and it rang like a bell. He hit it again, then shoved it up to reveal the white throat underneath and finished the job with his dirk.

He stood, panting.

The Vaix was just picking himself up a little farther down the hill.

The greffyn was bloodying its beak in the stomach of the Mamres knight.

Far below, he saw Fend and the wairwulf approaching Winna, Leshya, and Ehawk.

Please let me be right about this, Aspar said, but then he had no more time for doubt as the Vaix started for him.

Aspar did what he had planned, the only thing he *could* do.

He ran as fast as his legs could carry him toward his mount. A glance back showed the Sefry gaining even with his wounded leg, even with new blood showing all over him.

He made it to the horse, swung up, and kicked it into motion. The Sefry gave a hoarse cry and leaped at them, landing on his bad leg, which buckled. He threw the feysword at Aspar. It went turning by his head and cut through a young pine tree.

Then the yards were growing between them, and each glance back showed the Vaix farther behind, then gone.

Aspar didn't stop or even slow until after nightfall, when he reckoned he was at least a league and a half away.

CHAPTER NINE

THE HIDING
PLACE

WHEN THE PAIN of the knife wound faded and she ceased to feel her body, Anne for some time knew nothing but confusion and the sudden pull of a current so compelling that she had no thought of resistance. She let it take her, knowing what it was, having seen the lives of men leak away into its dark waters.

For an instant she thought she was ready, but then from the very center of her climbed dark, delicious, corrupt rage. It informed everything that remained of her as she sought to strike out through the ragged wall of death at her killer, but here she learned the obvious but unspoken truth: Without a body in the lands of fate, no desire of her will could she obtain.

That was death. That was why the promise of her had

forged an alliance with those who had gone before, to give all that rage and purpose, at last, a body again.

Now all that was failed and moot, and the chance would not come again.

She felt herself diminishing, melting, and knew that in time the very place she observed herself from would vanish. It wasn't fair; this was *her* domain, her kingdom. She had nearly had complete control of it, and now it was eating her. What it spit out would invade the dreams of another, be used by another—probably Hespero.

She caught the strains of a song, and as she focused her attention on it, it began to swell, and her throat yearned to open and join its strange harmonies.

For some reason that frightened her more than anything.

She suddenly saw light in the water and heard a familiar voice speak as if from another room. Then something caught her and pulled her in, and her thoughts suddenly became a confusion of voices, as in her Black Marys. At first she thought that it was the end, that she was merging with the river, but then she understood that she was thinking in only two voices.

Then a place shaped, and a face.

It took her a moment.

"Austra?"

"It's me, Anne," her friend said. "You've been here a while, but you didn't seem to hear me."

"Where are we?"

The light came up a little, diffuse strands of it made spidery by the tiny root filaments around the edge of the hole above her. She saw a little more of Austra now and noticed that between them was a stone crypt.

"It's the crypt," she murmured. "The one we found as girls. Virgenya's crypt."

"Is it?" Austra asked, sounding confused. "It looks to me like the womb of Mefitis, where we escaped the men who attacked the coven. See, there's light coming down the shaft."

Anne felt a prickling. She reached across the tomb.

"Take my hand, Austra."

The other stretched out her arm, but instead of the familiar grip of her friend's fingers, Anne felt not even the substance of a cobweb.

Austra nodded. "I tried to shake you awake earlier."

"Austra, what were you doing just before you found yourself here?"

"I was with Cazio," she said. "I had been hurt, and there was a battle. I was trying to go to sleep, when suddenly it felt as if something ripped me open." She looked up. "We're dead, aren't we?"

"I should be," Anne said. "Hespero—he stabbed me, in the heart, I think." She tried to touch the spot where the knife had gone in and found it as intangible as Austra. "But you were just trying to sleep. And why are we here?"

"Is this the same place we went that time we were trapped in the horz? The otherworld of the Faiths?"

"I don't think so, or at least not exactly. If that were true, I think Hespero—or the other—could find me. I think we're trapped somewhere, or maybe . . ." She drifted off, silenced by a sudden revelation.

"Austra, you walked the same faneway I did."

"I thought of that," Austra said. "There was a priest, doing things to me, and I—"

"I remember," Anne said. "I was there. I was looking for you."

"Saints," Austra breathed. "You *were* there. I'd forgotten. What does it mean?"

"I don't know," Anne said. "Maybe I'm dead, but a little of me is living on in you for a while. Maybe all of my power passed to you and it was too much for you. I'm sorry, Austra."

"Why did you send me away?" the girl asked.

"I saw you and Cazio dead if I kept you around me." The image flashed through her mind, and she suddenly recognized it. "Saints," she said. "You would have died, both of you, in the Red Hall, protecting me from Hespero. And you would have . . ."

"I thought it was because you didn't want us around to remind you of who you are."

"There's that, too," Anne said. "I have found new parts of me, Austra, furious ones. They are quiet now, because I'm here with you. I needed room for them to grow, to become strong. It doesn't matter now, does it?"

"I don't want to be dead," Austra said. And more softly: "Cazio asked me to marry him."

"Really?" Jealousy was quick venom.

"I know you love him, too."

Anne didn't answer for a moment. "You're right," she said. "Or at least I'm in love with the idea of him. It's part of the notion that I can do anything I want." She thought about telling Austra about Tam—had she ever called him that?— but she refrained. "Anyway, congratulations."

"I love you, Anne," Austra said. "More than anyone."

"I love you, too," Anne said. Without thinking, she reached for her friend again. This time their fingers touched. Austra's eyes widened. The room filled with white-hot flame.

"Hespero," Anne snarled, and *became.*

All the rage was there, waiting for her, welcoming her back into her poor abused—and nearly completely healed—body.

She reached out around her, looking for the praifec, brushing aside something near, a heavy, familiar presence that suddenly shrank away.

Then she saw the Kept, floating there, waiting for her.

At your service, great queen, the demon said. *I am here for you.*

"You promised to heal the law of death and die."

And so I shall, with your help, Qexqaneh replied. *But you have things to do first.*

"Yes," Anne snarled. "Yes, I do."

And the Kept took her up in his coils, and they went to Hespero's army.

Edwyn Mylton was graying, long-limbed, and awkward, but he had the eyes of a child with an active imagination and plans his parents wouldn't approve of.

"What sort of trouble are you getting me into this time, Leoff?" he asked.

"You won't believe it, I think," Leoff said, "and it is exceedingly dangerous. But I have to ask you. There's no one else I can think of."

Edwyn peered down his uneven nose for a moment. "I suppose I had better agree, then, before I know the details." He nodded at Areana. "Frauye Leovigild, it's wonderful to see you again."

"I wish it were as happy as the last occasion," she replied.

"Yes, well, the company is still good," he said. "Most of it." He nodded significantly toward the door.

"Berimund and his men are our friends," Leoff said. "Or at least we share some goals. We can trust them, I think."

"I trust your judgment, Leoff, but they were a little rough in collecting me."

"I'm sorry, old friend; that was a pretense to satisfy any curious Hansans watching."

"Yes, so they explained, but I had a bit of trouble believing it until now. So what are we doing, then?"

"We're going to sing with the dead," Leoff replied. Despite all his worries, he still managed to enjoy the expression on Edwyn's face.

Brinna handed Neil a small vial containing a greenish elixir.

"This should help," she said. "It's something I concocted from an old herbal, long ago, at my brother's request. He's hard on the drink."

Neil hesitated at the scent.

"What? Do you fear I would poison you? Or are you afraid it's a love philter?"

The elixir was as astringent and as strong as the drink he'd shared with Alis, but it did make him feel better. He'd been foolish; he might have to fight today. He should be at his best, even if that wasn't very good.

"Will this work?" he asked. "This thing you're going to do?"

She parted her hands. "I can't see that, if that's what you mean. But it might. That's something to hope on. But you and my brother, you must keep us safe until we are done. Then, whatever happens, we must find each other. I do not want to die without you."

"I don't want you to die at all," Neil said.

She placed her hand on his. "If we survive, Sir Neil, will you take me away?"

"Wherever you want."

"Someplace where neither of us has any duties," she said. "That's what I would like."

He gripped her fingers in his. Then he leaned toward her until her eyes were very close.

She bent her head, and their lips touched, and all he wanted was to take her away right then and there, forget the war, the law of death, everything. Didn't they deserve . . .

She touched his cheek, and he saw that she understood what he was thinking, and she turned her head just slightly from side to side. Then she got up and gently untangled her fingers from his.

"Remember your promise," she said. "Find me if I do not find you."

"How will we know when you've finished?"

"Somehow, I think you will know," she replied.

Marché Hespero drew on the faneway of Diuvo and made himself small in the eyes of the sky and of men.

The fighting had ceased at nightfall, at his order. Although his body was warded against steel, there were some things that might do him harm; the blow of a lance or mace, though it would not cut his skin, might well break bones and organs *through* the skin. And a splintered lance, a broken arrow—he frankly wasn't certain what they might do. During an open melee, any of those things might find him by sheerest accident even though no eye saw him.

He slipped through the lines of his men, past their fires and amid their grumbling. The enemy had withdrawn into Eslen-of-Shadows and crouched behind a low wall that had never been meant to serve as a fortification. Still, they had managed to hold it passably well. Crotheny might have lost its witch-queen and her ability to slay thousands with a wish, but if anything, the leadership of the army had improved.

He slipped over the barrier and wove through the alert front ranks, back through where men were sleeping, into the houses of the dead.

He knew his knights were questioning an attack that was not only sacrilegious and unprecedented but to their minds nonsensical. The only approaches to the castle from the shadow city were steep and fully exposed to anything the guards on the city walls might want to launch or drop on them for hundreds of kingsyards.

What he wanted, of course, was control of the throne, which finally had shown itself a few days after he had killed Anne.

He hadn't intended things to be this messy; he'd intended to seize control of Anne's gifts as he had the former Fratrex Prismo's. Her power married with his own would have made it easy enough to slay any who opposed him in Eslen and let his army walk in.

Instead, he had to make do with talents he already possessed, at least until he appropriated the sedos throne and then took control of the others. That shouldn't be so hard, with the Vhen throne empty and measures taken to keep it so. When he had both of those, he would find the keeper of the Xhes and dispense with him.

He had hoped to have Eslen-of-Shadows pacified to make the task of winning the throne easier, but he felt the power swelling toward the proscribed moment, and he also sensed the other foe he had dreamed about so long ago. He had no way of knowing who was stronger at this point, but he had taken plenty of risks, and this one last gamble for the greatest prize was surely worth it.

He was nearing the tomb itself when a soundless explosion of red-gold light came pouring from the door frame. He shrank against a cold marble wall, gathering his will to hide himself as completely as he could yet also ready for battle.

Something came flying out of the opening, a dark cloud, and a woman, glowing . . .

He blinked. It was Anne. It was the throne.

She was the throne. She was what he had come to claim. But how—

Anne was the flashing heart of a thunderhead, moving out over his men, bolts of blue-white lightning arcing out from her to the waiting earth, replacing silence with ear-aching thunder. He watched, frozen for the moment, as knights and soldiers and Mamres monks all perished alike, as Anne Dare—the Born Queen—only shone brighter and brighter.

His vision had started like this. Had he failed? Was there any chance to stop her now?

The Black Jester. If he could take his strength, add it to his own . . .

"Hespero!" a voice called over the din.

He jerked around and saw, to his great surprise, Stephen Darige.

"Brother?"

"Nice trick," Stephen said. "Good for sneaking about. Too bad you were distracted."

And with those words, their battle began.

CHAPTER TEN

BASICS

THE CANDLES all flickered when Brinna touched her fingers to the hammarharp, and the small room filled with the sound. Leoff waited, almost forgetting to breathe.

There it came, Mery whispering a note and then, suddenly,

the same tone issuing, clear and perfect, from the mysterious woman at the keys. It shivered up his spine to know that she was hearing the sound itself, not in this world but in the other. He wished with all his being that he could hear what Brinna and Mery did. He knew it in his mind, of course, but his ears hungered for it, too.

Now Areana joined in with the quick line, starting low but climbing higher separately from the first theme, never touching it, as if two deaf musicians were playing side by side, each unaware of the other. The melodies wandered like that for a while, tightening but still separate until, in a moment that shocked him even though he knew it was coming, they were suddenly in unison for three notes. It sent a thrill of pure terror through him, and he suddenly very much did not want to go through with this.

But now it was his turn to sing. He prayed he was up to the task.

In the house, a hammarharp sounded a single chord, and then a voice lifted in one high, clear note. Neil was startled; it reminded him of frightening a covey of quail along the side of the road. What was more surprising, that surprise or the startlement itself?

Because it was Brinna, and the depth of that single beautiful note opened a door on everything he still didn't know about her, everything he wanted to learn. He knew she played the harp, and beautifully, and he loved her voice, but he never knew this was hidden in it.

The note dropped and wavered, and a second voice joined it, another woman: the composer's wife. The song suddenly wasn't pretty anymore, and Neil remembered a time not so long ago when he'd been sinking in the sea, dragged down by the weight of his armor, and he'd heard the Draugs' lonely, jealous song, welcoming him to the cold land of Breu-nt-Toine, a country without love or light or even memory.

In this music—in Brinna's voice—he heard again the song of the Draugs.

He walked away from the house not so much because the music repelled him as because he was drawn to it, just as his armor had dragged him toward the sea floor.

But then another memory came.

He'd been seven, in the hills, gathering the goats. Goat gathering wasn't such a hard business, and he'd been doing some of the work on his back, watching the clouds, imagining they were islands filled with strange kingdoms and peoples, wondering if he could ever find a way up to them.

Then he'd heard the horns blowing and knew the fleet was in. He jumped up, leaving the goats to themselves, and rushed down the hill trail, racing along with the sea down below, until ahead he could see his father's longship with its broad blue sail and prow carved in the likeness of Saint Menenn's horse Enverreu.

By the time he reached the docks, the ships were tied up. His father already was back on dry land and opening his arms to sweep his son up in rough arms.

"Fah," he shouted. The sun that day had shown a kind of gold that Neil had never seen since, although he had watched for it and had seen something of its hue that day when he had fought for the waerd. And right there on the wooden planks, in front of all his comrades, his father pulled from his things something long, wrapped in oiled cloth, its head stockinged in sealskin.

He pulled off the cloth and sock in a hurry, and there it was, his first spear, with its beautiful shiny blade and plain thick pole.

"I had it made by Saint Jeveneu himself," his father said, but at Neil's amazed expression, he mussed his head and corrected himself.

"It was made by an old friend of mine on the isle of Guel," he said. "No saint but a good man and a good smith, and he made it special for you."

Neil had never been so proud of anything as that spearhead flashing in the sun and his father's hand on his shoulder.

When they got home, it was a different story. His mother

embraced his father and had begun bringing out the supper when she suddenly looked at Neil.

"And what of the goats, Neil? Did you just leave them up there when I told you to bring them in?"

"I'm sorry, Mah," he remembered saying. "I heard the bells—"

"And wanted to see your Fah, sure, but—"

"But you don't abandon your duty, son. Now go get them."

He got them and missed supper in the bargain, but when he finally made it down and the first stars were out, he found his father waiting for him outside the house.

"I'm sorry, Fah," he said.

"Now listen," his father said. "You're going to get older, we all hope, so let me tell you something. You've heard me talk about honor. Do you know what it is?"

"It's what a warrior gets when he wins battles."

"No. A man can never fight a battle and still have honor. A man can win a thousand and never have any. You'll hear all sorts of things in the future about what honor is; some, I'm told, in the courts of the mainland have written down all sorts of things a man must do to have it. But it's simple, really. Honor is about doing the things you know you ought to. Not the thing you think will win approval, not the most dangerous thing, not the thing that will win you the most glory, but the thing you know you ought. What was there more important today than doing what your mother asked and bringing in the goats?"

"I wanted to see you."

"And I wanted to see you, lad. But you lost honor doing so. You understand?"

"Yes, Fah. But that's hard, isn't it? How do you know what you ought to do?"

"You have to know yourself," his father said. "And you have to listen to your own true voice. Now, go get your spear, and I'll show you the proper way to hold it."

That had been long years ago, and not long after that he'd first used that spear. He'd broken it two winters later. It was years after, when his father was dead and he was with Sir Fail, that he learned the sword and shield and lance, wore lord's plate, and took on the trappings of a knight and the code of honor that went with it.

Alis was up talking to Berimund, whose men waited in silent formation, facing the gate. Neil went to join them.

"Excuse me, Prince," he said. "I was wondering if you had a spear or two I might borrow from you."

"You may have mine," the prince replied. "And a spare if you want it."

"Thank you," Neil replied. Berimund fetched the weapons: good, well-balanced man killers.

"Sir Neil," Berimund said as he examined the weapons. "We've reports of a force gathering up the road, about twice our number."

"Do you know why?"

"No, but I can guess that a messenger from Hansa has finally spread the news that my father has called for my head."

"We need only hold them for the space of another bell, at most," Alis said.

Berimund closed his eyes, perhaps listening to the music, perhaps to something in his own skull.

"No," he said. "We needn't hold them at all."

"What do you mean?" Neil asked.

"I won't let them come at me as they like," the prince said. "My wulfbrothars and I will go and meet them where they're gathering. Even if we lose, they'll have no reason to come here directly."

"They might, in search of Brinna."

"My men have spread the rumor that we put her on a ship at Saestath. Even if some doubt that, it will take time for them to be certain all of us are defeated; they wouldn't leave us at their backs." He grinned. "Or maybe they will choose their prince over their king. I was well received here until now."

"I can't go with you," Neil said.

"Of course not. I'll leave two men outside the gate, but

you stay here. What is that knife you people carry—the little one, the blade of last resort?"

"The *echein doif.*"

"Jah. You will be the *echein doif,* Sir Neil."

Neil watched them mount and ride through the gate. Then he stripped off the hauberk and laid it on the ground, flexing his shoulders under the light padded gambeson. He unbuckled his sword belt and carefully put the weapon next to the armor.

The night deepened, and behind him the music darkened and lightened weirdly, like the sun coming in and out of the clouds.

"There," Alis said.

Neil nodded, for he saw the shadows, too, padding through the gate on foot. Robert's guards hadn't made a sound.

"Remember our toast," Alis said.

"I remember," Neil replied.

Stephen was struck by a sudden impulse simply to close his eyes and sleep, and he almost laughed. Hespero didn't know who he was dealing with.

"Again," he said. "Nice try."

"We could be allies," Hespero said. "We could stop her together."

"I agree," Stephen replied, fending off another stab of Hespero's will. "Individually, neither of us has a chance against her, and we both know what that means. Surrender your gifts to me, and I'll stop her."

"We could work together."

"You're trying to kill me even now." Stephen laughed. "It's impossible. One of us would inherit from her, and the other would perish."

"Brother Stephen, I am your Fratrex Prismo. You owe everything in you to me."

"Now, that's just silly," Stephen said. "You won your position through lies, murder, and betrayal, and now you're asking for my loyalty? Would you like me to lie down and let you piss on me, too?"

"You aren't Stephen Darige," the fratrex said.

Stephen chuckled, then reached out with his full might. "You're going to wish you were wrong about that," he said.

Hespero reached back, and the lands of fate shrank away, and Stephen was holding Hespero, a waurm, Winna, Zemlé, himself . . .

It was the same fight all over again, the fight to keep himself whole as he had on the faneway, except before he had had Kauron's help. This time he *was* Kauron, the Jester, the Black Heart of Terror.

Which meant he was alone.

Still, Hespero's gifts seemed made to be broken by his. Until, that is, lightning ripped them apart and sent Stephen sprawling, his muscles pulled into balls like snails trying to retreat into their shells, pain shattering his concentration. He knew that somehow, against the odds, Hespero had won.

But he hadn't, Stephen realized as he opened his eyes and found Anne standing there, shimmering as if he were gazing at her through the heat of an oven.

"What have we here?" she asked.

It wasn't easy, but Stephen ignored her as best he could, because to stand a chance he needed Hespero's gifts and needed them now. The fratrex was unconscious, and that made it easier. He drank greedily from the well that was Hespero.

"I know you," Anne said, wagging her finger at him.

"You threatened me in the place of the Faiths. Not in that skin, but it was you."

A barrier of some sort suddenly snapped down between him and the churchman.

"Stop that," Anne said. "Listen to me when I'm talking to you."

Stephen backed away, trying to reestablish his connection with Hespero and finish the job, but the Fratrex Prismo might as well have been a thousand leagues away.

He looked at Anne and laughed.

"You think it's funny?" she asked, her voice almost a whisper in its fury.

"That was me," he said, "but I didn't know. Dreams, you

see? It was all in my dreams. Except in my dreams it was you terrifying me, when I believed I was only Stephen Darige. In your dreams it was me terrifying you, when you believed you were only Anne."

He rose up from his knees. "And now we are both almost who we were in our dreams. And I'll say now as I did then: We should join together, you and I, bright king and dark queen. Don't you see? We're male and female principle of the same thing. Nothing could stand against us."

Anne just stared at him for a long moment, those awful eyes slitted to hint at the mind whirling behind them.

"You're right," she said. "I see it now. I understand. But you know what? I don't need you. Nothing can stand against me as it is."

When Aspar was sure he wasn't being followed, he bound his wounds and slept for a few bells in the crook of a tree. Then he started back to the valley.

He reached it just before dawn and waited until there was enough light to see who, if anyone, was still there.

He made out a still figure in the grass about fifty yards ahead of him.

Closer, he saw it was Leshya, lying propped against a stone. Her head turned slowly as he approached.

"Another bell," she coughed, "and you wouldn't have seen me at all."

She glanced down and he saw that she was holding her bowels in.

"Doesn't really hurt anymore," she said.

He dismounted and pulled out his knife. He pulled off his broon and shirt and began cutting the shirt into wide strips.

"No point in that," Leshya said.

"There might be," Aspar said. "I know something Fend doesn't know, something you don't know, something only I and the Briar King know."

The slit down her belly was fairly neat. Fend's work, for sure.

"He wanted me to tell you he'll find you," she said. "Said he never imagined you could be such a coward."

"Werlic," Aspar replied. "He went in the Vhenkherdh, but he hasn't come out, has he?"

"No."

"Did he leave anyone to guard?"

"One fellow, hidden just in the entrance. I see him now and then. He's careless."

He handed her his water. "Drink it all," he said. "I'll be right back."

"Aspar—"

"Hush. Don't die."

And with that he went softly through the grass, coming around behind the strange growth of trees.

He edged around until he saw the man there and recognized with relief that it wasn't the Vaix.

He closed his eyes, trying to remember, back through a haze of fever and time. Trying to be sure.

He stepped around. The man looked up.

The passage into the Vhenkherdh wasn't covered with a door or any such thing. It was just a twisty little path back through the trees.

The man shouted at the top of his lungs, grabbed the hilt of his sword, and started to stand.

Aspar's ax hit him between the eyes. He sat back down.

Aspar went back and got Leshya. She still was breathing, and her eyes opened again when she saw him.

"Done?"

"Not by half," he said. "Come along now."

He took her arrows and put them in his quiver, then carried her to the Vhenkherdh.

"Now, listen," he said. "I need you to crawl on your belly until you're in there, do you hear?"

"I don't understand."

"When I went in before, it was just for a few moments. For Winna, out here, it was three days. Do you see?"

"I've lost most of my blood," she said. "It's hard to think."

"Yah. Can you crawl?"

"It's stupid, but yes."

"Just do it," he said. "It'll hurt, I'm sorry. But I have to see something. It will help me, werlic?"

He tried not to think about what she was feeling as she drew up onto her elbows and inched into the place. He followed a step behind her, wishing he could help, knowing it had to be this way.

The color of the faint light on her faded, and then she was gone.

He moved up to just that point and drew his hood to cut out any other light, and he saw her again, a bloody shadow.

Beyond Leshya he could make out a few vague shapes, all the dark red ghosts, all apparently immobile. He watched, knowing he had to make the right choices, glad he had a little time.

The Vaix was easy to make out because he held the feysword, and it glowed the color of gore dripped in water. Aspar took careful aim and shot at his neck. The arrow crossed into the same space as Leshya had, faded, and slowed to a snail's pace.

He shot at the Sefry three more times, then located another target, which, as his eyes grew used to the light, was pretty obviously an utin. Its head was turned away, but he aimed for the ear and then the inner thigh of one of the legs. He spent the rest of his shafts on the thing, because he couldn't be sure who the other shadows were.

He sat down and sharpened his dirk and then his ax. He had a bite to eat and let it settle. He walked over to the battleground and found a lance, which he broke down into a stabbing spear.

Then he went back to the Vhenkherdh and went in.

As before, his heartbeat sped quickly into a buzz, like a mosquito's, and time went strange.

CHAPTER ELEVEN

AWAKE

NEIL COUNTED only four men with Robert, all in black leather. They all carried themselves as if they knew how to fight.

"All alone?" Robert asked.

Neil didn't reply, but he noticed that Alis was nowhere to be seen.

He watched them get closer.

"You'll pardon me if I don't make a conversation of this," the prince said. "Given how our last talk went, I doubt that you're disappointed."

Robert drew the feysword, which glowed even more brightly than when Neil had last seen it. It looked like it had been forged from a lightning bolt.

"The music offends me," the prince confided. "An old friend thought I might like it, but he clearly doesn't know my tastes." He stopped and looked down at Neil's sword and hauberk where they lay on the ground. His eyebrows arched, and his eyes glittered oddly in the torchlight.

Neil had killed his first man when he had had eleven winters, with a spear. He had killed his second a nineday later. He wasn't strong enough to use a broadsword until he was fifteen.

He threw the first spear, feeling the motion come back to him, as natural as walking. His arm didn't protest at all, and the shaft flew true, straight into Robert's shoulder, where it sank deep and stuck. The feysword flew from his hand, and the prince's shriek was a piercing counterpoint to the strange music coming from the house.

Neil lifted the second spear out of the soil. Everwulf had been right—he still had his feet. He danced toward Robert's guard as they tried to encircle him, gripping the weapon underhand with his knuckles against his hip.

He rushed up to the lead man, forcing him to cut before he was ready while Neil skipped to the side. His arm shot out, and the steel head punched in at the navel, splitting the chain beneath the leather and coming out bloody. The man stumbled back choking, and Neil went on to deal with the others before the first one discovered that his wound wasn't critical.

One had come around behind him, so Neil jabbed the butt end back and ducked as something whirred over his hair. He felt the blow connect with a knee and turned, taking the weapon two-handed, and rammed the blade up through the foeman's crotch.

The spear stuck there, so Neil released it and rolled away, noticing as he did another of Robert's guards stumbling about headless.

The last man he could see coming from the left, but he was off balance, and there was no way to dodge the blow.

He threw up his forearm to meet the sword at an angle. He heard the snap of bone breaking, and white light seemed to explode from everything.

Between one footfall and the next, the arrows suddenly blurred back to speed, and Aspar followed right after them, vaulting over Leshya and drawing back the ax for a blow. The Vaix's head whipped around as the arrows hit him. The Sefry stumbled, and Aspar chopped him in the back of the head with the ax as he went by, thrusting at the utin's eye with the dirk. The dagger went in deep, but the monster hit him with a backhand that slung Aspar back against a tree, then sank its talons into his shoulder and gaped a mouthful of needles at him. Aspar hit the butt of the knife with his palm, driving it in to the hilt. The beast screamed and fell, writing so furiously in the cramped space that Aspar couldn't get by it for several long moments. When he was finally able to retrieve his knife and move on, he found two men waiting for him, and beyond he could see the wide opening inside the living lodge where Fend, Winna, and Ehawk were watching him with astonished eyes.

The men confronting him stared at him in what could only be terror.

"You can walk out of here," Aspar snarled, "or I can kill you."

A look of resolve flashed over the face of one of them, and he cut at Aspar with the sword. He ducked so that the edge thunked into a tree branch and stayed there while Aspar disemboweled the wielder. The other howled and swung wildly, hitting Aspar on the side of his head with the flat. Aspar stumbled back, ears ringing, as the man shouted something in a language the holter didn't know.

He threw the ax, and it buried itself solidly in the fellow's breastbone. He stared at Aspar as he walked up, yanked it out, and kicked him over.

"Fend!"

Fend drew a pair of knives.

"How did you do that?" the Sefry asked.

Aspar didn't reply. He just stepped into the leafy hall, feeling a sort of calm settle over him.

"Aspar!" Winna shouted. She was holding her belly, and her face was ashen. He thought there was blood on her lips, although in the dim light it was difficult to be sure.

"It's already too late," Fend said. "It's already begun."

"Not too late to kill you, though," Aspar said.

"Is that all you ever think about? I helped you."

"Only to get Winna here. You planned to kill me after that."

"Well, true. I really should have done it sooner, but I had a sense I would need you, and I was right. I only planned to do you because I knew you would slaughter me."

"And I will."

"You remember the last time we fought? You're even

older and slower now, and I'm more powerful than ever. I'm the Blood Knight, you know."

"No playing this time," Aspar said.

"We can still do this together," Fend said. "It needs doing."

"Even if it does, you said it's already begun. So what do I need you for?"

"I guess you don't."

"Aspar!" Winna screamed.

Fend leapt at him, faster than a Mamres monk, his right-hand dagger slashing toward Aspar's face. The holter ducked, stepped in, and took Fend's other knife in the gut, then drilled his dirk under Fend's jaw so hard that he lifted the Sefry clean off his feet. He felt the man's spine snap.

"I said no playing," Aspar told him. Then he dropped the gurgling man and slumped down to one knee, lowering his gaze to the knife still stuck in his belly.

He took another look at Fend, but the Sefry was gazing back from beyond the world.

"About time," he muttered, lowering himself down and scooting toward Ehawk to cut his bonds.

"You let him stab you," the boy said.

"If I'd fought him, he would have won," Aspar said. "I'd be dead, and he'd still be alive." He handed Ehawk the knife. "Cut Winna's bonds."

He got up and walked over to Winna. She was panting hard, and he could see her belly moving. She clutched his arm, but her eyes were closed.

"Sceat," he said. "I'm sorry, love."

"It's killing her," Ehawk said.

"Yah," he replied.

"What should I do?"

"I don't know," Aspar said. "Go bring Leshya here; maybe she knows. She's right near the entrance."

Ehawk nodded and left.

Aspar was finding it hard to take a deep breath. It was as if something were pushing down on him.

"Winna," he said. "I don't know if you can hear me. I'm

sorry for how I've been—always, but especially lately. There was a lot I needed to tell you, but I couldn't. I had a geos laid on me."

Winna started to speak, but then she cried out again. Her eyes opened, and he saw they were glazed with pain.

"Still love you," she said.

"Yah. I still love you. Nothing will change that."

"Our baby . . ." She closed her eyes again. "I can see her, Aspar. I see her in the forest with you, with her father. She's got my hair, but there's something wild in her, something from you, and she's got your eyes."

Aspar reached to stroke her hair, saw he had blood all over his hand, and wiped it on the ground first.

When his hand touched the earth, everything went still, and he felt his fingers reach into the soil, dividing, splitting, faster and faster, and his skin was expanding, moving out through the valley, across the hills, to the dying earth around it, and then he was back up north, staring into the eyes of the Briar King as he died.

Holter.

He lifted his hand and was back where he'd started, next to Winna.

Fend was looking down at him.

"Ah, sceat," Aspar said.

"It's time," Fend said. Except that it wasn't Fend at all, not anymore. It was the witch.

Cazio stood for a moment in a daze, wondering what had just happened, but then he realized that Austra was awake, looking at him.

"Love," he said. "Are you well?"

As she pulled up, the other people who had been in the crypt rushed out, probably to see what Anne could do now that she could fly.

"I'm fine," she said. "I was asleep."

"For days, yes," Cazio said. "Do you know what happened?"

"I was with Anne, or she was with me," the girl replied.

"It's a little confusing, but I think her soul came into me while her body healed."

"Do you know the way out of here?"

Austra looked around. "We're in Eslen-of-Shadows?"

"Yes."

"There's a path up to the castle, yes. But we have to find Anne."

"Well, she just flew off with the Kept," Cazio said. "Can you walk?"

"I feel fine."

"Let's go, then."

He helped her to her feet and kissed her.

"Come on," he said. "Let's go see what's happening."

"A moment there," a familiar voice said.

Marché Hespero stood in the doorway to the crypt. He looked disheveled, and his voice sounded strained.

Cazio drew Acredo.

"I just need her," Hespero said, pointing at Austra. "She's the link; she's the way to Anne. I can still save us all."

"You?" Cazio nearly laughed the word. "You expect me to believe you're trying to save us?"

"Listen," Hespero said. "The man who brought you here and Anne are fighting as we speak. Anne will probably win, and then she will come and finish me. If that happens, we will wish—beg—for the days when we were Skasloi slaves."

Cazio stepped in front of Austra.

"About all of that, I know nothing. You might be lying, you might be telling the truth. If I had to guess, I would say the first. It doesn't matter."

"He isn't lying," Austra murmured.

"What are you talking about?"

"Anne was trying to tell me something like that, even though I don't think she knew herself what she was getting at. And I am linked to her; we walked the same faneway."

"Listen to her," Hespero said. "There's not much time."

Cazio looked down at Austra. "Do you trust him?"

"No," she replied. "But what choice do we have?"

"Well, I'm not letting him have you," Cazio replied. "He might kill you both."

She closed her eyes and took his hands. "Cazio, if that's what it takes . . ."

"No."

"I don't know why I spent any time talking to you at all," Hespero said. Cazio saw that he had drawn a rapier.

"You remember that your weapon can't hurt me, I trust."

"Oh, we'll find a way, Acredo and I," Cazio said, taking up his guard.

Anne called lightning into him and for a moment thought it might actually be that easy. But the Jester grinned and regained his feet, and when she hurled another bolt at him, he twirled it around himself somehow and sent it back.

He laughed, just as he had laughed in the otherwhere she first had met him in.

What was so irritating was that she'd *had* him right under her nose—or at least the part of him that was Stephen. She could have killed him at any time, if only she'd understood, and this would never be happening. Worse, it had been her vision that sent him off to become—this.

How many of her other visions were false?

Well, there was still time to correct that mistake. She clapped her hands together and ripped him out of the world, into the sedos realm.

"A change of scene?" he said. "Very well, my queen."

The sky raged with her will; the land was all moors of black heather.

"This is mine," she told him. "All of it."

"Greedy," he said.

Her fury kindled deeper.

"I didn't want it. I didn't want any of this, but you all pushed me. The Faiths, you, my mother, Fastia, Artwair, Hespero—your threats and your promises. Always wanting something from me, always trying to take it by guile or trickery. No more. *No more.*"

She struck out then, filling the space between them with death of sixteen kinds, and with lovely glee she watched him falter. Yet still he kept smiling, as if he knew something she didn't.

No more. She saw a seam in him and pulled him open like a book, spreading his pages before her.

"You dare call me greedy?" she said. "Look at what is in you. Look at what you've done."

"Oh, I've been a bad boy, I'll admit," he said. "But the world was still here when I went to sleep. You're going to be the end of it."

"I'll end you for certain," she said. "You and anyone else who won't—"

"Do what you say? Leave you alone? Wear the proper hat?"

"It's *mine,*" Anne screamed at him. "I *made* this world. I've let you worms live on it for two thousand years. If I give you another bell, you should all beg me from your knees, kiss my feet, and sing me hymns. Who are you to tell me what to do with *my* world, little man?"

"There you are," he said. "That's what we've all been waiting for."

She felt him bend his will toward her, and it was strong, much stronger then she had thought. Her lungs suddenly seized as if filled with sand, and the more she fought, the more the weight of him crushed her.

And still he smiled.

"Ah, little queen," he murmured. "I think I shall eat you up."

CHAPTER TWELVE

✟

REQUIEM

NEIL FELL and rolled, desperately clinging to conscious-
ness. He fumbled for the little knife in his boot, but the man
kicked him in the ribs hard, flipping him onto his back.

"Stand him up," he heard Robert say.

Rough hands lifted him and slapped him up against the
wall of the house.

"That wasn't a bad performance," Robert said. "I had
heard you were in worse shape." He laughed. "Well, now I
guess you are."

Neil tried to focus on Robert's face. The other fellow had
his head turned; he seemed to be looking for something.

Neil spit on the second man. He turned back and slapped
Neil.

He hardly felt it.

Robert pinched Neil's cheeks. "Last time we talked," he
said, "you likened me to a mad wolf who needed to be put
down. And here twice you've failed to do that. There's no
third chance for you, my friend."

"I didn't fail," Neil said. "I did all I needed to."

"Did you? And what was that?"

"Distracted you," Neil said.

Robert's eyes widened. There was a flash of actinic blue
light, and then Neil was facing two headless men. Behind
the stumps of their necks a grim-faced Alis appeared, as if
stepping from a dark mist, the feysword held in both hands.

Neil fell with the dead man who had been holding him.
Robert's body continued to stand.

Neil wiped blood from his eyes and watched through a haze as Alis picked up Robert's head. The prince's lips were working and his eyes rolling, but Neil didn't hear him say anything.

Alis kissed Robert's forehead.

"That's for Muriele," she said.

Then she tossed the head away, into the yard.

Fend's dead eyes glimmed like oil on water as the witch of the Sarnwood stooped toward Winna.

"No," Aspar said. "Fend tricked you."

She paused, cocking her head.

"It won't work the way you want it to," he said. "It can't."

"It will," she said. "I know it."

"You can't have my child," he said. "*Her* child."

"*My* child," the witch replied.

"Not for long," Aspar said. He pulled the knife out of his stomach. Blood gouted.

"That can't hurt me," the witch said.

"I've been wondering," Aspar grunted. "Why *my* child?"

He dropped the knife and put one hand on Winna's belly and the other in a pool of Fend's blood. He felt the shock of the woorm's poison and what it had become in Fend's Skaslos veins before his fingers dug *down* again. This time they kept digging.

He closed his eyes and saw again the Briar King's eyes, stared into one of them as it opened wider and wider and finally swallowed him.

He had been sleeping, but something had awakened him; he felt wind on his face and branches swaying around him. He opened his eyes.

He was in a tree at the edge of a meadow, his forest all around.

A Mannish woman in a brown wool dress lay on her back at the foot of the tree, her knees up and legs spread. She was gasping, occasionally screaming. He felt her blood soaking into the earth. Everything else was still.

There was pain showing through the woman's eyes, but

*he mostly saw resolve. As he watched, she pushed and
screamed again, and after a time she pulled something pale
blue and bloody from herself. It cried, and she kissed it,
rocked it in her arms for a few moments.*

*"Aspar," she whispered. "My lovely son. My good son.
Look around you. This is all yours."*

*Then she died. That baby might have died, too, but he
reached down from the tree and took him in, kept him safe
and quick until, almost a day later, a man came and found
the dead woman and the boy. Then he drifted back into the
long slow dream of the earth, for just a little while, until he
heard a horn calling, and knew it was time to wake fully and
fight.*

"I'm sorry," Aspar told the witch. "I'm sorry your forest
was destroyed, your world. But there's no bringing it back.
Trying to will destroy what's left of my forest. That's what
Fend wanted, although I don't know why."

"Stop," the witch hissed. "Stop what you're doing."

"I couldn't if I wanted to," Aspar said. It was the last thing
he was able to say; agony stretched him as everything inside
of him pressed out against his skin. Then he split open, and
with the last light of his mortal eyes he saw green tendrils
erupt from his body. They uncoiled fast, like snakes, and
reached for the sun.

The pain faded, and his senses rushed out from tree to grass
blade and vine. He was a deer, a panther, an oak, a wasp, rainwater, wind, dark rotting soil.

He was everything that mattered.

He pulled life up from the earth and grew, pushing up
through the roof and absorbing the thorns into him as he
went.

The music lifted, the discord sharpened, and suddenly a
murmur grew in the air, the whisper of a thousand crystal
bells with pearl clappers chiming his music in all of its
parts. It seemed to spin him around, and the air grew darker
until even the flames of the candles appeared only as dim
sparks.

But the music. Oh, it went out of the house and into the vast
hollow places of the world. It rang in the stone of the mountains and sang in the depths of the sea. The cold stars heard it,
and the hot sun in its passage below the world, and the bones
inside his flesh. And still it went on, filling everything.

He almost lost his own voice. Mylton's voice did falter,
but then it came back, stronger, leading the lowest chords
up from the depths toward the still unseen summit.

On the music climbed, falling now and then but always
tending higher, never resolving and seemingly irresolvable.

He couldn't stop singing now if he wanted to; Mylton's
stumble had been the last time that was possible. He heard
many thousands of voices now sighing in the starless gulf,
then millions, and he began to panic, because he couldn't
remember how it finished, what was supposed to happen at
the end. The music on paper no longer mattered. The requiem had them all in its grip now, and it was going where
it wanted to.

He felt his body shiver like a dragonfly's wing and then
cease to be. Nothing remained of him but his voice.

The end came, and it was terrifying, wonderful, and then—
in a single, impossible moment—perfect. Every note fit with
every other. Every voice supported every other. Everything
was in its place.

The voices of the dead faded with his own.

Mery sagged against the wall and collapsed.

Out in the yard, the head of Robert Dare stopped trying to
talk.

Hespero came at him like lightning, lunging and thrusting at
Cazio's groin. He parried quickly in *uhtave,* but the blade
wasn't there, for the fratrex had disengaged. It was only by
wild chance that he managed to catch the blade a second
time and stop it from running through his throat.

Cazio stepped back.

"You know how to use a sword pretty well."

"I may have neglected to mention that I studied with Mestro Espedio."

Cazio narrowed his eyes. "I met another student of his not long ago. Acredo. This is his sword."

"An acquaintance," Hespero said. "You killed him, I gather."

"No. An arrow did."

Hespero shrugged and came at him again, using the attack of the Cuckold's Walk Home. Cazio countered it, move for move for move. Acredo nearly had killed him with that attack when they had fought because Cazio hadn't known the final reply, but he knew the point would be at his throat when it was all over, so he finished with a high *controsesso*.

Again he didn't find the blade, but Hespero's found him, slipping through the ribs of his right side. Cazio fell back, looking at the blood in utter disbelief. Hespero came grimly on.

You're going to be fine, Cazio thought. *He got lucky.*

He parried the next attack barely and then desperately struck deep. His blade grazed Hespero's off-weapon hand and drew blood.

That was a nice surprise.

"You're a better swordsman than I thought," Cazio said. "But you aren't invulnerable anymore."

"If you treat that wound now, you might live," Hespero said.

"Oh, you're not getting away that easily," Cazio said.

"I don't have time for this," the fratrex said.

Cazio renewed his attack, a feint to the hand, a bind from *perto* to *uhtave*.

Hespero punched him in the jaw with his off-weapon hand. Cazio reeled back, trying desperately to get his guard up.

Austra launched herself at the fratrex, leaping on his back and wrapping her arms around his neck. Hespero reached back with his left hand and grabbed her by the hair, but she didn't let go until he slammed her into the wall.

By that time Cazio was on his feet, albeit unsteadily. He lurched toward Hespero.

"Saints, you really don't know when to quit," Hespero said.

Cazio didn't waste his limited breath answering; he stamped and started an attack in *perto*. Hespero, a little impatiently, bound in *sesso* and riposted; Cazio ducked and lunged low but short.

Hespero started the Cuckold's Walk Home, and Cazio kept up with him, barely. The last feint came to his throat, and he desperately parried again, and again the blade wasn't there.

Neither was Cazio. As the final flank stroke came, he twisted his body out of the way and counterattacked rather than trying to parry. Acredo slid neatly through the churchman's solar plexus.

"Don't ever try the same thing on me twice," Cazio advised, yanking the blade out.

Hespero went down on one knee, then suddenly leaped forward. Cazio caught the blade and turned it in a bind, so close to missing it that the point dragged across his forehead. Hespero's low lunge exposed his back, and Cazio drove his sword down between his shoulder blades.

Then he slipped on his own blood and fell. As Austra rushed to him, he put his hand over his wound and closed his eyes.

Stephen cupped Anne's face in his hand and smiled ever more broadly.

"Are you ready, little queen?"

Anne felt as if her head were full of wasps, but she couldn't do anything but stare up at him with hatred.

But then she felt new strength enter her, strength of a sort she had never known before. It came boiling up in her not from the sedos but from the awful depths surrounding all, the chaos from which the world had been born.

My gift, o Queen, Qexqaneh said.

Her lungs cleared. The weight vanished.

The law of death is mended, the Skaslos said.

Stephen staggered back. "No," he said.

"Oh, yes," Anne said. "Certainly yes."

Her right hand was the sickle of the dark moon, and her left was the hammer of old night, and with them she struck so that he fell in pieces and she hurled the pieces out into the abyss, and she stood and grew until the world was tiny beneath her.

Now, the Kept murmured. *Now, my sweet, you only need kill me, and all is done.*

Anne stretched her grin. "And how do I do that, Qexqaneh?"

You are the rivers. You are the Night Before the World. Take me into you and destroy me. Give me oblivion at long last. You have my power. Now take my soul.

"Fine," Anne said. "I'll do that, then."

Cazio felt Austra stumble. He tried to put all his weight back on his own feet, but they just wouldn't take it.

"Stop that," Austra said. "I can support you."

"Not up the hill, you can't," Cazio said.

"I have to get you to a leic," she replied.

"I think it would be better if you went and found one," he said.

"I don't want to leave you."

"Then just sit here with me," he said.

"That's stupid. You're bleeding."

"It's not so bad," he lied.

"I'm not a fool, Cazio," she muttered. "Why does everyone take me for a fool?"

As they crossed the threshold of the crypt, Austra went rigid and gasped. Cazio looked to see what the matter was. Stephen Darige lay facedown a few feet away, but that didn't seem to be what she was looking at.

"Oh, no," Austra said. She suddenly felt very warm—no, hot, so hot he couldn't keep his arm across her shoulders. He stood away, teetered, and had to lean against the mausoleum wall to stay on his feet.

"No," Austra repeated. Her eyes suddenly incandesced, and yellow flame sprang from them.

"Austra!" he screamed.

She looked at him, and she wasn't Austra but a woman with fine, dark features and arching brows, then a Sefry with white hair. She was Anne, with flaming tresses. She was every woman Cazio had ever made love to, then every woman he had ever met. Her clothes had begun to smolder.

"What's happening?" Cazio screamed.

"She's doing it!" Austra said, her voice changing like her face. Then, more exultantly, "We're doing it!"

The ground suddenly was colored with strange light, and Cazio looked up and saw a sun descending toward them, a ball of writhing flame and shadow that made the oldest, most animal parts of him quiver and long to run and never stop running, to find a place where a thing like that couldn't be.

Instead he held on to the stone, panting, fighting the fear with all the life he had left in him.

"Austra," someone said quietly.

Stephen was standing a few kingsyards away. He didn't look good. For one thing, one of his eyes was missing.

"Austra," he said. "You're the only one who can stop her. Do you understand? He's tricked her. He'll die, yes, but he'll take the world with him. Anne will go mad; it's too much power. You feel it, don't you?"

"I feel it," Austra said. Her voice was that of a woman in the rising throes of passion.

"Fight her," Stephen said. "You have claim to the power, too."

"Why should I fight it?" Austra asked. "It's wonderful. I'll have the whole world in my veins soon."

"Yes," Stephen said. "I know." He stepped closer. "I didn't know what he was, Austra. That was what I was missing. He's been waiting in his prison for two thousand years, planning this moment, building it, planting the seeds in all of us. He doesn't want to rule, he doesn't want to return his race to glory, he just wants to die and take everything with him. Can't you see it?"

"Why should I believe you?"

"Don't," he said. "Go see for yourself."

Flames began to dance on her garments. She looked at Cazio, and for a moment her face was that of the Austra he loved.

"Cazio?" she asked.

"I love you," he said. "Do what's right."

Then his legs went out from under him.

Aspar would have laughed if he could, but the joy was there in the leaves and blossoms for anyone to see. He healed the broken, ended the hopeless, and pulled in the poison, spreading and diffusing it, changing it into something new. He found the heart of the Sarnwood witch and took her in, too, took all of her children in, and reckoned at last she understood, because she stopped fighting him and lent him her strength.

Or perhaps it was that she saw what he saw, the deadly fire kindled in the west, the one thing that would stop life's rebirth and send everything to oblivion.

The real enemy.

He didn't need a summoning, not now, and so he moved his weight across the world, fearing it was already too late.

Anne felt the black blood of the Kept flowing into her veins and cried out with glee, knowing that no one since time began had wielded might like this: not the Skasloi, not Virgenya Dare, no one. She was saint, demon, dragon, tempest, the fire in the earth. There had never been a name for what she was becoming. The Kept coiled around her as the life leaked from him, and his every touch sent shudders through her body, pleasure and pain so pure that she couldn't tell them apart and wouldn't if she could. Through his eyes she saw a hundred thousand years of such sensation and more, and the anticipation was its own luscious bliss.

More! she shouted.

There is more, the dying demon replied. *So much more.*

Stephen tried to keep his focus, tried to stay in the world, but it was difficult with so much of him gone. Only the ancient, terrible obstinacy of Kauron had let him keep anything, but even that was fading, and soon Anne would notice her mess and clean it up.

It depended on this girl. He ached to take Austra in his arms and drain the life and power from her; she was a vein that tapped right into the thing Anne was becoming, and he—if he had the gift—could bleed Anne through her. She would never see it coming.

But he no longer had that gift. He was less than a skeleton of himself.

He watched as she knelt by Cazio, murmuring, as her clothing finally exploded in blue flame and she was forced to step back from her lover to avoid charring him.

"You can't heal him, if that's what you're trying to do," Stephen said. "You can't heal anything. Neither can she. Always a storm, never a gentle rain. Do you understand? But you are her weak spot."

Austra stared at him with her blistering eyes for a moment, and then the flames began to subside, then smoke, until she was wreathed in dark vapor and her eyes shone like green lamps. Then she lifted toward the terror that hung above them.

Anne felt an ebb in her strength and sought jealously for the source of it. Had she missed someone? Was Hespero still alive?

But no, it was just Austra, bearing a fraction of her strength.

If you die, the Kept said, *she inherits all.*

She doesn't have the power to kill me, Anne said. *And she wouldn't if she could.*

She can betray you more than anyone. You know that.

"Don't listen to him, Anne," Austra said.

"Of course I won't," Anne replied. "We'll rule together, won't we?"

"Anne, Cazio is dying," Austra said. "Can you heal him?"

"No," she said. She hadn't realized until she said it that it was true.

Seize the Vhen throne, Qexqaneh interrupted. *Then you can heal any of these worms if that is your wish.*

"He's lying, Anne."

"Why should he? He's sacrificing himself for me."

"He's using you to destroy the world."

"So he thinks," Anne said. "But I'm the one with the power now. Anyway, what's so great about this world? You're part of me now; you can see what vermin people are. I'll create another world. I already see how it could be done. We'll make it the way we want it, the way it ought to be."

"That's crazy, Anne. That means killing everyone you've ever known, everyone dear to you."

"Like who?" Anne screamed. "My father? Fastia? Elseny? My mother is dead, too; did you know that? Everyone I care for is already dead except you and Cazio, and my patience is wearing a little thin with you. Now, if you want Cazio to live, either join me or give up your gifts, because we've got one battle left, and I need all the strength I can muster. After that we can have everything, Austra, just the way we want it."

Austra opened her mouth again, but then she looked beyond Anne.

"I'll save you, Anne," she said.

Anne turned.

She stood in a field of ebony roses, the pearls of her dress gleaming like dull bone in the moonlight. The air was so thick with the scent of the blooms that she thought she would choke.

There was no end to them; they stretched to the horizon in a series of low rises, stems bent by a murmuring wind. She turned slowly to see if it was thus in all directions.

Behind her the field ended abruptly in a wall of trees, black-boled monsters covered with puckered thorns bigger than her hand, rising so high she couldn't see their tops in the dim light. Thorn vines as thick as her arm tangled between the trees and crept along the ground. Through the trees and beyond the vines was only darkness. A greedy darkness, she felt, a darkness that watched her, hated her, wanted her.

"I've been here before," she told the forest. "I'm not frightened this time."

Something pushed through the thorns, coming toward her. Moonlight gleamed on a black-mailed arm and the fingers of a hand, uncurling.

And then the helmet came through, a tall tapering helm with black horns curving up, set on the shoulders of a giant.

But this time, standing her ground, she saw it wasn't mail but bark, and the helmet was moss and horn and stone. And of the face she could only see the eyes, wells of life and death, birth and decay—need and vengeance.

You have the power, the fading voice of the Kept told her. *Kill him and complete yourself.*

Anne gathered herself, but her peripheral vision caught motion, and she saw Austra running across the field, running straight for the Briar King.

If he gets her, you lose, the Kept said. *You must kill her now.*

Anne stood, watching.

Kill her, Qexqaneh said more urgently. *Do you understand? Through her he can defeat us.*

Anne lashed out at Austra, and the girl stumbled. She tried to rip through the connection between them, recover her power, but she saw what the Kept meant, how intimate that connection really was. Killing Austra was the only way for Anne to be whole, to possess everything.

She reached out, felt the life beating in Austra, knew the familiar smell of her, that little lock of hair that was always out of place, always had been since they were little girls. The Briar King reached for her, and Anne, hot tears in her eyes, started to squeeze Austra's heart.

Austra stumbled to her knees. She looked toward Anne, her eyes mortal now, wide as saucers, just another Mannish beast that didn't understand why it had to die.

Yes, the Kept sighed. *Finally.*

Somehow Austra stood back up, even as the strength drained out of her, as Anne took her in. The sky dimmed as she diminished and then went away.

"Our secret place," she heard Austra whisper in the darkness.

But it wasn't complete darkness, and Anne saw they were again in the chamber beneath the horz. But now the sarcophagus was open, and in it Austra sat, back propped against one stone wall. She looked as she had when she was nine, a pale waif.

"I knew better," the little girl said. "I knew better than to hope for anything for myself."

"Stop whining," Anne said. "You had a better life than you could have ever hoped for, born as you were."

"You're right," Austra said. "And I wouldn't trade it. You were always going to be the end of me, Anne. I knew that. You'll bury me here, and the circle goes on."

"You didn't know," Anne accused.

"Of course I did. I didn't know *how* it would happen. It nearly happened a dozen times when we were little."

"That's nonsense. I loved you."

"It's *how* you love," she replied. "It's how you love, Anne."

"I don't know what you mean."

"You probably don't," Austra replied, closing her eyes. "I love you anyway."

"He'll kill us both, Austra, if he gets you."

She nodded tiredly. "I know you won't, but please let Cazio go. Can you do that for me?"

Anne started to agree, but why should she? She didn't have to do anything Austra said or for that matter *listen* to anything she said. She was the only one who could make her feel like this, feel like . . .

Feel like what? she suddenly wondered.

But she knew that, too. When her mother—or Fastia, or anyone—disapproved of something she did, she knew she might be in trouble, but deep down she never actually felt bad.

When Austra disapproved of her, she knew in her heart she was *wrong*.

She didn't need that, did she?

She felt the Briar King, his power swelling, reaching for what remained of Austra, tearing through the illusory tomb.

Time was up. She had a heartbeat left to act, but it was all she needed.

No.

With a soft, chagrined laugh, Anne released her hold. The Briar King took Austra and loomed up to the sky. The Kept screamed once as he was ripped from her and hurled into the oblivion he craved, and then she felt as if all her veins had been opened, and the scent of black roses filled her lungs until there was nothing else.

EPILOGUE

✢

THE DAY *the last Skasloi stronghold fell began the age known as* Eberon Vhasris Slanon *in the language of the elder Cavarum. When the language itself was forgotten by all but a few cloistered scholars in the Church, the name for the age persisted in the tongues of men as* Everon, *just as* Slanon *remained attached to the place of victory in the Lierish form* Eslen.

Everon was an age of human beings in all their glories and failings. The children of the Rebellion multiplied and covered the land with their kingdoms.

In the year 2223 E, the age of Everon came to an abrupt and terrible end.

It may be that I am the last to remember it.

I was dying when the Briar King came. When the battle was done, he lifted me in his hand of living vines and opened those eyes of his upon me.

I knew my friend, and he knew me, and I wept at what he had given up, but more at what he had gained. He took me away, and in his long, slow way he mended me. He meant well.

Of all that died and lived that night, only I was left with the sight, and it was a faint reflection of what I once had. Like Aspar's Grim, my one eye can look beyond the horizons of days and leagues—but never again at my command.

The hour of treasured shadows had just struck in Vitellio, and in the little town of Avella, that meant everyone from the carpenter to a shopkeeper—or anyone who had sense—had found shade and a light snack. This was true even now, when the days were shorter and the shadows longer. Fewer duels were fought over the prime spots, and thus it was that this deep in the month Utavamenza, Alo was able to rest in the shade of the fountain of the Lady Fiussa without much fear of molestation, even given the current climate in town and the well-known fact that his skills with the sword were far from perfect.

He enjoyed the wine as best he could, knowing it would be his last for a while. He could wish for some bread to go with it, but he might as well ask Fiussa to weep sapphires.

He dozed on and off in the weakening autumn sun. A horse clopped across the stones of the piato; a girl sang from her window. He dreamed of better days.

He opened his eyes and found Lady Fiussa gazing down at him. She was young, fair, very pretty.

Only the lady ought to be naked, and this woman was dressed, oddly enough, as a man, in breeches and doublet, complete with riding hat.

"Lady," he said, scrambling to his feet.

"Hush," the girl said. "Are you the one they call Alo?"

"I am," he said. "I am very much he."

"That's good," she said. "I have something for you from an old friend."

She had a charming accent, Alo noticed.

"What is it?"

She held something out for him. It was a key.

"Zmierda," he swore. "That's Cazio's key. The key to his triva. Where did you get that?"

"It's a long story," she said. "He wanted you to have it."

"Is he well?"

She looked away, and Alo felt his heart sink.

"It was kind of him," Alo said, "but it won't do me any good. Some of Chiuno's thugs are using it. They broke in a while back."

"Chiuno?"

"The new lord of Avella," he said. He lowered his voice.

"A bandit, really. But with the Church in civil war and the Medicii all hurrying to take sides, little towns like ours get forgotten. I'm leaving myself this afternoon."

"I see," she said.

"Lady, who are you?"

"My name is Austra," she replied.

"Can't you tell me anything else about my friend?" he asked.

But she smiled a faint, enigmatic smile and walked away, mounted a scruffy-looking horse, and rode out of town on the Vio aza Vero.

Alo watched her go, then finished his wine and lay back, turning the key in his fingers.

He woke again, this time to a boot digging into his ribs. He opened his eyes carefully and found a rough-looking bearded man standing over him dressed much as the woman had been except that he had a rapier slung by his side. The woman, he saw, stood a few paces away.

"This is my spot, friend," the fellow said.

And then, behind the beard, Alo recognized him.

"Cazio!"

"Hush," his old friend said. "Let's go for a walk in the country, and you can tell me a bit more about this Chiuno fellow. He sounds unpleasant."

He offered his hand, and Alo took it, smiling.

I saw the Sefry flee for the deep and hidden places in the world. Most had not been involved with Fend, the Aitivar, Mother Uun, and her kin. Most never hoped that Qexqaneh would bring back their days of glory. But once their secret was out, the lands of men were no longer for them, and they knew it.

I saw Marcomir die of apoplexy. I saw the army of Hansa pull back to the border. I saw the Church descend into bloody civil war.

"Anne?"

Anne looked up from her reading. Her brother Charles

was sitting on the floor across the Red Hall, cross-legged, playing with some cards.

"What is it, Charles?" she asked.

Charles rubbed his eyes. He was a grown man, older than Anne, but his mind was forever childlike, and so were his motions. "When is Hound Hat coming back?" he asked. "I miss him."

"I don't think he will be back, Charles," she said gently. "But we shall find you another jester."

"But I liked *him*."

"I know."

"What about Mother? Is she coming back?"

"No, not her, either," Anne told him. "It's just us now."

"But I miss everybody."

"I do, too," she said.

"I'm sad," he said glumly, and went back to his cards.

Before she could return to her reading, she heard a soft voice near the door.

"Majesty?"

She glanced over and saw one of her pages standing there.

"Yes, Rob. What is it?"

"The earl of Cape Chavel, as you requested."

"Thank you. Show him in directly." She turned her gaze to the young woman standing behind her.

"Alis," she said, "why don't you take Charles to see the new horses."

"Are you certain, Majesty?"

"Yes, Lady Berrye, I am."

"Very well," Alis said. "Charles, could you go with me and show me the new horses?"

"Horses!" Charles echoed, bouncing to his feet. The two of them left arm in arm.

The earl entered a moment later. Rob left, too, and they were alone in the Red Hall.

Cape Chavel looked very fine, and she felt the ghostly tingle of the memory of his hands on her. Her heart felt very tender for a moment, very full.

"I'm so pleased to see you well," he said.

"I'm pleased to see you, Tam."

His jaw dropped for a moment. "You've never called me that," he said. "Of course I'm pleased."

"I'm sorry I haven't had time to speak to you before this," she said. "There was a lot to do. The circumstances of that night— I don't know how much you remember."

"I remember it well, until our own soldiers trampled me," he said. "I remember you rising from the dead, for instance."

"I was never dead," she said. "My soul fled my body for a time so it could heal, that's all."

"That's all," he said. "You say that as if it were nothing. I thought you were dead, Anne. I believed I loved you, but when I thought you were gone, I went mad. I don't know how you came back to me, and I don't care, only that you are back, and I love you even more dearly than before."

"I love you, too," she said. "Simply, honestly, without pretense. The way I have always wanted to love."

He closed his eyes. "Then why wait? You've already made me king of Virgenya. Surely everyone will agree we make a good match."

She tried to smile.

"We make a good match," she said. "We do not make the *best* match."

He wrinkled a confused frown. "What do you mean?"

Anne wished just for a moment that she had the cold, terrible nature of that night back, but that Anne was dead, stillborn. Whatever she might become now had never been foreseen, and she meant to make the best of that.

"I must marry Berimund of Hansa," she said.

"But you just said you love *me*."

"Yes," she agreed. "And so I wanted to tell you in person before you found out through the court. It will bring peace between us and Hansa."

"They hate you there. They think you're a witch."

"Marcomir died five days ago. He was the heart of that hatred, but even so, yes—in Hansa I will not be loved. But it is, very simply, what must be done."

"I don't accept that."

"You must. I hope to always be your friend, Tam, but no matter what, you *will* accept my word as your empress."

He stood there red-faced for several heart-wrenching moments before he finally bowed.

"Yes, Majesty," he said.

"That will be all for now."

He left, and so she freed the last of those she loved, and felt another crack in her heart, and knew that this was what being a queen was.

I saw Anne cede her power to the Briar King, and then I helped Aspar—I still call him that sometimes—conceal the thrones again, better than before, I hope. The power wanes, and Anne passed laws against the use of the fanes. Time only will tell, for men and women are foolish. I'm proof of that.

Leoff kissed his son's tiny forehead. The child looked about aimlessly with unfocused eyes, and he wondered what strange melodies might be in there, waiting for an instrument to give them life.

Areana looked pale and beautiful in her sleep, and the glare of the midwife forbade him to wake her. He gave the child carefully back to the old woman and went out onto the grounds, whistling.

"Not a new singspell, I trust?" a raised voice asked from some distance off. It was Artwair, approaching on a dun mare.

"No," he said. "Just a lullaby I'm working on."

"So, well?" Artwair dismounted and let the horse have its head.

"All is well," Leoff told him. "The child is healthy, and so is Areana."

"Saints bless, that's good news," Artwair said. "You deserve some good fortune."

"I don't know if I deserve it," Leoff replied. "But I'm grateful for it. How are things in Eslen?"

"Quieting slowly," the duke replied. "There are still rumors, of course, that the queen is really a demon, a saint, a man, or a Sefry beneath her clothes. Liery is still making noise about the wedding, and the winter was hard. But we have peace, and the early crops are good. Few monsters have been seen, and those only in the deep forests, far from town or village. And the Church—well, that might take time to settle out. Anne intends to establish her own, you know. One free of z'Irbina's influence."

"I wish her luck there."

"She actually sent me to talk to you regarding that," he said. "She'd like you to compose a hymn of thanksgiving to be sung at the lustration of the clergy."

"That's interesting," Leoff said.

"You don't want to?"

Leoff smiled. "I've already started on it."

"I think we're being followed, by the way," Artwair said.

Leoff nodded. He had seen the flash of dress through the trees.

"She has a bit of a crush on you, I'm afraid."

"And here I thought you were teaching her good taste."

Leoff raised his voice. "Come on out, Mery, and say hello to the duke. And after that we have work to do, you and I."

He heard her giggle, and then she appeared, skipping toward them.

When the law of death was mended, those creatures caught between fell one way or the other. He thanked the saints every day that she had fallen his way.

I see the last of the Faiths.

The boom swung and the sail caught wind, and the *Swanmay* cut through the rising waves. Neil leaned on the rail, staring out over the rough water at the rugged coastline.

"It's beautiful," Brinna said.

He nodded in agreement. "She's a hard old rock, but I love her. I think you'll like her, too."

She made a single fist of both of their hands. He winced

a bit, for the whole arm was still tender, but he treasured the touch.

"We'll stay here, then?" she asked.

He laughed, and she only looked puzzled.

"Would you make a liar of me?" he asked.

"I don't even know what you mean."

"I said I would take you away to where neither of us has duties. Now, the queen gave me my freedom and Berimund gave you yours, but we are still very far from that place."

"And where, husband, would that be?"

"We will have to hunt it," he said. "It could take the rest of our lives. Who knows how much of the world we shall have to see?"

And she kissed him and seemed young for the first time since he had known her. Together they watched Skern grow before them.

I saw Zemlé grow old, never knowing what happened to me. When I walked the world again, healed as much as I could heal, she was years dead.

So I returned to the empty Witchhorn. I grieve and write. And I remember what I can.

There is one thing I won't forget until the river finally takes me out into everything. That was the time I saw through his eyes.

I never imagined such a beautiful thing—to gaze with every eye of the forest, feel and hear through every leaf and fern. It was only once, years after the battle.

It happened where the tyrants once stood, the great ironoaks Aspar loved so well. They were all fallen, but acorns had sprouted, and for those first years things grew with un-natural speed. So many of the trees were already four or five kingsyards high, slender young things, but already starting to shadow out the underbrush, reconquering their territory.

A woman came there, still young, her face rosy from the winds, for that year was cooler. She was bundled in a wool coat, and she wore elkhide boots. I knew her, of course, for I once thought I loved her, and I did in a way.

Holding her hand was a girl of perhaps six or seven years. She had a bright, intelligent face that was full of wonder as she stared about the place.

"Here he is," Winna told the girl. "Here is your father."

And, through him, I felt every tree strain, and shudder, and yearn toward them, and all the birds sang at once.

It was the last truly human thing I ever felt from him, and not long after that he slept, as sleep he must.

When he slept, I awoke, and found the world changed.

—The *Codex Tereminnam*, Author anon.